THE PERFECT WOMAN

BOOK II OF THE ROSE GOLD SERIES

NICOLE FRENCH

raglan

For every girl who has been locked in any kind of tower, real or imagined.

You are not princesses, but queens.

PROLOGUE

From: Matthew Zola
To: Nina de Vries
Date: May 29, 2018, 9:10 AM
Subject: Last Night

Nina,

I know I don't have to say it again, but I feel like I should. There is too much on the line. You know it. I know it.

Last night can't happen again.

Matthew

————

From: Nina de Vries
To: Matthew Zola
Date: May 29, 2018, 9:21 AM
Subject: RE: Last Night

Ever?

Nina

————

From: Matthew Zola
To: Nina de Vries
Date: May 29, 2018, 9:23 AM
Subject: RE: RE: Last Night

Come on, doll. Don't make me feel worse than I already do.

————

From: Nina de Vries
To: Matthew Zola
Date: May 29, 2018, 9:26 AM
Subject: Remorse

I'm sorry.

————

From: Matthew Zola
To: Nina de Vries
Date: May 29, 2018, 9:31 AM
Subject: Remorse? Why?

Sorry for what? This isn't your fault. None of it is.

————

From: Matthew Zola
To: Nina de Vries
Date: May 29, 2018, 10:25 AM

Subject: Where did you go?

Nina?

———

From: Matthew Zola
To: Nina de Vries
Date: May 29, 2018, 10:57 AM
Subject: Starting to feel like a stalker…

Duchess?

———

From: Matthew Zola
To: Nina de Vries
Date: May 29, 2018 11:39 AM
Subject: Begging now…

Baby, please. Have a little mercy.

———

From: Nina de Vries
To: Matthew Zola
Date: May 29, 2018 11:52 AM
Subject: It hurts

I'm sorry I need you like I do.
I never wanted to make your life so difficult.

———

From: Matthew Zola
To: Nina de Vries

Date: May 29, 2018 11:55 AM
Subject: So damn much

A life not knowing you isn't worth living. No matter what happens, believe that.
I have no regrets.

———

From: Nina de Vries
To: Matthew Zola
Date: May 29, 2018 11:57 AM
Subject: At least there is that…

I love you, Matthew.

Goodbye.

Nina

PRELUDE

MAY 2018

Matthew

I stared at the last email for what seemed like hours. The last email, maybe, I'd ever get from Nina de Vries. Technically, her name was Gardner, but she didn't use it on this account, which I had a feeling she had set up for me. Just as I used my personal account to communicate with her. I hated thinking of her that way anyway, bearing the shitty name of a man no better than gum on the bottom of my shoe. As the tall, stunningly beautiful daughter of one of the oldest and richest families in New York, Nina was royalty in nearly every sense of the word. Her family's name fit her better than that rat bastard Calvin Gardner's ever would.

I swallowed hard, staring at the last few words of her final missive. The truth was, I didn't want this to be the end. I was already halfway to grabbing my phone and dialing her number. Telling her to meet me back at the Grace Hotel in the Lower East Side tonight so we could continue what we'd started last night.

Her text had been short and simple, but one I couldn't ignore, even though less than a week ago we'd decided to stop whatever this was between us in its tracks.

I need you.

Fuck me. I needed her too, and I'd have given her the world if I could. But life doesn't give most people a happy ending, and in our case, it had given us a straight-up tragedy.

Five months ago, I'd walked into a bar on a gloomy January night, wondering what the hell was missing from my life as a Brooklyn prosecutor, dutiful brother, and occasional philanderer. Well, I'd gotten my answer, I'll tell you that. It came in the form of an angel on a barstool, drinking a glass of red wine with her pinky raised in the air.

We'd taken that one night together, and then she'd disappeared. Three months later, I'd found her again as I took on the hardest case of my career—a secret investigation into one of the biggest human trafficking kingpins this city had ever seen. John Carson made Jeffrey Epstein look like Ned Flanders. As of last week, Carson was dead, but the case was far from over. Two other men had been photographed at the safe house in Brooklyn just a few weeks ago. One, Jude Letour, was safely awaiting trial at Rikers without bail. The other had been indicted and released.

He also happened to be married to Nina de Vries. Which, as of three weeks ago, meant that not only did the love of my life belong to someone else, she was also the one woman on the planet I could truly never have.

It was simple.

There was no one in the world who could prosecute this case but me. And these guys needed to be in jail. They needed to be locked up where they could never hurt anyone. Ever. Again. But the prosecutor shacking up with the defendant's wife, even after the trial was over? Definitely grounds for a mistrial. Hell, it was grounds for disbarment.

In five short months, being with Nina de Vries had become as essential as breathing. But being together would spell my ruin, and probably hers too.

I couldn't have that. Not for me. Not for either of us.

Even so, my heart felt like a fifty-pound anvil in my chest as I stared at her name and the blinking cursor beneath it, awaiting my response.

I love you.

She had said that the night before the world went to hell too. Until then, I hadn't really known if this feeling went both ways. She had shown up at my doorstep the night John Carson died by her cousin's hand. Frantic, alone, and out of breath.

And then she had done the impossible. The most perfect woman I could have ever imagined for myself jumped into my arms and told me she needed me. Begged me to throw caution to the wind and spend the rest of our lives together, social mores be damned.

For a few hours, we didn't care that she had a kid or a ring on her finger.

We didn't care about the scandal.

We didn't care about anything but what lay between us.

Need.

Lust.

Love.

And not just any love. The kind that goes beyond the grave. The kind that your kids and their kids tell stories about when you're gone. The kind that lasts for generations.

And then I'd gotten that fucking phone call and done the last thing I'd ever wanted to do. I'd sent Nina back to her husband. I wanted to keep her name out of my office's mouth. I couldn't protect her from this trial, but her husband could, goddammit. Spousal privilege would prevent her from having to defend his sorry ass. And then, when it was all over, she could leave him.

I just couldn't go with her.

I sighed, picked up the new file on Calvin Gardner from my desk, and absently flipped through it. We jumped the gun a little on the indictment, but given the suddenness of John Carson's death, we couldn't risk losing the last thread that held the operation together. We had been lucky Gardner's lawyers had waived their right to a speedy trial in favor of a lengthy discovery process. We had sixty days, said the judge, but based on the obliqueness of the information so far, I was guessing we'd end up asking for sixty more.

His life was confusing, to say the least. Derek Kingston, the special investigator with the Bureau of Organized Crime, hadn't been able to determine his exact relationship to the safe house where he had been spotted, and neither had I. Carson was identified as the owner of that particular house, and it was still empty. But girls from Cypress Hills, the nearby housing project, were still disappearing. Twenty so far, with a lot of other leads in other neighborhoods too. With Carson and Letour out of the equation, that had to mean Gardner was in charge of that scheme, or he was working with someone else.

The problem was finding out who, and where, they were. And if it was outside Brooklyn—outside of our jurisdiction. As yet, the U.S. attorney, once on John Carson's payroll, had been unwilling to tap into the investigation. Carson's ability to cover up the crimes of his cronies seemed to extend beyond the grave.

A knock at the door pulled me out of my misery. Derek, in his typical street clothes of jeans, a faded Yankees jacket, and a backwards baseball hat, stood in the doorway, one sneaker crossed over the other. He didn't exactly fit in with the suited lawyers here on Jay Street, but what made Derek the best investigator we had was his ability to blend in everywhere else.

Today, though, he didn't look like he was particularly enjoying his job.

"Be honest," I said as I swiveled in my chair. "You wish you were writing traffic tickets right now, don't you?"

Derek snorted as he walked in. It was a frequent joke between us, actually. He'd been about ten seconds from leaving the NYPD when he was called up for the special investigator position, right when I was also ready to abandon the DA for some private-sector contract bullshit. Derek and I ended up saving each other's careers, and we'd been friends ever since.

"Different jobs, same dead ends," he said, flopping into the other chair in my small office. He shook his head. "We're getting outside our jurisdiction, Zo."

"You've been saying that for months."

"This is different."

I frowned, glancing at the still-open door. Derek turned in his chair and kicked it shut before swiveling back to me.

"What do you mean?" I asked. "The Pantheon filing was a dead end too?"

I'd asked Derek to investigate the LLC that was technically on the lease of the house. We already knew Carson owned it, but I was betting there were other names associated with it too. There had to be if the operation was still in effect after the man was dead.

"The LLC was registered in Delaware," Derek said. "A no-name shell corporation, of course. That tiny fuckin' state has more corporations than people, did you know that?"

I nodded. I did actually know that—most of the legit corporations in New York were registered in Delaware for the tax and anonymity benefits, not to mention the underground operations I made my living going after. So, the fact that the LLC listed as the lessee for the safe house was registered in one of four states that allowed anonymous ownership wasn't particularly surprising.

"Well, John Carson was a criminal mastermind, not an idiot," I said. "We thought this might happen. He made the mistake of putting his name on one deed, but the others are someone else's problem now. I just need the documents. Somewhere, there's a name. Who's associated with the LLC?" Delaware state law required that an anonymous LLC must name someone who knows the owner, even if that name wasn't the owner himself.

Derek shook his head. "Dead end. It was John Carson."

I raised a brow. "Shit. So we don't even know if he was the owner. The utilities, maybe?"

Derek shook his head. "Garbage, water, sewer. All the same LLC."

I drummed my fingers on the desk. "But the job hasn't stopped. Girls are still disappearing. Someone else besides Carson owns that company."

"Fuck, Zola, I know that."

I frowned but ignored my friend's sharp tone. Given the fact that he was from East New York himself, I wondered if this case was more personal for him than most.

He seemed to feel it too, because when he spoke next, it was a bit more measured. "Look. We only found two other houses in New York owned outright by Pantheon, and they've both been cleared out too. If Gardner is still moving anything—girls or guns—he's doing it outside of where we can get to them."

"So let's look. No harm in that. Nothing says we can't snoop around, even if we can't make an arrest."

"What do you want me to do, Zo? Call the Delaware staties?" Derek snorted again at just the thought of it. "Tell them to be on the lookout for a masked company zooming down the highway? You want me to go driving around with them too?"

I rolled my eyes. "Give me a break, man. That's not what I meant."

"This is a job for the Feds, Zola. It's across state lines. We're not voyeurs."

"And if we give it back to the Feds, you know exactly what's going to happen," I retorted. "You, me, Cardozo, and anyone else working this case are suddenly targets."

I frowned toward the door, like somehow looking in that direction could get me closer to the gun safe in the bottom of the building, where my Beretta and its holster were stowed along with those belonging to other people like me working for the Kings County District Attorney. We were some of the lucky ones. Not all district or state's attorneys allowed their prosecutors to carry to and from work, despite the fact that prosecutors faced consistent death threats as a result of just doing their damn jobs. But the reality was, when you went after bad guys for a living, sometimes the bad guys came after you.

It got complicated when the bad guys were supposed to be on your side.

"I just need the documents," I said again. "Something that shows Gardner's involvement beyond a shadow of a doubt. Right now, we don't have enough for a conviction beyond accessory, and that's only a year tops, more likely just a fine. Keep following the money, King. Here's what I think: you keep nosing around Brooklyn, and I'll contact a few people I know in Newark. Not everyone's a crook. There have to be a few good eggs out there."

Derek didn't look particularly pleased by this idea. I understood. If the crimes we were looking for had in fact moved someplace like New Jersey, we were basically turning over a year-long investigation free and clear, allowing for another prosecutor to run off with the conviction. It was painful. But not as painful as Calvin Gardner getting off scot-free.

"Someone is going to turn up," I said. "And I'll bet my last dollar it's Calvin Gardner."

Derek continued to study me. "Zola, don't take this the wrong way, but...did you ever think that maybe he's not actually the guy?"

The look on my face must have told him I abso-fuckin'-lutely hadn't.

Derek worried his jaw around a little bit. "Look, Zola. I—I don't know how else to say this but to come out and ask. Could your attachment to Nina Gardner be fucking with your judgment here?"

If I had looked up any quicker, my head might have popped up. "I'm sorry, what? What the fuck are you talking about?"

Yeah, I know. The lady doth protest too much. Or in this case, the irritated fuckin' prosecutor.

"Whoa, whoa, whoa. It was just a question, man." Derek held his hands up in surrender. "I'm not saying I know anything. I'm not saying I've seen anything. And to be honest, I don't really want you to tell me if I'm right. Because if I am, that puts me in the weird spot of having to report you to Ramirez and your bureau chief. Since you're the only paper pusher I've ever liked, I don't want to do that."

I snorted. The animosity between the NYPD and the prosecutors' offices in the city was legendary.

"Fuck you," I said. "I'm not a fuckin' paper pusher, and you know it."

Derek shrugged, though he cracked a good-natured grin all the same. "The point remains. Is there any chance you want this guy to be guilty more than he is?"

"King, we already took it to trial. It's not just me that needs the guy to be guilty of more than a single count of aiding and abetting."

"Yeah, but what if he's not? Just because you got a thing for his wife doesn't mean he's the worst guy on the planet, Zola. I know you want him to be more than one of Carson's lackeys, but I gotta be honest, my friend. I'm not sure it's there."

We sat together in silence, ruminating over the possibility. I knew

Derek was right. So far, the evidence against Calvin Gardner was weak, and nothing more had come up in the last three weeks.

And yeah, there was a girl involved in my investigations, possibly swaying my judgment (though I was never going to admit as much to Derek). But I couldn't shake the idea that this went beyond my feelings for Nina. My gut hadn't led me astray once in seven years at this job. I wasn't ready to concede the first time. Not yet.

"Look, we still have another month until trial, more if I can extend discovery. I have an idea." I nodded as the rest of it came to me. "I want to come back to the person associated with the Pantheon."

Derek scowled. "Zola, we covered this already."

"Yeah, but don't you see? That's where whoever owns Pantheon made his big mistake." I nodded again, sitting up straight. "He named a dead man, but everything associated with the LLC is still running like he never died. Pantheon wasn't included in his will either. Which means the person or people who actually own Pantheon are still alive."

Derek blinked. "Okay…"

"Don't you get it?" I clapped my hands together. "You can't know someone if you're dead, King. They have to change it by law, and we can ask them to do it. The owner names a known compatriot, and boom—we have a whole new suspect with a whole new bunch of connections, not to mention weaknesses to exploit."

Finally, Derek's eyes brightened. He nodded.

"Okay," he said. "Okay, so you'll…"

"You just keep watching those houses, keep interviewing people at all the other fronts, and file a request for the known associate, my friend. Within a month, we'll have a new target. And this case will be back on track."

I

PROSPETTIVA

THEN

CHAPTER ONE

MAY 2008

The subway screamed overhead as Nina Evelyn Astor de Vries stepped onto the corner of Sixty-Seventh and Roosevelt, smack in the middle of Jackson Heights. Queens. Out of habit, she pulled out her sunglasses—a cheap pair purchased at CVS just for today. Flimsy and uncomfortable, unlike her favorite Guccis tucked deep in her purse, but without the name brand recognition. Because nothing about today was normal. She wasn't normal.

Nina had worn nothing but designer name brands and couture since she was ten. Had made semi-annual trips to Milan and Paris with Grandmother and Mother since she was twelve. And now she was standing in the middle of Queens in a pair of ill-fitting Gap jeans and a "Big Apple" baseball cap atop her golden blonde hair, hoping to God no one would spot her for the fraud she was.

The neighborhood was only twenty minutes from the Upper East Side, where Nina had grown up, but it felt like another country. The fact was, Nina was sheltered. Spoiled. Naive in the worst possible way. And the reality of that hadn't really struck her until she had left the streets of the Upper East Side for college and spent the last year studying abroad. Wellesley, of course, was still a fount of privilege, but was at least something different. Florence wasn't exactly the developing world either...but it certainly wasn't New York. Nina hadn't expected nine months in a foreign country to completely turn her perspective on its axis. But it had. It had changed everything.

There, she was no longer an Astor, or Nina de Vries, daughter of not just one but two centuries-old New York families. She was simply Nina. A girl in a class. A woman walking along the Arno. No one special at all.

Perhaps she might have stayed.

If only.

Nina closed her eyes and saw the face that haunted her dreams, day and night.

Giuseppe.

Or Peppe, as his students called him. Just barely an inch taller than her. Slight and willowy, his shoulders stooped from years of bending over his books. A few hints of silver threading his otherwise shiny dark hair. Skin the color of soft, pounded leather, a pair of glasses perched over a patrician nose. Not a particularly handsome or young man, but one who became utterly beautiful when he talked about the great artists of Florence. His deep eyes crinkled at the edges and danced. His hands came alive.

Two weeks into Nina's course on classical Renaissance art, Peppe had lectured on Botticelli and took the class to the Uffizi to see the master's work.

Long after the class had moved on, Nina stared at the *Birth of Venus*, absorbed by the curling strawberry blonde hair of the naked goddess and her unabashed curves as she stood on her shell. The fullness of her breasts, her thighs.

She had turned to find her professor equally entranced.

"Hypnotizing, is she not?" He stared at her while he spoke, waving his lithe, graceful hands toward the picture.

It was the first time Nina had imagined those hands on her. The first time she had imagined or wanted anyone's hands on her at all.

Principessa.

That was what he called her, even before he learned who and what she was. The first time was when Nina had wandered to his office hours wanting more information about Botticelli and other masters.

She was his *principessa* a few weeks later when he took her on a private tour of the lesser-known art hidden in Florence's cathedrals, then kissed her in the shadow of the Cathedral of Santa Maria del Fiore while the Arno river shushed in the distance. And again in the golden light of his family's deserted olive farm after making love to her in the cool spring night for all of Tuscany to witness. Once more when he had told her goodbye at the train station, cupping her face between those beautiful hands and promising her he would never forget her in a thousand years.

She couldn't stay with him, nor him with her. Nina had a family to return to, and so did he. Two daughters and a wife, all waiting for him in their apartment near the edge of the city. A life that in her heart Nina knew could never be hers, but that she had wanted badly, nonetheless.

She pressed a hand over her stomach, over the remainder of that dreamlike farewell.

If only.

"Hey, lady! Get out of the road!"

Nina opened her eyes just in time to stop herself from falling into the street. Two cars and a taxi blared loudly as she stepped backward on a sharp breath and bumped into someone else.

"Oh my! I'm so sorry," she said to an elderly Asian woman taking small, solid steps.

"Need some help, sweetheart?"

A warm hand steadied Nina's arm, and she looked up to find a pair of dark, kind eyes twinkling with interest. A delivery worker, stopped mid-shift, unloading boxes of produce into the basement of a Dominican restaurant. He was handsome in that way some of her friends liked—the ones who engaged in short-lived affairs with their doormen or cleaning crew members, trying to avoid (or maybe provoke) their parents' ire.

Such affairs never lasted, and, to be honest, Nina found them distasteful. The way her friends used men like these as objects, not people. And the way they used them back, like trophies, not women. They lasted a few weeks, a month or more. If there was any trouble, money took care of it. And if there wasn't, even better.

Nina had managed to avoid those sorts of things, instead allowing her cousin Eric to act out enough for both of them. Truthfully, she had always enjoyed the way he goaded their grandmother, the matriarch of their great New York family, whenever she forced them through another etiquette lesson or dance class together. But while Eric was like a brother, he was also the dashing heir to the de Vries family fortune. His boyish misbehavior was chalked up to strength of character. Permitted, even if not fully condoned. Nina, on the other hand, couldn't leave the house with a hair out of place.

Rules were always different for women.

Even so, Eric wasn't always the golden boy. Nina remembered his face the first time Grandmother had told him that Penny, his Greek girlfriend from a working-class neighborhood, was utterly inappropriate for him. She remembered his stubbornness when he had kept seeing Penny and even brought her with him to Dartmouth the following year. She remembered the fiery defiance when he had announced their engagement last Christmas, just a few months before his graduation.

"He won't get away with this," her grandmother had said privately to Violet, Nina's mother, once the couple had left.

Five months later, days before Nina had arrived back in New York, Eric had found the girl lying in the bathroom of their apartment, both wrists slit to her elbows. This after months—no, years—of harassment and embarrassment, courtesy of the de Vries family and their friends. So the rumors went.

Nina had never needed her cousin more than she did now. For, truthfully, she had never been more terrified of her own kin. Of what they were capable of.

But Eric was gone, done with the lot of them.

She couldn't blame him.

But she did wish he were here.

"Oh, no, thank you," Nina said, pulling away from the man's warm, if slightly greasy touch. "I know where I'm going."

"Well, try not to get run over, honey," he replied with a cheeky grin, then disappeared underground with his box of limes.

"Yes," Nina murmured. "I'll try."

Pulling her cap farther over her face, Nina turned around, looking at the street signs to get her bearings. The corner was overwhelmingly green—not from plants, but from the green iron castings of the elevated train tracks and the green-painted entrance to the Roosevelt Street subway station, which spanned nearly the entire block. It took her a moment to figure out where she was—she didn't dare bring out her phone. Most people in this neighborhood didn't seem to have iPhones yet. Nina didn't want to bring attention to herself, if at all possible.

She crossed the street, sidestepping cabs and people, and all the other forms of life here in Queens. She turned a corner and made her way down a quieter street, grateful that her hat shaded her face from the suddenly glaring sun.

One block, two. And then, there it was. The address on the slip of paper. A nondescript brick building with graffiti on the bottom and a simple glass door marking the clinic's entrance.

God, was she really here? Her of all people? Standing in front of this grungy building?

Nina wasn't stupid. She had taken enough history and women's studies classes to know exactly how common abortion was. Women had been trying to figure out how not to carry unwanted children since the beginning of civilization. What made her any different?

But that was the problem in a nutshell. Was this child really unwanted?

No.

Nina's vision blurred with sudden tears. This had been happening more and more over the last few weeks. Pregnancy hormones, according to the internet, meant a lot of uncharacteristic crying along with sensitive nipples, morning sickness, and general all-over puffiness. She had told Grandmother she'd picked up a parasite in Italy, and the old woman seemed to believe her. For now.

Nina turned suddenly and tripped over a large crack in the sidewalk.

"Shit," she muttered as she pulled herself upright, leaning against the crumbling brick. The word felt strange in her mouth—Nina never swore, following her grandmother's edicts to a T. "Oh, damn."

She stared at her heel, which had broken clean off. Even in jeans, even in a cap, Nina hadn't completely been able to eschew her clothes completely. With an extra three inches that made her taller than most men in the city, heels made her feel powerful. Even ones like these, purchased at the same ninety-nine-cent store as her hat.

She could just hear Grandmother now: "Cheap is as cheap does. We get what we pay for, my girl, do we not?"

"Nina?"

Nina's head jerked around in a panic, though her vision was still blurred with tears she now swiped at viciously.

"Nina Astor, is that really you?"

As he approached, the stranger became slightly familiar, but his name eluded her. In all honesty, the man himself wasn't particularly memorable. Everything about him was average. In heels, she topped his height by several inches, which meant he was likely no more than five foot six, five-seven at most. His light brown hair was thinning at the temples, cut slightly too long so a few thin strands waved in the hot summer breeze. His body, clothed in a poorly fitted beige suit, had the sagging look of a man who spent too much time behind a desk and not enough at the gym.

But it was his face that was most mediocre of all. Nina thought of the one drawing class she had taken as part of her art history major. They had learned about the composition of bone structure, how to identify the lines in a face that gave a subject its foundations. This man's face was perfectly round, with two small eyes, a thin mouth, and a weak chin lightly dusted with graying stubble. He reminded Nina of an oatmeal cookie that had too much butter. The kind that, when baked, could not retain its shape, but would simply melt outward on the pan.

"Calvin Gardner," the man helpfully supplied as he reached Nina and held out a hand. "I was with Craig and Jeffries Fund, helping your dad with an investment. Or trying to. Christmas Eve, 2003." He winked. "I made you laugh by the punch bowl, remember?"

"Oh," sniffed Nina. "Oh, yes. That's right." She didn't remember at all. So instead, she cleared her throat. "I, um, I use de Vries now."

She vaguely remembered meeting this Mr. Gardner at some dinner party or another the last time her father had visited from London, maybe four or five years ago. Her father hadn't had time to spend with his daughter at Christmas, so Nina had been shuttled to a business party and watched men like this one beg for his attention all night.

If there had ever been a night to run off with a busboy... Perhaps she might have if she had thought her father would have cared at all.

Nina tried to suppress the rest of the memories. How she had begged her grandmother for the rights to her maternal family's name rather than her absent father's. Or how she had only been given permission with the awareness that it wouldn't change her chances at inheritance.

She'd get a trust like every other female member, but the de Vries fortune and company were patrilineal. Meanwhile, its single heir had run away in fury.

Fuck Eric, Nina thought with sudden vengeance, the word sounding as strange in her head as it would have on her lips.

"Nina?"

She shook her head, yanked back to the present.

"It's really too bad that deal never went through," Mr. Gardner was saying, chatting on about the night they apparently met, though his words didn't translate as Nina's own mind started to cycle.

Had he seen her hand on the door?

Had he seen her about to cry?

Did he know why she was here?

Gardner's eyes flickered to the title on the door, clearly printed in peeling white letters: Clinic: Abortion Services and Other.

There it was. Plain as day.

"I—oh." His small brown eyes flew back over Nina, landing on her stomach, where her right arm was clasped around her waist.

She dropped it immediately, all sorts of inappropriate language flying through her mind. Well, if he hadn't known before, he did now.

To his credit, though, Gardner's face softened.

"Ms. Ast—de Vries," he said. "Nina. Do you—can I help you with something? Is there someone we should call?"

Nina glanced around. "I—oh, no. There is no one here."

That, she would realize later, was her first mistake.

Mr. Gardner's head tipped. "Really?"

"Really," she insisted weakly. "And you know, Mr. Gardner, I should probably be going…"

He took her wrist before she turned away completely. Nina stopped and stared at it.

It had been two weeks, four days, and seven hours since someone had touched her. Since Peppe had slipped his hands around her neck and pressed his lips to her cheeks at the train station, one at a time, before letting her go.

Buon viaggio, principessa.

"You don't need to be ashamed," Mr. Gardner said, glancing at the door again and then back at Nina. "I don't judge. Really."

"Oh, Mr. Gardner, it's not what it looks—"

"Calvin, please." Gardner offered a kind, if somewhat forced, smile that made his otherwise dull features warmer. The hand on Nina's wrist relaxed but didn't let go. "You shouldn't be here alone. If there isn't anyone you'd like to call, I could come in and sit with you. If you want. Only until—until you need to go in."

As awkward as the offer was, he almost looked eager. And as alone as Nina felt, it almost seemed sweet. More attention than anyone had given her recently. Except, of course, one.

She opened her mouth to tell this Calvin everything she knew she should say. That he was mistaken. That she was in the neighborhood looking for a fabric store, or got lost on her way to the Queens MoMA, or some other tall tale that would protect her reputation and keep him at arm's length.

But suddenly, the idea of walking into this crumbling building, up the stained carpeted steps to a waiting room that was probably just as depressing made Nina want to cry all over again. Calvin seemed to understand, pulled her close enough that she could smell his mild scent of cheap deodorant, aftershave, and sweat. His light brown eyes were unwavering, unwilling to let her look away.

"Oh—okay," she said, surprising even herself. "Yes, I would appreciate that. Thank you."

Gardner released her wrist then, but only to prop open the door. He then took her other hand and helped Nina limp up the stairs in her broken shoe, all the way to the clinic on the second floor. Into the waiting room that was as predictably beige and decrepit as she had imagined. Where three other women sat with their toes touching, trying as hard as she was not to make eye contact with anyone else in the room.

Nina sat down while Calvin went to the receptionist to check her in. He returned with a form in hand.

"Do you want me to help you fill it out?"

Nina's hands were shaking. Shame and dread pressed on each of her shoulders.

Principessa. I love you.

Oh, would Peppe still say that if he saw her now? Or would he be relieved that she was saving him from another kind of shame and ruin?

"No," Nina said. Suddenly, she couldn't stop shaking her head, back and forth, back and forth. She couldn't do this, could she? No, she should. Or maybe she shouldn't.

She was twenty years old. Too young to be a mother. Too young to weather the tabloids, the press, all the unwanted attention when she was discovered pregnant out of wedlock. Too young for her family to turn on her like they had turned on Eric.

Would Peppe be the next to die in a bathtub?

She was much too young for that, just as Eric had been.

Ultimately, she was too young for love.

Principessa.

Nina turned to Calvin, a man she hardly recognized, but who was the only person in that moment who seemed like he knew her at all. His face was blankly sympathetic, like a character on a sitcom. Practiced and flimsy, but still kind. Like he was doing what he thought he was supposed to in this awkward situation, rather than what Nina actually needed.

It was all she deserved anyway.

Nina stared down at the paper and raised the pen to the first line of the intake form. It wanted her name and address.

She scratched a line.

Terror shot through her.

Everything was wrong.

She dropped the form to the floor and turned to Calvin.

"I c-can't," she said, her voice barely a whisper. "I need to go home. Can you take me home?"

Calvin swallowed, looked at the empty form on the floor, then back up to Nina. "Are you certain?"

That same strange eagerness pervaded his voice.

Do you want me to get an abortion? Nina almost asked. But instead: "Y-yes. Yes, I'm sure."

Calvin eyed her for one moment more, almost like she was an animal in a zoo doing something out of the ordinary. But the expression only lasted a moment before several others consumed him. Sympathy. Kindness. Friendship.

And then...knowing.

"Don't worry, princess," he said as he helped her back up onto her ruined shoes. "I'll take you home. And we'll take care of everything."

CHAPTER TWO

JUNE 2008

"You're going to have to do something about that, you know."

Nina turned from where she was watching a few tourists in a canoe push away from one of the docks in front of the Boathouse on the Central Park Lake. When Calvin had asked her to meet him at the tourist trap, she'd agreed partly because it was a nice day, and partly because he'd simply been so nice to her in the four weeks following their awkward meeting in Jackson Heights.

Well, perhaps nice wasn't the right word.

Knowing.

Attentive.

Invested.

These were more accurate, and Nina wasn't sure how she was supposed to feel about them. But Calvin was the only one who seemed to care what happened to her these days. And he was the only one who understood what was going on beneath the surface since that strange, hot May afternoon.

"I'm sorry?" Nina asked as she pushed a bit of lamb around with her fork. Everything was disgusting right now. "Do something about what?"

Calvin took a large bite of his hamburger, and Nina tried to ignore the way grease pooled slightly at the corner of his mouth or when a fleck of ketchup landed on his shirtfront. His clothes were always stained, either from food like this or the uneven bleach he used to get it out.

Nausea roiled in her stomach.

"Well, you're getting bigger every day," Calvin said through a mouthful of meat. "You must have gained an inch around the waist in the last two weeks alone."

Nina glowered at her salad, as much put off by this man who had known her barely a month inspecting her body like a broodmare, as she was by anything about her being considered "big." She wanted to ask what right he, a thirty-eight-year-old whose belly looked like it was filled with Jell-O, had to comment on her physique.

That said...he was right. Her waist had lost its perfect twenty-three-inch circumference a long time ago, and in the last four weeks, her breasts had popped a full cup size, to the point she couldn't zip half her delicately fitted silk dresses or anything else without elastic in her closet. All that couture might as well have been window drapings.

"Go on," Calvin said, shoving Nina's plate toward her. "I ordered you the lamb because you need some iron. I read about it on the internet."

She perked a brow. "You were reading up on what pregnant women need to eat?"

He scoffed through his food. "Someone had to. I can't trust you to take care of yourself, obviously."

He made comments like that a lot. Nothing overt, but it was clear what he was talking about. The fact that he had found her, crying, shoeless, and contemplating abortion gave away something critical about her character. And, apparently, its defects.

Nina pushed her fork at her lamb again. She shoved a bit of lettuce into her mouth, chewed, and swallowed. "I'm surprised you had time to research," she said. "Considering how busy you've been with your...property development now, isn't it? In Newark, right?"

He frowned. Calvin didn't like it when Nina asked about his business. Nina knew that. She was pushing his buttons now, a little tit for tat.

A few questions around her milieu had informed her that Calvin Gardner was currently "between ventures"—upper-class nomenclature for unemployed. Apparently, he had bounced between hedge funds for several years before deciding recently to dip his toe into real estate—hence his presence in Queens, where he was looking at property when they met. The problem was, he didn't have the connections to procure the investors he needed.

"Grifter," one person had said.

"Social climber," said another.

Well. He wouldn't win any people to his side if they thought he didn't belong there in the first place.

Not that he told Nina any of this. The few times she'd asked, Calvin had just clicked his tongue, told her not to worry her little royal head about his business, and changed the subject to the baby in a voice much too loud for her comfort.

Now he barely masked a glare at her before taking another enormous bite of his burger. "God, you really are a princess, aren't you?" he said through a full mouth. "Can't do a little research on your own. Think everything about everyone has to be handed to you on a silver platter."

Nina glared at him. Calvin just chuckled. She watched, cringing as he polished off the rest of his sandwich and tossed his napkin on the plate before wiping his hands on his pants.

"You're lucky you have someone like me who actually cares about you."

"I have—" Nina started, but he continued.

"I mean, the next thing you'll say is that you're planning to go back to school in the fall."

The look on Nina's face must have made it clear that was exactly what she had been planning to do. There were no laws about pregnant women staying out of classrooms.

"Nina, you can't be serious." Calvin shook his head, dumbfounded. "What kind of life will this kid come into if its mother doesn't care enough to prepare for it?" He reached across the table and plucked an untouched potato off her plate. "Now, don't tell me you're planning to go back after the birth too. Do you care more about froufy paintings than a baby who needs its mother?"

He snorted, like it was preposterous. Nina kept her mouth closed, unwilling to admit that too was her original plan.

"Since you've already decided to flee the father," Calvin continued, "the least you could do is give it a mother who's actually present. Or do you want to be like your own? Like mother, like daughter, eh?"

Nina opened her mouth, but nothing came out. All her indignation was suddenly replaced by doubt.

He was right. She didn't even have a place to live with her baby. She hadn't given it a single thought.

"Hey, princess."

Calvin's voice, suddenly soft, pulled her gaze up. Tears welled, and she hated that she couldn't stop them. She was everything a de Vries wasn't: empty of self-control.

He reached out with his soiled napkin and dabbed at her eyes. Nina was too upset to bat it away.

"Calm down," he said. "Listen, princess. I have a plan. It could save you some grief." He sat back and looked pointedly at Nina's still-full plate. "Eat. That wasn't cheap, you know. At least care enough to nourish your kid."

Nina didn't bother telling him that she was more than capable of paying the bill. Instead, she cut a small bit of the lamb, did her best to ignore the nausea rising as she lifted it to her mouth, and waited for Calvin to continue.

"We all know you'll end up in the papers no matter what—this city loves its royalty, and you, pregnant at twenty, were always going to get some attention."

The way he said it, like Nina was a specimen they were evaluating together, made her gag. Although that might have also been the mint sauce, which the lamb was absolutely doused in. But she couldn't deny that, again, Calvin was correct. Even now there were potential photographers meandering through the park, hoping for a glimpse of a celebrity or a socialite. They preferred film or music stars, but they would (and had) settled for someone like her. She and Calvin had avoided the papers thus far, but it was only a matter of time. And when she was visibly showing…

Nina drooped. She'd never have any peace, would she?

The olive farm drifted through her mind. The lazy afternoon. The taste of dry red wine on Peppe's lips.

Her eyes welled with tears all over again.

"So, the plan is simple," Calvin said as he plucked a roasted carrot off Nina's plate and popped it into his mouth. "We make an honest woman out of you."

Nina almost choked on the over-chewed piece of lamb in the back of her throat. Carefully, she managed to swallow. "We what?"

Calvin leered, his half smile revealing coffee-stained molars on one side. "Look, it would be simple. Your family already thinks we've been seeing each other for several months."

"Well, yes. Only because you told them that."

Nina cringed again, remembering the awkward meeting. When she had asked him to take her home, she'd only meant to her building, not all the way up to her grandmother's Park Avenue penthouse. He'd promptly introduced himself as Nina's "beau," like they were characters in an Edith Wharton novel, not twenty-first-century humans. Grandmother had eyed his sweaty, unwashed hand like he was handing her a rotten fish. And then she had turned her gaze to Nina with surprise. And disbelief. And then…disappointment.

"I took the heat off you when you disappeared for the day, didn't I?"

"Well, yes, but—"

"And haven't I been here since, helping you through the most difficult time in your life?"

"I suppose, but, Calvin—"

He shook his head. "I'm not going to be made a fool of, Nina. Not by you or anyone else. I've come too far."

She frowned. He had only told her once that he was from somewhere in New Jersey, but beyond that, Nina really knew nothing about his origins except when he made statements like these. He said it wasn't important, and she never pressed. But it didn't exactly help the perception that he was the social climber others accused him of being. Especially when she had no idea what he was climbing from.

Calvin polished off another oily carrot from her plate, then caught her examining him. He leaned over the table, his tie hanging dangerously above his empty, but still grease-spotted plate. "Don't think I'm good enough for you, princess?"

Nina paused, unsure how to answer the question. To anyone else, she might have said "No, of course not!" as vociferously as she could manage, but that would have been more for their comfort than for the sake of honesty. Because she was different from the average person. And she had no reason to question that either.

Her family was one of the oldest in New York, but it went beyond that. Celeste de Vries was the first woman in their four-hundred-year history to retain the title of Chairman of the Board of De Vries Shipping Industries while she waited for her grandson to come of age and inherit his birthright. Countless times, Nina had watched her grandmother handle the sniveling, self-righteous, insecure men who considered themselves titans of their class and of the city. Men who had questioned her every move. She'd torn them all to shreds.

Through all of that, she had raised Eric and Nina. Together.

Still…Nina was not her grandmother. She would never be Celeste de Vries. And it was time to be honest. In all likelihood, she would also never live up to the impossible standards this family set for her.

Nina forced herself to meet Calvin's eye. "I—of course not. You've been very kind to me, Calvin. I'd never say otherwise."

He relaxed, plucked an oil-soaked beet from her plate, and sat back again. "Good. Then we're clear."

Nina frowned. "What? But I—"

"But you what, princess?"

Nina frowned at the cold hunk of meat on her plate. He wasn't really going to make her say this, was he?

He was.

"To be honest, I really only ever imagined myself marrying someone for love," she told her food. And immediately flushed red. As soon as the words were out of her mouth, she wanted to take them back.

Not because they were wrong. Nina did feel that way. But there again was Peppe, his kind, weathered face crinkled with a melancholy smile. Wondering at her naivety, even if he never said anything out loud.

Nina felt as though her chest was twisted into a solid knot. Love. What did that matter now, when the man who owned her heart wasn't someone she could ever have? Especially in a world where most of the women she knew married for reasons that had nothing to do with their hearts. The notion now seemed childish. Like she was, in fact, the naive young princess Calvin accused her of being.

Calvin looked at Nina like he was sorry for her. "Good lord, did you think I meant forever?"

Nina looked up. "Um, I—I'm sorry, what do you mean by that?"

"I meant temporarily, you silly girl. Obviously this would be an arrangement. We'd share an apartment—separate rooms, of course— for a year or two. However long you think it would take for the bloom to fall off the rose or whatever so I can make an exit that won't land you in the papers for too long. What do you think your grand- mother would prefer? Divorce after a year or a baby out of wedlock?"

It sounded so crass, the way he said it. Nina's first thought was neither.

As if he could read her mind, Calvin clapped a wide, moist palm on top of Nina's, its heavy weight trapping hers to the linen tablecloth.

Nina had to fight not to pull her hand away. "And what do you get out of this?"

Calvin shrugged. "It's simple. I know you've been asking around about me, princess. You're not that subtle, you know."

Nina had the grace to blush. To whom had he been talking?

"And you're at least smart enough to know I've got some irons in the fire, since you keep asking about them. But I need connections to make them happen." Calvin shrugged as he finally removed his hand, though he swiped an oil-soaked potato from her plate and popped it in his mouth. "So, you get to avoid disgracing your family and keep your good name. I get to be a part of the de Vrieses, if only for a little while, and I'll have some doors opened that I need right now." His face darkened significantly. "Unless you're looking for a repeat of what happened to your cousin?"

Nina swallowed. The family hadn't even come close to recovering from that debacle. Eric continued to go rogue, so to speak—currently gallivanting his way around California, as far as Nina could tell from friends—and *Page Six* was still having a field day speculating about the city's missing heir.

Calvin knew just as well as she did that her family was not to be trifled with. And that her grandmother wouldn't take to another scandal.

"I will be a success in this life, Nina," Calvin said. "It's the only thing worth doing right."

Nina opened her mouth to ask what exactly he meant by that, but before she could, they were interrupted.

"N? Nina, is that you?"

Nina turned with shock to find her best friend, Caitlyn Calvert, weaving her way between the tables.

They had formed a friendship as children when Caitlyn received a scholarship at her preparatory academy, where she had boarded instead of commuting from her hometown of Paterson. She had even stayed with Nina's family several times when her own home life had been more...difficult.

Even so, the girls had somewhat drifted apart over the last few years. Nina had gone away to college, but Caitlyn had stayed put on the Upper East Side, by what means, Nina really wasn't sure. Now, however, Caitlyn looked...different. While they had both grown up over the last few years, the short, pudgy girl with unruly brown hair, a slightly crooked nose, and even more crooked teeth had disappeared. Everything was straightened and bleached, and she must have lost at least twenty pounds since Nina left for Florence. Her glossy hair was now closer to dark caramel than black coffee. In fact, Caitlyn would have been nearly unrecognizable had it not been for that voice.

"Ahh!" she shrieked as Nina stood to greet her, grateful she wore a very loose-fitting sundress. "It is you! The girls didn't think you would be back until July at least. Maddie was convinced you'd spend the summer on the continent, but here you are!"

They traded air kisses, and then Caitlyn joined the table without an invitation.

"You look wonderful, Cait," Nina said honestly. "Your hair, your—"

"Nose?" Caitlyn snickered. "Florian Hendricks actually paid for me to have it done—can you believe that? Men will do anything."

Nina's brow wrinkled. Ah. Any questions about how Caitlyn could afford to stay in New York's wealthiest neighborhood vanished. "Florian Hendricks? Isn't he…"

"Older than the earth? Balder than a golf ball?"

Beside them, Calvin's face blackened, and he touched his thinning hairline self-consciously.

Nina hid a smile. "I was going to say a bit older than you, but I suppose that works."

Caitlyn shrugged and flipped her hair over one shoulder, appearing not to notice the other person at the table. "Age is nothing but a number, and the man is crazy about me. Paid for this, this, and these on top of the nose." As she spoke, she pointed at her lips, hair, and then her breasts, which yes, did look a little bigger and…higher… than before underneath her fitted summer dress. "Of course, you can't say a word. You won't, my love, will you?"

Some people were overwhelmed by Caitlyn's somewhat manic energy, but Nina had always enjoyed it. Like Calvin, she was a social climber, but Nina found her honesty about it refreshing in a world of veiled references. Caitlyn knew what she had to offer the world, and what she didn't. And somehow, someway, she managed to make it charming. Almost as if she saw herself with the same tongue in cheek that everyone else did.

"No," Nina assured her with a smile. "Your secret is safe with me."

"Good." She grinned. "Because I'm aiming for some jewelry out of this too, before the old coot gets bored with me. Can't have a reputation, if you know what I mean. And this all goes for you too, whoever you are." She turned to Calvin. "Who are you, anyway?"

They turned to find Calvin eyeing Caitlyn with an expression Nina couldn't quite understand. Irritation? Greed? Admiration? Everything?

"Oh, I'm sorry," Caitlyn chattered on. "How rude of Nina not to introduce us. I'm Caitlyn Calvert, her oldest friend."

She offered her hand, dangling a bright diamond tennis bracelet as she looked Calvin over, taking in everything from his ill-fitted suit to his stained overshirt to his cheap shoes. Calvin took a large gulp of beer, leaving a thin line of moisture on his top lip, then accepted her hand.

"Calvin Gardner." He glanced at Nina. "I need to use the john. I'll leave you to reacquaint. And I know you'll make the right decision, princess. You did before."

He stood up, causing his chair to screech on the deck and a cascade of crumbs to fall to the ground. As he left, another wave of nausea swept through Nina. Midday "morning" sickness. Or maybe just the idea of committing herself to a sham marriage. Or perhaps the prospect of telling Grandmother that she was pregnant with her professor's illegitimate child.

It could have been any of them. Nina had no way of knowing.

"So what's his story?" Caitlyn asked as she watched Calvin go. "Obviously, I wouldn't blame you for an affair with an older man, but you don't have the same needs I do. A few more years and your trust will pay for any new body parts you want. But that man? Those Macy's shoes and the Men's Wearhouse special tell me he's not worth more than five figures, even—and he's not packing much anywhere else either."

Nina snorted lightly. "That's ridiculous, Cait."

"Hey, in my experience, what they say about a man's foot size definitely applies to the rest of his extremities. That guy's feet are no bigger than a size eight. Nine, tops."

Ironically, Grandmother had said something similar after meeting Calvin. Well, not about foot size, but about his financial prospects. Nina had actually considered offering to take him for a fitting at Armani, if only to help him make a better impression with the people whose assistance he wanted. His potato-shaped physique probably wouldn't fit the Italian lines anyway.

Nina kept quiet when a waiter returned and took Caitlyn's order for a dry Chardonnay. Like most restaurants in the city, he did not request identification.

"And for you, miss?" he asked Nina. "Anything else?"

"Some sparkling water, please," she said absently. "And maybe ginger tea if you have it?" Anything to wash the taste of minty animal flesh from her mouth.

"Right away, ma'am. Would you like me to box that up for you?"

Nina pushed her plate away. "No, thank you. Just remove it, please."

Caitlyn's sharp blue gaze flickered back and forth between Nina, the plate full of food, and the waiter as he left. Then she leaned close.

"Be honest. You're pregnant, aren't you?"

Nina had just sipped her ice water and nearly coughed it across the table. "What?"

Caitlyn grinned. "No wine? No eating? Plus, it's not just the lake, love—you look green in the face. And you're hanging out with that." She wrinkled her surgically enhanced nose in the direction Calvin had gone. "Why don't you just take care of it? Then you wouldn't be stuck with him. We all get Prosecco goggles from time to time, but there's no reason to martyr yourself to a one-night stand. Especially when it looks like that."

Nina swallowed as the pit in her stomach tightened again. "I—it just wasn't right. Not for me."

"So it is his?" Caitlyn pressed.

"Hmm? Whose?"

"Whose do you think, silly? Calvin's, of course. I'm just asking, N. We don't really know what you were up to in the last year. For all I know, you had some delicious love affair with a hot Italian rogue." She chuckled, as if the idea was absolutely hilarious. "Don't worry," she said with a conspiratorial wink. "I won't tell a soul."

Caitlyn had no idea how right she was, Nina thought. For a moment, she considered confiding in her. She thought about saying that's exactly what had happened. And more than that, she had fallen so desperately in love with the most wonderful and unavailable man in the world that she couldn't bear to give up any other piece of him, including his baby.

But if she did that, she might as well call *Page Six* and have them run a spread.

The photographers would find Peppe. They would destroy his family. His entire life. And that, despite everything, Nina would never ever do.

So, she let the assumption of Calvin's paternity stand.

"Caitlyn, really," she said quietly. "You can't say anything until I speak to Celeste. At least for a few days."

Immediately, Caitlyn sobered. She reached out to clutch Nina's hand, and for a moment, Nina felt her heart rate calm.

"Oh, N," she said with a soft squeeze. "Of course. You don't even have to ask."

Caitlyn really could be a good friend when she wanted. As had Calvin thus far, Nina had to admit. Perhaps he was being honest about the suggestion that a marriage between them would be a temporary arrangement. If he was truly her friend…would that be so bad?

"Thank you. I appreciate it."

"We've always kept each other's secrets, haven't we? You're like my own sister."

Nina sighed. "You can imagine what's going to happen, after everything that happened with Eric."

At the mention of Nina's cousin, Caitlyn looked truly pained. It was no secret that she had nursed an intense infatuation with Eric since they were all children. His engagement had nearly ruined her. And now that he was gone…well, Caitlyn couldn't be happy about that either. Florian Hendricks or not.

"It's all just terrible," she agreed in a voice that cracked. "Have you —have you heard from him?"

Nina shook her head. "Nothing. He hates all of us now. And I don't blame him. Why wouldn't he, considering what they did? Our kind of people can be so awful to others when they don't fit in."

Caitlyn pressed her slightly fuller lips together. She'd been on the receiving end of a few of those comments herself over the years.

"Which means you can't disappoint them either," she said with full understanding. "Of course not. But if your grandmother finds out about this baby, she will be enraged. Oh, N, what are you going to do if you're not getting rid of it?"

"Did you tell her the news?"

They both turned to find Calvin back at the table, still adjusting his pants and wiping his damp hands on his jacket. Caitlyn's lip curled with slight disgust. Nina trained her face blank. Was she really going to…marry…this man? Would anyone in her family believe she'd willingly attach herself to someone so uncouth?

Calvin sat down and smiled at Caitlyn, who looked like she was fighting to maintain a straight face.

"News?" she asked. "What news is that, N?"

"I'll let you tell her, princess." Calvin raised one brow, and his gaze darted between Nina and Caitlyn as he grabbed his beer and took another thick, messy gulp.

Was that a threat or a reminder? Nina couldn't tell. But fear danced up her spine regardless. Of what, she couldn't quite say, but if she closed her eyes, she could still see the pictures of Eric at Penny's funeral. And the smug look on Grandmother's face behind him.

Ostracization.

Financial ruin.

Total humiliation within and outside of her family's home.

Maybe someone's death.

These were the things facing Nina if she went it alone.

"You have to keep this to yourself too, Cait," she told her friend with as much conviction as she could muster. "At least for a few days. But you might as well hear it first."

Caitlyn leaned in, bright blue eyes dancing with anticipation. She loved nothing better than a secret.

Nina swallowed thickly. Her throat was so dry.

"Yes," Calvin said as he set a hand over hers. "I've just asked Nina to marry me. Do you want to tell her what you said, princess?"

A breeze floated off the water, catching a leaf of lettuce Calvin had dropped earlier and carrying it away into the pond.

Nina swallowed hard. Calvin's thick fingers didn't move from hers. Her stomach turned, reminding her of what she was harboring.

"I—I said…" She drifted off, then finally managed to drag her gaze back to Caitlyn's. Her voice was barely a whisper. "I said yes."

CHAPTER THREE

"Nina. Nina."

The name bounced through the dusty chapel, echoing off plaster walls beyond flowered hats and polite faces.

Nina blinked and found Calvin Gardner, her husband-to-be, glaring at her from the other side of the altar while the officiant blinked through oversized glasses like a bemused owl.

"For God's sake," Calvin hissed, pulling for the tenth time at the part of his stiff tuxedo collar that dug into his jowls. "Can you answer the man's question?"

Nina took a moment to remember where she was. A church. In a white dress. In front of friends, family, and an assortment of people who had come to watch the novelty of an heiress marry a nobody.

Marry.

The strength of the word hit her in the stomach yet again. The same way the word "object" had just a minute or two before.

When the minister had asked the assembly in a bored tone whether anyone objected, Nina had chanced a peek through her veil. No one had raised a hand.

She had looked to the doors at the back of the hall, half expecting to see Peppe, or maybe even Eric, crash through them.

The doors stayed firmly shut.

Nina took a deep breath, trying and failing to ignore the way the boning of her dress—yes, her wedding dress—dug into her expanding ribs. It had only been days since her final fitting, and at almost ten weeks along, she was already outgrowing it.

It didn't matter. She wouldn't have chosen this dress for herself under normal circumstances anyway. Too much lace covering her arms and bodice, the full skirt wider than it was tall.

But then again, this wasn't the wedding Nina would have chosen either. No little girl dreams of getting pregnant out of wedlock and marrying a man who vaguely resembles a banana muffin, all before she's twenty-one. She had always seen herself getting married on the beach, perhaps near her family's estate in the Hamptons. Wearing a slip dress like Catherine Bessette-Kennedy, not one like Grace of Monaco. Dancing in the moonlight in the arms of a man who loved her.

She should have known it was time to forfeit those dreams the second she met Peppe. She should have known in that moment that she would never be worthy of them.

Nina swallowed as she looked between Calvin's livid face and the minister's. "Um, I'm so sorry. Can you repeat the question?"

"Oh, for God's sake," Calvin muttered.

The minister adjusted his glasses and patted Calvin kindly on the shoulder like he was calming a toddler about to throw a tantrum. It didn't seem to work.

"Of course, dear. It happens all the time." He cleared his voice and repeated, in a louder voice: "Nina Evelyn Astor de Vries, will you have this man to be your husband; to live together in the covenant of marriage? Will you love him, comfort him, honor and keep him, in sickness and in health; and, forsaking all others, be faithful to him as long as you both shall live?"

St. Mark's Church in-the-Bowery was silent, the only noise the occasional whisper of paper fans and screech of rented chairs on the wood floors. It was hot, even for late June in New York, and the second-oldest church in the city did not have working air-conditioning that day.

One hundred and four of New York's most elite people—her people, as Nina had been told all her life—were crunched onto the chairs, fanning their sweat-soaked faces while they awaited her response. It was a small crowd by de Vries standards. Even Aunt Heather's second wedding was twice this size at the Vineyard, and that had been called a modest affair.

"Ahem."

In the front row, Celeste de Vries's light cough spoke volumes. She, like the rest of the family, looked perfectly put together in her light pink Chanel suit, her silver hair pinned into a classic French twist, and a wide-brimmed hat tipped elegantly to one side. Beside her, Nina's mother, Violet, watched with only a slightly less bored than usual expression through her typical Chardonnay glaze. Edwin Astor, unsurprisingly, had elected not to come. Too short notice, he'd said. And with only two weeks between the announcement and this strange procession, he was right.

It was short notice. For everyone.

Nina looked down to where Calvin cuffed her shaking hands with his thick fingers, his thumb brushing over the diamond engagement ring that Nina had purchased for herself only a week before. She studied the lace that covered her body from wrist to neck like a straitjacket and forced herself to breathe. Then she looked to the floor, where the tips of her Zanotti pumps peeked from under the layers of tulle and taffeta.

Everything suffocated. Everything.

Don't cry, she thought to herself as she pressed into her feet to stand tall. *Don't cry. You mustn't cry. They'll never stop talking about you if you do.*

And wasn't that the point of today? To fade into obscurity, away from their prying eyes? Marry a nondescript man in a nondescript dress and live a nondescript life until it didn't matter anymore?

All she had to do was not cry while she did it.

It was very, very hard.

"Nina."

For a moment, she saw him. Peppe. The slightly worn skin from too many summers under the olive trees. The salt-and-pepper hair curled a little too long over his ears. The large friendly eyes protected by the glasses that constantly slid down his long nose.

She imagined he was the one standing at this altar, clutching her hands, waiting for her to make the promise that would bind her to him for life. She imagined that they hadn't said goodbye that terrible day at the station. That he hadn't gone back to his wife and children. That she wasn't here. Pregnant. Alone.

Well, she was alone. Wasn't she?

"Nina!"

Nina blinked again, and it wasn't Peppe's voice calling her back to the present, but Calvin's. The man who had stumbled upon her somewhere outside a nameless Queens clinic, then sat with her in silent support as she made a decision that would change the rest of her life.

For that, she supposed she owed him everything.

In front of them, people were openly whispering. Celeste scowled. How one person's expression could contain all number of threats, Nina would never understand. But she felt them. And would endure all of them if she embarrassed herself and everyone there by doing what she desperately wanted—to walk out of this church and leave it all behind. Even if it meant she risked the sincere wrath of Celeste de Vries to claim her freedom.

Because it would be wrath.

Make an honest woman out of you.

It wasn't a proposal. It wasn't even a question. Calvin had made this marriage seem like he was doing Nina a favor. Her. One of the two apparent heirs to the great de Vries fortune. Him, a no-name, amateur investor. Doing her a favor.

Eric hadn't shown today. Of course he hadn't. Because of what Celeste had done to his girl. His love.

So many ruined because of her grandmother's vengeance. Nina had witnessed the blackness in her grandmother's face when she swore that no one in the family was above punishment. She had felt the sear of her threats when she announced to the entire family, time and time again, that she would not tolerate disgrace.

An honest woman out of you.

And so, Nina had said yes.

The announcement was placed the next day. St. Mark's was booked two weeks later. And here they were.

Grandmother knew it was a farce. Of course she knew. Celeste de Vries loved a spectacle, and Nina was this family's princess. This wedding was supposed to be at St. John the Divine, with a thousand guests, three separate receptions, a *Vogue* spread, and a season full of engagement parties and events that would last at least a year. Not this. A paltry hundred and change smashed into this sauna of a church. A quick garden party reception with chicken breasts instead of king crab. A weekend-long honeymoon on Long Island instead of Europe for the summer.

This was Celeste de Vries's version of a shotgun wedding. And if Nina dared run away now...she was terrified to find out what Celeste's version of the actual shotgun might also be.

"Nina."

This time, Calvin's voice was a hiss again, full of serpentine consonants. Frantic and incensed.

Nina blinked, and Peppe's face was replaced by Calvin's. He was wearing lifts today, and her, only kitten heels, so for once they were almost eye to eye. It was Calvin who had insisted on this absurd dress in the middle of summer. Who demanded Nina choose (and pay for) the gaudy engagement ring at Tiffany's when she would have done with something smaller and more tasteful, or nothing at all.

"Can you say something?" he whispered fiercely.

A thin line of sweat drew a streak through his face. The man was wearing makeup, Nina realized. She was about to marry a man who was wearing makeup, sweating like a pig through his tuxedo, and was looking at her across the altar like he wanted to beat her black and blue.

"Ms. de Vries?" ventured the minister, who now looked equally uncomfortable in the afternoon heat. "Do you need a moment?"

But Nina's tears were gone.

Her heart was numb.

Peppe was gone. And Nina already had the only thing from him she could keep.

A baby. Who would maybe, one day, have a father.

She cleared her throat and stood up straight, now taller than Calvin again, even in his lifted shoes.

"No, I'm sorry," she said quietly. "I'm ready."

And then, in a much louder voice:

"I will."

NOW

CHAPTER FOUR

JUNE 2018

Nina

I counted to one hundred before opening my eyes.

Waited for the door to catch.

For the footsteps to recede.

For the invasion to cease.

Yes, okay. Perhaps it was a bit extreme. But to be candid, I think you would do the same if you had put up with the man for ten years.

You would fake sleep to escape that ham-fisted touch. The intrusive fingers. The painful slap.

It's the least you would do. Truly.

It wasn't until the shuffle of leather soles on parquet and marble completely faded, and the faint ring of the elevator announced my husband's departure that I finally greeted the day. On the other side of the triple-pane windows, the sun shone, but New York threatened. I couldn't hear her, of course. Such was my privilege, ensconced in my tower. Twenty stories above traffic horns and subway rumbles. Silence is one form of currency in this city, and only the rich—like me—have it.

But even here, the tips of the high-rise buildings of midtown, just across the park, still threatened to pierce. New York is a dangerous city.

A city full of weapons. Some I'd been learning to use all my life. Others I couldn't touch.

There was a soft knock on the door, and I sat up, checking that my injuries from last night weren't visible.

"Mrs. Gardner?" The familiar, timid voice of my personal assistant sounded through the oak.

I sighed. What an unemployed housewife needed with a personal assistant, I really couldn't say. It was even more pathetic than the fact that I couldn't do without her. I wasn't sure when Moira Lemon and I began our daily routine of wake-up calls like I was the dauphiness of France, but close to a decade later, here we were.

"I'm up," I called as I swung my legs out from under my duvet. "Come in."

Moira strode in, followed by a maid wheeling the espresso cart, just as I was wrapping a gray silk dressing gown over my torn chemise. The maid left, but my assistant remained outside the door as I walked into the en suite to examine the damage to my body in the mirror over the vanity.

"Nice busy day today," Moira called cheerily. "Would you like your cappuccino, Mrs. Gardner?"

I pulled open the robe, frowning distastefully at the rip in the silk nightgown. Another one for the trash. "Yes, please, Moira."

As the sounds and scents of the coffeemaker filtered in, I continued my inventory-taking. I was married to a man who gifted me his negligence ninety percent of the time and made up for it in the worst possible way the other ten. But what had once been an occurrence two or three times per year, when my husband was actually home, had become almost nightly since Calvin's arrest five weeks ago for racketeering, bribery, and human trafficking. Since his travel was stunted while the trial began, I was a convenient place to take out his frustration. Particularly since January, when I refused to comply with his other wishes.

Frigid bitch.

It could be worse, I thought numbly. From the neck up, I looked relatively normal. My blonde hair was a mess, but Mikael, my stylist, would fix that later. My light gray eyes, a little too big for my face, were framed with dark circles, but I had concealer. My bottom lip was puffed slightly, but nothing lipstick wouldn't hide.

We had a deal, after all. Anything but the face. And he only broke that deal sometimes.

Elsewhere, there were a few small bruises at the base of my neck left over from last Tuesday, but I thought I could cover those up too. It was the large one I could feel forming on my inner thigh, deep under the skin, that might make it difficult to walk properly later.

A decade ago, I had been called sharp. Striking. Full of promise. Now look at me. Thirty years old, haggard, beaten.

And what's more, I deserved it.

The fuck you do, doll.

I suck in a sharp breath as the voice—deep, coarse, and utterly hypnotizing—echoed in the back of my mind. Uncalled for, but when was it ever? Matthew Zola's voice was a bell whose ring never faded. Once I'd heard it, I couldn't sleepwalk through this life anymore.

I still wasn't sure if that was for better or for worse. These days, maybe the latter. Since, of course, he turned out to be the man prosecuting my husband.

I splashed a bit of water on my face, wincing as it dribbled over my lip. I ignored it and went about the mundane tasks of cleaning myself up for the day.

There was another knock on the door. I opened it to let Moira in. The older woman set my coffee on the vanity, then began running through the day while I brushed my teeth.

"Spencer will be here in twenty minutes for your morning Pilates. After that, you have cycling at seven forty-five. Your gym kit is on the bureau. You reached three hundred miles last week, so I picked up some new sneakers too. Be careful about blisters."

I quirked a smile in the mirror. Moira had started laying clothes out for me when I was in the throes of postpartum depression and had never stopped. I didn't always use them, but it was a sweet gesture. My own mother had never even done that.

"After that, you've got acupuncture at nine around the corner from the studio."

I winced as the marble countertop pressed into my thigh.

Acupuncture would be good today, but the look on the practitioner's face when I removed my clothes would not. "Reschedule that for next week, please. And then?"

"Blowout with Mikael, then lunch with your mother at noon. She wants to discuss the Met luncheon she's planning in honor of your cousin's recent contributions. I assume you're planning to go?"

I sighed. Once upon a time, luncheons, charities—all of these were daily occurrences, things that, if not particularly fulfilling, at least gave my shadow of a life some meaning. Now, I couldn't help wondering how much of our "charity" work was simple self-congratulations. I'd rather just write a check and be done with it.

I spat, then rinsed and replaced my toothbrush in its charger. "Mother really is pulling out all the stops to kiss the ring, isn't she?"

Moira didn't respond, which was basically her way of agreeing with me. It didn't take rocket science to figure out what was going on. Less than a year ago, my cousin Eric had returned to the family fold after a ten-year absence. He might have been the black sheep of the family, but he was welcomed as its prodigal son. The last of the line of birthright de Vrieses. Heir to the bulk of our now-passed grandmother's considerable fortune, including controlling ownership of the family company).

Now that Grandmother was gone, Eric was the de facto head. Which made Mother and me nothing but poor relations, relatively speaking. I realized that we weren't exactly in line at the food bank, but considering that De Vries Shipping was valued at something close to twenty billion, my supposed fifty-million-dollar inheritance and the similar amount handcuffed in my trust were paltry in comparison. Mother too had her own, plus the estate near Southampton, but again, neither came close to Eric's newfound wealth.

I couldn't lie. When the will was read, I was hurt. Really hurt. Not because of the money. And I loved Eric. I had even come to love his wife. What did I care if my portfolio or theirs expanded by a factor of ten or ten billion? No, it was the fact that in the end, Eric's last name mattered more than the decade I had spent with our grandmother while he had been off doing God knew what. They say blood runs thicker than water, but in our family, gender trumped all.

My husband, however, definitely cared about the money. After all, it was the reason he married me. And it was why, six months after the will was read, he was still quietly trying to get my other family members to fight it in probate. So far, he hadn't succeeded.

So, for now, Eric paid the bills. And Mother would want to do what was needed to keep that faucet running, which included sucking up to the new head of family and the wife that no one thought belonged on the Upper East Side.

"Okay, lunch," I repeated after splashing water on my face and grabbing a towel. "What else?"

"An appointment with Dr. Raleigh at three."

I dropped the towel. "Is it that time already?"

Moira shrugged. "It's been six months. You missed your last appointment, and the receptionist called." She looked up from her list. "Shouldn't I have made it? I assumed you'd want to look nice for tonight. Not that you don't always, of course. But since it's special…"

I frowned into the mirror. "Special how?"

Moira blinked. "Well, since it's your anniversary, of course."

We both stilled as my sudden awkward silence landed in the middle of my bathroom like a wet blanket. Moira wasn't stupid. She had been my assistant for nearly ten years, which meant she understood at least something of the distance between Calvin and me, even if she didn't know what happened behind closed doors.

"Mr. Gardner's assistant hasn't said anything to me about it," Moira said quietly. "I assumed you were planning something at home. Might be nice not to think about…everything."

It was her kind way of suggesting I should probably do something to distract from the embarrassingly public trial we were facing in a matter of weeks. And offering to help, should I need it.

I cleared my throat. "Um, yes. I suppose I am. But nothing you need to worry about. Thank you, Moira."

I leaned closer to the mirror again, more in order to avoid Moira's gaze than because I really saw anything. I pressed at my skin, eyeing the minuscule, practically nonexistent wrinkles at the corners of my eyes. I didn't have nearly the work done regularly that many of my friends had. But they also didn't smile. Or laugh. Or love. And until recently, neither did I.

I love your laugh, doll. That voice again, reprimanding me. *Don't you change a fuckin' thing.*

I stood back from the mirror. Matthew wasn't the only person who had ever called me perfect.

But in front of him was the only time it had ever felt like the truth. When I had had less sleep than this. When my face was tear-stained and blotchy. When my lips were swollen and hard-kissed.

To him, I was perfect. If only for a moment.

"Cancel the appointment with Dr. Raleigh, please," I said to Moira as I straightened and picked up the coffee on the counter. "I've decided to see what life is like without the needle for a while."

Moira nodded and made a note. "Very well. Do you have a preference for breakfast?"

I shook my head. I didn't like much more than coffee before my trainer. "Just a poached egg and grapefruit, please."

"I'll be sure it's in the dining room, Mrs. Gardner. After that I'm taking out the dry-cleaning and then making sure Patricia is available to nanny again this month and in August. We want to have everything in order before Miss Olivia returns this weekend."

I smiled at the mention of my daughter. "It will be nice to have her home for a bit, won't it?"

Moira smiled back. Olivia wasn't just the light of *my* life. My assistant, the cook, the maid, the doorman—they all adored her as well. "Yes, it certainly will."

She didn't say, as she had years before, that she wished Olivia could stay longer, and why didn't we just hire a nanny for the entire summer, not just for a few weeks. Moira never explicitly stated that she understood why my daughter attended school in another state or why she would go to a sleepaway camp in England. Instead, her eyes dropped to the bruise on my chest where my dressing gown had fallen open, then flickered back up when I tugged it closed.

I willed myself to look her in the eye. What would she say if she knew I'd given that one to myself?

Moira turned toward the door. "I'll be on my cell phone if you need me, of course. Have a wonderful day, Mrs. Gardner."

Her footsteps echoed my husband's, as did the sound of the bedroom door opening and closing, leaving me alone again. I turned back to the mirror, pausing for a moment. And then, slowly, I pulled off my robe.

The bruise on my chest was flowering a bit more now, and the bottom of my lip was positively purple. I turned my hip out to examine my inner thigh—just a hint of color there, but the skin was tender and swollen.

You have to take care of yourself, doll.

My lower lip trembled. It had been nearly five weeks since I'd seen him. Seven since I'd toppled into the small brick house on the edge of Brooklyn and confessed the truth buried in the depths of my soul.

I love you.

And Matthew, of course, loved me too. For a few brief, shining moments, I had envisioned a future away from this plush jail. Seen myself living in that tiny townhouse, breaking bread with his raucous family in the Bronx. Fleeing the man I was chained to for the man who set me free. Since meeting Matthew, I had craved freedom. And for scant moments, I tasted it in his arms.

Until he told me I couldn't. Until he had broken my heart. And told me I had to come back.

———

"Nina," he said in a voice portending certain doom. "Baby, I don't think you understand. You have to go. You have to go back home."

My eyes popped open with shock. Disbelief. "What? Why?" After the night of passion—no, love—how could he be saying this?

"Because," Matthew said. His head dropped. Shame emanated from his beautiful body like some sort of sick halo. "I can't protect you from this investigation. But being married to Calvin..." He shook his head, looking ill. "That will."

———

SUDDENLY, I was gasping for air.

The problem with addiction is that once you start, you physically can't stop the wanting.

The problem with love is the same.

The course of the day seemed utterly impossible. I touched a finger to my swollen lip. The flash of my diamond—a gaudy, glittering lie—made me squint. I couldn't do this anymore.

I just want to see him, I told myself. *Nothing illegal about that.*

Before I knew it, I had trudged back into the bedroom, sunk into the covers, and taken my phone from the nightstand. It took only a few more seconds to pull up his name—or the pseudonym I had given him—in my contacts.

I couldn't.

I shouldn't.

Just like last time, the text was short and sweet, and before I knew it, flying through cyberspace.

Me: I need you. Please.

The phone lay silent in my hand for a long time. But just when I was about to give up and shove my legs into Lycra like it was my armor against the world, the phone vibrated.

Maya: What time?

I closed my eyes in relief, my chest expanding at just the thought of his face in front of mine.

Nina: Two o'clock. Our room.

CHAPTER FIVE

Golden slumbers kiss your eyes,
Smiles awake you when you rise.
Sleep, pretty wantons, do not cry,
And I will sing a lullaby:
Rock them, rock them, lullaby.

Care is heavy, therefore sleep you,
You are care, and care must keep you;
Sleep, pretty wantons, do not cry,
And I will sing a lullaby,
Rock them, rock them, lullaby.

Peppe turned from the window, a smile playing over his lips as Nina finish reciting the poem. Thomas Dekker, one of the many assigned for his class on Renaissance literature and art this summer. Nina hummed the tune from The Beatles' "Golden Slumbers." Peppe loved The Beatles. She clung to these small details he offered like cellophane.

Still wrapped in sheets like one of Botticelli's models, Nina preened in the bed, ignoring the crumbling plaster overhead. This apartment might have been falling apart, but it felt like a palace when her lover was in it.

"Very good," Peppe said, ever the professor, even after sex. "Full marks for you, principessa.*"*

Nina stretched, allowing the worn linens to fall from her limbs, drawing him to her like a moth to a flame.

"All right, Professor," she whispered as he returned to the bed and brushed the hair from her face. "Your turn to recite a little poetry."

"There are many kinds of poetry, my principessa.*" His voice was a hummingbird's wing as it found the curve of her shoulder and set her skin aflutter. "Let's explore another."*

———

THE KNOCK AT THE DOOR, brisk and quick, shook me out of my daydream. I turned from the floor-to-ceiling window of the Grace Hotel penthouse, from which the Lower East Side spread, cooking with the rest of the city in the summer heat. The room was air-conditioned, but even so, my silk shell was sticking to the back of my neck. I needed to get these clothes off. I needed a cold shower

But I needed something—some*one*—else more.

"Nina?"

His voice pulled me to him, and before I could help myself, I was skipping over to the door and yanking it open like a child on Christmas morning. There I found the man who had stood in court and charged my husband with counts of racketeering, trafficking, and bribery.

It had been only a few weeks since the last time I had begged Matthew to see me one last time, but it felt like years. In this room. Where it all started. For one final night.

We can't do this again.

So wrong.

The last time.

He had said them over and over again as he peeled the garments from my worn body like he was unwrapping a gift. Breathed the words as he set my skin alight with his touch. Whispered them against my lips before taking kiss after torrid kiss.

Still, he had meant them, and so had I.

Still, we were here.

He looked as dapper as ever. A man straight out of any woman's fantasies, somehow belonging as much to an older time as his own. I'd seen this light gray Ferragamo suit before. It was the sleek, almost mod Italian cut he generally preferred, immaculately tailored to make his waist trim and his shoulders impossibly broad. A straw fedora—always a fedora—was tipped rakishly to one side as he looked me over with sooty, dark green eyes.

Matthew Zola, assistant district attorney.

Zola to friends, Mattie to his family.

But to me, he was just my Matthew.

I frowned.

His smile immediately morphed into a mirror image of my own. "Not exactly the welcome I was expecting, doll."

"What's your middle name?" I asked. "I just realized I don't know."

For some reason, I *hated* that I didn't know. I wanted to know everything about this man who had somehow taken one half of my heart for his own.

The smile reappeared, roguish and slightly crooked over gleaming white teeth. Matthew resembled a pirate in many ways, most particularly because of the chiseled jaw and the graze of black over cheeks that he usually kept clean. He was also very observant, seeming to catch every stray glance of mine.

No one could read me like this man. Considering how trained I was to be unreadable, he might have been the only one to do it at all.

Or perhaps he just undid that training.

"I…well, I don't have one, actually."

I frowned more. He chuckled.

"Truly?" I asked.

"I have two first names, though." He tipped his head. "Italian custom, according to *Nonna*. They get two first names, but no middle name. If this were Italy, you'd see them marked on the census with a comma. Matthew, comma, Luca Zola. But here it just looks like a middle name on my birth certificate."

I reached out and fingered his lapel, then ran my touch over the collar of his polka-dotted shirt, the bright red tie. Matthew wasn't the most well-dressed man in the city—not on a civil servant's salary, and not with secondhand suits like this from his sister's consignment shop. But he might have been the most stylish. Unlike most men I knew, for whom clothes were perfunctory uniforms, Matthew was like a character from one of the old movies he loved so much. With a good tailor and interesting textiles, he managed to blend quality and fashion together in a way that was anything but cookie-cutter.

"So." His voice lowered in a way that made my toes curl. "You going to invite me in, doll? Or do I need to toss you over my shoulder?"

Suddenly, I had a hard time swallowing. Nearly six months I had known this man, and that particular growl never failed to have the same effect. Undoing each one of my careful reserves. Unweaving my—

Control yourself. It was a mantra I'd practiced my entire life. The creed of the de Vrieses and their ilk. Never show emotion. Never show vulnerability. Never lose control.

That was the problem with Matthew. He undid those knots with a single word and had since the moment we met.

So, I realized with sudden clarity, *why fight it?*

That's right. I didn't have to. Not here. Not with him. For a fraction of time, I could just let go.

So I did. The hand around his lapel tightened, and I yanked him to me with an ardor that knocked his hat to the ground as the door slammed shut behind him.

He didn't even seem to notice. As my fingers slid into the shining thickets of his dark hair, his lips found mine with similar force. He walked me backward into the suite, hands sliding up and down my body. It was always the same with him, the way he explored me each time like he'd never seen me before. Never touched me.

"God," he breathed after he took one kiss, then another, and allowed me to take the same. "I thought this would *never* come."

Our tongues warred with each other like this was the first time we'd ever given in. Six months after we had started our affair, it was still like this. It didn't matter how many times he took me, in how many ways. As soon as he was done, that craving came right back again.

A pirate indeed. I was a new world, and he was here to pillage it.

"How long do we have?" I wondered as I pushed his jacket from his shoulders.

He was hot, like his skin was burning up. His shirt was slightly dewy, an effect of the heatwave ravaging the city. But it only made his scent—something musky mixed with the subtle cologne he used and the more typical odors of coffee and paper—that much more alluring.

"Ninety minutes, maybe. I have to be in court by four, and the trains are running late again. God, get this thing *off*," he snarled, more at the jacket than at me as he shook it off with a snap onto one of the chairs. "The city is an absolute fuckin' sauna. Ninety-eight degrees this afternoon, and they say it will get up to a hundred tomorrow. In June, do you believe that?"

With reluctance, he stepped away to continue undressing on his own. I used the opportunity to catch my breath and get us both glasses of water from the bureau. The cool glass pressed to my lips, I watched him pull off his tie, then his button-down shirt, shoes, and socks with neat precision until he was standing in just his gray pants and a white tank undershirt.

I licked my lips. I knew very well what treasures were underneath that thin layer of cotton, but the in-between was nearly as enjoyable. The man made simple undergarments look like couture. Especially when sweat caused them to cling to his sculpted body just… like…that…

"Nina."

I continued to stare. The tight muscles flexed, guiding my gaze over his flat belly, down to the waistband, then to the—

"*Nina.*"

I blinked and colored. Lord, he had caught me again. "Yes?"

He raised one dark, rakish brow. My cheeks heated even more as his fiery gaze slid up and down my body. After spinning class, I'd slipped on a demure white sundress appropriate for the heat and a pair of nude sandals that wrapped around my ankles. My hair was blown out and tossed around my shoulders, but with a bit more volume than usual from the humidity. It was even starting to curl a little at the ends.

Nothing special. But the fire in Matthew's dark gaze made me feel like I was practically naked.

"Well, you got me here, beautiful," he said. "Now what are you going to do with me?"

I couldn't reply. I could barely remember my own name when he looked at me like that.

"Thirsty?" he asked as he spied the water in my hand.

I looked down at the glass and back at him. "Like you said, it's very warm."

He closed the space between us, and for a moment I fought the urge to run. I had tried it before, and to my delight, he had stalked me across the room like a panther tracking its prey. When he pounced, I had forgotten my name completely.

Well…I had the same power. If I wanted to use it.

I jiggled the ice in my drink, then pulled out one cube and held it up to my mouth, tracing around my lips, delighting in the dilation of his eyes as he watched.

"Nina…" His tone was equal parts warning and praise.

I sucked on the ice cube, then trailed it down my neck and over the swells of my breasts. This wasn't a particularly revealing dress—none of mine were—but it was flattering and showed enough of my chest that Matthew could complete the picture using his imagination. And I already knew that was quite avid.

"Sweetheart," he growled. "It's been five fuckin' weeks. If you don't drop the ice and get the fuck over here, I'm going to—"

"You're going to what?" I interrupted gently.

He didn't bother to answer, instead closing the space with two long strides, grabbing the glass from my hands, and upending the entire thing over my chest.

"Matthew!" I shrieked as the ice and water soaked my dress, causing goose bumps to fly up everywhere.

But before I could shout again, his mouth, hot and hungry, closed over mine, shuttering my cries. One hand slipped under the hem of my dress to find my backside, the other found my breast and squeezed. Our tongues coiled together all over again before he broke the kiss and looked down.

"I knew you weren't wearing a bra."

I followed his cocky inspection. The water had made my dress completely transparent. "How could you have possibly known that?"

"Because." Both hands now closed over my breasts. "I know this body like I know my own. I know its shapes. Every peak"—his thumbs drifted over my erect nipples, making me shiver—"and valley."

I watched transfixed as he leaned down to take one nipple into his mouth through the soaked silk. He sucked, using his teeth to lightly worry the sensitive nub.

I gripped his hair even tighter. "Matthew."

He moved to the other side as he plucked at the buttons down the front of my dress. "Hmm?"

"Matthew, p-please."

Lord. I never stuttered. Just like every de Vries child, I had been taught to enunciate perfectly. But he brought that out of me, just like everything else.

Matthew stood straight again just as he undid the last of the buttons, then peeled the fabric to survey his spoils. "Perfect," he murmured.

I pulled back enough to allow the dress to drop to the floor.

"I should pick that up and lay it to dry," I said. I didn't move, though. I was shameless, standing before him in my heels and a pair of nude silk panties.

"You'll do no such thing." Matthew's voice was thick with desire— just like the bulge in the front of his pants. He looked like he was two seconds from tossing me backward onto the bed.

God, how many nights had I fallen asleep dreaming of that exact expression on his face? In front of him, I was the center of the universe. Nothing existed other than the two people in this room. Two bodies aching for each other.

"A work of art," he murmured as he had time and time again.

He never ceased to make me feel so much more beautiful than I really was.

I tipped my chin up, giving him a view of the neck he loved to praise as swan-like, though I was no pinup. Thin rather than curvy, but he loved me just the same.

Or so he had said. Once.

Matthew stepped toward me, but just as he was about to kiss me again, he stopped. "What's that?"

"Hmm?" I was too ready for his touch to even notice his change in tone.

"That. Nina, what the hell is that?"

My eyes flew open in panic. I had taken such care before coming, but perhaps the ice water had washed away some of the cover-up. Perhaps our kisses had made the one on my lip that much worse. Or maybe the bruising on my thigh had gotten worse…

Relief flooded me as I realized he was staring just above my left breast.

"Oh, that. You gave me that."

Matthew reared. "*I* gave you that? It's been five weeks. I remember dropping a few hickeys here and there, but…"

He drifted off, as if our last encounter rendered him speechless. I knew the feeling.

He shook his head. "But nothing that would look like that after five days, let alone five weeks. The whole area is yellow, like a bunch of bruises almost done healing. Jesus, doll, you look like someone's been smacking the shit out of you."

My cheeks reddened. The tightening in his voice told me he was suspicious. He didn't need to know how correct that was—some days, anyway. But not about this, at least.

"I—I might have helped it along," I admitted.

Matthew raised a brow. "You helped it along."

Sheepishly, I nodded. "I did." I pinched the skin lightly, demonstrating how. "See? I wanted the reminder of you."

Matthew frowned. "You wanted my…"

"Mark. Yes."

It sounded so vulgar, so barbaric, but that's how he made me feel.

Matthew was in full inspection mode now, and I was torn by the desire to keep him from looking for other flaws—flaws I did *not* want him to examine—and the need to feel him close. Thankfully, they were both solved the same way.

I slipped a hand around his neck again and pulled him closer, so we stood only inches apart. His nose touched mine, and he nuzzled me with a sweetness that ached.

"I can't stand this." I ran my nose over his neck, then bit softly, enjoying the shivers it produced all over his body. "Don't you know I want your marks everywhere?"

He shuddered. I shuddered. For a moment, I imagined what it would be like. How it would feel if I didn't have to spend twenty minutes in the mornings slathering makeup all over my body to hide the evidence of my home life. How it might feel to spend an entire night together with nowhere to go the next morning. To wake up with the knowledge that the day would continue together, and the day after that, and the day after that...

What it might be like to live with my daughter again?

He looked equally despondent. "Nina, maybe we shouldn't—"

"Please," I interrupted before the sadness became too unbearable. "Please, Matthew. I know this is just for today. But I told you—I *need* you. I'm begging. Mark me again."

Like an animal, he growled and yanked me close so my almost-naked body was flush with his. His erection pressed against my thigh through his pants as he set his teeth to my neck.

"With fucking pleasure."

He whirled us around, and then I was flying through the air and landed on the bed with a very unladylike shout. With swift, efficient movements, Matthew removed the rest of his clothing, then fell on top of me. Caging me with his arms, his smooth, muscled chest, his sleek, solid body.

"Your legs, baby." He dropped kisses over my face, then moved around to take my earlobe between his teeth. "Wrap them around me."

Obediently, I hooked my ankles around him, causing the heels of my sandals to dig into his backside.

Matthew hissed, but with more pleasure than pain. Instead, he pressed against me, teasing between my thighs. His teeth bit harder. I arched in his arms.

"Is this what you want, Nina?" he asked, moving his mouth over my neck, my chest, my breasts, and around again, sucking hard everywhere before releasing the skin from his mouth with a pop.

I gasped for air, but at the same time felt like I was breathing again for the first time all week. "Yes, Matthew. Oh, *please.*"

He slid into me, and I arched against the intrusion. He was big— bigger than anyone would expect of his inch or two over six feet. Enough that it usually took a moment or two for me to get used to him.

His teeth bit into my neck, and I squirmed.

"Do it back," he ordered as he thrust even deeper. "Mark me too, baby. The way you know I love."

My hands slid over his shoulder and I dug my nails in, pulling them up his back hard enough to leave trails. He arched and moaned from the pleasure and pain.

"*Fuck,*" he grunted, losing the last vestiges of his gentlemanly control. "*Fuck,* just like that!"

I panted like a dog in heat as he started to move. But as pleasure vibrated through me, another thought echoed along with our hot, deliciously animal instincts.

The same I'd heard since the first time I'd met him. Since the first time I welcomed this man into me.

Not lust, though we were coated in it.

Not love, though that was always there too.

As we gave ourselves up to the rhythm that was so instinctive, I was convinced it was written into my DNA. The world melted into oblivion. Matthew was no longer Matthew Luca Zola, brother, uncle, grandson, assistant district attorney currently prosecuting my husband. And I was no longer Nina Evelyn Astor de Vries Gardner, second grandchild to the de Vries family, mother, and wife of an alleged criminal.

Together, we had no positions, no people, no pasts to keep us apart.

I cried out, but the sounds were swallowed by his kisses, by the rumble of his voice. Matthew gasped, and his movements shook the bed beneath us, the very core of who we were.

Together, we had no names. We ceased to be two separate people.

Lost, yet found.

Wild, yet tamed.

That word swelled again.

Together we were *home*.

CHAPTER SIX

"So, what happened today, doll?"

I looked up from where I was still buried in a nest of down comforter and Egyptian cotton. Not quite the same as the fifteen-hundred-thread-count sateen I usually slept on, but in its own way nicer, courtesy of the warm afternoon light pouring through the drapes and the deep green eyes of the man with me. It was funny, in spite of the being the epitome of luxury and comfort, my suite at home still felt like the center of a jail. And my jailer could unlock the doors and violate that sanctity—as he had done last night—any time he wanted. Especially now.

Dread settled over me like a thick mask. The idea of leaving this room, this man, was utterly asphyxiating.

The desire between Matthew and me had quieted to a simmer instead of the hot summer boil.

I still wanted him. I'd always want him. But reality pressed on the cool glass walls of this lovely room.

How could something that felt so unbelievably right be so terribly wrong for both of us? I was married. Matthew was investigating my husband. We were both at risk, even with just a text.

But the thought of leaving all over again made me feel like I was cutting off my own arm. I had never felt anything like this before. Not for Peppe. Certainly never for Calvin. The closest thing was for my daughter. And even with her...no, it wasn't the same.

Our time was nearly up. Matthew was already half-dressed in his pants while he ironed out his shirt. His smooth, even motions made the sinewy muscles of his chest, arms, even his abdominals move in elegant concert. He had no idea what a graceful creature he was—I truly loved watching him complete even the simplest tasks. If the city was a jungle, Matthew was its panther. A king cat, always on the prowl.

When I didn't answer his question, he stopped ironing and looked up. His full lips curled into another roguish grin.

"Enjoying the view?"

I didn't even bother to hide it. I never had to with him. "Of course I am. You're beautiful."

Matthew opened his mouth as if to joke again, but frowned at my tone. I was trying for light but couldn't quite manage it. In less than a second, he had abandoned his shirt and moved back to sit beside me on the bed. He twirled a lock of my hair, winding it around his finger like a ring before letting it go.

"There it is again," he remarked. "That face. I don't like it. Five weeks since we talked or anything, and you text me out of the blue. What's going on?"

My stomach squeezed. He couldn't possibly know how badly I wished the rings on my finger matched one on his instead of the husband I would rather never see again. I'd give up every dollar in my bank account, every sumptuous fabric in that penthouse if it meant I could stay here with him.

"Is it the guilt?" he asked quietly. "Is it too much?"

He dropped my hair to toy with the white gold chain around his neck. On it dangled a crucifix and a medallion of San Gennaro, the patron saint of Naples, where his grandfather was born. He was given the cross at fourteen—after his father died and Matthew was confirmed. The other piece was his grandfather's, who had passed some years back. Both were grim, almost gruesome reminders of family, pride, and faith.

I understood the first two very well. After all, until I met this man, my entire life had been shaped by the fact that I was a member of the great de Vries family and needed to maintain their pride (and thereby, mine). We had room for one black sheep, but by the time I became pregnant, Eric had already taken that spot. So I sculpted myself in the matriarch's image out of fear. I'd gone to the right schools. Worn the right clothes. Married the right man. Or, as it happened, the very *wrong* one. And for what?

Family. Pride.

Faith, though. That wasn't as clear to me, but Matthew seemed to have it in spades despite his own history of loss.

I never probed. Things like that were personal—nothing I would ever ask about, having been trained assiduously to leave politics and religion firmly *out* of polite conversation. But I knew his faith was deep and nuanced. I knew he attended Mass frequently with his grandmother and sisters in the Bronx. I knew he confessed what he considered his "sins" to a priest and had been going to confession more often since we met. I knew that he carried his faults around like the cross was on his back, not around his neck, and often believed he was beyond redemption.

I also knew he was mistaken.

The squeeze in my stomach tightened. Not because I felt particularly bad about being here with him.

I simply didn't. Not anymore. Calvin Gardner was my husband in name only. He was a bad man. And the only reason I had to stay with him now was to protect myself and my daughter during the trial. Matthew said it was for my dignity. He still didn't know about the other secrets I carried.

It was fear, not guilt, that kept me up most nights.

Better to live in the moment. Not to yearn for a future that could never be.

Even so, there was no use pretending completely. Not with Matthew.

"No," I said. "It's not guilt. It's…today is my anniversary. Number ten, as it happens."

Matthew's face darkened. "That's right."

I turned on my side toward him, drifting a hand over his bare chest, then down across the solid ridges of his stomach. "You knew?"

Of course he did. Matthew had researched me and my family long ago as part of an ongoing investigation related to Eric, and now for the case he was building against Calvin.

My husband.

Live in the moment.

I rolled onto my back and stared up at the ceiling. "Ten years." I sighed. "It's a little hard to believe."

Matthew bared his teeth, again resembling a cat that desperately wanted to hunt. "It's a fuckin' tragedy, is what it is."

I shied, as I often did when his bitterness about my marriage took over. I wasn't afraid. I just couldn't do anything about it, and it hurt. So, so badly.

Matthew's face softened. "Shit, doll." He slumped, then stood and returned to his ironing. "I'm sorry."

"No, you're not." My voice was sharper than intended. Almost defensive, though I wasn't. Not of Calvin anyway.

But I knew that tone well, and it never went anywhere good. Matthew and I had had more than one argument on the street about the state of my marriage. *Why?* He'd always demand, before the complication of Calvin's criminal behavior presented itself. *Why do you stay?*

Eventually the truth came out.

That I had been pregnant with another man's baby when I'd married Calvin.

That none of my family had known about the affair, and at only twenty, I was too afraid of their reaction to say anything.

That my daughter, Olivia, also had no idea.

Family. Pride.

How could things so important also feel like dead weights?

I shouldn't have resented them the way I did.

But I did. I really did.

"So what does old Calvin have planned tonight, huh?" Matthew couldn't quite keep the vitriol out of his voice. "A room at the Plaza? Maybe a trip to Tiffany's?"

I sat up against the headboard, then drew the sheet and my knees to my chest, shrinking more with each suggestion. They were jokes, clichés, productions of jealousy. But Matthew couldn't know how much they hurt. If that was the sort of husband I had, I probably would have never ended up at this hotel in the first place.

No. That possibility burned as well.

"Nothing," I said. "We generally don't celebrate our anniversary."

Matthew looked up. "You're kidding."

I shook my head. "Why should we, with such an arrangement? It's not as if we love each other. Or ever did."

"Because you love me now, right, baby?"

"Well…yes."

At my frank admission, Matthew put the iron down again, and we stared at each other across the room. The air crackled.

Then he crossed over to the bed in five long strides, pulled me into his arms, and delivered a long, deep kiss. It was anything but decorous. It was messy. All-consuming. And exactly what I needed.

When he released me, I gasped. But my limbs were no longer stiff and folded into themselves. Once again, I was relaxed. Fluid.

At peace.

"For what it's worth, I love you too," Matthew said, equally out of breath. "And I'm sorry. I'm a jealous asshole."

I reached up and pushed a few strands of hair off his forehead. His hair was a deliciously deep brown that shone like the sides of a skyscraper in the rain.

"You're just frustrated," I said. "I understand. I am too."

Matthew pressed his forehead to mine, eyes closed as our breathing returned to normal.

"When…" he started, seeming to search for words. "Fuck it. If you were my wife—"

"Your *wife*?" I practically squeaked, arching back to look at him.

A broad, cocky smirk—the one that always managed to enthrall and irritate me at the same time— spread across his face. "Well, yeah. My wife. What do you think I'm so jealous of?"

"I—I hadn't really thought about it, to be honest."

It was the truth. Or was it? I'd be lying if I said in moments of weakness, I hadn't imagined what it would be like to come home to this man night after night. Wake up with that smirk greeting me each morning. Be his "doll" for the rest of our lives.

He seemed to understand this as he leaned in, touched his nose to mine, then kissed me again, ending it with a light nip on my lower lip.

"Like the stars, baby. Remember?" He stood up again and tipped my chin with one finger. "If you were mine, I'd celebrate the hell out of our anniversary. We'd be swing dancing at a hundred. You can believe that."

The visions returned. This time they were fifty years from now, both of us old and gray. Me with finger-rolled hair curls, and Matthew, stooped and gray with his ever-present fedora, holding hands by the river while we watched the sun drop below the New York City skyline. I settled back into my pillows and let myself swim in the idea for a few moments more. We both did, until the truth sank in.

It would never happen. It couldn't.

Matthew pressed one more kiss to my forehead, sighed, and returned to his clothes. "Is he at least home? Will he bring you flowers? Maybe a card or something?"

I shook my head. "Unlikely. Actually, you might like to know he was making some phone calls last night, and—"

"Don't." Matthew shook his head as he finished with the iron. He pulled on his undershirt, then the Oxford. "Even if it would be helpful, it shouldn't come from you."

I watched as he did up his buttons and tucked in his clothes, making sure everything aligned correctly with the zipper of his pants. Neat, no fuss, but always precise in a way most men couldn't manage anymore. Classic.

It made me forget for a moment how irritatingly reticent he was to take any information I offered about Calvin. This wasn't the first time I had offered. And every time, he always refused.

"Honestly," I said. "What is the point of any of this if I can't help?"

"The *point*, duchess, is that we have to keep this case clean. And out of our damn bed, if you don't mind."

"Well, the sooner it's over, the sooner we can spend more time in it, don't you think?"

"Nina."

I stopped and sighed, feeling very much like a petulant child. I didn't like not getting my way. I never had.

Matthew cocked his head, looking at me like he felt sorry for me. It was utterly infuriating. "Nina," he said again.

"I only want to help."

"You are helping. By staying safe."

The word rattled. He had no idea how unsafe I really was.

He pulled his tie around his collar and came to sit with me on the bed, offering the two ends. It was as big a compliment as I could get from Matthew Zola—the honor of looping his half Windsor knot.

I went straight to work, if only because it allowed me to focus on the crimson paisley and avoid getting lost in those deep green eyes again.

"Look, Nina, you know you can't tell me things like that. We're in the middle of the discovery process right now, which means that at some point before the trial, I have to divulge every single thing I learn to Calvin's lawyers. Along with where I got the information. If they find out it came from you…well, it will probably get thrown out anyway once he claims spousal privilege. But then it will bring a rain of fucking fire down on your head too. A hell of an investigation on *your* potential part in Calvin's dealings. That's the only way the DA will get around it—by naming you as an accomplice to his crimes."

"And what part would that be?" Did I protest a little too loudly?

Matthew didn't seem to notice as he stood and picked his jacket off the chair near the door. Exquisitely put together. The perfect gentleman, but with a distinct and delicious dark side.

I closed my eyes, if only to fight the urge to drag him back to bed and have my way with him all over again. It was ridiculous, this desire.

This complete and utter need.

"Spousal privilege, baby," he said as he returned to the bed one last time. "You need it. *We* need it. I don't want you or Olivia anywhere near this case. All right?"

"But I have spousal privilege even if we're divorced, don't I?" I tried again.

"It only protects what was said during the marriage," Matthew replied through clenched teeth, like talking about my marriage physically pained him. "If you're divorced—and if it ever comes up that there was any kind of threat or rancor in the marriage...well, the whole thing could potentially split wide open anyway." He shook his head. "Not to mention my career falls apart too. And then I can't protect you anymore. The case gets turned over to a much more bribable ADA. Calvin gets off, and we're both fucked."

We'd had this conversation countless times. That for everyone's sake—especially Olivia's—I needed to remain Calvin's wife until the trial was over. Matthew thought I was willing to be Mrs. Gardner to protect myself from the threat of his investigation. He didn't realize that our humiliation wasn't the only or even the worst threat. It was the knowledge that if he ever discovered the truth, he'd never look at me the same way.

It made me a coward, but I couldn't take that chance.

"Do you have any idea how much it kills me, sending you back to that monster?"

I shivered at the rumble of his quiet, forlorn voice. He didn't know the half of it.

Matthew slipped his palm around my neck and stroked my cheek with his thumb. We gazed at each other for a long moment. Then he leaned down, past my mouth, and dropped kiss after kiss along my neck, my bare collarbone, before pushing the sheet out of his way so he could take my nipple between his teeth. He sucked, then worried it hard enough that I hissed. When he pulled away, the skin above it was red again. Marked.

I loved it. Just like I loved him.

Maybe because he listened to me. He looked for the line where pain and pleasure met and found it every time. Unlike the other man in my life. The one who sought out my pain, but only for his own pleasure.

"It's all right," I murmured as my fingers threaded into his thick dark hair. "I'll bear it."

He sat up, quiet as his thumb drifted over my skin, then down to my wrist, which he encircled with his fingers. "He doesn't actually hurt *you*, though. Right?"

Matthew's dark green eyes were searching, almost pleading for me to say no. He looked as desperate and trapped as I felt. As utterly helpless.

And after all, what could he do if the answer was yes? I knew this man. He would throw every caution to the wind if he believed I was unsafe. Including himself.

How could I betray that?

"Of course not," I said, recalling every bit of conditioning I had to keep my face straight under Matthew's probing gaze.

"Those bruises on your inner thigh—"

"I told you. I stumbled getting off the spinning bike," I lied.

Matthew was quiet for a long moment. Then: "I would never hide anything from you that I didn't have to, Nina. You know that, don't you?"

Now guilt strummed through my insides like the strings of a guitar. Did I know that? Wasn't he purposefully shielding me from his work? Did he *have* to?

I knew what he would say.

In order to save you from it.

I shook away the thought and did what I was best at. I changed the subject.

"How did you get in?"

Matthew gave me a curious look while he stood to put on his jacket. "The service stairs. I'm assuming you took them too."

I nodded. "You know me and elevators."

At the mention of my terrible claustrophobia, a sly grin crept across Matthew's face, causing me to blush in response. We were thinking of the same thing. An evening when we were trapped by some absurd circumstance in a faulty elevator in the Metropolitan Museum of Art. I had believed I'd never see him again, but fate had thrown us back together—just as my claustrophobia attacked like never before. Somehow, his presence had calmed me. His entire *body* had calmed me.

Desire, I had learned that day, is stronger than any fear.

Or maybe that's just love.

He dropped the sides of his jacket and began a slow crawl across the bed, caging me into the pillows once more.

"I didn't mind being trapped in an elevator with you." His lips were soft against mine, the rub of stubble delicious on my skin.

Instinctually, my hands slipped over his shoulders, feeling the grace of taut muscle under the refined cotton. I wanted to strip it all off again—not to repeat what we'd just done, but more to hold him close. When I was in the hospital after giving birth, the nurses had suggested bringing Olivia to my bare chest, skin to skin, to utilize the bonding effects of oxytocin. It's the reason we should hold our children so close from the start.

I was never touched as a child. My father was gone, my mother more familiar with her wine collection than with me. So I never understood how much I was missing. Not until I met him.

Touch heals. And none so much as Matthew's.

"I don't want to go," he said between kisses. "But I have to. Fuck, it feels wrong."

Reluctantly, I let my hands fall. "Go. I'll try not to call again. I'm sorry I did this time. I just couldn't..."

"Help it," he completed with a bittersweet smile. "Trust me, I know the feeling."

The heaviness of the circumstances descended all over again. The reasons that made even sneaking around like this so dangerous. Some weeks ago, my husband's name, and mine, had been splashed all over the local papers. Sometime soon, likely in a matter of months, it would happen again once the trial began (although Matthew assured me there were all sorts of ways to delay the inevitable).

On the one hand, I was eager. If he was successful, I'd finally be rid of the nightmare I was chained to. But in a way, I was also dreading it. Because there was another truth neither of us was willing to say out loud: this was our last remaining connection. Even after the trial was over and I could file for the divorce I desperately wanted...we still couldn't be together. I wouldn't put Matthew's career in jeopardy. And he wouldn't risk bringing me under possible investigation.

We were written in the stars, he said.

But apparently that just meant we were star-crossed.

"I love you," I whispered as I framed his beautiful face between my hands. This time it was almost painful to admit.

Matthew sighed, nuzzling into one palm. "I love you too. Goddammit, but I do. I'd give you the whole fuckin' world if I could, baby. You deserve it."

He kissed me again, this time slower, as if it might be the last time. I didn't rush him, just enjoyed the last few tastes he was willing to give me. I didn't fight it when at last he stood up, grabbed his hat off the floor, and set it on his head.

Matthew paused, drawing his eyes over me one last time, as if to memorize what I looked like in this bed, still rumpled from the effects of his passion. Of his love.

I didn't look away. Didn't assume any sort of mask or attempt to hide a single bit of what I was feeling.

"I'll see you, doll," he said as he turned for the door.

It was then I closed my eyes. I couldn't bear to watch him leave. "Goodbye, Matthew."

When I opened them again, he was gone.

CHAPTER SEVEN

"This looks amazing, Marguerite. Thank you."

The diminutive cook nodded politely and backed out of the dining room to let me eat. She had never had very good English, but that mattered less than the fact that she was excellent at making just about anything we possibly wanted. A meal for one or forty.

This room, much like every room in the apartment, was ridiculously over-decorated. Part of my husband's never-ending campaign for legitimacy in this social set. Sweeping window treatments, Romanesque statues beside the ornate wainscoting, bright teal jacquard wallpaper, and an enormous chandelier suspended above a table for eighteen...all for an audience we had never had. Parties we had never hosted.

And why would we? It would only be inviting guests into a den of lies. To view the charade of our life up close. Neither Calvin nor I were willing to risk that. It was maybe the one thing we had in common anymore. Or had ever had in common.

I turned to the meal in front of me and the empty place setting to my left, at the head of the long, empty dining table. It was nine o'clock at night. I couldn't honestly say I'd been waiting for hours for Calvin to come home from "work," but I'd learned the hard way some three weeks earlier that he did not find it acceptable for me to eat without him when he was in town anymore.

My jaw still ached from that particular lesson.

Fuck that, doll. You gotta eat.

I smiled as I turned to the plate of linguine and clams. Apparently, today I was quite the rebel. For a moment, I considered snapping a picture of my meal and sending it to Matthew. An inside joke of sorts—he was always trying to get me to eat pasta. I'd consumed more simple carbohydrates with the man over the last six months than I had in ten years. It meant doubling up on my trainer's hours to keep my pants fitting correctly...but it was worth it. So, so worth it.

I was just lifting a sumptuous forkful of noodles to my mouth when the elevator doors chimed open, and Calvin's heavy footsteps sounded, followed by another pair of shoes that were identifiably female from the way they clicked on the parquet.

In a hurry, I emptied my fork, wiped it clean on my napkin, and set it to the side. Acting as though I had been waiting patiently instead of about to stuff myself silly.

"I'm guessing she's in here waiting for me," Calvin was saying as he walked in with his guest. "Ah, see? I was right, as usual."

Perhaps my cheeks would have reddened if I hadn't been so numbed. Or if I wasn't that much more surprised by his companion— my once-best friend, Caitlyn Calvert. Even my composure had its limits.

Calvin clicked his tongue as he took in the empty table, his place setting, and my untouched food. "You're so predictable, princess. Do you always do as you're told?"

I repressed the urge to throw my fork at him for using the pet name "princess." He had called me that from the very beginning, disregarding every request I'd ever made for him to stop. It didn't have the same lilting fondness as Peppe's *principessa*. It never sounded anything but condescending. Resentful. Even nasty.

"She does," Caitlyn chimed in as she delivered air kisses to my cheeks. "But that's why we love her, don't we? Not everyone can be a leader."

I swallowed. "No. I suppose they can't. Hello, Caitlyn. This is a surprise."

"Calvin and I ran into each other at Madison Fletcher's engagement party tonight. Why weren't you there, by the way?"

I opened my mouth to say I hadn't been invited, but they would have already known that. It costs to break with your set. Madison was one of the many who had distanced themselves from me over the last several months. That was what happened when you sided with your black sheep cousin and his eccentric wife over the schemes of petty ring-seekers. The moment Eric had returned to the Upper East Side it was clear that nearly every single woman under thirty-five understood him as her "territory" and had *not* taken kindly to the fact that he was marrying a half-Korean nobody from Chicago instead of one of them. This had actually included Caitlyn, who had done her best to disrupt their wedding.

At one point, I had been sympathetic. After all, Caitlyn had grown up with us and nursed a terrible crush on Eric since she was small. Her feelings for Eric had been deeper than the average socialite bent on a good marriage. But I had come to like Jane quite a lot since the wedding last November, and I didn't take kindly to betrayal.

Which was why it was so curious that my husband had been at this party too.

But before I could say as much, Caitlyn kept talking. "Anyway, there will be others. I'll make sure you get invited next time."

I coiled some pasta around my fork and tried not to smart at the idea. A decade ago, it had been the other way around. *I* had been the one responsible for conducting Caitlyn through our social milieu. When I had first met the girl, she was a frumpy, frizzy-headed no one with a New Jersey accent a mile long. Now she was swanning all over the city with blond extensions, two ex-husbands, and a brand-new face (among other things).

And I was the charity case? How rich.

"You look...refreshed," I remarked tactfully before taking a bite. "Did you do something new to your hair?"

Caitlyn's cheeks pinked as she took a seat across from me. "Just a few new highlights. Thanks for noticing."

"It looks nice," I said demurely. It did look nice. It also looked exactly like my color, which happened to be perfectly natural. But no, that wasn't it.

Caitlyn seemed to sense my suspicion as she mischievously tapped her chin. "Not everyone can have the impeccable de Vries jaw line without a little help. Mum's the word, of course."

Ah. So it wasn't her hair, but her chin. Yes, now that I was looking, I could see the change. A bit more pronounced, a sharper angle. She'd always had a weak profile, but now that was mostly hidden by what were probably some injections.

"I asked Caitlyn over to cheer you up," Calvin said as he shoved a fork into his pasta and took a bite roughly appropriate for a hippopotamus. With his mouth full, he continued. "She's been—I don't know— lost, somehow. Maybe you can help her. I can't take living with such a damn grump all the time."

He patted my hand with a few flat thumps, and I resisted the urge to jerk it away. I only kept it there because if I didn't, I'd pay for it later.

"Calvin, dear, really. Can you blame her? Your arrest wasn't exactly easy. And people have been viciously unkind to her since Eric's wedding, you know."

I stared at my pasta. They had been unkind, in part, because of *her*.

Calvin rolled his eyes. "How has any of that affected her? I'm a damn pariah with the great de Vries family these days, through no fucking fault of my own. First, I get totally jilted with the old lady's will…"

I opened my mouth to point out that hardly any people who had married into the family had inherited anyway, but quickly realized I was wrong. Jane had, of course, and she had literally married Eric on the same day Celeste died. And then, of course, there was his mother.

It was the men, then, whom Celeste ignored unless they were literally born into the family. My father, who hadn't been a part of the family in years anyway. And my husband, who had forced his way in.

"And then I'm the one who was carted away like an animal, thanks to that sniveling DA." Calvin took his phone out of his inner jacket pocket and pulled up a picture. "Can you believe he had the guts to call a press conference last week? Look at that guy. What a greasy rat."

He displayed his screen around the table. I resisted the urge to rip it away and gawk at the picture of Matthew standing in front of a number of microphones in front of his Jay Street office building. He looked like a character from one of his favorite Hitchcock movies, full of panache and *savoir faire*, his natural charisma practically jumping off the small screen. My chest ached.

He was beautiful. Intelligent. Perfect.

Not as perfect as you, doll.

Oh, God. It really did hurt.

"*That's* the prosecutor?" Caitlyn guffawed. "Goodness! I've seen him before! At the opera this spring. Nina, wasn't he with you, or did you forget?"

I looked up sharply. I hadn't forgotten that night at the opera with Matthew. So sweet, salacious too…until we had bumped into Caitlyn and Kyle, and it had been obvious that she and Matthew had had their own extramarital affair at one point. It was before I really knew him, but I hadn't been pleased.

I was much *less* pleased that she was bringing it up now.

"He was nosing into the family before, believe it or not," Calvin said, oblivious to the sudden tension. "Even guilted Nina, so Eric forced her to take him, if you can believe that. Slimy little worm was digging into us even then, wasn't he, princess?"

My face felt wooden, though visions of that night flashed behind the mask. The way he looked in his tuxedo, a red rose pinned to the lapel. The look on his face when he'd seen the red Valentino dress that had literally been sewn onto my body hours before. The feel of his hand sliding between my legs as the tenor's voice rose.

Oh, yes, I remembered. I'd never forget any part of that.

"Fucking freeloader," Calvin sputtered.

Caitlyn flashed her blue eyes at me, then turned to Calvin. I mentally begged her not to say anything.

She turned to Calvin. "My, that *is* devious of him."

"Yes," I said a little too loudly, more for Calvin's benefit than for Caitlyn's. "It was. He's perfectly *awful*."

"He's a crooked, conniving little fucker," Calvin agreed. "And he has no idea what's coming to him. No. Idea."

The sudden violence that rippled through my body caught me by surprise. I wanted to ask what in God's name he meant by that. I wanted to demand he take it back or suffer the consequences. More than that, I wanted to reach across the table, grab my husband's tie, and strangle him with it. All that at even the hint of a threat toward Matthew.

Good lord. Who had I become?

"Anyway, let's not let one bad apple spoil the dinner," Calvin said. "Happy anniversary, princess."

He slapped a familiar blue box on the table in front of me. I put down my fork.

"Ooh, Tiffany's!" Caitlyn crooned. "Aren't you lucky, N!"

I smiled grimly, still trying to swallow back my rage as I picked up the box. "This is a surprise."

"Ten years. Thought I needed to do a little something, even if you didn't. I never even bought you a real engagement ring. You got that ugly thing yourself, remember?"

Caitlyn snorted. "It does look like something we would have picked out when we were twenty, doesn't it, N?"

I examined the enormous pear-shaped diamond on my left hand. Well, they were right about something. The engagement ring I had worn almost continuously for ten years was legitimately hideous. I had hated it when I was twenty, and I hated it now, and not just because everything it represented was a lie. The only reason I had even purchased it was to protect the pride of the man sitting next to me. Calvin had insisted I had to wear *something*, and unbeknownst to me, he was broke at the time. But when we had walked into Tiffany's that day and I had pointed at a much smaller, plainer stone that would be more realistic for a man of his means to supposedly give me, he simply shook his head and found this one instead.

I won't be embarrassed, princess. Not by you. Not by anyone.

"Open it," Calvin said. "Come on. It's an upgrade, I promise. No one will laugh at us now."

Were they laughing before? I wanted to ask. Whispering, maybe. But Calvin had always imagined so much more.

Conscious of my audience, I slowly pulled off the white ribbon, then removed the ring box and opened it.

It was awful. A strobe light. A very, very pink one. I removed a ring bearing a massive, carnation-colored diamond encircled with not one but three wreaths of tiny white diamonds, all nestled in a setting of flashy yellow gold. It was the jewelry equivalent of Studio 54. And not in a good way.

"Oh…my," Caitlyn said, quickly recovering the flash of revulsion that crossed her face

"The guy at the store said it was a princess cut," Calvin said proudly. "It was the most expensive one they had. A princess for the princess. So…how about it?"

I looked up, dumbfounded. "How about what?"

"You. Me. Vow renewal. This September. It's been ten years, princess, so I figure it's time to have the wedding we never got. A big horse and pony show at St. John's or maybe St. Patrick's. We'll get you the biggest dress with the longest train or whatever, and really show New York who we are. No one will ever laugh at us again after that. And besides, a little good PR won't hurt with all this trial bullshit going down."

I stared at the ring with a different kind of horror. He wanted another *wedding*? In front of the entire city? Eric and Jane had done the same thing less than a year ago. Was he jealous of the attention? Did he not see how ridiculously tacky it would be to have a similar affair for a marriage that had already taken place? Not to mention that the idea of saying vows again to this man literally made me nauseous.

But before I could find a way to say anything else, another thought crossed my mind.

"You bought the most expensive ring at Tiffany's?" I asked.

Immediately, Calvin's face clouded. "Of course I did. You act like we're paupers or something here, Nina."

"Of course we're not," I said quickly. "No, it's, um, it's really something, Calvin. It's just…"

"Just what?" he spat, looking quickly between me and Caitlyn, embarrassment rising on his face.

But I couldn't stop. "It's just that given the situation we're in...and the lawyers...don't you think maybe...this should have..."

"What are you saying?" The question slipped between his crooked, yellowing teeth.

I took a deep breath. I couldn't stand down now.

"I'm saying," I said as gently as I could. "Perhaps it's not the best optics for you to be spending several million dollars on a piece of jewelry and then millions more on a fake wedding when you've been indicted for less-than-savory business practices."

As the steam started to rise on Calvin's face, my heart sped up. Oh, dear. Oh, that was a big mistake.

You said what you said, doll. It's not your fault he can't fuckin' handle it. Wasn't it?

Calvin looked like he wanted to toss his dinner all over me—what little there was still left of it. And if Caitlyn hadn't been sitting next to us, he very well might have, along with a few other things. I could easily imagine it. The way my body would fly out of the chair. The way my cheek would crack against the sideboard edge. The way I'd be forced to my knees, my hair yanked, face slapped until my ears were ringing.

But Caitlyn, to her credit, did not make the sleek exit most people would do in her situation. She simply sat beside me and waited.

At last, Calvin sucked in a deep breath and stood. "I'm sorry it doesn't meet your lofty goals, *your highness*," he gritted out. "I'm going to the john, and then I have to make a phone call. When I get back, maybe you'll have learned to appreciate the things your husband does for you instead of being so goddamn selfish." He glared at me, then Caitlyn, then back at me again. "Happy fucking anniversary, you callous bitch."

CHAPTER EIGHT

H e stormed out, leaving us sitting at the table in awkward silence
—me staring at my plate, Caitlyn staring at me.

After recovering myself, I looked up at her. "I'm sorry you had to
see that."

Caitlyn looked pityingly at me. But unsurprised. I wasn't sure why
Calvin never felt the need to censor himself around her. Maybe it was
because they came from similar backgrounds, but I supposed it
provided some relief. Someone knew who he really was. Even if she
couldn't do anything about it.

"No need to apologize," she said quietly. "I'm sorry things haven't
changed much."

I shrugged, willing the dread that had suddenly settled over my
chest like a fifty-pound weight to lift a bit. "It is what it is."

We both were quiet while I pushed pasta around my plate. My
appetite had fled.

"How are you?" Caitlyn asked after a minute. "How are you
really?"

I stilled my fork. My resentment about her behavior over the last
year returned with a flourish. "How in God's name can you ask me
that?"

Caitlyn had the decency to look slightly ashamed, despite the fact that her face couldn't actually move very much. "Look, N, I know things have been off between us since my little stunt—"

"You mean the part where you tried to trick me and the rest of my family into ruining my cousin's wedding?" I demanded. "Or the part where you showed up with his nemesis at New Year's and shoved it in his face just before he was arrested? You know my family, Caitlyn. You know we don't take kindly to treachery."

Caitlyn flinched at the sudden sharp edge in my tone. Any other time, I might have lowered my voice. I might have apologized. But right now, I was tired of being run over roughshod. Matthew, even if imagined, still chanted in the back of my mind.

Don't take their shit, baby. You deserve better.

Caitlyn seemed to sense it. After a moment, she sighed. "Yes, well. I do regret all of it, you know. Can you blame me for being a teensy bit jealous? After all, I did have such a terrible crush on Eric when we were kids."

"And that makes it okay?"

"No, of course not. But I've apologized a million times over. Is it really worth it to end our entire friendship over one mistake? Besides, that all happened months ago. I'm happily remarried now. Kyle and I are just two peas in a pod."

I couldn't help raising a brow at that one. Kyle Shaw, Caitlyn's third husband at this point, was at least thirty years older than her. I'd known the man most of my life as a passing acquaintance of my parents—what he and Caitlyn had in common, I could list on one hand.

Caitlyn tilted her head, like she was in on the joke. "Okay. So maybe we're not in the same pod. But he's nice. And I can't say that about the last two, can I?"

I released a breath. Sometimes I spent so much time thinking about Caitlyn's and my differences, I forgot about the things we had in common.

"I'm glad you're happy," I said. "You deserve it. Really."

"So do you." Caitlyn glanced in the direction Calvin had gone, then back at me and leaned a bit closer. "Which is why, between friends, I have to ask—do you really want to be entertaining other men right now? Especially knowing what yours is capable of?"

I jerked. *"What?"*

Caitlyn looked at me like a child who had lost its toy. "N, please. It's all over you."

I couldn't help but look down at myself, as if my indiscretion was somehow evident on my clothes. "What could you possibly mean by that?"

"Well, for one, your lips look like that Jenner girl. And since I know you don't do injections, I'd assume you were kissing someone."

"I wasn't—"

"And secondly"—she glanced toward the bathroom again—"the bug bite excuse only works once, darling. Next time, tell your 'friend' to keep his teeth to himself. For both your good."

I peered at my open collar, then hurriedly did up an additional button to hide the bright red mark peeking over the silk. Lord, she was right. Matthew hadn't exactly been gentle, but it also hadn't been that bad six hours earlier.

I laid my hands on the table and forced myself to look at Caitlyn straight on as I willed every bit of the mask I had worn my entire life back into place. "I'm only going to say this once. I am *not* having an affair, Caitlyn."

"Come on!" she hissed. "I saw you at Lincoln Center in your slinky red dress. Are you *really* trying to tell me that you and the lawyer were only there as 'friends'?"

"As Calvin said, I was there as a favor to Eric. Besides, I am not *you*, Caitlyn." I gritted out the lie, glancing over my shoulder toward the door. Calvin was nowhere to be seen. "And for the record, Mr. Zola was very forthcoming that night about *your* previous rendezvous with him."

Caitlyn reared like she'd been bitten by a snake. "He didn't."

I arched a brow. "He did. He felt, given the work he was doing for Eric and Jane, that he needed to be transparent."

"Did you...did you tell Calvin?" she asked.

I frowned. Why would it matter if Calvin knew about Caitlyn's extramarital activities? I would have thought she'd be more concerned about her husband discovering the connection. Or Eric, given her feelings for him.

I set my wineglass back on the table. "No. And if we can stop this ridiculous conversation, I'll continue keeping it to myself."

Caitlyn exhaled with relief. "Thank you. Really. I just—well, I don't want to make more trouble for *you*." She looked me over again. "But really, how do you explain the puffy lips and the—"

"It was Calvin," I said finally. "And it was *not* from kissing, if you must know."

Caitlyn sat for a moment, digesting my meaning. It wasn't like she hadn't seen it before. We'd had these conversations more than once over the years, though not for some time. She was the only one who ever knew anything about what my life was really like. Not all of it. Not even most of it. But the important parts. The parts that kept me in my place.

"Oh," she said finally. "I see. And it's been—"

"More since he's been home," I admitted. "Since the indictment, he's under a stay-at-home order. He can't leave the state."

She was still, understanding completely what that meant for me. "Have they interviewed you at all?"

I shook my head. "Who?"

"What do you mean, who? The lawyers or whoever. Zola."

Just the sound of his name on her lips made that protective urge ripple through me all over again. With effort, I shoved it back down. "No. I'm covered by spousal privilege. Calvin has claimed it."

Caitlyn exhaled. "That's good." She reached over and patted my hand. "Calvin will get a good settlement, or just get off, N. I'm sure of it. Your lawyers are too good for a puny district attorney to manage. Then everything will go right back to normal."

That's what I'm afraid of.

We sat in silence a bit longer, forking our food, but not really eating it. Caitlyn, of course, didn't eat carbs any more than I used to, so she wasn't particularly interested in the pasta to begin with. And my appetite did not return.

"Are you—are you okay, N?" she asked finally.

I looked up. "Why?"

It was then the old version of my friend resurfaced. The one who used to spend hours and hours in my room with me after school. The one who wasn't only interested in boys. The one who, at one point in my life, knew me better than anyone.

"You just seem...I don't know. Different. Lost, I guess, though I don't mean to repeat what Calvin said."

I stared at my plate. If Matthew was here, he would have taken my hand under the table and squeezed it just to let me know he understood. Or maybe he would have leaned over and whispered deep-voiced encouragement in my ear.

I like you different, doll.

But that wasn't going to happen again. Even if we had any number of other illicit meetings at the Grace or some other clandestine location. What I wanted, what I thought he wanted—a life, a *future*—that could never happen. Matthew had been very clear. If Calvin won, he would look for any reason to have Matthew disbarred and shamed. Ruined. And if he didn't...any hint of misconduct would ruin the entire case, and Matthew's career along with it.

I thought of the people at home he supported. The house he had bought not just for him, but his sister and his niece. The grandmother in the Bronx whom I was certain he helped financially here and there. The sister at whose shop he purchased all the suits he needed for court.

It wasn't just my future at stake here. It was Matthew's, and one of the warmest, most loving families I'd ever met. I could never forgive myself if I ruined a thing for any of them.

But unlike Caitlyn, I did believe in Matthew's abilities. My love wasn't the only one who could do research. My assistant, Moira, had done a little digging and discovered that while he was still young, his conviction record was easily the best in his bureau, and one of the best of all three hundred and some attorneys employed by Kings County. He was very, *very* good at winning once he put his mind to it.

It was inspiring, actually. The more I learned about how much he had done to create the life he had, the more I wanted something like that for myself. And so, perhaps Caitlyn was right. Perhaps something *was* different about me after all.

"I want something more," I admitted for the first time. Out loud. Or to myself.

"What do you mean?" Caitlyn asked, not quite able to keep the envy out of her voice. "You have everything you could ever want. Well, for the most part. And you could have that too if you were just a little more careful." She winked conspiratorially. "Once Calvin can travel again for work, it shouldn't be too hard."

I ignored her innuendo. "You don't know what it's like, not choosing anything for yourself."

"Don't I? I've only had to shackle myself to other people's things to survive," she said bitterly.

I compressed a smile. "So, you and Kyle aren't a match made in heaven, then?"

In response, I received a dry expression that almost made me laugh. The Caitlyn I knew before. Frank and honest, even about her own deceptions. It was nice to see her again.

"I've made my choices just like you have," she said. "Which has been even harder since I can't have kids, of course. Otherwise I'd just sail that child support ship for as long as I needed. But spousal support doesn't last forever, and this time I was able to negotiate a solid prenup. Even if I can't outlast him—Kyle has a bad heart, you know— I'll walk away with real security. It's all I've ever wanted."

I nodded. Perhaps I was being a bit myopic. Unlike me, Caitlyn had come from next to nothing. She was a scholarship student at the preparatory school where we met. Had never gone to college, instead attaching herself to wealthy men and marrying multiple times to keep herself afloat. She had no useful skills other than the socializing she had learned from, well, people like me.

How could I blame her for doing what she needed to support herself? How could I blame anyone for doing that in such a cruel world?

"Okay," I said. "Then you do. I just..." I shook my head. "I don't think I can do this anymore. This 'normal.' I'm just not sure what that means yet."

"Does that mean you and Calvin..." She glanced at the obscene diamond ring still sitting on the table in front of me. "Won't be renewing those eternal vows after all?"

I shook my head in a hurry. Even if she was playing the friend right now, I was under no illusions she wouldn't possibly use a bit of currency—like my intention to leave Calvin after the trial—against me should it benefit her.

"No," I said. "I don't know about a big ceremony, but I'm not planning anything else, if that's what you're asking. I just mean I want to do something more with my life besides attend benefit luncheons and meet with my trainer. I'm just not sure what that is yet."

Caitlyn examined me curiously as she took a long drink of her wine. But before she could reply, the dining room door burst open again, and Calvin rushed in, phone in hand.

"I have to go out," he said. "A deal I was working on today went south, and I have to go downtown."

I turned. "At ten o'clock at night?"

"Yes!" Calvin snarled. "And I have more bad news too. It's probably going to take me weeks to fix this mess, so I'll probably just stay at the office for the week so Olivia doesn't get in my way. I'll be back tonight to get my things."

My mouth dropped. "You're kidding. Livy's only home for a week before she leaves for camp. She'll be crushed if she can't see you."

"Olivia will deal with it," Calvin snapped. "Honestly, Nina, whose side are you on here? I'm the one who's been accused of these bullshit charges that are currently ruining my life. I'd think you'd have a little more consideration for your own husband instead of your turncoat cousin and that trampy little chink he married."

Caitlyn and I both recoiled at the racial slur. I gripped my fork, wanting to throw it at him. But my best hope for avoiding a repeat of the night before was to choose my battles. Ignore these moments. Try to let the dust settle.

"I have to go," he said again. "But when I get back, I expect a little more gratitude. And that ring on your fucking finger."

My mouth dropped. I literally had no idea what to say to that. I had absolutely no intention of walking down any sort of aisle or parading this sham of a marriage beyond the next few months.

But before I could reply, Calvin turned to leave. "Caitlyn, I'll help you get a car downstairs if you want."

Caitlyn looked mildly irritated at our conversation being interrupted, but nodded and stood up with him, pulling her purse over her shoulder.

"Call me, N," she said. "Let's get lunch soon. Or any time you just want to talk."

I nodded and took up my wineglass, grateful more than anything else to be left alone again. "Thank you."

"Don't bother with her when she's in a mood," Calvin grumbled.

———

HE DIDN'T RETURN until early the next morning, shuffling past the dining room to pass out in his suite just as I was sitting down to a light breakfast after my morning run. I didn't ask where he had been. Because I didn't particularly care, but also because I was fairly certain I already knew.

Some things were better left alone.

What was the phrase?

Plausible deniability.

But lastly, I was too consumed with the other thoughts running around my mind. Waiting up to see if my jailer would pay me a visit, I didn't fall asleep until nearly three in the morning. As I waited, I stared at the crown molding of my ceiling, all the conversations I'd had that day running through my mind.

I'd give you the world if I could.

I've made my choices just like you have.

I want more.

I was struck suddenly by how true it really was. Since January, I had thought "more" meant Matthew, but as it became clear that relationship was doomed from the start, I couldn't help thinking about other options.

What would my life be, if not ensconced in this ivory tower?

What else lay for me outside of being a mother, a wife, a vapid socialite?

What would I do instead?

And just as my body forced me into a restless slumber for the first time in what seemed like forever, I permitted myself to imagine a life where I wasn't just Mrs. Calvin Gardner or Celeste de Vries's grand-daughter.

A life where my name was only Nina.

And I belonged to myself.

INTERLUDE I
AUGUST 2018

Matthew

The line for confession was long, even for a Saturday. It wound around the corner of the apse where the big wood box was housed, down the left aisle of the church until it was halfway to the main entrance. And because I had nothing else better to do while I shuffled along with this week's collection of sinners in Belmont, I shot off a quick picture to my sister, Frankie.

> **Me:** I'm going to be here all damn afternoon. Tell *Nonna* to leave a plate for me. I won't make lunch.

Her reply was almost immediate.

> **Frankie:** What do you expect? School doesn't start for another week, and everyone's guilty about yelling at their kids all summer long.

I snorted. They were doing more than that, I was willing to bet. Domestic violence cases involving minors did go up in the summer, partly because, yeah, everyone was at home with their kids. I could speak to that from personal experience. My old man was a mean fuckin' bastard when he was drunk, ten times worse when I was home mouthing off in ninety-five-degree heat with no air conditioner. New York was a swamp in August. I started running errands for my grandfather's garage when I was just eleven, as much to get out of the house as for extra pocket money for me and my sisters. The little ones could go to *Nonna's* to escape the chaos of our house during the day, but at night, we all had to go back to the belt, and later, for me, the fist.

I peered down the line, looking for the guilty ones. The guys with extra bruises on their knuckles or the mothers holding the collars of their kids' shirts a little too tight. None today that I could see, but they were out there.

Me, I didn't have any kids, but I had a lot to atone for.

Cursing, sure.

A few white lies here and there, okay.

But the coveting. Yeah, by far, the coveting was the worst.

I hadn't exactly slipped back into my old ways that involved too many one-night stands with too many taken ladies. It was because even now, two and a half months since I'd last seen her, Nina de Vries was still stuck in my mind and my heart, right where I knew she'd probably stay until I took my last breath.

Okay, so even that wasn't totally true. Because like a maniac, I couldn't help but stalk her a bit. I was like a junkie who needed just a little hit to get through the day. I'd justified it by telling myself her building needed to be watched. Her husband was a suspect, and Derek was busy enough.

It was how I knew that, like always, she spent most of her time alone in her penthouse apartment.

It was how I knew that her daughter, the little blonde girl with sun-kissed skin and dark, brooding eyes, had come home for exactly a week this summer before leaving again (I was guessing for camp).

It was how I knew that Nina spent most days and nights alone at that apartment, waiting for someone to come find her.

God, I wished it could have been me.

She must have known I was there. Why else would she linger

outside her building, chatting up her doorman for several minutes longer than necessary when she returned from the gym or some ladies' lunch? Or turn suddenly to gaze up and down the street, lingering on parked cars or the street's shadows with the intensity of a hawk scouting its prey? Though I knew she couldn't possibly see me from where I sat in the back of a cab or under the awning of the building across the street, I knew she felt me, just like I felt her, as immediate and sensory as the wind on my cheek or the hum of the subway beneath my feet.

"Fuck," I mumbled, momentarily forgetting where I was.

The woman in front of me, who looked maybe ten years older, but maybe a little too overdressed for confession, gave me a dirty look over her shoulder. I almost said something, but was interrupted by a text.

Jane Lefferts: Got plans in a few days? We're hosting a big party up at the house on Long Island. Come be the only other normal person there with me?

I smiled. Jane de Vries, still listed as Lefferts in my phone, was a good friend from way back. We hadn't talked much since the terrible night her husband had shot John Carson point blank in the middle of their apartment—while the guy was holding Jane hostage. Yeah, I probably wouldn't want to talk to anyone either if that had happened to me. It was pretty damn impressive that she was feeling good enough these days to host a party.

Me: How very Great Gatsby of you. Are you dressing up like Daisy?

Her reply chimed almost immediately.

Jane Lefferts: Ha ha. Only if Daisy has a bunch of magenta streaks in her hair.

I chuckled. Jane would never fit in with the ice cream cones that inhabited the Hamptons, but that was part of why I liked her. She walked to the beat of her own drum, just like I did.

Before I could answer, she texted again.

Jane Lefferts: Seriously, tho. Last year's white party was such a damn disaster. Now Eric's entertaining investor peeps, and I'll go insane without one normal friend there.

I hovered my thumb over my screen. I shouldn't ask. I had to ask. No, I shouldn't.

Fuck you, you big pussy. Just ask.

After all, it *was* my job. Wasn't it?

Me: Are the Gardners going to be there?

The three little dots appeared on the screen and seemed to hover indefinitely. Then:

Jane Lefferts: Nina maybe? But prob not Calvin. Eric still isn't feeling the most forgiving toward him.

I smirked. Yeah, if I suspected a family member of landing me in jail, I wouldn't be too welcoming either.

I could go. I had a reason, and if Calvin wasn't around, I wasn't technically breaking any rules. The line to the confessional shuffled forward, like it was reminding me to walk toward absolution instead of the Long Island beach and a leggy blonde who would probably look fuckin' incredible sunbathing at a pool party.

Shit. Nina.

Just her name was a punch to the gut.

The fact was, I missed her. The logical side of my brain wondered how I could miss someone I had barely spent any time with, but here I was, two months through a long, *very* dry spell with no end in sight. Summer was usually a time when women around the city let their hair down a little. They prowled the streets like cats in heat, and I was more than happy to take advantage. This year, however, going home with a new girl every weekend had about as much appeal as a weekly dentistry visit.

The problem with trying the best chocolate in the world is that everything else tastes like shit after.

And for a short time, I hadn't just had a taste. I'd been consumed. Nina de Vries had ruined me for life.

With a sigh, I punched in a quick response.

Me: I don't think so. I have a lot of work coming up. Probably not the best time to leave.

Jane Lefferts: No worries. If you change your mind, the offer stands. All jokes aside, it should be nice.

I sighed. Yeah, I bet it would be nice. The salty sea air, a cocktail in my hand, and Nina in a bikini? That didn't sound nice. It sounded like paradise.

Before I could contemplate and talk myself into it all over again, my phone buzzed, this time with a message from another number.

Derek: Call me. We finally got a name change for Pantheon.

I didn't waste any time. On top of fighting with my conscience for the last two months, I'd also been fighting an uphill battle on the Gardner investigation. Everywhere we turned, there were roadblocks. It wasn't just that we were running out of time to find witnesses to the trafficking we suspected him of doing. It was bureaucratic. Every record we requested on the guy, every paper trail we tried to follow, all of them were stymied again and again. Too often for there not to be some kind of motivating factor.

The Delaware Chamber of Commerce had been the worst so far. Three times, I'd sent in requests for the name change associated with Pantheon. Two had been "lost," and the other had only been done with the threat of a federal subpoena (they didn't need to know we didn't yet have any Feds willing to take the case). But even they couldn't skirt us forever. We needed a breakthrough. Bad. I was really fuckin' hoping this was it.

"Yo," Derek answered on the first ring. "Where are you?"

"Standing in line for confession."

"On a Saturday? I thought Sunday was the church day."

"It takes time to cleanse the soul, man. Especially when you're a damn dirty sinner like me."

The middle-aged woman in front of me turned with a scowl. "This is a church!"

"I apologize, ma'am," I said with a tip of my head. "Obviously, I need to be here more than most, don't I?"

When I winked, her mouth dropped, and she turned back around, shuffling forward a step or two, as if she needed the extra space to protect herself from my sinning ways.

"Are you done making trouble yet?" Derek asked on the other side of the line.

I smirked. "For now. What's the name?"

"I don't know if this will help. Kate Csaszar."

I frowned. "You look her up yet?"

"Zola, you must really think I'm stupid."

"Sorry. I don't think you're stupid. You're a fuckin' champ, King. You're the best detective I've ever met, and I bow to your investigative prowess, all right?"

"Thanks, and go fuck yourself," Derek said.

"You're very fuckin' welcome," I rejoined.

The lady in front of me whirled back around with a hiss. "Language!"

I grimaced and held one hand up in surrender. "I promise I'll say an extra Hail Mary if it makes you feel any better, ma'am. At least I'm here, right?"

She scowled hard enough that it made her look like a gargoyle, and I almost started laughing right there in the middle of the apse. Wouldn't have been the first time I got kicked out of a church for bad behavior, but I had to admit, it had been a while since secondary school.

"You're a real ne'er-do-weller, aren't you?" Derek said.

"Terrible influence on God's flock," I agreed. "So what do you know about this Kate character?"

"That's the thing. Absolutely nothing. Cliff ran the name through a bunch of systems and even asked a friend at the Newark DMV to check it out. There's a Katarina Csaszar listed on the 1990 census in Paterson, but I don't know if that's the same person, given the name difference. I think it's a dead end, man."

I, however, did not. "That's pretty close. She could have changed her name," I said as I shuffled forward in line. "They sound Russian or something."

"Bulgarian, actually," Derek said irritably. "I know how to google, Zo."

I ignored him. "Who else was on the census?"

"Head of house was listed as Benjamin Vamos, forty-two. Household includes a Sara Berto, a few years younger, and another man, twenty, named Károly Kertész. Then Katarina, age one. But I checked with immigration. Sara went back to Hungary the next year and took the little girl with her. I'm telling you, man. It's nothing."

I wasn't buying it. "You by a computer?"

"Yeah, why?"

"Look up the names Berto and Csaszar in the social security database. Check for any name changes."

As I waited, I could hear the clicks of the keys under his fingers.

"Nothing," he said. "In New York or New Jersey."

I frowned. "How about the other kid? The boy. Kertész."

More keys.

"Holy shit. Zola, you slick motherfucker. What do you have, a sixth sense for slime?"

I might have smiled if I hadn't known it to be true. After all, it takes one to known one. "What did you find?"

"I still can't—this is insane. Zola, in 1996, Károly Kertész changed his name to—get this—Calvin fucking Gardner. You asshole. You fucking nailed it."

"Fuck, yeah, I did!" I crowed, loud enough that the "fuck" bounced around the stone arches of the church like the tolls of its bell.

"Shh!" This time it was several people in line hushing me, not just the witch in front.

"Sorry, sorry, sorry," I muttered to everyone. "I'll keep it down, I promise."

"You should just leave!" hissed the gargoyle lady.

"Tell it to the priest," I snapped at her. Then, back to Derek as quietly as I could: "I knew it!"

"All right, all right," Derek said. "You figured that out. But we still don't know who this Csaszar girl is and what happened to her. Is she Calvin's sister? Are they related?"

"Someone does," I said. "And we're going to figure out who. Calvin Gardner doesn't keep his associates under wraps, and he isn't smart enough not to tell at least *someone* he trusted with Pantheon. This thing was run by one of the richest, most powerful men in America. The others working with him know. Someone knows. These slimy uptown fucks all known each other's business."

"So, what, you thinking a surveillance warrant?"

I nodded, even though he couldn't see me. "We got cause, and we're under a tight deadline."

"Good. The fucker has just been holing up in his office all summer. He's not doing shit right now—someone has been doing it for him."

"I got the extension on discovery, but we're not getting more than another two months, no matter how much the judge hates Gardner's lawyers. I think she'll give us the warrant if we ask."

"Okay, but if she doesn't?"

I shrugged. "Keep following him, but we should focus more on known associates. Anyone who might be in his social circle, you know?"

There was a long pause.

"Derek, what?"

"Zola, we need another way to figure this out."

"No," I cut in. "No Feds. You know what's going to happen. They'll drown the whole damn case."

"I don't mean that, asshole. I'm talking about...look, Cliff and I can follow Gardner all you want around the city, but we gotta be real. On the Upper East Side? We stick the fuck out."

He didn't have to say what he meant by that. The Upper East Side was the whitest part of New York. And my detectives were definitely not.

Shit. I shouldn't. This was *not* a good idea.

And yet somehow it was.

"Well, I did just get an invite to a party in the Hamptons. Hosted by Eric de Vries. His wife asked me to be her plus-one because she said the party was going to be full of business types."

"Shit. You gotta go. All those assholes love jerking each other off."

"Yeah, but I figured Gardner might be there."

Liar. I wasn't going because I knew she might be there.

"Hmmm," Derek said. "Look, if we had a bigger investigative team, I'd say stay away. But, it's not against the law for you to attend a party."

I ground my teeth. "Yeah, but—"

"Besides, I thought you said the family hated him ever since Eric got pinched."

I searched for another way, *any* way that we could possibly get this kind of information. But surveillance was hard enough when we could count the people we trusted on more than one hand. And it wasn't going to get easier than this to poke around. See who knew what.

Derek knew it too.

"Zola, I'll be straight with you. If there is any way you can nose around that party and find out who this chick is, it could potentially save this investigation a shit load of time," he said. "Find out if Gardner's going to be there or not. I think you need to get your ass on the Jitney, man."

I sighed. All sense of victory had suddenly morphed into fear, plain and simple. Not because I was worried about Calvin Gardner. Because I was worried about *her.* And the fact that when she was around, I couldn't seem to control anything I did.

But just as quickly, another landslide of questions rattled through me.

How much did Nina know about her husband's past identity?

Was she aware of Pantheon's existence?

Did she know the name Katarina Csaszar?

Maybe she had been trying to tell me these things the entire time. And I, of course, had blocked her out as a potential source completely, as much to protect my own hide as to protect hers. I had said it myself: the only way for her to evade spousal privilege was to name herself as an accomplice in the crimes.

I hadn't ever once considered that maybe she actually was one.

I shook my head toward the apse to my right, where several rows of candles stood flickering in red votives, symbols of the prayers offered by parishioners for their loved ones. Gestures of faith, grace, and hope.

No. I knew this woman. Knew her on a soul level. I had seen her with her daughter, watched her break bread with my family, worshipped her as she fell apart in my arms. There was no way Nina would ever be a part of a sick racket like this.

But then again, there was only one way to find out for sure.

"All right, man," I said heavily. "I'll do it."

We hung up. The line shuffled forward.

"Fuck," I muttered with each footstep. "Fuck, fuck, *fuck.*"

"Language!" The gargoyle reared back from her place in line, which was now next for the priest.

My head snapped up. I hadn't been in the mood for this before, and now I *really* didn't give a shit about protecting these parishioners' pretend-virgin ears. "Ma'am, with all due respect, go fuck yourself."

"*Ex*cuse me?" she hissed. "*What* did you just say to me?"

"We're both in line for the priest," I cut back, ignoring the astonished looks behind me. "I'm pretty sure you aren't any more of an angel than I am. So why don't you focus a little more on your own fuckups and leave me to think about mine, all right?"

She opened and closed her mouth like a fish, and for a moment, looked like she wanted to punch me. Hell, I probably would have let her. With a comment like that, I probably deserved it.

But I never promised anyone I was a nice guy. The best I could offer was saying sorry afterward. That was, after all, why I was here.

Gargoyle lady apparently couldn't bear my presence long enough for her weekly dose of absolution, however. She jumped right out of line and scurried out of the church, muttering something to herself in

Spanish that I couldn't make out. I was pretty sure it was no better than anything I'd said.

The door to the confessional opened, and another parishioner stepped out, crossing himself. I took his place, for the eighth time in as many weeks. Sank to my knees, faced the screen, and ignored the smell of stale cedar and incense that threatened to consume me. This wouldn't take long. After all, the priest already knew the story. I'd been telling the same one for weeks and weeks.

About the woman I wanted but couldn't have.

The sins I'd committed but could never repent.

The future I craved but could never produce.

I could talk all I wanted, but I knew it wouldn't save me. Because you can't have grace without true repentance, and I could never truly regret anything Nina de Vries and I did together.

Still, it couldn't hurt to try. I'd keep coming back, going through the motions until something clicked.

Except now that I knew I might see Nina in just a few days, I was pretty sure those motions were going to get about ten times harder.

"Matthew," droned the familiar voice of Father Deflorio. "Causing an unusual stir today, aren't we?"

"Yeah, well. It's an unusual day, Father."

There was a long sigh from the other side of the screen. "Why don't you tell me about it, then?"

I crossed myself and took a deep breath. "Sure, all right. Bless me, Father, for I have sinned. Or at least, I'm pretty sure I'm about to."

II

PAESAGGIO

THEN

CHAPTER NINE

AUGUST 2008

A bird was chirping at the window. Not a pigeon or sparrow, which wouldn't be particularly notable for New York City. This one had a higher cheep, a pretty little warble that whistled through the air, chipper and light as the summer breeze on the balcony outside Nina's rooms, left open through the night while she tried to sleep through nausea and heartache.

She turned on her pillow to find the bird hopping along the sill of the open window as if dancing to its song. It was yellow—a goldfinch, maybe. Pretty and bright. Impossible not to notice.

"Hello," Nina murmured.

The bird cocked its head skeptically.

"I know," Nina replied. "I barely recognize myself these days either."

At the sound of her voice, the bird emitted another dancing song, then flew away, leaving Nina alone again with the ambient noise of cabs, pedestrians, and the general roar of the city twenty stories down. This morning felt different, she realized, than the last forty-two or so. Vaguely, she wondered why.

She still wasn't used to this apartment. Of course, Nina still wasn't used to much of anything about this situation. The fact that a small part of her trust became available upon her marriage had been a surprise to everyone, something her grandfather had set up for future progeny before they were even born. Everything else was off-limits—married or not—for another ten years at least, according to the board.

But immediately after that surreal day at St. Mark's, the executor of Grandfather's estate had pulled Nina and Calvin aside and handed them the deed and keys to a penthouse on Ninety-Second and Lexington Avenue. Calvin had swept them up with the glee of a child finding an extra toy at Christmas. Nina had simply blinked and nodded. And they had moved in directly after their "honeymoon" weekend on Long Island, during which Nina had spent most of her time trying not to vomit.

Normally she found this space oppressive, like the whole building was weighing down on her despite the fact that they occupied the entire top floor. But this morning, everything seemed lighter. It took her a few moments to realize what was different. But when she did, she laughed out loud for the first time in weeks.

She wasn't feeling sick. Her head wasn't about to burst. Her ankles didn't feel like swollen lead. And the sweaty threat of losing last night's dinner wasn't lurking in the back of her throat.

Nina rolled to her back and used the moment to peer around the room, which she had barely noticed before, too busy dashing for the bathroom or sobbing into her pillow. The decor was hopelessly old-fashioned, like it hadn't been touched since its pre-war days. Between the brass fixtures, mahogany four-poster, blush-colored carpets, and heavy, flower-sprigged drapes that matched the wallpaper, Nina rather felt as though she were trapped in a thirty-year-old soap opera.

"It will all have to change," she muttered.

Strip the sprigged wallpaper and trash the matching drapes. Lighten everything with a fresh coat of white, including the box-molded ceilings. Yank the carpets and install new floors, maybe parquet. All but a few pieces of furniture could be donated, or perhaps put to use in one of her other family members' equally over-decorated homes.

It would be fresh and minimalist, the hardwood furniture replaced with simple, luxurious pieces. And then there would be art. Beautiful, glorious art to take advantage of the high ceilings and natural light pouring in through the tall, original lead-paned windows.

She found she could imagine it all quite clearly.

She also found that she didn't particularly care. For this place, no matter what she did to it, was unlikely ever to feel like home.

"You're awake."

And just like that, the rush of her first morning in three months without immediate nausea faded. Nina sat up and found her husband standing in the door to the suite, which she hadn't even noticed had been opened. "I am, yes."

Calvin looked the same as ever in a pair of creased chinos and rumpled button-up that made his slightly stocky body look shorter than normal. He said he had made use of their new joint bank account to hire a stylist, have several new suits made up, and trade his Third Avenue barber for someone at the Plaza, among other things. His graying hair was now a bit more chestnut, but other than that, Nina couldn't see any discernible differences in his appearance. A stylist couldn't stop crumbs, stains, and a predisposition toward wrinkles.

"Not sick this morning?" Calvin strode in, his tasseled loafers leaving heavy footprints in the carpet.

Nina shook her head. "No, thankfully. Yesterday was only in the morning too."

Calvin nodded curtly. "So Cook said when I got in last night."

Nina frowned. "Cook?" Even her grandmother didn't call her staff simply by their positions.

Calvin shrugged. "Whatever her name is."

"Marguerite has been really wonderful so far," Nina replied. "And since you like her chicken parmesan so much, perhaps you can tell her."

Calvin's eyes narrowed, but Nina was careful not to betray any other sign of her disgust with the way her husband ate slabs of cheese-laden chicken he rather resembled at times. As he sat down on the edge of the bed, his beady gaze traveled over Nina's body. He did that sometimes, with the same kind of attention some men used to check their cars for scratches.

Nina didn't like it. At all. But when she had asked him what he was looking for, he had snapped at her so virulently that she never asked again. More and more, it seemed that something was boiling just under the surface of the husband she had initially considered so placid.

So, she tried again to strike a lighter tone. "Well. How was our 'honeymoon,' darling?"

It was meant as a joke. After their "honeymoon" in the Hamptons had gone awry when Nina's morning sickness had taken over the entire thing, Calvin had scheduled an actual trip to France and England—for work, he said, despite the fact that he used her black Amex to book everything.

"Hilarious," he said. "People kept asking me where the fuck my wife was."

Nina frowned, confused. "You actually told people it was your honeymoon? You said this was a business trip to secure investors."

"Well, originally I thought you would be going on it with me, so I didn't think it would hurt to tell the hotels we were newlyweds. Which just made me look like a scammer when you decided not to show and embarrassed me all over again. Cost me a fortune to reschedule all of that, you know."

His hand, which had been gesturing wildly as he spoke, settled on her shin with a clap over the blanket. Nina fought the urge to move her leg, but didn't. She had a feeling it would make him that much angrier. And, after all, it was just her shin.

Instead, she sighed and sank back into her pillows. What else was there to say? One month into this sham marriage, and she was already weary, explaining away every perceived slight Calvin had. "What are you wearing?" he asked suddenly. "It's a damn rag."

Without waiting for her to respond, he pulled the comforter down, baring Nina's thin white nightdress to her knees. She resisted the urge to press her hands over her chest. The material wasn't sheer, but somehow, she still felt naked under Calvin's roving gaze.

"Two weeks away, and you swell up like a balloon," he said. "Just look at you. How is having a trophy wife going to help me secure investments if she's nothing worth showing off?"

Nina followed his gaze to her stomach and set her hand over her navel, trying not to let the words sting. At just over four months along, the small bump was clearly evident, as were the changes in her breasts, which were double their usual size. She felt swollen and ripe, like a peach that could bruise with the lightest touch. And maybe, if it were with anyone else, she might have actually enjoyed it. If it were Peppe sitting beside her, she would have already pulled him down to explore these new sensitivities.

But the prospect with Calvin only made the nausea return.

"You're still kind of pretty, you know." His voice had changed, a ragged attempt at a purr instead of a snap. The hand on her shin rose and began to float up her leg, over her body.

Goose bumps rose up and down Nina's arms.

"That hair. This skin." His finger ran over Nina's shoulder and toyed with the strap of her chemise.

Wait. No. This was wrong. It wasn't what they had agreed to.

Friends, Calvin had said just days before they entered the church. *We'll live as friends, I promise.*

"Calvin," Nina ventured as his hand pulled the strap down. "What are you doing?"

He leaned in close enough that she could smell the sweet and sour residue of a Bloody Mary on his breath. Someone had been out to brunch.

"They said no," he said as he pulled the strap back up, then down again, hypnotized by its progress. "At breakfast today. At every fucking meeting I went to in Paris, London, Manchester, Edinburgh. No, no, no, no, no. They didn't believe I was part of the family. I told you we should have had more press at the wedding."

Nina didn't respond. She happened to know that her grandmother had personally requested most local newspapers not cover their wedding, and Nina had not argued at all. While the rest of her family had traditionally enjoyed the benefits of *Vanity Fair* profiles, large Style section features in the *Times*, or at the very least, a mention in the *Post*, her marriage was not something she had wanted to publicize.

"And Celeste, of course, was conveniently unavailable every time I tried to call," Calvin continued. "Everyone said they'd wait for you to make a move." He grimaced, yanking on the strap now so that it dug into her skin. "Honestly, it's just property, not interior design. You don't know shit about this in the first place. But how am I supposed to become the next Trump when I'm handicapped by your idiotic trust limitations?"

Again, Nina stayed silent, fighting the urge to slap his hand away from her shoulder. This tone, this unreserved resentment was new. She honestly wasn't sure what to make of it.

She had heard Calvin complain about his failed business ventures before. Just as she knew of his plans to replicate what honestly sounded like a slumlord model of purchasing decrepit properties around New York and raising the rents until the poor tenants could be evicted. She didn't know much about real estate, but it didn't sound like a very nice way to make money.

She also knew it wasn't working for him.

"In a month, though—maybe less—you'll look like a cow," he continued, still mesmerized by the strap pinched between his thick fingers. "No one will want to fuck you, and that's half the charm, isn't it? So I should probably take advantage of it now, don't you think?"

He pulled the strap far enough that the top of her nightdress began to fall with it, baring some of her new décolletage.

A sinking feeling grew in Nina's stomach. "I'm sorry. Wh-what do you mean?"

"Women always do that. Apologize for things when they aren't the slightest bit fucking sorry." Calvin scowled, but his hand didn't move. Instead, he pulled the strap down farther, enough that the fabric threatened to topple over her nipple.

"What do you think I mean? We're married, aren't we?"

Nina jerked. His hand fell from her arm, but instead of giving her space while she pulled her nightdress back into place, he slipped it under her sheets to grab her thigh. Skin to sweaty skin.

Nina squirmed. "Calvin!"

"Don't be such a fucking prude, Nina," he snapped as his hand tightened. "The jig is up, isn't it? Considering the state I got you in, I don't think you're really in a position to pretend you're all that modest."

"Calvin," Nina tried again, stilling like a deer staring at headlights. Did that mean he was the semi? "Calvin, please stop."

"I'm tired of this little game."

"Tired of what game? We had—I thought we had an arrangement. We have separate bedrooms, and—"

"Did you really think I was going to marry you and not act like an actual married couple?" Calvin snorted as his hand moved up her thigh, gripping even harder. "That's part of the perks, isn't it? You might be ruined goods, but I've never been too good for the bargain shelf. Especially when I can't get anything else I need."

"What—what are you talking about?" *Move* screamed a voice in the back of Nina's mind. But for some reason, her body was stone.

The hand on her thigh crept upward.

"This whole marriage was supposed to set me up for life. No one would give me the time of day without my child fucking bride. The one with the de Vries pedigree." He practically spat the words. "But I'm on an *allowance* from dear old Grandma. I have to ask for fucking pocket money from my child bride. Well, if I can't get what I want out there, I might as well take advantage of it in here."

Nina gasped as Calvin's hand shoved underneath her nightgown, a blunt intrusion against her thin silk underwear.

"Calvin! What are you doing?!"

Suddenly, Nina was all action, finally in her right mind. She sprang off the bed and to the other side, breathing only slightly easier when there was a king-sized mattress between them. She yanked her robe from a chair beside the bed and wrapped it tightly around her body, ignoring a desire to jump straight into a hot shower.

"Look," she managed. "I don't know what you thought this was. And I'm sorry if I misled you. But I wasn't expecting us to...you know..."

"Fuck?" Calvin snarled. "Come on, princess. It's not like you've never done it before."

Nina gulped. "You said the plan was to remain strictly platonic!"

"Plans change."

Calvin stalked around the bed, and, suddenly, Nina wished dearly she had run the other way, toward the door. As it was, she was trapped in the corner, with nowhere to go unless she scampered back over the mattress like a monkey.

And maybe she might have if she hadn't been stymied by a sudden wave of nausea flinging her back again.

In a few surprisingly quick steps around the bed, Calvin cornered her against the chair. A ribbon of sweat broke out across Nina's forehead as she tried to fight the rising tide in the back of her throat.

"You won't put me off forever, you know," Calvin said as he curled a hand around Nina's wrist. "Those hoity-toity assholes in suits might, but you won't. I won't fucking have it."

Nina looked down at his hand, then back up at her "husband." She snuck a glance down the hallway.

"The butler isn't here. None of them are." One of Calvin's light brown brows quirked upward as he leered down her robe, openly examining her cleavage. "I told them to leave for the day."

Nina gasped. "You dismissed our entire staff for the day without telling me?"

Calvin shrugged. "You sure think you're something of a mistress, don't you? You're a child, Nina. And that's exactly how they all think of you."

"If I'm a child," Nina snapped, "then what does it say about you that you want to sleep with me?"

His other hand found her cheek with a sudden, ringing smack. Her skin burned, her neck throbbed with the sore reflex of being hurled to the side.

"You will never talk to me like that again!" Calvin roared. "I have to take all their fucking belittling outside this house. I won't have my wife doing the same. You *will* respect me!"

He grabbed her other wrist and shoved her against the wall so her head thumped hard against the plaster, enough that there would be a sizable knot there later.

Every cell in Nina's body tensed. Every muscle seized. She wanted to fight. Wanted to yell, run, punch, kick. But at the same time, a sensible voice in the back of her mind reminded her that she was a pregnant woman trapped in a corner with nowhere to go. And something in Calvin's eyes told her he could potentially do far worse to her and her unborn child.

Think.

"A-all right," Nina whispered. "All right. Let me. Calvin, please let me help you. What—what can I do to help? Is there anything I can do to make it better? Call those men? Get you the meetings you need? I'll tell whoever you want that we are married. I said I'd help. I will."

His small eyes flashed like beady peppercorns in a mashed potato face. His vodka-tinged breath was hot on her neck. Nina's stomach roiled.

"The princess wants to help her pauper 'husband,' eh?"

"Calvin, p-please. Just tell me what I can do."

He stared at her hard for a long time. Then, at last, his iron grip dropped. Nina's arms fell, and she rubbed her sore wrists as Calvin pulled a crumpled paper from his pocket and shoved it at her. Nina took it. It bore a list of crossed-out names that she recognized as board members of the De Vries Shipping Corporation. Many were on the board of her trust as well. Including her grandmother.

"I need seed money for some properties in Brooklyn and Newark," Calvin said. "Five million to start. If I put that down, others will follow."

Nina gasped. "That's—that's a lot of money." She couldn't imagine her grandmother would ever agree.

"There's a lot more than that in your trust, and you know it, princess. They'll make an exception for your new married venture. You just have to ask."

"Calvin, I don't know…"

As quick as lightning, one of his hands found her wrist again while the other slipped back between her legs.

"All right," Nina breathed as she clamped her thighs together. "All right, I'll call them today. I-I promise."

He removed his hands and examined her, as if to see whether she was telling the truth. But instead of stepping back, he leaned closer. Nina stilled. They had kissed once at the altar. Never since. But right now, soaked in a sheen of vodka and canned vegetables, Calvin's thin

lips hovered just over her own, breathing heavily—with anger, frustration, or lust, Nina couldn't tell.

Her voice was small. Terrified. "Please—please don't."

"Oh, shut up, princess. It's just a fucking kiss."

His lips smashed against hers like a pair of rubber worms. It was
only for a second. But a second was all it took.

Nina gagged. "Oh. Oh God."

With a sudden rush of nausea-fueled adrenaline, she shoved
Calvin's chest violently and made a decidedly ungraceful beeline for
the bathroom, barely making it to the toilet in time to lose what was
left of her dinner the night before. It came and came. And then, when
Nina remembered where she had stood and what had happened right
before, it came again.

A few minutes later, when her stomach was empty and the heat in
her face was starting to recede, Nina looked up to find Calvin standing
in the doorway of the bathroom. His own forehead was reddened and
sweaty, his ugly striped tie loosened around his thick neck as he stared
down at her. Her wrinkled chemise pushed up her thighs, her bare legs
splayed across the marble floor like a broken deer's.

For one terrifying moment, Nina thought he might join her there on
the floor and continue what he had started in the most brutal way
possible. Even more terrifying, she was certain she wouldn't have been
able to stop him if he had.

But then, he turned. The second mercifully passed.

"Disgusting," Calvin muttered as he pushed off the door. And then,
over his shoulder as he left: "Make sure you call the board today. I
won't wait any longer."

CHAPTER TEN

SEPTEMBER 2008

"Is your husband here, Mrs. Gardner?"

Nina looked up from her toes, wriggling at the end of the exam table. She had a good view of them from here, lying on her back, feet propped in metal stirrups. No dignity, but at least she had a pedicure.

Her toes were so much more swollen now, to the point where she would require a larger size shoe before long. So strange that only a few things seemed to be growing. Her belly, of course, which housed the baby. Fingers too, so much that she couldn't wear the rings she'd first put on in June (not that she was particularly disappointed about that). Breasts, toes. But that was it.

She cleared her throat. "Oh, um. No. No, he won't make it."

The tech kept her face carefully blank, but Nina didn't miss a flicker of pity there as she glanced at her before looking back at the screen. Most of the other women in this office had their partners with them. Nina's hadn't made a single appearance at any of her prenatal appointments thus far.

The bigger difference, though, was that she didn't want him there at all.

It had been a month since that terrifying morning and almost as long since Nina had begged her grandmother for an audience with the board. Celeste, of course, had probed and re-probed every aspect of the potential deal before even consulting her calendar.

In the end, it was only an appeal to her sense of propriety that had done it.

"Grandmother, be honest. How will it look if I'm the only person in the family married to a failure?"

Thankfully, Calvin had been better prepared for the inquisition. He had stood next to Nina with his business plan in hand—a binder full of projections, numbers, property history, and so forth. Nina didn't know what half of it meant, but in the end, it had still come down to her. Grandmother, sitting in her place at the head of the long table, had looked Nina in the eye and asked: "Is this truly what you want? Another five million out of your trust fund liquidated early?"

Her name would be on everything, Calvin had promised her. An investment for them both.

Nina didn't care so long as he never touched her again. Five million from an account containing hundreds seemed like a pittance. The money itself was an illusion anyway, considering she wouldn't even be eligible to access most of it past her monthly allowance until she was over forty. If begging for a paltry piece would pay for Calvin's inattention, it would be well worth it.

Permission had been granted. The money deposited into a fund under both their names the following week. And Calvin had disappeared for several weeks, appearing only a few times in the early mornings after nights out with his new "associates." Sitting beside her bed, sometimes with a drink in hand.

But he hadn't touched her since.

"Nice strong heartbeat," remarked the tech as she moved the ultrasound transducer over Nina's swollen belly. "Oh, look! There're some good kicks going on. You'll probably start feeling those in another three, maybe four weeks, I'd guess."

Nina nodded. The baby's heartbeat was a hushed lullaby around the dim blue room. But instead of watching the screen, she closed her eyes while the tech continued to take photos and measurements. It was strangely soothing, this touch via machine. Impersonal, of course, but at least it wasn't threatening.

How long until you can get yourself back to normal?

Calvin had asked her that only two days earlier, the last time she'd woken to find him staring at her from the chair at her vanity. Still no touches, but the way he looked at her made her feel like a treat about to spoil.

I'm not interested in a wife with an ass like cottage cheese, you know.

Would Giuseppe have said that?

Peppe's face appeared again, as it often did now when Nina felt sad or alone. She nuzzled into the pillow, pretending it was his lean chest. His warmth instead of the coarse linen. His touch on her belly, loving his unborn child, instead of a machine. At night, peace only seemed to come when she imagined Peppe spooned around her.

Principessa, he'd say dreamily. Before he'd return to his family. His wife.

Since that terrible morning with Calvin nearly a month ago, Nina had started and thrown out five different letters and twice as many emails. More and more, she was starting to feel Giuseppe had the right to know about his baby.

This heartbeat, this child. It belonged to him too. She didn't expect anything from him. Didn't want to ruin his marriage or his family, and she had more than enough to care for the child herself. It could still be a secret, just between them. No scandal necessary.

But every time she tried to write the words, her tongue got stuck in her throat and her fingers froze.

Peppe, I'm sorry.

Peppe, I lied.

Peppe, I miss you.

Peppe...I'm preg—

"All right, Mrs. Gardner. It looks like everything is in order."

Nina opened her eyes as the heartbeat faded away. The curtains barring entry to the small ultrasound room parted, and the tech traded places with Dr. Jenkins, who took the seat near the machine while a series of pictures printed from below. She replaced the transducer on Nina's belly. The heartbeat returned.

"Yes, yes," said the doctor. "Everything looks perfect." She smiled warmly. "Would you like to know the sex?"

Nina blinked. She honestly hadn't even thought about it, and Calvin, of course, was more interested in her changing body than the child that was causing it.

"I—oh, yes," she found herself saying. "Yes, I suppose so."

Dr. Jenkins sighed and stilled the transducer. The baby's heartbeat remained audible, like it was squeezing the room with each hushed thump. Nina kept her eyes on the dark, beating spot in the center of the screen.

"Mrs. Gardner. Before we do that, I wanted to say—the baby is healthy...but I am concerned. You're twenty weeks into this pregnancy, and you've gained maybe two pounds."

Back to her toes went her gaze. "There's nothing wrong with keeping trim," Nina mumbled. Hadn't her mother said so as soon as she heard the news?

"There is when it prevents your baby from flourishing, and that's what I'm concerned about. By your third trimester, the baby may be putting on as much as a pound per week. That can't happen if you're not taking care of yourself."

Nina didn't answer. She wasn't sure what else there was to say.

The doctor tried again. "Look, there's nothing wrong with feeling however you feel. In fact, prenatal depression occurs in approximately fifteen to twenty percent of—"

"I am *not* depressed," Nina interrupted with emphasis that surprised even her.

Lord, it was like Grandmother had spoken right through her, with a steel-sharp tone that brooked no alternative response. De Vrieses didn't get depressed. Just like they didn't get overweight, ugly, or emotive in any real way.

Dr. Jenkins tipped her head kindly. "Mrs. Gardner, no one can always control what your hormones are going to do at this time. There's no shame in it. But I must ask—is everything all right at home? I have noticed your husband hasn't accompanied you to any of your appointments."

And there it was. The sad fact of Nina's complete and utter solitude in all of this. Her friends couldn't have been less interested in the fact that she could no longer join them at brunch spots and nightclubs. Her family was too busy hosting luncheons to inquire about her health. And her husband…

She bit back a bitter laugh along with a few tears.

"I'm from the Upper East Side, Dr. Jenkins," Nina said, trying for a bit of levity. Failing miserably. "Our husbands often work more than eighty hours a week. Does it really surprise you that one of them isn't particularly concerned with a child that hasn't been born yet?"

The doctor just offered a sympathetic expression, then patted Nina gently on the knee and turned back to the screen. Nina tasted the sweet tang of blood when she bit her lip hard to stop from crying.

"I'd like you to eat more," Dr. Jenkins was saying. "And I'm going to write you a referral to a very good therapist. Just in case you need someone to talk to. Otherwise, you could potentially take—"

"No medications," Nina cut in, surprising herself again. Then, a bit softer: "They aren't good for the baby."

So that's what maternal instinct feels like, she thought. It was strong, pulsing through her for the first time, right along with the baby's heartbeat. She smiled, and this time, even through her heartache, it was genuine.

The doctor smiled back. "All right. But if you need anything, please don't hesitate to ask. That's what I'm here for."

Nina watched the fuzzy screen, where the baby's heartbeat pulsed and the legs kicked in unison. "I'll eat," she said. "I promise."

Dr. Jenkins nodded. "Good. Are you ready for the big reveal? Or are you doing something at home to celebrate?"

Nina stared at the screen, fully transfixed. There were its legs, its arms. The shape of a head that could fit in her palm, maybe even now. "Please," she said. "Just tell me."

The transducer moved a bit. Then a bit more. Dr. Jenkins craned her head, squinting to look more closely.

"Ah! There it is." She turned to me. "Sometimes they don't want to show us, you know."

"What…what is it?" Nina asked uncertainly.

"Congratulations, Mrs. Gardner. You're having a girl."

A girl.

Like me.

For a moment, a bubble of jubilation filled Nina's chest, her mind, her entire being.

She saw her daughter as clearly as anything in the room. A beautiful, golden-haired child. Or maybe dark, like her father. Her real father.

She would coo and smile and laugh and cry. And she would be loved. So, so loved.

Or would she?

Almost as quickly, the vision of the little girl faded, and Nina saw the rest of her daughter's life ahead of her. The one she had led herself.

Endless nannies, etiquette lessons, and meals at huge empty dining room tables. Playing alone in a nursery without a sibling or many friends. Day school, then boarding school, plus finishing lessons of every kind. Expectation after expectation piled on her, until one day she would burst if she didn't make at least one mistake for herself at last.

And when she did, she would turn around and find hardly anyone there to hold her through its inevitable fallout.

And on her daughter's behalf, Nina never felt more alone. Because how could she love a child when no one had ever taught her how.

I love you, principessa.

Had that even been love? How could it have been when he had found it so easy to leave her? Peppe had looked at her with such fondness, had touched her body with such reverence.

But love?

This far away, Nina wasn't so sure anymore.

I'll be there, she thought fiercely as she watched the baby move. *I'll protect you from all of it. No matter what. We might be alone, my darling, but I promise, you'll always stay safe.*

CHAPTER ELEVEN

NOVEMBER 2008

"Oh God!" Nina shrieked. "Oh God!"

"Just hold on, Mrs. Gardner. This will pass."

The nurse's voice was calm, indulgent, masking the pity that every single person at Mount Sinai Hospital had demonstrated in one way or another since Nina had been admitted two hours earlier in the care of a servant. Her cook. Marguerite seemed to like her, but not enough to stay through labor.

Since then, Nina had been alone in one of the luxury suites of Mt. Sinai, waiting through contractions for her daughter to be born.

The staff's whispers were hushed, but not hushed enough.

"Newly married."

"Husband out of the country."

"De Vries family."

"All alone."

She didn't have it so bad, she tried to tell herself. How many women around the world gave birth at home every day? Without the benefit of a hospital like this? Without all the things the de Vries name commanded in this town: the best medical staff in New York City waiting on her hand and foot, a private room in the most exclusive hospital, ice chips, flowers?

Things, Nina thought bitterly as she groaned through another heavy contraction. They were just things. And in this room, when her body was starting the process that literally every mother on the planet had endured before her, what did things matter when she had no one to hold her hand?

Not one. Fucking. Bit.

Yes, fucking. Because that was what went through her mind when the iron band around her belly crushed her like this. They didn't. Fucking. Matter at *all*.

Nina. Evelyn. Astor. De Vries. Gardner.

Her names were staccato shots through her mind as the contraction throbbed—they were all she could think about as she had this baby. Almost six weeks early.

Nina for the daughter she was.

Evelyn for some unknown great-aunt.

Astor for the father she'd barely known since she was a child.

De Vries for the family she had striven her entire life to please.

Gardner for the man she was chained to.

All family. And where were they now?

Her mother was in Cabo, sunning herself on a friend's yacht. Her husband was in Thailand with some fool named Letour. Eric was still lost somewhere else around the world. And Grandmother was too old and too much of a hypochondriac to set foot in a hospital at all.

Nina had no one. She was completely by herself.

"Ahhhhhhh!" she shrieked as the contraction reached its zenith. "Goddamn you, Peppe!"

Yes, her aversion to cursing had definitely disappeared this evening. But the nurse didn't even blink.

"Breathe, Mrs. Gardner. Just breathe. Remember what you learned in your classes."

"I didn't finish the fucking classes!" Nina spat as her face scrunched up in agony. "I stopped after the second one."

After seeing all those ridiculous couples flashing smiles and cooing at each other, she had simply been too mortified—and sad—to continue. Dr. Jenkins had told her to do whatever it took to keep her spirits up. Well, that class definitely did nothing for her.

"Didn't go to the..." The nurse shook her head, but was wise enough not to finish her sentence.

Nina shook hers back. "No." Stupid, stupid. When was she going to learn? "Ahhhhh!" she cried as the third and final spasm passed through her.

And then, just as quickly as it had come, it left. Nina rolled to her side and rubbed her lower back viciously. If it wasn't one part, it was another.

"Hello!"

Nina and the nurse both turned to the door, where an unfamiliar man in a lab coat entered the room.

"Who are you? Where is Dr. Jenkins?" Nina asked.

"Oh, she's on vacation in Belize, lucky girl," the doctor replied. "I'm Dr. Conrad, the on-call obstetrician here this evening. I'll be helping you through this birth, and I promise, Mrs. Gardner, we'll take good care of you." Dr. Conrad turned to the nurse. "Is, um, Mr. Gardner here?" he asked out the side of his mouth.

The nurse shook her head mutely and made a covert sign across her mouth, signaling it was a no-go subject before she darted out of the room.

Internally, Nina raged.

"Looks like it will be tea for two, then!" Dr. Conrad turned with an over-jovial grin as he sat on a stool at the end of the bed. "Let's have a look, shall we?"

Nina forced her awkward, massive body onto her back and pushed herself to the end of the bed so the doctor could measure how far along she was. Still trying to catch her breath, she found it much harder to ignore the fact that she was effectively on display to a complete stranger. And a man, at that. It was funny, though. She was having a hard time caring either way.

"Seven centimeters!" cheered Dr. Conrad. "And you refused an epidural, that's right?"

"Yes," Nina said wearily. She was almost regretting that decision now, but was too stubborn to say anything.

"I'd say at this rate, you'll be ready to push in three hours or so, hon." He pulled down his mask and grinned at her. "Are you ready to meet your little one?"

Nina slumped into her pillow and pushed the tiny, sweat-soaked hairs from her forehead. "Can I have some ice chips, please?"

The doctor frowned at her lackluster response. "Ah, yes. I'll get a nurse." He pushed away from the bed as Nina folded her legs back together. "Chin up, Mrs. Gardner. It will be over sooner than you think."

As the doctor left, Nina pressed her face into the pillow, trying not to cry. Would it be over soon? And what would that look like? She'd have a daughter...a baby...and what in the world was she going to do after?

She had finished the letter to Peppe but never sent it. It was on her desk. His face, thin and mournful, rose in Nina's mind. She choked back a sob. Another contraction began.

"Oh, God," she wailed into the coarse cotton.

That same vise grip wrenched her belly even tighter than before. She gasped at the ceiling, then rolled onto her side. The pain throbbed in harsh, consistent waves for thirty seconds, forty-five. Nina squeezed her eyes closed, but tears came anyway.

"Peppe," she gasped, again and again. "Where are you?"

And then, as suddenly as it had arrived, the contraction faded. Nina's tears did not, but as soon as she decided to really let go, she was started out of her misery by a knock at the door.

"What?" she snapped, wiping viciously at her face. "Who the fuck is it?" Who could possibly be here for a social call at a time like this? Who could possibly think this was important? "Calvin, I swear, if you are knocking right now—"

"It's not Calvin."

The door opened, and instead of Nina's husband, another familiar face popped in: Caitlyn Calvert.

Immediately, Nina relaxed some. "Oh, it's just you." She lay back on her pillow, suddenly conscious of the fact that she was half-drenched in sweat in a rumpled hospital gown. "I thought it was another insipid idiot from the hospital board or something like that.

Someone trying to kiss Grandmother's ass. At least two have made appearances since I checked in."

Caitlyn chuckled as she slipped into the room. "You're a dear. And you were swearing at Calvin, not them, so you can't fool me. N, I've never heard you speak like that before, you beast."

Nina grunted, still catching her breath, both from choked sobs and the remnants of the contraction. "Well, I've never been in labor before. I think I'm allowed a pass."

Caitlyn laughed again as she sat down in one of the bedside chairs. "Agreed. I'm sure if I were in your shoes, every bit of Jersey in me would be coming out in spades. Here, one of the nurses said this is for you." She handed Nina a cup of ice.

Nina accepted it gratefully and popped a few chips into her mouth. The chill was a welcome relief. "Thank you." She took a closer look at her friend. "You look different. Where have you been?"

The Caitlyn Nina knew these days never looked anything less than perfect. Today, though, Caitlyn was simply dressed in a pair of jeans and a t-shirt, her caramel-colored hair pulled back into a ponytail. She looked more like an average, twenty-year-old college student than a budding socialite. Like the girl Nina had met when they were kids— the trust fund brat and the yearly scholarship student.

"I came as soon as I heard," Caitlyn said. "Maddie said your mom bought everyone drinks at El Farallon when she got your call."

Nina tried hard not to think about how the idea of Violet treating a restaurant full of strangers instead of coming to see her own daughter in the hospital made her feel.

"I went home to change first, though," Caitlyn continued. "I didn't think Chanel was really appropriate for the birthing room. Florian would kill me if I ruined it."

Nina blinked. Ah, there was the new Caitlyn, loud and clear. But before she could reply, another sudden, much more violent contraction seized.

"Oh fuck!" Nina could barely breathe, but still managed to hiss a long stream of profanity for close to a minute.

When it was finished, Caitlyn was bracing herself against the chair, like she was expecting to be hit in the face or something.

"Sorry," Nina breathed. "That was terrible."

Caitlyn shook her head. "Honestly, it's a bit of a relief to see you like this. Nina de Vries finally breaks." She chuckled. "I never thought I'd see the day."

Nina slumped into the pillows. Everything hurt. Everything. Too much for her to care about Caitlyn's passive-aggressive punches.

"So...you want to tell me who Peppe is?"

Nina froze, eyes closed. Even through the heat, the sweat, the exhaustion, her skin grew cold. "What?"

"You were crying for him when I walked in." Caitlyn bent closer, eyes gleaming. "Is it...is it the baby's father?"

Nina opened one eye. "What are you talking about?"

But there was no guile on Caitlyn's newly perfected face. Just care. Just sympathy. "N, come on. We've known each other since we were kids. I mean, we practically still are kids."

Nina snorted. It was true, but like so many people from this city, they had grown up faster than most. Even in high school, half her friends were already starting to date men ten years their senior.

The habits of New York's elite class.

"You were supposed to come home in triumph," Caitlyn said. "Cynthia Devon went to Smith, you to Wellesley, and so forth."

She sniffed. Nina knew it was because, unlike the rest of them, college hadn't been an option for Caitlyn. Not with her grades or interests.

"Instead, you turn up after your year abroad engaged to...him?" She shook her head. "And now he's not even here?"

They both stared at Nina's bare hands, which had been too swollen for months for the ugly pear-shaped diamond.

Nina swallowed. Even then, she couldn't reply, though she desperately wanted to. In all honesty, it would've been so nice to tell someone about the way her life had changed completely in Florence.

"So...Peppe?" Caitlyn asked again. "I'm guessing he was Italian. Handsome?"

Nina shrugged. Handsome, yes, but not in a typical way. It wasn't quite the right word to describe her dignified professor.

She closed her eyes again. Just thinking about him was painful.

"Does he know?"

Eyes open, Nina shook her head in defeat. "No."

But Caitlyn didn't look away. Instead, she just watched somberly as the next contraction arrived.

"It's okay," she said as Nina's eyes started to water. "You can tell me. I won't say anything."

"I want him to know." The words tumbled out as the contraction tightened its iron grip once more. Nina grasped the rails of her bed, leaning forward, face contorted with pain. "I never t-told him! But now —oh fuck!—I want him to know!"

Caitlyn grabbed for her hand as Nina began to moan louder.

"It's all right, N, it's all right. Just…well, I don't know what you're supposed to do. I guess breathe, right?" Caitlyn started to mimic Lamaze-style breaths the way people did sometimes in movies or TV shows.

"Gah!" Nina shouted, though she almost started laughing through the gut-wrenching pain. Caitlyn looked absolutely ridiculous with her cheeks puffing out like a fish.

Caitlyn started laughing too. "Does that help?"

"No!" Nina squealed. "Ah, they are so…c-close!" Each word came out through a painful huff. The contractions were so fast now. Things were happening. She didn't have time to think about anything other than the baby.

"All right!"

The door opened again, and this time the doctor swept in with a nurse beside him. "Who's ready to have a baby?" he asked, his over-pronounced joy bouncing off every surface in the room.

Nina wanted to murder him.

"We are!" Caitlyn rejoined, squeezing Nina's hand even tighter.

Nina turned, even as nauseating levels of pain swept through her. "We?"

Caitlyn turned back to the bed with a weak smile. As the contraction grew, she squeezed as hard as Nina did, biting her lip with effort but never once letting go.

"We," she said with surety Nina couldn't feel. "I'm here, N, I promise. Until the end."

CHAPTER TWELVE

DECEMBER 2008

"Here we are, Mrs. Gardner. Looks like they're all ready for the season, aren't they?"

Through the backseat windows of the big black Escalade, Nina peered up at her grandmother's familiar Park Avenue building. The Escalade was new, just like the chattering driver, Davis, whom Calvin had hired after the birth. He had insisted that it was ridiculous for them to take taxis or hire town cars. *People like us have their own drivers,* he'd argued.

Us? Nina wanted to ask. *Or me?*

Either way, she didn't really care about the answer. And she had learned quickly over the last few weeks not to provoke the beast.

This was one of her first nights out since the birth. From the wide window sill in her suite, she had nursed Olivia and watched Christmas bloom in the city streets below. The world had been quiet. Calvin was gone most of the time, thankfully, showing even less interest in his supposed "daughter" after she was born than he had before. And for the last nearly two months Nina had been given a sanctuary from her marriage.

It also gave her time to think about its end.

A year, they'd said. Enough time for Calvin to get his business off the ground. Enough time for her to avoid the scandal of having a baby out of wedlock. It was half over now. She could hire a lawyer, make sure the terms of the prenup would be upheld. Plan a life outside of her tower for her and the baby. Together.

Nina sighed as she looked up at the traditional garland and lights decorating the familiar brick building. The problem with getting out of the marriage was that she didn't know what that life was supposed to look like afterward. Money wouldn't be an issue. But it wasn't like she would be able to jump right back into being an impetuous college student. She had a child to care for now. She had to think about where she wanted to raise her. Whom she wanted in their life.

Giuseppe.

The letter had sat on the desk in her room for over a month until she finally got up the nerve to send it to the university.

Peppe—

Buongiorno from Novo York, as one might say! I hope you're doing well and have a good Christmas planned with your family. The museums here are dressed in garlands, but every time I visit the Met, I take a peek in the Renaissance section and remember your lectures on perspective.

I am planning a visit to Florence again next year with some family to show them everything you taught me. If you have time, it would be lovely to get an espresso and learn a bit more from you.

xNina

It was harmless. Nothing more than a polite hello from a former student, in the event anyone else discovered it. More importantly, she couldn't imagine telling Peppe they had a child together in a simple letter. Some things had to be said face-to-face.

Regardless, over a month later, she hadn't heard back. Now she was wondering if she and the baby would have to make a surprise trip. If she got up the nerve to do it at all.

Once, she'd had a bit of nerve. Down several blocks, the light marking the entrance to the subway blinked, a beacon for the constant stream of people pouring in and out of the tunnels. For a moment, Nina could see herself, glancing this way and that to make sure none of the family's security or staff were following before darting underground where no one could find her. A sixteen-year-old girl's small act of defiance. Girls like Nina weren't supposed to take the subway. But she had. Just like she'd attended Wellesley instead of Smith. Studied in Florence instead of London. For a short time, she had been a girl willing to stage small rebellions, but rebellions nonetheless.

She wasn't a girl anymore, though, was she?

Nina turned to the tiny bundle in the car seat next to her. She wasn't even twenty-one yet, but not quite eight weeks since the birth—most of them spent at Mount Sinai's NICU—she felt much older. Strange how something that weighed less than two pounds could change your entire life.

"But you're not two pounds now, are you?" Nina whispered to the tiny figure, who was still fast asleep, and thankfully, healthy as ever. "And now everyone wants to meet you. So let's do our best to shine, shall we?"

————

THE DECORATIONS CONTINUED into Celeste de Vries's grand penthouse, the same place where Nina had essentially grown up. Technically, her mother's townhouse a few blocks away had been her official address, but considering her father's absence and Violet's preference for yachts in Palm Beach over town cars on Park Avenue, Nina had spent the majority of her childhood here, with Eric. Under the wing of Celeste de Vries, being coached on all the things expected of them as part of this tribe. For Eric, that had meant golf and tennis lessons, public speaking education, and gradually learning about the family business. For Nina, it had meant a barrage of etiquette and finishing classes along with incessant critiques of her hair, skin, nails, clothes, posture, and anything else related to her looks. The best part was the ballroom dance classes, to which Caitlyn often tagged along.

Yet despite all of her grandmother's autocratic tendencies...this had been home until just six months ago. It was the reason Nina had fought so hard to change her name from Astor to de Vries when she was a mere teenager. It was once a place that was at least stable in its tyranny.

Now it felt surreal.

"Mrs. Gardner." Garrett, the decrepit old butler who had been with the family since Nina's mother was born, bowed slightly from the waist when he greeted her in the foyer.

Nina set the baby, still in her carrier, on the large table bearing nothing but a massive vase of white poinsettias. Like the lobby, the apartment was lit up with Christmas splendor. The Ming vases gleamed on their stands under the garland and lights strung around the elaborate crown molding. More clusters of poinsettias garnished the few open doors and the foot of the salmon-colored wainscoting that led through the maze of hallways.

"Is Eric here?" Nina wondered hopefully as Garrett helped her remove the white, fur-lined wool trench she had gifted herself as a "push" present. After all, it wasn't as though her husband would do such a thing for her, and she rather thought she had earned it.

"I'm afraid not, Mrs. Gardner."

Nina kept her face pointed away from the old man while she worked to hide her disappointment. Eric had been gone now for nearly seven months. Occasionally news had filtered to her through Caitlyn or other friends. He'd been spotted bouncing around Ibiza at one point; someone had supposedly seen him biking around Bali in November. Once the summer ended, she had hoped he might have resurfaced, if only to tell their grandmother off. But there had been nothing but silence, and then Nina had been too busy at the hospital to notice that he still hadn't returned her emails, or that her calls now went to a number that had been disconnected. While she no longer blamed him for not coming to the wedding...a part of Nina expected him to show up here. Now. To meet the newest addition to her family.

Eric was more than her cousin. He was practically her brother.

He wouldn't abandon her completely.

Would he?

"Nina, please, Garrett," she said as she turned to pick up the carrier again. "After all, you've known me since I was this age."

The butler simply sniffed as he brushed off Nina's coat and hung it in the closet. "As you wish, madam."

Nina rolled her eyes to her baby girl. "Madam" was even worse than "Mrs. Gardner."

Garrett escorted the two of them through the penthouse, which was still structured in the classic pre-war style, with a maze of corridors blocking each section of the house from another. *The help know their place and we know ours,* Celeste had once said. She had never cared for the modern fashion of open-concept apartments like the lofts downtown or in Brooklyn, though Nina quite liked them. Perhaps one day she could remodel her own apartment so it less resembled a series of cellblocks and more the open, joyful home she wished she had.

They wound around to the main drawing room—the ornate parlor centered around a large fireplace could easily hold twice the hundred or so people who had come to Grandmother's annual Christmas salon. Celeste de Vries would never hold something so pedestrian as a simple party. A *salon*, by unspoken decree, only included a specially curated group of people deemed worthy.

There was Violet, of course; Aunt Heather, Eric's mother, and her husband; Celeste's brother Rufus, and several of his children and their children; plus a few other distant de Vrieses and van Dusens. The other guests rounded out a veritable "Who's Who" of Upper East Side society. These weren't so much the local celebrities that generally populated Page Six (though a few did from time to time). No, these were old money, people with names like Astor and Vanderbilt. People Nina had known all her life. People her family had known for centuries.

But before they entered, Garrett stopped in the hall and cleared his throat. "This arrived for you, madam."

He then produced an envelope. A crisply folded piece of cream-colored card stock with Nina's name scrawled across the front in familiar curling letters.

Nina's stomach leaped as she took it.

"Thank you, Garrett," she said, then turned into the smaller parlor across the hall—a more private room that also had its own crackling fireplace. She set the baby, still snoozing in her carrier, to the ground and sank into one of the armchairs to read the note.

She knew what it was before she opened it. Giuseppe wasn't given to extravagances, but he loved his stationery. How many small notes had he affixed to her papers when she was in his class, all embossed with one of his gold and red insignias? She had saved them all, and would at times take them out of a shoebox in her closet, where, on her worst days before the baby was born, she would sink to the ground under the swirl of hanging skirts and read them before crying herself to sleep. She hadn't done that for a while, but something told her tonight might be different.

CARA,

THANK you for the kind letter. It was a wonderful surprise to hear your voice, if only on the page. I trust you are well in New York for the holidays and enjoying life as only one your age should.

I TOOK my family back to the olive farm for my sabbatical this fall. Do you remember it? As soon as we arrived, I knew I never should have brought them. You are a golden ghost in the air, a beautiful dream that will haunt me in the grass until I die. This is our place. You are everywhere. In the trees. By the fire. Dancing in the vineyard. In every corner, I see you and all the things I should have said before you went away.

I MISS YOU, principessa. This life is wrong without you. But it is a life I must have. After Christmas, I will return to Firenze, and I will sell the farm like my wife has always wanted. I will be a good father to my girls and try to remember the life I am supposed to live for them, not for myself. I will let the dreams of what might have been sleep, for that is the only place they may be real.

· · ·

FOR THIS REASON, I must ask that you do not follow me back to the city. Stay in America and live your own life. You gave me such beautiful dreams, principessa, but they can never be real. And I cannot allow a dream to ruin my family's real life.

BUT TONIGHT, one last time, I will drink this wine and eat these olives and think of the way you looked with the firelight in your face and hair. My own perfect Venus, alive in the night.

CON TUTTO IL MIO CUORE,
Peppe

NINA READ THE LETTER ONCE, twice over before she truly understood what it said. Then she looked back at the baby, who slept soundly in her seat, another firelight flickering over her chubby cheeks.

"You look like him," Nina told her in a low voice.

It was true. The baby had blonde hair, but her eyes were as dark as the Arno, and her lips were as full as a ripe Italian plum. She was tiny and beautiful and would probably always be a slight, perfect thing.

"He has to see you," Nina whispered fiercely as she rocked the seat with her toe. "He must!"

"I see you've nearly gotten your figure back already."

Nina started, then turned to find her grandmother entering the room, the normally crisp click of her heels masked by the thick Oriental carpets. Celeste de Vries was clad in her typical Chanel suit— this one a lush winter cream with gold buttons, appropriate for the holidays. Her silver hair was pinned in its perennial elegant twist, and her fingers, wrists, and ears were tipped with their ever-present glints of diamonds and gold.

As priceless and classic as ever. And as rich.

"I—thank you. It's good to see you, Grandmother." Nina stood to deliver kisses to her cheeks.

"I'm very glad to see you haven't allowed yourself to let go completely after the birth," Celeste replied as she took the other seat by the fire, then crossed one ankle over the other. Unlike most women of her station, Celeste de Vries had chosen to age gracefully without the aid of needles or scalpels, but she was still remarkably well preserved for a woman of her age. Most people thought she was Nina's mother, not her grandmother.

"So many do now," she continued. "I didn't even allow your grandfather into the hospital room until we could find a stylist to reset my hair, you know. Nowadays they let everyone roam the halls like a pack of wild chickens. It's why we didn't come to see you there. We wanted to allow you a bit of dignity."

Nina bit her lip to keep from sniping at her. She honestly wasn't sure what was worse: that Celeste thought she was actually doing Nina a favor by giving her time to look the part of a de Vries woman, or that she was lying to cover up the family's general apathy.

"We'll take you shopping to celebrate," Celeste proclaimed as she looked Nina over. "Your hair is quite overgrown, and it's time for you to get out of your maternity clothes. You can't be a new mother and look like a ragamuffin student."

Nina looked down at her dress—a white silk thing that, yes, she had worn while pregnant, but only because its flowing silhouette had been forgiving, even during the last trimester, when she had gained a bit more weight. She had purchased it in Florence last February. Giuseppe had said it made her look like a goddess. And then he had slowly unwrapped it from her body until she was undressed before him.

Peppe.

Nina clutched the note tightly.

"Your professor certainly has some gumption, sending that here."

This time, Nina actually did start as she looked up again. Her hand uncurled, leaving the note crumpled in her palm. "Y-you read this."

It wasn't a question, and that was because she wasn't completely surprised. Peppe's note hadn't been sealed, having obviously been sent in another protective layer and opened before it was given to her. And this was Celeste de Vries, after all—someone who took what she wanted, when she wanted. And no one said any different.

"It was my right. It did bear my address."

"But my name, Grandmother."

"Not anymore." Grandmother tipped her head. "Why, might I ask, must I keep reminding you of that? Your husband says you never filed the name change with social security. He's not particularly happy about it either."

Because you wanted the wedding, Nina wanted to insist. *You said it would maintain respectability. Keep me from being a laughingstock, save the family from social ruin…*

Had Celeste actually said those things? Or had it been Calvin, while Celeste nodded? At this point, Nina didn't even know anymore. So she just fingered the paper, gazing at the insignia at the top—a curling, crimson and gold G—before folding and refolding it back into a tiny square.

"Nina."

Nina looked up to find Celeste holding out her hand, palm up. She pressed the letter into her skirt and looked down at the baby, whose lashes, so unusually lush and dark, fluttered on her cheeks. "What?" she mumbled.

Celeste's fingers beckoned. "It was generous of me to let you have it in the first place. But like he said, it's time for you both to return to your families. You can't bring him with you any more than he can bring you back."

Nina stared at the note. It wasn't like it was the only one she had. Even if it couldn't join the others, she could still hide it with her other things from Florence—cashmere scarves, bottles of wine and olive oil, pieces of art she wanted to hang but didn't want to spoil with the lie of her new life. Things she was saving for after. When she was free. Maybe when she would see him again.

He had to know about the baby.

"Was this…Peppe…before or after you met your husband in Florence?"

Celeste, Nina realized, had never said Calvin's name out loud. Not once in seven months. He was always a thing that Nina was responsible for, like a dog or a houseplant. "Your fiancé" or "your husband." An object. Something that could be thrown out.

The two women stared at each other, and for a moment, Nina wondered if Celeste knew her secret. If underneath her barely masked contempt for Calvin, Celeste had allowed her only granddaughter to marry a scab of a man, had been willing to sacrifice Nina's happiness and her great-granddaughter's paternity simply to save face. It would have been one thing for Nina to protect the family from her shame. It would have been another completely if they had actively been a part of the deception.

What would that say about Celeste?

What would it say about Nina?

"Nina." Celeste's tone sharpened. Her hand stretched out farther. She wouldn't ask again.

Nina swallowed and pressed the note to her heart. But eventually, inevitably, she handed it to her grandmother. And, like the parchment was an errant piece of kindling, Celeste immediately tossed it into the fire, ignoring the way her granddaughter fought sudden tears as she watched the paper singe and curl as it caught aflame.

"Now," Celeste said. "I want to meet my namesake."

She leaned over the carrier, and Nina fought the urge to yank the baby away from this family's inspection. Suddenly, she wanted to run her back to the elevator and into the Escalade, away from anyone who might and probably would find her wanting. She was perfect and always would be. In all her imperfections.

"Oh, God, finally. There you are, princess."

Celeste and Nina straightened at the sound of Calvin's voice. Was that irritation on Celeste's face, or just her normal dissatisfaction with most people? It had been a long time. Nina found she couldn't quite tell.

"Where have you been?" Calvin hissed as he hurried to stand beside Celeste—beside her, not his supposed new family. He was over-dressed in white tie, while Nina knew most of the men in the salon would probably be in suits appropriate for a cocktail party. Was he taking his cues from *Upstairs, Downstairs*? Did he think the New York upper class changed into formalwear before every meal?

Nina forced her face to remain blank. Calvin had appeared in the hospital exactly once after the baby was born, wondered aloud why she looked like a "wimpy little slug," and then promptly left for another "business trip" that had taken him to God-knows-where for the rest of the time the baby was in the NICU and Nina was praying for her life.

"Did you expect me to do this alone?" he asked her. "Your entire family is in there wondering where you are."

"Calm yourself," Grandmother ordered, leaning away from him slightly, as if he exuded some kind of stench she wanted to escape. "She has a new child. And it's Christmas. We can be a bit more forgiving, can we not?"

Nina simply ignored him as well as the idea that anyone in her family could be the slightest bit forgiving. She hadn't forgotten what had happened three nights earlier. The way he had stumbled into her room sometime past two, swimming in bourbon. The way he had collapsed onto her bed and fumbled around the duvet, grasping for her bare limbs while mumbling something about "doctors" and "more than six weeks" and "done waiting." And then he had promptly passed out.

Nina had spent every night since in the nursery.

"It seemed easier to make our entrance once she was already asleep," Nina said. And then, because she couldn't help it: "She is precious, isn't she?"

"She is," Celeste admitted as she bent over the tiny bundle. "Quite beautiful, really."

"Just like her great-grandmother," Calvin ventured, wet-mouthed.

Celeste did not look impressed. Nina could have told her idiot husband that naked compliment wouldn't curry her grandmother's favor any better than hopping around her shoulder like a pigeon would, but she doubted it would do any good. Celeste valued acumen and competency in her men. Calvin seemed to have neither.

Nina reached down and picked her daughter up. The baby cooed slightly in her arms and smacked her tiny lips before sinking into a deeper sleep. Just the act of holding her calmed Nina's racing heart. Suddenly, it was as though her pretentious family or foolish husband didn't matter anymore. All that mattered was this tiny person. And doing whatever was needed to protect her from this world.

"But we can't call her Celeste, of course," Calvin put in as he squatted next to Nina, causing his pants to pull around his thick thighs. "After all, we've already got one of those, and she's irreplaceable."

He looked up at Grandmother exuberantly, reminding Nina of a soft-headed golden retriever looking to be pet for returning a ball. Instead, Celeste examined him as if he were gum on the bottom of one of her Stuart Weitzmans, then turned back to the baby.

"There is nothing wrong with honoring family with namesakes," she said. "Many of the men in this family have borne variants of Jacob and Jonathan for four hundred years. No reason the women shouldn't have their own traditions."

Her thin, painted lips quirked at one side with satisfaction. It had actually been a last-minute decision to name the baby after Celeste. A sort of insurance, Nina supposed, done in a fit of panic at the hospital. But she could already see that might pay off one day.

Sometimes flattery did work with Celeste de Vries. If it was the right kind.

"Has she a middle name?" Grandmother asked as she hovered a finger over the baby's angelic face. "We'll call her by that. And for God's sake, Nina, don't tell me it's Violet."

Nina shook her head and peered down at her daughter. Warmth burned in her chest as the baby's tiny hands curled into the bodice of her dress. The silk would wrinkle, but Nina couldn't care less.

Nina could think of only one other place where she had ever felt such peace. A place with sunshine. Fields and fields of olive trees, as far as the eye could see. If she closed her eyes, she could bring herself back there. Grandmother could burn a note, but she couldn't torch those memories.

"Yes," Nina said, remembering the hue of the oil before Peppe would serve it to her on a drenched piece of focaccia. Golden. Warm. Just like this baby's face in the firelight. "She does. It's Olivia."

Calvin frowned, clearly confused.

But Celeste didn't look the slightest bit surprised.

"Olivia," she said as her sharp eyes flashed with recognition. "Yes, Olivia. I see."

NOW

CHAPTER THIRTEEN

AUGUST 2018

Nina

"What time is it?" I asked Moira for the third time in the last ten minutes. "They should have landed by now."

My assistant tapped her sturdy brown pump on the vinyl floors of the Thirty-Fourth Street Heliport lounge, then dutifully checked the Cartier watch I had given her as a Christmas gift two years ago. "Two oh three p.m., Mrs. Gardner. She's a few minutes late, but they should be here any—oh, look, I think that's them."

I followed her finger toward the southeast horizon, where an aircraft had just appeared through the haze of the afternoon sun and smog over the crest of the Brooklyn Bridge.

Moira and I watched as the helicopter carrying Olivia, plus Jane and Eric, slowly landed. Once the heavy rotors started to slow, I pushed through the glass double doors and went out to meet my daughter.

"Mama!"

Olivia's small voice still managed to carry over the remaining hum of the engine as she sprinted across the tarmac, small blonde braids flying in the wind. She looked like most children did after a summer spent outside—a bit windswept. I just managed to catch her as she flew into my arms and allowed me to fold her into a tight embrace.

"Hello, my love."

I rocked her back and forth. It was the only time we were like this—after a long separation or when she was about to leave (which often happened at the same time). The rest of the time, we both struggled with open affection. But right now, we couldn't bear to be apart.

"I missed you," I whispered in her ear.

"Me too."

She hugged me tighter for several more seconds before finally, to maybe both our regrets, she seemed to remember whom she was again. Or at least whom she was supposed to be. A member of the de Vries family, even if a Gardner by name.

"Is Daddy here?" she asked as she released me and looked around curiously, straightening her back.

"Oh, no, darling. He's at his office. But I think he'll be home tonight to see you."

Was it my imagination, or did she relax more at the news?

"That's good," she said. "He wasn't there last time."

It wasn't that Calvin was a particularly good father. Really, he wasn't a father at all except in name. But Olivia's eagerness to see him, despite his demonstrable apathy reminded me of the universal truth that had bound me to my own dysfunctional family: all children love their parents. And all children want their parents to love them.

"Did you have a nice time at camp?" I asked, turning back toward the lounge as porters unloaded her bags from the back of the helicopter.

She nodded. "I did. The horses were really splendid this year. I was really mad about this one Andalusian named Lucy."

I smiled at her casual use of British slang, the same sort I had picked up as a girl from similar experiences. She was becoming quite the rider, so I had sent her to an English equestrian camp this year, hoping all the time outdoors with horses would give her the same pleasure it had given me at this age. Olivia would have plenty of time to learn the rigid rules of society, and God knew she got enough of them at her regular boarding school. During the summer, I wanted to give her space to play. To be a child. To get a little bit dirty.

Everyone deserves to get dirty sometimes, doll. Not just kids.

I blinked and shook the voice away. Over two months since I'd last seen him, his distractingly velvety voice was still there, popping up at the most inopportune times.

You love my voice, baby.

I squeezed my eyes shut as Olivia and I reentered the lounge. *Stop it, stop it, stop it.* I just wanted peace. That was all. Just a little vacation from this eternal emptiness. This strange longing that never seemed to abate.

"Hello, Ms. Olivia." Moira crouched down when we reached her. "Have a nice summer, honey?"

Olivia nodded shyly, despite the fact that she had known Moira for most of her life.

My assistant smiled kindly. "Marguerite asked me to bring you this from the kitchen."

Olivia's eyes popped as Moira offered her a small piece of chocolate wrapped in wax paper. "Marguerite made caramels?"

Moira smiled as she stood back up. Olivia popped the candy into her mouth and chewed blissfully.

"It's *so* good," she confirmed through a full mouth. But then, as she caught me watching with interest, her expression shuttered. She swallowed and covered her mouth with one hand. "Sorry, Mama."

I blinked. Sorry? For what? It took me a few seconds to realize she had expected to be reprimanded for talking with her mouth open. "Oh, it's all right. You're excited. And Marguerite's caramels *are* really good."

Olivia nodded shyly.

"Please tell me someone brought that kid some candy."

Jane's sardonic voice broke through our little staring match as she and Eric strode over, followed by the porters. They had been visiting friends in Boston for the week. When they discovered that her return flight from London went through Boston, Eric had offered to bring her the final leg with them on the company helicopter rather than forcing the girl to sit through another flight alone to Teterboro.

"Moira did," I confirmed as I accepted kisses from each of them. "Thank you for bringing her back with you. I hope it didn't mean cutting your trip short."

Eric shrugged. "Not at all."

"She's a good kid," Jane agreed. "A little too quiet, though. Olivia, I expect some more mischief out of you at the beach, all right?"

Olivia looked up at her and smiled shyly. "Auntie Jane, you're silly."

"I'm just doing what needs to be done. Eric needs someone to teach him a lesson, and it can't always be me."

"What beach?" I asked, momentarily sidetracked as we turned toward the exit, where each of us had cars waiting.

"Mama, are we going to the party at the big house?" Olivia asked.

"We decided to throw the white party again this year on Long Island after all," Eric said. "Mostly because I have some new investors in town this weekend."

"I mean, is it really a party?" Jane asked. "I'd call it more of a back-yard barbecue that you thrust on me last night."

Eric sighed. "Jane…"

She offered us all a contrived grin that had Olivia hiding giggles all over again. "It's going to be fun, see? Really, though, Nina, you guys should come. Your mom's helping us host, and she'd probably love someone to teach me how to do this correctly."

I blinked. "Oh, well. I don't know. We hadn't—"

"You should," Jane said. "And by that, I mean, dear God, *please*. I won't last through all the boring business talk without someone there to chat with."

"You should come," Eric said. "Aunt Violet said she'd like to see Olivia anyway."

"*Please*, Mama…I want to show you what I learned this summer anyway, and I want to see our horses before I go back to school."

What could I say? Under normal circumstances, I would have determined whether or not Calvin was out of town before committing my time, particularly for an overnight trip. Only Calvin wasn't travel-ing, and undoubtedly, he would want to come. But the idea of sharing a suite with him, right now in particular, seemed unbearable. Dangerous, even. It's much harder to keep a secret behind just a few walls than behind an entire apartment building.

"We'll see," I said. "We have to talk to Daddy and figure out his plans too."

We exited to the curb, where two large SUVs were waiting, complete with drivers and Eric and Jane's security detail in front.

"Jane?" I asked. "Would you like a lift uptown if Eric's going to the office?"

"Actually," Jane said, "he'll just drop me in Soho. I'm interning with Lake McHugh this fall so she can recommend me for FIT next year. Can you believe it? Good thing I went to law school so I could become an unpaid intern all over again."

"Hey, pretty girl. Stop."

Olivia and I watched in awe as Eric's quiet phrase immediately shuttered Jane's self-doubt. She beamed, refilled with sudden pride as Eric slung an arm around her waist and guided her toward their waiting vehicle.

Envy hummed through me. But not just at their closeness, I realized. Also for their direction. Only a few months after they had both come out of one of the darkest episodes of either of their lives, neither Jane nor Eric seemed to be lost at all. Eric had dived even further into his role as chairman of De Vries Shipping, and Jane had embraced her love of fashion in order to create a new career for herself here in New York. It wasn't that they didn't have difficult moments or struggle with their trauma. It was that their knowledge of themselves helped them through. Right along with the way they so clearly advocated for each other too.

What would it be like, I wondered as I rode in the back of the Escalade with Moira and Olivia, to have someone like that who would stick up for you in that way? What would it be like to have a partner so intent on protecting you from harm that he wouldn't even let you do it to yourself?

Just know that you have someone in your corner. That someone out there thinks you're incredible like no one else. Know that, and remember it when you're feeling down.

Matthew's words swept over me like a tidal wave. Where had he said that? On the street? In the hotel?

I found it didn't matter. Because as soon as the joy of them arrived, it disappeared just as quickly.

Because he wasn't mine.

He couldn't be.

I had no direction in this life, and even more, I was so very alone in it still.

And so, I focused on the little girl next to me, who had watched my cousin and his wife with an expression that told me their interaction was as much a mystery to her as it was to me.

The reality dug a pit deep in my stomach.

My darling girl deserved to know what that kind of love felt like. Maybe I could try to do that for her.

For us both.

———

I GAVE Moira the rest of the day off, and thirty minutes later, Olivia and I entered the apartment to the sounds of several unfamiliar voices. My darling girl had waited patiently by the lifts while I climbed the twenty flights of stairs. I often wondered why she never went in without me, but I was too charmed to inquire lest she stop.

"What about Kate?" said a brusque male voice from the drawing room.

"What about Kate?" came Calvin's even brusquer reply. "She doesn't know anything. It's a moot point."

"Then all the better to put her on the stand," said the other man, whom I now recognized as Merrick Reynolds, the primary attorney representing Calvin against Matthew's office. "They're grasping in the dark for evidence, Gardner. They'll be desperate for anything they can rip apart. But *you* need some character witnesses, and she's the best you've got."

Olivia shuffled with me toward the drawing room, where we found Calvin sitting with Merrick. The gruff older man nodded at both of us with a courteous, if steely glance. Calvin just scowled at me, then blinked indifferently at Olivia.

"Oh, it's you. Has it really been two months already?"

Olivia shied behind me and nodded. "Hi, Daddy. Um, yes. More, actually."

Calvin frowned. "What did I say about calling me that?"

Olivia's cheeks reddened as she stared at the floor. "I—sorry. Father."

"That's right. You're too old for that Daddy crap. Listen, I have to finish some business, so do us a favor and go to your room until dinner, all right? God knows we've bought you enough things to entertain yourself with. They just sit there the rest of the damn year, so you might as well use them now."

Olivia's jaw quivered, but she stuck it out nonetheless and turned to me.

"I'll come find you in a moment," I told her quietly. "Would you like to play a game and tell me about your horses? Patricia will be here tomorrow."

Olivia's face brightened—whether at the prospect of spending time with me or her nanny, I didn't know.

"Okay, Mama," she said, then scampered off down the hall, her footsteps quickly swallowed by the large apartment.

I turned in the direction of my suite but was called back almost immediately.

"Nina, come over here. This concerns you."

Swallowing back my irritation, I returned to the table and took a seat beside Calvin, who clapped a paw on my knee and started massaging it vigorously.

"I still don't see why we can't just put her on the stand. Look at her. She'd make me look great. She always has."

"No, no, no, you don't want to do that," said Merrick. "You waive spousal privilege, and suddenly the prosecution is all over every little thing you might have told her *ever*. Trust me. Keep her silent."

"What's this about?" I asked quietly.

"That greaseball from Brooklyn submitted a new list of witnesses this week," Calvin said.

"It's nothing to worry about," said Merrick soothingly. "My main concern at this point is how they're trying this already in the court of public opinion. There was a lot of press around the death of John Carson and the arrest of Jude Letour. The fact that he confirmed you as an associate doesn't look good. But if you're only an investor in the property, you're certainly less culpable."

I frowned. "Is that really all they have? His name on the property?"

"And that grainy photograph of me and Letour outside the property. You remember, the one they used to arrest me the first time?" He chuckled, clearly more for Merrick's benefit than for mine. "Talk about picking the worst time to do an inspection, eh, princess?" Then the hand on my knee tightened as his voice sharpened. "Why, what did you think they would have?"

I opened my mouth, but found I had nothing to say. This was yet another reason Matthew had kept me purposefully in the dark, no doubt. Plausible deniability worked both ways.

"Nothing," I said demurely.

"Well, Merr here agrees with me. It's time to fight fire with fire." Calvin's gaze dropped to my left hand, on which I still wore my original engagement and wedding rings. And his gaze predictably turned to ash. "Where is your ring?"

I looked down at the pear-shaped diamond that was somehow so much better than that new monstrosity he'd given me. "Oh, um. I'm having it resized. It was a little too small."

"Again?"

I nodded. "They did a poor job the last time. Now it's too small. And then, as you remember, the cleaners damaged the gold, so I needed to have that replaced."

None of these things were true. I had simply been drumming up as many excuses as possible to avoid wearing the eyesore.

"Small, eh? Are we putting on a few extra pounds?" Calvin chortled at Merrick, who kept his face predictably blank.

I pressed my lips together and shook my head. "I'll pick it up next week." I also added a mental reminder to drop it off in the first place.

"Good. We'll need a photoshoot, won't we, with the new gem. A wedding planner is coming tomorrow. You'll set it all up with her."

My head snapped up. *"What?"*

"I asked Moira to find one. Thought it might be a nice surprise." Calvin's face darkened as he realized it wasn't anything of the sort.

In two and a half months, I had somehow managed to evade the question of vow renewal again and again. It wasn't that difficult. For one, Calvin was often gone despite technically being restricted to just the city. It was clear to me that he was trying desperately to cover up whatever business he was doing that he didn't want Matthew to discover, though I couldn't have said for sure, given that he did most of it outside the apartment.

I had honestly thought he'd forgotten about it. Apparently not.

"A nice white wedding would certainly help things," added Merrick unhelpfully. "Pretty wife all in white. Little girl. Make you look like a family man. There are all sorts of ways to manipulate the press."

"I—" I swallowed. I had no idea what to say to these two men who were examining me much as they might a mannequin in the displays at Bergdorf's. "I really don't know. Don't you think it's a bit…much?"

Calvin looked between me and Merrick irritably. My insides shrank. I knew that look. That look was not good.

Merrick stood and packed his briefcase quickly. "I should be going. Gardner, I'll see you at my office tomorrow morning. We need to go over the rest of the files they sent today. There are a few things I think we can get thrown out if we play our cards right."

Calvin nodded, his beady eyes still firmly on me. "Tomorrow."

We waited tensely until Merrick left. Then I edged my thigh away from his sweaty touch.

Wrong move.

His chair screeched on the floor as he suddenly swept around and caged me against the table.

"What did I say?" he demanded in a low, nasty voice tinged with vodka. "What do I *always* say? Don't. Embarrass. Me."

"Calvin," I said quietly. "Please. Olivia is here."

"Unless you'd like me to bring up your part in all of this. I'm sure that smarmy DA would love to learn how you and the great de Vries family provided the money that started this whole thing."

I swallowed. My chest prickled. It was a familiar threat.

Truth: I didn't exactly know what happened anymore in the houses and buildings purchased in part with the money I had given Calvin from my trust. Massage parlors, he had said once. Adult video stores, he had admitted another time. Nothing illegal. Technically. Perhaps some small-time gambling. But nothing like the first year, he swore up and down. Nothing like the things Carson and Letour had done without his knowledge. And the second he had seen it the night he was photographed, he had walked away.

I wasn't sure I believed that. I didn't want to know. Because the other truth was this: If Calvin was locked up and I was too, by virtue of my involvement, Olivia would be alone. She would go to my mother because there was no way that Calvin would change our living will to give Eric and Jane guardianship. She would lose both her parents, not just one.

I couldn't do that to her, no matter what the cost.

Calvin shoved me against the table hard enough the wood dug painfully into the small of my back.

"I want this wedding, Nina," he said. "Is that clear?"

His beady eyes stared at me while a drop of sweat lingered over his left brow. My stomach clenched as I braced myself for the slap.

"Is that clear?" he said again.

I still couldn't bring myself to say yes. I had walked down the aisle to this man once before, my stomach full of knots, a child inside me. The thought of doing it again, in front of everyone I knew? It made me want to vomit right here, all over the heirloom table and Aubusson rugs.

I squeezed my eyes shut, waiting for the inevitable blow. It was always worse when I said no. But instead of doing what he so clearly wanted, Calvin took another tack. He touched my chin with one thick finger—his gesture of tenderness.

"Look, princess. I understand it's a surprise. But I'll be honest. The vows—they're obviously not just for you. I know you wish they were, but they're not."

Obviously, I thought. But I didn't respond.

"The truth is, we need some better PR, like Merrick said. I'm getting hammered in the damn press, Nina, and it's only going to get worse once this fucking trial starts. The judge hasn't even set a date. Did you know that oily wop actually filed for an extension of the—whatever the fuck this period is called—and the judge actually gave it to him? It's all turned against me."

Resisting the urge to spit in his face at his denigration of Matthew, I only offered the term I knew. From him. "Discovery?"

Jane and Eric had already walked me through it. After the indictment, the discovery began, wherein the evidence that was provided to the grand jury was released to Calvin's legal team, and then both sides had more time to investigate each other and trade their evidence. It was a long process, and in a case like this, it could take months.

"Yes," Calvin snapped. He did not like being corrected. "Which means he thinks he's going to find more. I don't know what, yet, but I can't wait. I need to be a family man. More than ever, I need to be seen as legitimate." His hand slipped down and traced my collarbone, sending shivers of revulsion down my spine. "Think about it. A nice white wedding. Hell, we could even get you knocked up again. You could finally let me do what you've been avoiding for what, six months now?"

My entire body recoiled at just the idea. *Never again.*

"Keep your voice down!" I whispered fiercely, surprising even Calvin with my ferocity. "Olivia is here!"

"Ah, yes, Olivia…"

To my surprise, Calvin stood up completely and paced in front of me for a moment, steepling his fingers. "I almost didn't recognize her, you know. She's becoming a looker. And she does love her daddy, doesn't she?"

I straightened with a mother's innate sense of protection. "Do not even think about using her for your PR campaign, Calvin. It's not her job to save you."

Calvin blinked, no doubt whatsoever in his eyes. "Try me, princess. She means nothing to me. Never has."

I wanted to hit him. To take the open bottle of wine on the table and smash it over his shiny head and watch him fall to the ground for even suggesting what I thought he meant.

Still, I hadn't gotten through the last ten years without knowing how to acquiesce when I had to. How to say the things that needed to be said simply for survival. To buy myself—and my daughter—some time.

"Okay," I said. "I will think about it."

"When?"

I stirred. "After this—this w-weekend, all right? I'm taking Olivia to Southampton to visit Mother. Get out of your hair. And when we get back, I'll have an answer."

He could have said no. He could have slammed me against the table as he sometimes did when I stuttered like this.

But instead, Calvin's face spread into a wide, sweaty smile.

Maybe at the thought of being alone. Or maybe because he knew he already had me.

"All right, Mrs. Gardner. You have a deal. And when you get back, I expect a response. Do you understand?"

His threat was explicit. If he was going down, he would bring me with him.

"I'm not Eric and Jane," I said quietly. "I've never liked a show. I'm not the type to be the center of attention. You have *always* known this about me."

"No, you're just the type to tease," he sneered.

Violence flashed through his eyes, and I could see the idea of teaching me the price of my supposed coquetry cross his mind.

"Sunday," he said, then turned back to his vodka, like I wasn't even there.

CHAPTER FOURTEEN

"Do you think Grandma will be there?"

I turned away from the Escalade's tinted window, through which I was watching as the smaller roads off Montauk Highway gradually gave way to the long, isolated entrance to my family's estate. Over the ridge, tall grass waved merrily from the dunes, while the trees to the east masked deep green fields and the stable.

"Hello, darling, you woke," I said to my daughter. "Don't let her hear you call her that."

"Oh, right. Sorry. Grandmamá."

Olivia yawned and stretched her arms toward the ceiling, and I was struck again by how much she had grown over the last year, though she was still small for her age. Maybe that actually made the extra half inch or so look like even more.

"I expect she'll be there," I replied. "It is her house, after all. Or it will be eventually."

Despite the fact that my grandmother's will was still in probate and probably would be for another year (or longer, if Calvin successfully undermined it), Mother had moved right into the grand estate she'd inherited last November. Neither Eric, who paid the bills, nor the executor, who was technically in charge, seemed to mind, and Mother seemed content to morph into one of the eccentric old people who live year-round in their empty mansions, drinking too much gin and talking to the lawn ornaments.

"But it's Uncle Eric and Aunt Jane's party," Olivia protested in that way small children argue for nothing.

I shrugged. "So it is. But it's her house. She'll be there."

Although Eric had jokingly called it the "white party," I already knew this would be a far cry from the family's previous years of August decadence. I sincerely doubted Jane had any desire to host two hundred of Long Island's wealthiest residents in front of a full orchestra, fireworks, and thousands of dollars of Cristal. Instead, Eric was determined to use the estate to impress new investors he was courting from Singapore and China, men apparently eager to experience the heights of rich American customs. I could have told them French catering, horseback riding, and a private firework show was probably the farthest thing from what most Americans experienced. But then again, what authority did I have on the matter?

Still, Eric was adamant about starting his own traditions.

"You're a part of this family. Wouldn't you rather spend time with the people who actually make our lives possible?" my cousin had asked when I'd questioned whether I should even be there. "Instead of wasting your time schmoozing with the same old stuck-up assholes?"

A year ago, I would have said no. A year ago, I would have stuck with the family tradition, with whatever our grandmother said we should do. Drank the right cocktails. Worn the right dress. Made polite, conversation with the right people. A year ago, I was focused on being a perfect member of the de Vries family, even if that was no longer my name. Now I was starting to understand why Eric had stayed away for so long. More than that, I envied him.

I rolled down my window a touch, welcoming the salty sea breeze into what had suddenly become a suffocating back seat.

"Mommy! Won't that ruin your hair?"

I turned to Olivia. Poor girl. Never allowed to eat in front of the TV. Or wear a t-shirt to bed. Or roll the car window down. And yes, I probably had given my hair as a rationale for that in the past, if it wasn't Calvin saying something similar.

So I just rolled it down farther, letting the wind catch pieces of carefully blown-out tresses. I smiled at Olivia. "We're on vacation, aren't we? Time to let our hair down."

Slowly, my daughter began to smile back, a lovely thing that made her face glow between two blonde braids.

My heart twisted. I didn't see that enough.

I reached back and pulled out the pins that kept my hair in place, then leaned toward the window to let it all whip into my face as it liked.

She giggled. "Yes, Mama. We're on vacation."

I turned to find her pulling out her own braids, and together we rode for a bit like dogs with our heads halfway out the window, loose locks flapping like flags in the wind.

After a bit, we rolled the windows back up—most of the way, but not quite all. I turned to Olivia as I pulled my hair back again.

"Nearly there now. What's the first thing you'll do?"

Olivia considered the question much longer than I would expect from most nine-year-olds. Was my daughter inordinately pensive, or was that only because I didn't know children well enough to say?

An image came to mind of three young boys shooting up the stairs of Matthew's grandmother's house. The one he called *Nonna*, the sweet, familiar word for Grandma that allowed everyone in that house to acknowledge their shared heritage as well as their fondness for the woman. I remembered the look on her elegant, wrinkled face when Matthew leaned in to kiss her cheek like it was the most normal thing in the world. The way they clutched each other briefly. So much love in such a brief touch.

"What are you thinking about, Mommy?"

I blinked and straightened my face. "Oh, nothing. Just considering the question myself."

"I've never seen you look like that about Long Island," Olivia observed. Lord, if she was pensive, she was also shrewd. That I *knew* she had learned from the family.

"Have you decided?" I prodded, ignoring the question. I needed to be more careful with my expressions.

Olivia tipped her head from side to side. "I think first I'm going to say hello to Sunshine in the barn. Patricia said she and I could go shell-hunting on the beach when she gets here. Then I'm going to ask the cook if we can make chocolate cake. Then I'll go swim—oh, look, there it is!"

Davis turned a corner, and suddenly, the grand compound came into view. We passed the closer outbuildings: the tennis courts, indoor pool, guest houses, and then the main house at the end of the circular drive where several vans were open to a catering crew busy setting up for the party the next day. There were also a few other luxury cars in the drive. The event wasn't until tomorrow, but apparently some people had arrived early.

"I don't know if the cook will have time for cake, Liv," I said. "Something tells me she might be busy getting ready for tomorrow."

Olivia's face fell, but not for long, as Davis pulled to a stop and the front door opened to reveal Jane, emerging to greet us.

I had to give it to my new cousin-in-law. In only a year, she had adapted to the family's ways remarkably fast and with unique panache. It wasn't that she had completely assimilated to the neutral tones of luxury adopted by the ultra-rich. Honestly, I doubted Jane could truly fit in anywhere. Aside from the fact that she was a half-Korean woman in a family full of blonde-haired Scandinavians, she was also a former lawyer turned budding designer. She walked through life to her own particular beat, right down to the loud blue streak in her otherwise black-brown hair, the psychedelic-printed cover-up swathing her tall, thin body, and the red and black polka-dotted glasses she was wearing this afternoon. And that was just looks. With a host of strong opinions and a tendency to hold nothing back, Jane might have been the most honest, genuine person I had ever met in my life.

It was easy to see why Eric loved her. She was everything we were not. Everything we secretly wanted to be.

"Is that my niece I see in there?" she asked as soon as Livy opened the door. "About time you showed up!"

"Auntie Jane!"

I watched as my daughter, so normally reticent and careful, scrambled across the pebbled drive into Jane's arms. She immediately swung her around and around, causing the multicolored silk of her caftan to float around them like feathers. She wasn't really her aunt, of course, no more than Eric was her uncle. Second cousins, technically—one by marriage. But considering Eric was the closest thing I had to a brother (or had been, once), it was nice to know that Jane embraced the role as well.

My heart squeezed. Olivia hugged me too, of course. For a good long time after she had arrived home. And again last night before bed, long enough that Calvin had barked at her to go to her room. But not with this kind of freedom. This kind of naked joy.

Perhaps with Jane, Livy knew no one would ask her to stop.

I wished more than anything else it could be me.

"I'm glad you two were able to make it," Jane said as I approached, clutching my shoulder briefly as she kissed my cheek.

"Shall I bring these to your regular suite, ma'am?"

I turned to Davis, who was holding my weekender along with Olivia's, then back to Jane. "Is that all right? Or have you given it to someone else? I know we were a little unclear about our plans."

Jane just scoffed, one of her thin arms still draped around Olivia, who looked to be in seventh heaven. "We are just lucky guests this weekend. This is your place so much more than it would ever be ours."

It wasn't. Once I had thought it might be. Before Eric had come back. At first, Calvin thought I might inherit it from my mother, who had gotten the compound in Grandmother's will, but then it became clear she only had rights to its use before it deferred back to Eric after her death, just like everything else. And it *was* Eric who paid the bills now that Grandmother had passed away. It was his name at the top of the checks that paid the maintenance fees. He who supplied the gardeners, the pool man, the household staff, the security guards.

So, yes. Perhaps for now the residence might have "belonged" to my mother. But ultimately, the keys were in Eric's hand.

"It's for all the family," was all I could say. "I don't want to impose on your plans, though…"

"Please," Jane said, batting the idea away like a fly. "Go on, Davis. She and the munchkin here are taking their usual suite. Come on, you two."

Something inside me relaxed. "Thank you, Jane."

Jane looked behind me. "No...Calvin?"

Her voice strained slightly over my husband's name. They had no physical proof, but Jane and Eric thought Calvin may have been the one who framed Eric in January for securities fraud. The case was dropped, but that was when my relationship with Calvin truly took a turn for the worse. When I had found the line at last I never thought he could cross.

It was also when I had run from my home right into a sea of passion and guilt. Drinking in a bar, in a part of New York I had never been to, a dark corner of the city where no one would find me...I had met Matthew. And for the first time in my life, I had really understood what it meant to fall in love.

I shook the thoughts away. No. I couldn't go *there* this weekend, not after giving in to those desires so egregiously only months ago.

My stomach knotted at the thought of the man I never stopped craving and also at the memory of the truth: that had I not left the apartment that night, I might have prevented the worst. Eric in jail. Jane gone to Korea in search of her mother. Abducted, nearly killed. Her unborn child murdered as a result.

It's in the past. When will they ever let it go?

My husband's impatient, irritable voice again, announced at every slight, every absent invitation. Nothing had ever turned up explicitly about his involvement in Eric's arrest. But there were hints. Little snide comments.

We'll just make things a little harder, princess. He deserves it, after all those years away.

Don't play so innocent. You and I both know what you've done.

No, I couldn't go there. Never. I'd lose everything.

Jane's black-painted fingernails snapped suddenly in front of my face. "Earth to Nina," she said with a grin. "Man, you de Vrieses *really* know how to go to la-la land, do you know that?"

I swallowed. "Pardon?"

Jane smirked. "Eric does the same thing. Just zones out, lost in a vision like he's Madame Esmerelda looking at her crystal ball. One day he's going to get stuck there, and it'll be off to the looney bin with him. I don't care how cute his butt is."

I blushed, though I couldn't help smiling. Jane might be a little crass at times, but there was no doubt she was entertaining.

"Well, I'm not stuck now," I told her. I checked my watch as we crossed the foyer. "Is my mother here?"

"Violet? Oh, sure, she and the ladies who lunch have set up shop by the pool. Pretty sure it's gin o'clock over there. You want me to let her know you're here? Get you a drink?"

I shook my head. "No, I'm sure she doesn't want to be bothered."

Jane's mouth quirked, the way it always did when she noted our family's odd reticence with each other. She and her mother had a loud, if often contentious relationship. Very different from my family's icy, imperious distance.

"Livy said she wanted to see the horses first," I said as we walked through the first parlor, which led directly to the outdoor pool and patio in the back of the house. "Where did she go?"

"Um, I don't know if she's going to have horses on her mind *right* this second."

Jane pointed through the glass of the floor-to-ceiling french doors. Olivia was standing at the edge of the pool, arms outstretched for Eric.

"Uncle Eric, can I get in too?" she asked, her voice just audible through the glass.

Eric stood up in the water, where he'd been swimming laps, beyond which the Atlantic Ocean twinkled. Next to me, Jane swallowed visibly at the sight of her shirtless husband. I hid a smile. Objectively, Eric did keep himself in good shape, with the help of our family's genetics. But what I really loved was the way Jane couldn't hide her attraction and didn't even bother trying. What was even more entertaining was the fact that he generally couldn't be bothered to mask his feelings for her either—something our family was *very* good at doing.

"Fine by me, Liv," Eric said. "Go ask your mom, all right?"

"See?" Jane asked as Olivia scampered back inside.

"Mommy?" she asked. "Can I go swimming with Uncle Eric?"

I nodded. "Of course. Davis took our bags upstairs. Your suit should be there."

With another rare, bright grin, Olivia skipped back toward the grand staircase. I turned to Jane, who was still watching Eric. And he, I noticed, was now watching her back.

"Maybe you should get in too," I teased gently.

Jane coughed. "What? Oh, ha. No. No. Maybe later…" She adjusted her glasses, then turned back to me, her skin visibly pinker. "You?"

I shrugged. "Perhaps. I was looking forward to seeing the horses myself, but I should probably stay here and keep an eye on Livy until the nanny arrives."

"Oh, don't worry about that!" Jane said with a friendly hand on my shoulder. "Go on, have a little fun. We've got her."

She winked at me, and warmth pooled in my chest.

"Are you sure?" I asked. "I really can wait for Patricia…"

"Are you kidding? Other than the helicopter ride, we've barely seen the munchkin since March, and I was such a mess. You go for a ride, and we'll see you when you get back."

Slowly, I nodded. It was strange. Having people offer to do me a favor without being paid. Or without wanting something in return. But I had come to realize that was simply how Jane was.

"All right. I'll just get changed, then," I said.

"Have fun!"

I made my way back through the parlor to follow my daughter upstairs. But when I rounded the corner into the foyer, I stopped again for a very different reason.

There he was. Standing in the middle of my family's grand double staircase like he belonged there. Like it was made for his polished reserve, even for the occasional profanity that peppered his speech.

"Matthew?" I gasped.

He turned, and when he found me, his face broke into a bright smile, which was quickly replaced with horror.

"Hey, doll," he croaked. "I—shit. You're, um, you're here."

CHAPTER FIFTEEN

"What the hell are *you* doing here?"

As soon as the words escaped, I clapped a hand over my mouth, the metal of my wedding rings scraping my teeth. Reminding me, as they always did, of how simply looking at this man made me a very bad person. Lord, if Grandmother could see me now, she would have been appalled. I sounded rude. Impatient. And most of all, very, very guilty.

But Matthew was here. Against all odds, he was on my family's estate, in the middle of the marble-encrusted foyer, looking like he owned every square inch of it despite the fact that his actual net worth was a tiny fraction of ours. And his presence was, like always, making me feel more at ease than ever and completely out of my comfort zone.

For an instant, I saw all the times I had visited this house with the man I'd actually married. Every time Calvin made some absurd (and usually inaccurate) comment about an expensive piece of furniture or mixed up a modern artist with an older one. Stupid things. Shallow things. But things that a connoisseur of any kind would be able to discern, and anyone else wouldn't bother to identify. Things that only revealed how much Calvin hungered for some notion of class that he had no idea was just a myth. But which also revealed how he would never belong here, no matter how much he tried.

And then there was Matthew. The kind of man who took the time to do things right, whatever they were. He didn't have everything, and he knew it, but he took pride in what he did have. I knew, for example, that he had poured years of research, sweat, and labor into his small Brooklyn house. I also knew without asking that the white shirt he was wearing fit him perfectly not because he had paid an enormous amount of money for it, but because he had probably taken a bargain piece to the tailor he had known most of his adult life.

It was so unfair. Too late, much too late, I had met a man who seemed to fit into the corners of my life with the precision of a puzzle piece. It had nothing to do with class or background, as I'd always assumed, and everything to do with simple compatibility. It didn't matter that Matthew and I were effectively from different worlds. Together, we made such perfect harmony.

And yet...we couldn't work. We both knew that very well, even though we weren't always successful at abiding by the facts.

Like right now.

When Matthew was in my house, not looking very happy to see me.

"What am *I* doing here?" he asked, clearly recovered from his shock. "What are *you* doing here, Nina? Is Calvin here?"

"No, not that it's any of your bus—"

"Eric said you probably weren't coming when I talked to him last week."

"*Eric* doesn't keep track of my social calendar," I replied, perhaps too haughtily. "He and Jane invited me a few days ago. My plans changed."

Matthew glanced from side to side, then took a step toward me. "Well, they need to change again. You have to go back."

I frowned. "What? Absolutely not."

"Nina, I'm not kidding. Get your shit and go. This is too important. I—"

"You what?" I demanded, suddenly unable to hide my irritation.

This was why he was so dangerous. Not just because he made me feel things I had no right to feel, but because when I was around him, my filter seemed to disappear completely. And that was going to get me into trouble.

It also no longer mattered. "This is *my* family's estate," I rattled on. "I don't know why you think you can order me off it, but you can't. And you still haven't answered my question. What are you doing here anyway?"

He said I was the one who evaded questions, but he did it too with ease. "I thought it was Eric's estate," he corrected me. "He inherited it, right?"

"Actually, my mother did." Why did men always think they knew better? Even this one? "*My* mother. Or, she will, once they are finished with probate. Eric just heads up the board of trustees."

The explanation sounded as pedantic as it felt. What did it matter which part of my family supplied the money for which part of its holdings? The point was, it was *my* family. And this cocky, overly self-assured know-it-all *still* hadn't explained his unannounced presence here.

Matthew was silent for a long time, as if he were evaluating my response. Lord, the man never did stop investigating, did he?

"Well?" I prodded.

He pulled his hat lower over his face, like he was trying to hide his expression. "I was invited too," he said again. "I just thought I'd come a little earlier than the bigger party."

"An entire *day* earlier?" The actual barbecue for Eric's clients wasn't until tomorrow.

"Do we really have to argue about this, Nina? Yes, Jane and Eric invited me too—we are actually friends, in case you forgot—"

"I did *not* forget," I bristled, but he just kept going.

"Eric thought I would have a good time."

"And you really thought it was appropriate to spend days with my family given that you're trying to lock one of us up?" I lowered my voice, stepping closer in case anyone heard us.

Mistake. His scent of ink, sweat, and the light cologne he favored swept past my nostrils. I crossed my arms to keep myself from reaching for him.

"Us, Nina? Really? Since when do you care if your husband gets put away? Or have you had a change of heart?"

My entire body seized up at the sudden defensiveness in his voice. "How could you *possibly* say that to me?"

He raised a black brow. "I don't know. It's been a few months. Maybe that last time did it for you. One last ride on the horse, so to speak, before you went back to your perfect life. Maybe in the end you don't really want me to bust it wide open."

At my side, my hand twitched with the need to slap him. Lord, when he got like this—stubborn, with the uncanny ability to stab at every insecurity I had—I really just wanted to take every bit of frustration out on him.

"I cannot believe you would suggest such a thing."

Matthew examined me for a moment more, then sighed. "Shit. You're right." He pulled off his hat, ran a hand over his brow, then put it back on. "I'm sorry. I had no right." He shook his head. "Look, I couldn't say no. It was too good an opportunity to pass up."

"Opportunity for what?"

"Observation."

He quieted again, apparently waiting for me to piece things together. When I didn't immediately, Matthew blew a long breath through his teeth.

"Nina, part of learning about a particular suspect is exploring the people around him."

And then, of course, everything clicked. "You're here to investigate, aren't you?"

His chest dropped as he exhaled. My own tightened. I was right.

"Yes," he admitted quietly, looking around for potential eavesdroppers. "I am. Calvin's into some deep shit, but the investigation is at a standstill. He and his known associates are cockblocking my office's attempts for interviews. I have to get at the people who know him another way. And before you offer anything, you *know* I have to figure this out on my own."

"So, what, you're going to dig into the rest of my husband's life?" I asked. "His family and friends, go snooping around all our private lives instead of just allowing me to give you what you need in the first place?"

His jaw was clenched so tightly, I wondered what he wasn't saying. It almost sounded like he was trying to convince himself more of that than me.

"Nina, it's sort of the gig. You knew this was going to happen."

"I didn't know you were going to dig for evidence around my family home—"

"*Shh*," Matthew interrupted as a kitchen staff member came scurrying through with a tray of beverages. "This isn't the time or place." He shook his head. "Goddammit. I really wish you had told me you were coming."

"I don't have to run everything by you, Matthew."

"Oh, really?" He clearly did not believe me.

"Yes, really," I protested, finding I had to stop myself from stamping my feet. Good lord, as much as I loved him, the man really did bring out the worst in me.

I opened my mouth to argue, but found I couldn't. It was odd—of the two of us, you would think that I'd be the one to maintain propriety. But no, as usual, I found all I could think about was flinging decorum out the wind in order to do all number of things with this man. Argue. Fight. Kiss. Fuck.

Yes, fuck. The word, one I hardly ever uttered, suddenly seemed poised on the tip of my tongue. Matthew's eyes dropped suddenly to my mouth, like he could sense it there. His brow furrowed in that way that made me want to kiss him and smooth it out. He looked torn between wanting to drag me into a closet and toss me out of the room.

"Nina."

"What?"

Matthew removed his hat again, the same straw fedora he was wearing when I had seen him at the Grace. Memories of the way it had tumbled to the ground made me shiver. And from the way his left brow rose knowingly, he could see exactly what I was thinking. Damn this man. I loved him, but I also hated the way just his presence seemed to remove every barrier I had. When we were alone, that transparency was liberation. But out here, it was treacherous.

Finally, the tension in his shoulders released. They were such fine things—I admired the shape of them more than he knew. Broad, but not too broad. Svelte enough that he fit into the lean cuts of his favorite Italian suits with ease, though the power he nurtured at the gym each day couldn't quite be hidden beneath wool and gabardine.

"Fine," he said at last. "You're right. This is your home—I have no right to kick you out. But I can't leave either." He shook his head. "I'm an investigator, Nina. We need some information, and this is a good place to listen."

"But Calvin isn't coming," I protested.

"No, but a lot of his business associates are. Most of them won't know who I am."

"I don't know," I demurred. "You *were* in the news, weren't you?"

That irritating half smile appeared again. "Keeping tabs on me, duchess?"

I didn't reply. Eventually, the smile disappeared, and he just shrugged.

"I'm willing to take the chance that most of these penguins don't memorize faces any more than they remember the names of their servants, especially after a few martinis. I can test the waters without Calvin around to poison the well." He tipped his head. "Unless you're going to do that for him by telling people who I am."

The way his tone suddenly sharpened again cut me to the quick.

I took a deep breath. "Matthew, of course I won't." Darting another look from side to side, I continued: "In fact, I could help you…"

He paused. But a second later, the shake of his head told me he was sticking to his guns. When our eyes met, his mirrored the guilt that seemed permanently lodged in my stomach.

"No, doll," he reminded me. "On my own."

We stared at each other for a long time, the sad reality of the situation settling between us. What I wouldn't give to be able to take his hand and guide him out to the patio. Introduce him to the crowds of people who, yes, might look down their noses at first, but who would eventually come to love him just as much as I did.

A pipe dream. Especially since if he ever uncovered what I thought he might, we'd be finished anyway. Husband or not.

"So, your daughter. She's here too?"

I swallowed and nodded.

"Can I meet her?"

I looked up in surprise. "Are you going to interrogate her too?"

Matthew's brow furrowed. "What? Absolutely not. I only—"

"Because she's a child," I said. "It's going to be hard enough for her to see her father dragged through the mud. I won't have you doing it to her too."

"Nina—" he started to argue, then stopped himself. "Everything I'm doing is for you," he said finally.

"Don't lie," I whispered. I noted he didn't say *us*.

He relented. "Okay, maybe not everything. But I can save you, baby. If you'll let me. You just need to trust a little bit."

Trust. What did that feel like? And how could you trust another when you couldn't even trust yourself?

I breathed. "It's fine. I usually spend most of my time here at the stables anyway."

Matthew nodded. "All right. And if anyone asks, I'm a friend of Eric's from law school."

"Then it's settled. I'll stay away from you. You stay away from me. And that includes—"

"Mommy?"

We both froze at the sound of my daughter's voice echoing across the marble. We both took immediate steps away from each other and turned. Olivia stood in the hall, a large towel wrapped around her small body, goggles in hand.

"Mama, who is this?" she asked as she approached.

I opened my mouth to answer, but before I could, Matthew strode forward and extended his hand as he squatted in front of my daughter.

"Hey, kiddo," he said. "I don't believe we've made a proper introduction. I'm Matthew."

Matthew. For a moment, I was riddled with jealousy. That was my name for him. He'd told me so himself. No matter that it was his given name, the one on his birth certificate, the one anyone on the planet could call him if they liked. For some reason, I resented anyone else but me using the full, deliciously formal version that I had somehow claimed as my own.

Even my daughter.

I shook my head. Ridiculous. I was absolutely ridiculous.

"I've seen you before," Olivia was saying as she shook his hand solemnly. "You walked my mother home one night. You had a hat like that, but it was gray."

Matthew's full mouth crooked to one side as he looked at the fedora in his hand. "Good memory." He tossed the hat back on his head with a rakish tilt that made my heart skip and Olivia bite back a grin.

"My name is Olivia. Patricia says I have a good mind for faces." She tipped her head at him as he stood. "That's my nanny. She says I'm an elephant. I never forget."

"Patricia is right," Matthew said. "How about names? Are you good with those too?"

I watched with awe as Olivia stuck out her chin, almost as defiant as I myself felt with this man. Did he have that effect on all women he challenged, or just us?

"Depends," Olivia said.

"On what?" Matthew asked.

"On whether the name deserves to be remembered."

"Olivia!" I put in. "That was very rude."

"Ah, let her be, Nina. We're just getting to know each other," Matthew said as he tipped his hat up so the afternoon light revealed his entire chiseled face. He pointed to it. "See this, my little *elefantessa*?"

Olivia laughed outright. I started. It wasn't a sound I had heard in a very long time.

"What?" she asked. "Your face?"

"Yeah. This ugly mug."

Matthew grinned. The giggle grew louder. I pressed a limp hand over my heart.

"I promise you that by the end of this weekend, you'll never forget it or my name. And if you do…that's an ice cream on me, kid."

The whites of my daughter's teeth shone through her full-faced smile. "Is that a bet?"

Matthew nodded. "No, it's a deal, kid." He stuck out his hand again. "Shake on it."

Olivia eyed his hand again, but smiled wide enough that two dimples touched the corners of her cheeks.

"Shake," she murmured as she took part in the ritual.

"Olivia." I cleared my throat, finally able to locate my voice over the thump of my heart. "I think you can leave Mr. Zola alone now. He's here to see Eric and Jane, not us."

Her gaze shuttered and turned to me as she pulled her hand away. "Mama, do you have to go to the stables right away? Can't you come for a swim at least once this weekend?"

Next to her, Matthew's eyes bugged out. It was clear the idea of me in a swimsuit had produced the effect.

I should have said no. I should have continued with our plan. Maintained my distance while he kept his.

Really, I should have done as he originally demanded and taken Olivia home. But instead, I smiled at my daughter, enjoying the way Matthew swallowed heavily.

"Yes," I said. "I think I will come for a brief dip. Let me just go upstairs and change."

CHAPTER SIXTEEN

"It's just a swimsuit," I told my reflection for the fourth time. "Everyone wears them."

Everyone except you.

Lord. My internal monologue was really getting out of control.

I'd been in this room for forty-five minutes and I'd changed in and out of these two bits of fabric four times. Every time I turned to leave, I'd come right back and strip it off in favor of another sundress. And then when I got to the door, Olivia's eager, surprised face and the flash of lust on Matthew's would turn me on my heel. Back on went the suit.

"It's a *suit*," I muttered. "You're not Lady Godiva. You're still dressed, for God's sake."

And it was true. The white bikini was tasteful. Unremarkable. No more revealing than anything others would wear. Yes, the floor-length white cover-up I wore over it was sheer and open, but it was still floor-length. Beyond that, I'd pulled my hair back in a neat bun at the top of my head and kept my jewelry to its quiet minimum with only my wedding rings, a pair of diamond studs, and the small pendant around my neck that had been a gift from my father when I graduated high school.

"No one will notice anything," I told myself through my teeth. I blinked. I was lying. And terribly too.

Because the truth was, this was more of my body anyone in my family or circle of friends had seen in ten years. I would walk down to that patio and they would all stop and gawk. Gin-soaked comments would be made, like: "Aren't you the cute little showgirl?" or "My, my, who are we trying to impress?"

I'd become the one thing I'd tried never to be: a spectacle.

Anxiously, I toyed with my necklace as I turned from side to side, examining myself. I had nothing to be ashamed of, after all. Daily sessions with a trainer on top of spinning classes, Pilates, and Barre kept everything perfectly tight along with the balanced, carefully allotted calories Marguerite provided. I might have been thirty and a mother, but everything was still, for the most part, where it had been for the last decade. And I intended to keep it that way, thank you.

Sometimes I had to remind myself I *was* still only thirty. Only half of my childhood friends were even married, and even if they were, many still lived like they were ten years younger. Lounging around in the smallest scraps, their bodies waxed, polished, and, yes, artificially inflated in some parts. Never too lavish. Never cheap. But always on display for their husbands, their lovers. Always there for *someone*'s pleasure, even if it was just to look.

I, on the other hand, had been prim and proper to the point of eccentric. Everyone believed me when I said it was for my daughter. For my family. That I had a role to fill. No one questions statements like that when they're coming from a family like mine. The de Vrieses didn't just follow the rules of propriety—we made them. And so, if the granddaughter of Celeste de Vries intimated that it was improper for a young mother to wear a string bikini, no one whispered a word against it. No one wondered if the expensive cover-ups hid more than just maternal body. No one checked for bruises.

No one had ever bothered to look beneath.

Until him.

I pulled the sheer fabric aside. There was a shadow of one bruise still lingering on my thigh, but it was practically gone now. The worst was the one on my inner thigh, but I could keep that hidden if I just kept my legs together.

I chuckled. That sounded like an admonishment I would have received from Grandmother before coming out.

A lady keeps her legs crossed, Nina.

I shook my head. I wasn't a lady. Not anymore. Maybe not ever.

With a bit of defiance, I grabbed my lipstick off the vanity and held it up. I had thrown another tube of this at Matthew in the middle of the street…and then replaced it the following day. Never in my life had I worn this color until I met that man, and I hadn't worn it in over two months. Not since I had last seen him.

I shook my head. I shouldn't. Really. But even as the thought crossed my mind, I found myself drawing the deep crimson carefully over my pouted lips. If I was going to make an entrance, I might as well do it. And if the stubborn man insisted on being here this weekend, I wasn't going to make it easy for him. Maybe I should…but I was starting to learn that when it came to Matthew, I had very little control.

———

BY THE TIME I finally drew up the courage to walk out to the patio and pool, a large party had assembled. Eric's guests of honor weren't due until tomorrow, but everyone else was well known to me: neighbors, extended family members, and society acquaintances, all likely summoned by Mother, who was sitting on one of the loungers at the far end, presiding over the party like Cleopatra. It all looked very…normal.

The staff wove in and out of the crowd with trays of canapes while Marcus, Mother's butler, mixed drinks under a large umbrella. I recognized several neighbors and their children splashing around the large kidney-shaped pool along with Olivia while a few board members cornered Eric near the lawn. Jane, with her blue-streaked hair standing out in a crowd of polite neutrals, sat on one of the lawn chairs making conversation with a few distant cousins. She brightened and waved when she caught sight of me, but I could barely respond when I spotted him.

Matthew sat on a lounge chair next to my mother, each of them nursing what looked like Marcus's famous gin and tonic. Like me, Matthew had changed into more appropriate poolside clothing. But as much as I missed his shirt sleeves and tailored trousers, I couldn't deny that he still made the simple black shorts and short-sleeved button-down work well, particularly with the tawny, rigid lines of his stomach flexing under the open shirt front, the silver cross and saint's medallion on his chest gleaming in the sun. Add the vintage browline sunglasses and straw fedora, and he looked good enough to eat.

Not for the first time, I wondered how a man like him could exist in the twenty-first century.

He opened his mouth and laughed at something my mother said, his teeth shining white from across the lawn. Mother tittered into her drink and tossed a hand into the air, gesticulating a little too much. I rolled my eyes. She was a terrible flirt—always had been, much to Grandmother's disapproval.

For a moment, I considered turning back. It wasn't too late. No one else would notice me, and Jane certainly wouldn't say anything.

"Nina!"

Well, I could have turned back.

I turned to find Edith Stacy, one of my mother's oldest friends, winding her way around the pool to give me a kiss. Just beyond her, Matthew turned at the sound of my name, and started when he found me. His mouth dropped open, and his glasses slid down his nose so that his deep green eyes betrayed the expression of pure lust—and yes, love too—as they swept over me.

I swallowed and stood a little taller, thankful that the large shades I'd popped on before coming down were firmly in place. Who knew what kind of emotions were reflecting back at him?

"Come join us," Edith said, taking my arm and guiding me around the pool before I could answer. "Your mother has been asking about you for the last hour. We've all been dying to say hello."

I was summarily deposited on the lounger beside Matthew, who shifted uncomfortably as our thighs touched.

Mother sat up in her own chair. "Edith, be a darling and ask one of the staff for an umbrella out here, will you? We're positively roasting."

Edith, acting more like a handmaid than an equal friend, immediately darted off at the command. I barely masked a snort. It hadn't taken my mother long to adjust to her self-appointed role of queen bee of the family.

"Well, look at us," she said, tipping her enormous sunglasses down her long de Vries nose to look me over. "Putting on quite the show, I see."

"Mother," I said. "I just changed. I promised Olivia I would go for a swim."

My mother's gaze wasn't anything as penetrating as Celeste de Vries's, but Violet de Vries still had at least some genetic ability to look through a person like they were made of glass. Everyone in my family was like that.

It took everything I had not to grab at the sides of my cover-up.

"I see," she said as she eyed me up and down. "Well, I daresay you can't now. They're animals in there. Just look at that. Olivia positively tore Mr. Zola here apart. She got a side ache from laughing so hard, the poor thing."

I chanced a look at Matthew, who had by now replaced his sunglasses, though I could still feel his stare drilling into me from beyond the opaque lenses. His shorts were still a bit damp, sticking to his lithe, powerful legs, and his white shirt clung slightly to his shoulders from the remnants of the water. For a moment, I could imagine him climbing out of the pool, muscles gleaming. My heart caught in my chest. And then it moved to my throat when I imagined him making my daughter laugh.

"Oh—oh," I breathed. "Well, I'm…I'm sorry I missed that."

"Well, at least you look fabulous," Mother replied as she leaned back in her chair. She turned to Matthew with a lazy smile. "Isn't my daughter beautiful, Mr. Zola?"

"Mother," I muttered. "Please stop before you embarrass yourself."

"Oh, pish," Mother replied.

She waved her hand at me, and the bracelets around her wrist clinked together. A decade's worth of consolation prizes from my missing father.

"Don't pay attention to her, Mr. Zola," she said. "She's more obsessed with propriety than even my dear mother was, may she rest in peace. Won't put a toe out of line, not ever."

"Is that right?"

Out of the corner of my eye, I spied a black brow rising over the rim of his glasses.

"Please flirt with her, Mr. Zola. God knows that husband of hers never does." Mother clicked her tongue, then took another long drink. The motion made the bracelets on her wrist clink again. "My fault," she said in slightly slurred speech. "I married a man who put an ocean between us. Makes sense Nina ended up with someone just as absent."

"Mother!" I snapped. "Please stop."

"You stop. And get a cocktail, for heaven's sake. You're at least three behind all of us. Yoo-hoo! Marcus!"

"Yes, madam?" Marcus looked harried, weighed down with a tray full of drinks for the increasing party. I turned my attention fully on the butler in order to avoid the handsome, green-eyed pity I was sure I'd see from Matthew.

"Marcus, Nina needs a cocktail," Mother said lazily. "She's a terrible bore without one."

"Mother, honestly. It's not even two. And, Marcus, I can just get a sparkling water from the kitchen. You have enough out here—"

"Nina, now *you* stop it," Mother interrupted. "This is what we pay him for. Marcus, you know what she always has. Aperol spritz, light on the Prosecco."

Marcus swallowed, clearly struggling under his tray of drinks. "Of course, madam. If you'll just wait for me to deliver these, I'll return with yours—"

"I got it, Marcus." Matthew interrupted. His thigh brushed against mine as he stood, sending shivers all through me.

"Oh, Mr. Zola, that's not—"

"Mrs. Astor, it's really no problem. Anything for such a beautiful woman. And her daughter, of course," Matthew said, charm dripping from every syllable.

My mother blushed. A woman of fifty-five blushing like a fifteen-year-old schoolgirl.

"Oh, Mr. Zola, it's Violet. Please."

I rolled my eyes.

Matthew flashed the crooked grin that made my own stomach drop. "It's no problem. I happen to make an excellent cocktail. Shall I make us a couple too?"

"Yes, please!" Mother replied, fanning herself.

He nodded. "If you'll follow me, Mrs. Gardner, I'll get you that drink."

And just like that, the swirling in my stomach clenched into a tight fist of dread. How could a name affect me so? It was just a name, but coming from him...oh, I couldn't bear it.

Call me duchess, I wanted to beg him. *Doll. Nina.* Anything *but Mrs. Gardner.*

Instead, I followed Matthew silently through the crowd to the cocktail cart by the patio entrance. He spent a few minutes locating the ingredients for my drink. I leaned against the cart, enjoying the way he kept darting quick glances from the sides of his glasses at my legs. Matthew always did like my legs.

"You. Little. Tease."

The words were barely audible over the clink of the ice. But I could hear them. Just for me.

"I'm not sure what you mean," I murmured back.

The quick, dark glance over his glasses made the pool of desire in my belly splash again before he went back to pouring Aperol and soda.

"I thought we were done playing games, doll," he said, overly focused on our drinks. "We had an agreement. Keep our distance, no matter what. And then you walk out in that."

I looked down at my body, then back up at him. "It's just a swimsuit."

"And I'm just Eric's friend from Harvard. Give me a break, Nina."

Once again, that odd streak of defiance only he brought out reared its ugly head again.

"This is a pool," I said. "A swimsuit is hardly inappropriate."

Matthew sucked in a labored breath, then exhaled through his teeth. "I can see every damn curve you've got. Every gorgeous inch of those long legs." He shook his head ruefully and pulled on the collar of his shirt, despite the fact that it was hanging open. "Christ, baby, your nipples are practically staring at me, begging to be bitten."

I reddened. "Oh, please. The material isn't *that* thin, Matthew."

He grinned as he slowly peeled a bit of orange. The muscles in his forearm rippled with the simple movement. "Well, no. But the fact that I know them so well makes it easy to imagine."

I bit my lip. He growled, low.

"Well, sauce for the gander, as they say." I accepted my drink, trying not to look affected as our fingers brushed.

"What's that supposed to mean?"

"You could have at least buttoned your shirt."

Matthew looked very much like he wanted to laugh, more so when the muscles over his stomach tightened. Somehow, he managed to swallow back his mirth as he prepared a twin cocktail for my mother and another for himself. Then he leaned toward me—not so much that anyone would notice, but the minuscule difference was enough to set my heart racing.

"You want me to cover up, baby?"

Another shiver traveled down my spine despite the ninety-degree heat. It was hard—so hard—to stand next to him like this and not touch him. I wanted to run my finger down the slick plane of his chest. Touch the divot where his necklace hung. Lick away the tiny drops of sweat that lingered there.

"Well, you seem to think I should," I said. "And yet you act like it doesn't go both ways."

I forced myself to look away and took a sip of my drink. Of course he made a perfect cocktail. Of *course* he did. The spritzer was refreshing. Exquisite. Just like him.

His gaze traveled up and down my body, searing right through his glasses. It didn't matter that I couldn't see through them. In fact, maybe it was better. I doubted I could take the intensity otherwise.

It occurred to me then that he might say yes. He wasn't exactly happy I was here. And he was right—I was going out of my way to be a distraction, wasn't I? He wouldn't be unreasonable to suggest that I make myself less provoking with a caftan. Or just disappear altogether, out of sight.

But the thought anchored another, much more familiar feeling in my stomach—fear. Not fear that someone would discover us, but fear that Matthew—*my* Matthew—was like everyone else. That he would want me to maintain propriety above passion. That he would want to hide me away.

Or punish me if I did not behave.

Please don't, I found myself begging internally. I really didn't think I could take it if he did.

But before I could say anything, he pulled down his glasses so his eyes could meet mine. The force of his gaze almost made me take a step back.

"Don't mistake my struggle for censorship, doll," Matthew proclaimed quietly as he stirred the drinks. "Any man who'd hide a woman like you should be locked up himself. A man who won't let you shine doesn't deserve the light of day."

God, how did he always do that? One moment we were all witty repartee, and then, just when I thought I was getting my bearings, he would completely undo me.

"Matthew, I—"

He cleared his throat roughly, replaced his sunglasses, and looked across the pool, explicitly away from me. "Nina, you need to shut your mouth and stop looking at me like that."

"Like—like what?"

"Like you want me to drag you onto that lounge chair and ruin this whole damn charade. Right here. Right now. Don't think I wouldn't do it, either." He hissed another breath through his teeth, like he was having trouble catching it. "You have sunglasses?"

I opened my mouth again to argue with him, but he just cocked his head as if to say *See?*

So I just nodded. "Yes." I held up the pair I had brought out with me.

Matthew set the stirrer on the cart. "Good. You win, all right? You look stunning, and it's going to drive me crazy in ways you can't even imagine. But right now, I'm going to stay on my side of the party and keep your mother company while she runs her mouth and introduces me to important people. You keep your shades on and stay on yours. For both our good. Deal?"

I nodded again, suddenly feeling like a chastised schoolgirl and fighting the urge to yank the sides of my cover-up together. "Yes. Fine."

Matthew picked up the other two drinks and made his way back to my mother without another look my way. I turned to face the pool, cocktail in hand, and without thinking, tipped it back in one go. Oh, he was right. I shouldn't have come out here. I shouldn't have stayed at all. The next few days would be harder than I had ever imagined.

I turned in the other direction and found Jane watching me carefully from the other side of the pool. Beside her, Eric seemed to be fielding questions from an assortment of extended family while she sat alone, looking bored. I waved at her half-heartedly, and she tipped her head to one side as if to beckon me over. Questions were written across her wry features, through the thick cat-eyed glasses that somehow made her look both quirky and shrewd.

"Mommy? Mama, are you actually wearing a swimsuit? Are you really coming in?"

Grateful for the intrusion of Olivia's uncertain voice, I turned my attention to the pool, where she had swum to the side with a hopeful look on her face.

I knelt down to the edge and forced myself to smile.

"Yes," I replied with more enthusiasm than I felt. "Yes, I believe I am."

CHAPTER SEVENTEEN

Two cocktails, endless hidden glances, and one swim with Olivia later, I had made small talk with every one of my family's associates and acquaintances, and steered my great-uncle Rupert away from the drink cart, all while assiduously avoiding Matthew's quick green gaze even while being astutely aware of his presence as he also made his rounds about the party. From time to time, I caught bits of conversation floating about. He was using his skill with cocktails to his advantage—getting on Marcus's good side by helping out the staff and using my mother's large stores of liquor to loosen the lips of my family's social circle.

To them, he was a lark. A charming, well-mannered boy with just enough edge to give them a thrill. He knew exactly the right kinds of things to say, to the point where I found myself quite disgusted with it all. Was that how I had been when we met? Had he sized me up across the bar, known that if he touched my shoulder in the exact right way, called me "doll," and looked at me with those deep green eyes, I'd melt into his touch just like my cousin Carolyn was right at this moment?

I found myself stewing on exactly that when my name was called from across the party. I turned and froze when I saw the second last person I expected here today: Caitlyn Calvert. Well, I suppose it was Shaw now.

"Will this day never end?" I muttered to myself.

"Nina!" she called out with a flick of her wrist. "N, darling! Oh, I'm so glad you made it this weekend!"

On the other side of the party, Jane froze mid-conversation with her mother-in-law, Heather, with whom she'd become quite close recently. She immediately set her empty glass on a side table and made a beeline over to Eric, who was encircled by two neighbors comparing golf courses in loud, domineering voices. Eric's face lit up with relief when he saw his wife approach, but immediately hardened when he followed her nod toward Caitlyn.

"Shit," he mouthed, then found me. His meaning was clear. What was Caitlyn doing here? I shook my head, hoping he would understand that I was not the one who invited her.

"Hello," I greeted Caitlyn as she offered air kisses. "This is a surprise."

I waved a hand for Marcus's attention, but he was already starting a cocktail for Caitlyn, as well known as she once was in our family.

"I'm so sorry to drop by unannounced," Caitlyn replied. "Violet called to let us know about it this morning, and Kyle's desperate to get Eric's ear on something. But I'm glad I came—look at you! In a bikini, no less!"

"Oh. Yes," I said. "Did you lighten your hair again?"

"Do you like it?" Caitlyn toyed with the sunny blonde ends of her waves. "Just a touch-up."

I tipped my head. "It's nice. I haven't seen it this blonde for years, though."

There was a loud throat clearing beside her. Caitlyn turned to her husband as if he were gum on the bottom of her shoe. I glanced between the two of them. It was clear that Caitlyn hadn't filled him in on her last interactions with Eric and Jane.

"Well, go on now," she said to him like she was shooing away a bug. "He's over there. You made me ruin these people's evening, so you might as well do what you came here to do."

Kyle Shaw shot his wife a bored, irritable look, but straightened his shirt collar underneath his seersucker suit and strode toward Eric.

"He's dying to get his hands on this development project," Caitlyn said. "Somewhere in the Bronx, if you can imagine anywhere up there worth developing."

I blinked, thinking of Arthur Avenue. Of Matthew's childhood home and the warmth there.

"There are some lovely places in that part of the city," I said.

Nina snorted. "If you say so."

"Mommy, Patricia said she would take me and some of the other kids upstairs to watch a movie. Is that okay?"

Caitlyn and I both turned to find Olivia standing in front of me, wrapped in a towel. She looked tired, shivering, but more content than I'd seen her in a long time. The afternoon with a group of children had done her good.

I blinked. "Yes, darling, but don't you think you ought to say hello first?"

Olivia looked obediently up at Caitlyn, who softened as she looked down.

"Hello, O. How's school?" she asked. "Tell your aunt Caitlyn all about it."

Olivia eyed her. "Well, you're not really my aunt."

Caitlyn's smile turned slightly sour. "I was there when you were born. I think that makes me an honorary aunt, don't you?"

Olivia blinked back and forth between me and Caitlyn—looking, I supposed, for some confirmation from me. Well, I couldn't argue with facts.

"I—I guess so," she said. "But I'm not in school either. We don't go back until September."

"Well, that's nice." Caitlyn looked at me too, clearly out of questions to ask. I didn't say anything, though she obviously wanted me to step in.

After a few moments of awkward silence, I took pity on them both. "Go on, darling. Enjoy the movie."

Olivia nodded and scampered off. On the other side of the pool, where he had sidled into the conversation Eric and Kyle were now having, Matthew's eyes followed Olivia out of the party, then flashed back at me before he resumed listening.

"Let me guess. You're dying for her to go back already."

I turned back to Caitlyn and shrugged. "I wouldn't say that. It's been lovely having her home."

"Does Calvin think that too?"

I didn't answer. I didn't have to. Caitlyn knew. She knew exactly why I sent Olivia to Andover every fall instead of enrolling her in one of the many excellent schools in New York. Why she had spent the entire summer in England and would go straight back to Massachusetts in just another week.

"Oh, N," Caitlyn murmured as she squeezed my hand. "I know."

I bit my lip and was grateful for my sunglasses. For some reason, all of a sudden, I was finding it terribly difficult not to cry.

"Yes," I murmured. "Well."

But by that point, Caitlyn was clearly no longer engaged in the conversation. Instead, she was staring openly at someone else on the other side of the pool. Someone currently making her husband laugh hysterically while mixing the man what looked like a very generous high ball. Someone with more natural charm and charisma than everyone in this party combined.

"What *is* he doing here?"

I turned to follow her gaze toward Matthew.

"Blending in, I suppose," I said.

"Blending in? With that ridiculous hat? And that absurd chain?"

"I don't know. It's stylish, I think. Classic."

Caitlyn snorted. "He looks like a *Mad Men* extra." She turned to me. "Like he's dressed in some costume of what he thinks rich people wear. He looks like he's really from—"

"Paterson?" I interrupted, more sharply than I intended. I couldn't help it. I had absolutely no interest in hearing a single word deprecating the best man I knew. And certainly not from someone who came from equally humble beginnings.

Caitlyn looked wounded. "Do you know why he's here?"

I shrugged. "Eric and Jane invited him. They knew him from Boston, I think."

"Harvard? How is that possible? Zola is from New York, isn't he?"

I blinked. Oh, dear. "Um, yes," I sputtered. "But—"

"And he only went to some grubby state school, isn't that right?"

I frowned. How much did she actually know about Matthew?

The night at the opera clanged in my head like a bell. Not just the memory that Matthew had undoubtedly slept with Caitlyn at some point, but also that I had wanted to throttle her—and him—for it.

That instinct hadn't exactly faded over the last few months.

"How do you know that?" I asked a little too sharply.

Caitlyn flushed. "I—I—well, it's common knowledge, isn't it?"

I raised a brow. She was embarrassed. Strange, actually. Usually she was more than happy to regale me with all her extramarital exploits. Three marriages to equally philandering, old rich men. She had no shame.

I glanced again at Matthew, who caught me looking this time. He winked before finding Caitlyn beside me. Then his face froze before he smoothed it back to its previously affable smile at Eric and Kyle.

I shook my head infinitesimally at him before turning back to Caitlyn, who was staring at him as well.

"You know," she said. "I think I'm going to go say hello myself. Make sure that Kyle isn't embarrassing himself too much."

No, I wanted to say. To be frank, I wanted to do more than that. I nearly pushed her in the pool to stop her from going over there and sinking her well-manicured claws into Matthew. I knew that tone. I knew my friend's *modus operandi*. She'd ask for a drink. Run her nails up his back. Laugh at all his jokes before whispering a room number or a closet destination.

I couldn't watch as she left me poolside. I wasn't sure I could stay here anymore.

"You look like you need another one of these."

I turned to find Jane approaching with a pair of cocktails, including another Aperol spritz for me.

"Compliments of Sam Malone over there," she said, nodding at Matthew.

"Sam who?"

Jane blinked. "Sorry. Eighties TV reference. Only latchkey millennials get those."

I shrugged, still not sure exactly what she was talking about.

"He certainly seems to be the life of the party," she said, looking back at Matthew.

"He does, doesn't he?" I took the cocktail from Jane, but then stared at it for a long time before setting it down on a small table. "That's very kind, but I think I've had enough."

"Have you?"

I sank to another lounge chair, and Jane joined me. She, however, was still happy to take my drink instead.

"Are you okay?" she asked. "You're a little...I don't know. I still can't read your family well, but you don't seem your usual chipper self."

I bit back a smile. Jane and I both knew I was many things. Chipper was not one of them.

"I'm fine," I said. "I'm just not my mother. I know when to stop."

As if on cue, Mother's gin-soaked laugh knocked around the pool like a hyena's. I shuddered. Jane masked a smile.

"It doesn't have anything to do with Medusa over there crashing the party, does it?" Jane asked.

I arched a brow. "Medusa?"

Jane shrugged as she shot daggers at Caitlyn. "Cruella de Vil. Maleficent. I have lots of names for the she-devil who tried to break up my wedding. It's only because I promised Eric I'd be on my best behavior this weekend that she and her extensions aren't already in the pool."

I chuckled. She had no idea how close I'd come to doing the same thing. "Well, we're not exactly close right now either. I wasn't happy with what she did to you two."

"That's good to know. But it's hard anyway, I imagine, losing your best friend."

Jane's kind, frank statement again made the tears threaten all over again.

"It's not just that," I admitted.

"I didn't think it was."

I looked up. Jane's face was unlike everyone else's in my social circle. I had liked her immediately, even when I wasn't supposed to. She was candid and kind, and she always expected everyone else to be the same too. Without judgment.

"Lately," I admitted. "I've been feeling a little…"

"Frustrated? Irritable?"

"Lost," I filled in softly.

Jane eyed me sympathetically. "Ah. Yeah. I know the feeling."

I turned. "Do you?"

"I do. Six months ago, I was still planning to keep practicing law in New York. And then I thought I was pregnant. And then I wasn't either of those things anymore. You could say I've been drifting for a while now."

At the mention of her horrific loss, guilt swept through me. She talked about it like it was nothing, but the real chain of events was so much more complicated. If Eric hadn't been imprisoned over false charges, I wouldn't have been staying with Jane that weekend when she left for South Korea to find her mother. And if she hadn't gone, she wouldn't have been abducted, drugged, and lost her baby. And she wouldn't have done any of it if I had been there that night to stop her. Because that night, of course, was the night I met Matthew.

Like she read my mind, Jane reached out and patted my hand.

"Hey, I didn't mean to make you uncomfortable. It's not a competition between sob stories. I just meant I understand."

"Am I really that transparent?" I wondered, watching as Caitlyn set her hand on Matthew's arm. Was it my imagination, or did he encourage her? Eric seemed to be ignoring her completely. Why couldn't Matthew?

"I don't think I could accuse anyone in your family of transparency, Nina."

I sniffed. "We are a stiff bunch, aren't we?"

Jane gave a very unladylike snort. "That's maybe putting it lightly."

I didn't respond. Caitlyn was now whispering something into Matthew's ear. I couldn't see his eyes behind his sunglasses, but his smile momentarily disappeared. My fingers curled over my knees, hard enough that my nails dug into my flesh.

"So, what do you want to do?" Jane asked, crossing one leg over the other like she was settling in for a good chat.

I turned back from my voyeurism. "Hmmm?"

"Have you given it any thought? If you're feeling lost, where do you want to be? What do you want?"

The sudden candor caught me off guard. It wasn't that I had never considered the question. For some time now, I had known that a life of planning fundraisers and luncheons, sitting on endless charity committees and boards of directors wasn't something I found particularly fulfilling. But it was in January that this feeling, this empty ache, really took root. When he was temporarily imprisoned, Eric had entrusted me to oversee the smooth running of De Vries Shipping. And while that really hadn't consisted of more than observing board meetings and making sure no one was making crooked deals behind his back, it had been a relief to know that regardless of what happened, I was at least competent enough to step into those shoes should the need arise. But it was also equally demoralizing to discover that I didn't particularly want to. And so, when Eric returned, I was more than happy to hand back the reins to the family carriage, so to speak. And render myself rudderless once more.

"I—I honestly don't know," I admitted. "I wish I did."

"Can I ask you something?"

I tore my attention back to Jane. She seemed to be doing everything she could to wrest my attention from the scene at hand.

"Sure," I gave in. "I mean, of course."

She tipped her head knowingly as she adjusted her glasses. I didn't like that look. I didn't like it at all.

"You stayed with me for a while, Nina. Before I left for Korea, you were really fucking down," she said bluntly. "And then, this spring, things seemed different. Up and down. You were decidedly...unstiff. Sometimes you seemed really sad. But others...almost happy. Did everything just magically get better with Calvin over the last few months? Or—and I'm just taking a wild guess here—did a certain dashing Italian with a penchant for jaunty hats have something to do with it?"

Ah, yes. The other fedora-wearing, cataclysmic elephant in the room (or today, the patio) who had sent shock waves through my life last January. I stared at my feet, resisting the urge to dive into the pool away from this line of questioning. Was my guilt written so plainly? Oh, Grandmother would be disappointed.

"I don't know what you're talking about," I mumbled.

Jane looked around the party like we were discussing the weather. "Well, if that's true, then I'll tell him to stop looking at you like that when he thinks no one notices."

I looked up. "Don't you dare."

Jane cracked a wry smile. "I wouldn't. I just wanted to see your face when I said it. You might want to avoid being in the same room for too long, though. This crowd is just self-absorbed enough that they'll be slower on the uptake than most, but eventually, he's going to give the game away."

I was doused in fear. And it must have been perfectly obvious, because Jane's smile disappeared.

"Hey," she said. "Don't worry. Your secret is safe with me and Eric, if you say anything to him. Fair warning, though—he's a wily bastard. He probably already figured it out."

I blinked. "I'm not saying any of this is true. But if it were…why would you…"

"Well, we like Zola pretty well. And we're not exactly fans of Calvin. Speaking of, maybe one day you'll tell me why you're still married to the guy."

Across the party, Caitlyn broke into high laughter as she clutched Matthew's arm. Eric looked bored while her husband continued talking his ear off. Matthew looked as charming as ever, though he darted another glance my way.

Jane cleared her throat. And at that, I finally managed to find my legs again.

"Maybe one day we can investigate the state of my marriage and life's purpose," I said as I stood. "But for now, I think I'll go riding for a bit before dinner after all. Will you let Olivia know if she comes looking for me?"

Jane nodded, still watching me carefully. "Sure," she said. "But, Nina? Be careful."

I didn't have to ask whether she meant with the horses or my heart. Her meaning was perfectly clear.

CHAPTER EIGHTEEN

I was fourteen the first time I was allowed to take a horse—my horse —out without a trainer. Coral was a ring sour Andalusian—trained too young, scared of the whip, and unable to compete. To make up for missing yet another birthday, my father paid a small fortune to make her my "beach horse" instead of a brood mare for her irritated owners. She was as skittish and temperamental at seven as I was at fourteen. But perhaps that made us kindred spirits, because from the moment I approached her, apple in hand, it was love at first sight for us both.

How many evenings had I escaped here as a teenager from my mother's vapidity, my friends' shallow behavior, my grandmother's tyranny? How many times had I sat on the stool just inside and leaned on Coral's warm, big body, seeking comfort and affection from the only person—yes, my horse was a person to me, in all the ways that mattered—who would give it in those days?

When I returned from Italy, pregnant and heartbroken, I had come straight to Long Island, straight to this stable. And then again after meeting Calvin. It was here, in the hay, after I had cried all my tears out with my horse, that I had really decided to be a mother, much more so than that day in the clinic.

Coral's velvety gray nose poked out of her stall almost as soon as I entered the stables, nickering softly, almost as though not to disturb the other horses chomping quietly on their hay.

"Hello, Cor." I offered her the apple I'd nicked from the kitchen on my way out. "How've you been, my love? Hmm?"

Coral made quick work of the apple, then snorted as she shoved her nose under my arm, looking for another.

"Well, aren't we a little porker?" I teased, rubbing a hand over the white spots that dappled between her eyes and admiring the way her long lashes curled as she leaned into the touch. "I know, I know. It's been a while. Livy's been home, and I've been busy…with things. I'm sorry. I'll be out every weekend this summer, I promise."

Coral chuffed lightly, much like she was calling me on my bluff, and stomped one hoof on the ground.

I chuckled. "Okay, maybe not every weekend. But more, I promise."

I pulled a carrot from my pocket, which she chomped quickly. When she was done, she didn't look for more, though, just stood stock-still, allowing me to run my hands over her cheeks, between her eyes, over her long, graceful neck. Her willingness to accept love, whenever and wherever, was, as always, my undoing. My chest squeezed. Why couldn't people be this simple?

Coral chuffed again, and this time nuzzled toward me, looking for my neck.

I sighed as I pressed my cheek to hers. "I can't talk about it. Not here."

She didn't move, almost as if she knew I needed the extra contact. For all her skittishness around others, she was ever-patient with me.

I patted her cheek and stepped back. "Come on, my love. Let's get you ready. I'll tell you everything once we're out in the open."

I opened the stall and went inside to loop a harness around her head before leading her to the tack room, where she stood obediently, waiting for me to get her ready for a ride. The other riders in the family usually called down to have the trainer prep the horses before they got here, but I preferred to do it myself. It was soothing, connecting, brushing Coral's warm flanks, cleaning her hooves, laying the blanket, then the saddle. Connections, touches, between her big, warm body and mine. In some ways, hers was the longest relationship I'd ever had.

I lifted the bridle to her mouth. She accepted the bit, then gave another soft nicker, as if to say, *come on, then.*

"All right, all right."

I checked the saddlebags to make sure we had enough water and food for the ride, then stepped into a stirrup and swung myself up with ease. Coral pawed at the ground, eager to get going. I took a deep breath. Things really did seem easier to see, to feel from up here.

I patted Coral's neck and leaned forward. "Okay, Cor. Let's go."

———

WE TOOK one of the trails through the trees at the east end of the property, then wound down to the part of the beach that bordered a wildlife sanctuary—where the neighbors were less likely to intrude. Here it was just me, Coral, and the occasional gull or sandpiper among the grassy dunes that eventually gave way to the long, white sand and then the ocean. Vast, open. Exactly what Coral and I both needed.

"No one here today, Cor," I said to my misanthropic horse. "Aren't we lucky?"

Coral tugged on the reins a little. I'd given her control through the paths she knew so well but had picked up the slack down here.

"Stop," I said, pulling more on the leather. "What do you want to do, bolt?"

She gave a soft neigh and trotted impatiently, more like she was a two-year-old filly, not a twenty-three-year-old mare.

"Oh, you think you can run, my love?"

Another sharp pull on the reins told me she did indeed. Coral was eyeing the long, empty expanse of beach with lust. Kellan, our trainer, took her out regularly, but I doubted she was given much in the way of free rein.

I swallowed. I knew what it was like to want to run.

I leaned over her neck and gave her the slack she desired.

"All right, Cor," I whispered. "Go."

She didn't need more than that to take off. Coral was a dressage horse, not a thoroughbred, but she was still fast enough. The wind whipped through her hair as she charged down the beach, and I laughed, even closing my eyes to feel the cool Atlantic breeze across across my face.

Freedom. That's what this was. At least, one of the only tastes of it I'd ever known. On Coral, I was able to let go of my fears, my frustrations. The trappings of a life that sometimes it truly felt I'd never chosen at all.

Lost.

My answer to Jane's question echoed through my mind, an immediate rebuke. If I was being honest—which, apparently, I was today—I'd been more than a little lost my entire life. Kept on a bridle like my horse. Led from place to place, from show to show. From master to master. Perhaps a tiny rebellion here or there, but my biggest and dearest one—my daughter—was also my greatest secret. And in many ways, the one that had cost me the most.

My life had never really been my own.

What do you want to do?

They were two different things, weren't they? Living and doing. Or maybe one would help me accomplish the other.

Well. What did I want, then?

Matthew.

His smile, his warm, mischievous eyes, his urgent, tender touch. It all filled me, along with a yearning I was certain would never fade. At twenty, I had thought I was in love. But that was nothing compared to this. Now I understood just how little I had known Giuseppe. How small I was in comparison with the magnitude of his family, accomplishments, passions, works. I was only a girl. Sometimes still learning who she was. And it went both ways, really. How could he had loved me either? How could have known me at all when I hadn't really known myself?

That love, just a dalliance, was nothing compared to the man I couldn't have.

So what, doll? Even then, Matthew's warm timbre echoed through my conscience. *Even if you could have me, I'm a person, baby. Not a life.*

What did I want?

I had given up everything for so many others.

Never finished college.

Never traveled again.

Never had a job, real interests, passions that belonged only to me. My life was a mind-numbing collage of luncheons and fundraisers and trainers.

And fear.

Always fear.

By the time Coral and I made it back to the stables, we were both tired. We had walked most of the way back while I poured my heart out to my horse. But, unfortunately, I had no more idea of the answers to my questions than when I began.

"Tuckered her right out, did you?"

Kellan, the trainer, appeared from the barn, where he was feeding the other horses. I smiled as Coral stopped in front of the stable door for me to dismount. She snorted at Kellan with a half-hearted greeting.

"You want me to cool her down for you, Mrs. Gardner?"

I shook my head. "No, that's all right. I can take care of her today. We'll finish what we started together."

The old trainer nodded. "Just as well. I need to take out Night-shade. Should be about an hour, maybe more. You need me to finish anything, just leave a note in the office."

I nodded. "Will do. Thank you, Kellan."

I slid off Coral and led her into the barn to remove her tack, hang my helmet alongside, and get her cooled down and something to eat and drink. When I reemerged from her stall, I was in a daze from the ride, enough that I didn't notice the person waiting for me outside.

"I didn't know you rode."

I jumped at the sound of the familiar voice behind me, then turned to find Matthew leaning against the wall of the stable, elbow propped against a post, watching me carefully.

I shoved a hand through my hair. Lord, I was sweaty. And hot. And in need of a drink.

"Here."

Matthew held out a chilled bottle of Perrier, likely brought from the house—he must have been chatting with Marcus, who would have known my preferences.

"Thank you," I said, accepting it, then guzzling half the bottle in one go, stopping only to catch my breath, and then emit a small belch as a result of the carbonation. Immediately, I covered my mouth with my hand. "Excuse me. That wasn't particularly ladylike, was it?"

Matthew grinned. My heart pumped a bit harder.

"It was fuckin' adorable," he said. "Besides, you know I like seeing you enjoy things with your mouth, doll."

That only made me blush. And I couldn't help the way my gaze dropped over him, remembering all the things about this man I had, in fact, enjoyed just like that.

Lord. I was like a teenager all over again.

"Why—why are you here?" I asked. "I thought we needed to stay away from each other."

The flirtation on his face disappeared. "I—well, yeah. We do. But there's no one here, is there?"

I shrugged. "Kellan, the trainer, will be back soon. He's harmless, but chatty."

Matthew shoved his hands into his pockets. "Well, something just seemed…off. When you left, I mean."

I ground my teeth. "You seemed to be having a lovely time. Caitlyn appeared to be *very* entertaining."

Matthew sighed, then removed his sunglasses and tucked them into his shirt pocket. "Don't tell me you're jealous. Baby, you *know* there's nothing there."

"Do I? It certainly didn't look that way," I snapped, then was immediately irritated with myself. I sounded petty and childish. What a waste of a lovely ride.

"Well, I had to watch every midlife crisis-battling man over thirty ogle you for ninety straight minutes, so yeah, doll, I think I can sympathize." He shook his head. "You'd think the bastards hadn't ever seen a pair of legs before." His gaze trailed up mine, which were now covered in my riding breeches. "Of course, yours do take the cake."

We stared at each other for five hard seconds. Matthew, however, was the first to give.

"Nina," he said softly. "Please. Let's not do this."

I opened my mouth to argue with him, but found that for once, I didn't want to. Because what was the point? I had no claim to this man. And never truly would.

The thought made me completely deflate.

He took a step toward me. "Anyway, I came because I was worried. I told Eric I was going to explore the property a bit and came to find you."

"How did you know I would be here?" I wondered. "Twenty acres is a lot to explore. I could have been anywhere."

"Jane."

"Ah." I pushed a hand through my hair, ignoring my grandmother's mental admonishments not to make it greasy. It probably looked frightful after my ride anyway.

I didn't really care. At the mention of Jane, our conversation came back all over again, along with guilt, and I lapsed into another silence while Matthew watched. He adjusted his hat, then fussed with his watch for a moment. I peered at him. Matthew wasn't typically one to fidget—if anything, he had grace and confidence rarely seen in most people. He was here for something beyond just concern and curiosity. He was nervous about something too.

"Are you too tired for another short walk?" he asked. "We, um, we need to talk."

I swallowed, glanced from side to side, then hated that I even had to do it. Guilt and resentment lodged in my gut all over again. And after an hour of undoing them too.

"I—I suppose."

Matthew sighed. "Please, doll. Just a walk."

I sighed too. "It's never just a walk with you, Matthew."

But I still went with him. I had a feeling I always would, as long as he asked.

CHAPTER NINETEEN

W e meandered into the woods, but this time stayed away from
the beach as if by silent accord. Too much open space. Too
easy for someone to see us.

"You looked happy," Matthew remarked as we passed a large
beech tree. "When you were with your horse, I mean."

I nodded. "I—yes. I was. Happy and tired." I sighed. "Riding
always has that effect on me."

"You just took off. I looked up from the pool and you were gone.
Your mother was looking for you too."

I shrugged. "There didn't really seem a point to me being there."

"No?"

There was a strange note in his voice. Reluctant disappointment.

I had to nip it in the bud, so to speak. "I'm sorry I got jealous about
Caitlyn. I have no right to that. No claim on you."

"Don't you?"

I stopped and turned. "Are you just going to keep repeating the
same questions over and over again?"

To my utmost irritation, Matthew cocked his head. "I might."

I sighed, but found I couldn't maintain a scowl. The mischievous,
boyish glimmer in his green eyes could only make me smile.

Until I remembered the truth.

"I'm sorry I stayed," I said quietly as we continued to walk. "You were right. I should have declined the invitation and returned to the city when I found you were here. It would have been kinder to you. And certainly more supportive to what you're trying to do here."

"I know," he said. "But would you have really gone, knowing I was here? I wouldn't have. I couldn't. It seems I can't stay away from you either, even when I have to."

His candor, blended with the same hopelessness stirring inside, broke my heart.

We approached a big oak tree near a clearing. It was familiar, bearing many small, weather-worn marks where Eric and I used to carve our names and hearts and other small insignias into the trunk.

"I can see you here," Matthew said as he drifted his hands over the wood. "Like Olivia. Cute little blonde girl, playing hide-and-seek in the woods." His wide mouth quirked crookedly. "I would have liked chasing you."

"Matthew—"

"It might be a good idea," he interrupted suddenly, "for you to get out of town for a while."

I paused at the sudden change in his tone. "That's what you came to tell me."

Dark green eyes wide and serious, he nodded.

I bit my lower lip, thinking. "Why?"

Matthew hesitated, like he knew he shouldn't say anything. "Shit," he muttered. "God fucking dammit."

"Matthew, if it's against the rules, you don't have to—"

"It's a rock and a hard place, is what it is, doll." He sighed, long and low. "If I tell you, I'm crossing a major ethical line as a lawyer. But if I don't, I'm crossing another as a man." He looked up. "A man really fucking in love."

Another arrow. Another spear.

I closed my eyes, trying to will the pain away.

"Fuck it."

When I opened them, he had already closed the three feet or so between us. His hand slipped around my waist like it belonged there, the other threading through the hair at the back of my head. My arms automatically wrapped around his neck to pull him closer, moving of their own accord as if this were the most natural thing in the world. Our mouths found each other, and for a few minutes, it was like we could both breathe normally again. His kiss, warm and urgent, was oxygen.

After a few minutes, we broke apart, gasping for air between reddened lips. Matthew pressed his forehead to mine as he caught his breath.

"The investigation just got a surveillance warrant for Calvin," he said. "The judge approved it yesterday."

The revelation was like a bucket of cold water dumped on top of me. "What?"

His arms released me, and he stepped back as he removed his hat and started rubbing his neck. "I'm sorry, Nina. But that's all I can really tell you. And I shouldn't even tell you that."

"Have you—have you been watching him before now? Us?"

I wasn't stupid. Unofficial police surveillance was the worst-kept secret in America, and the NYPD was one of the most egregious offenders. Still, I didn't want to believe that Matthew would have invaded my privacy without telling me.

Suddenly my chest felt like it was made of ice.

Matthew shook his head. "We've been tailing him for a while, watching your building and his office, yeah. But nothing tapped. So far."

I sighed with relief. The idea that he might have seen anything that went on in that apartment…and said nothing…it was unbearable.

"You can expect the apartment to have eyes and ears after Monday, though," he continued. "I'm supposed to confirm that you're here or when you leave."

I stepped farther away, leaned against the old oak tree, and wrapped my arms around my middle before I started shaking. "What —what—what does that mean?"

Matthew watched me sadly. "It means no privacy, baby. It means they'll be planting cameras and audio in every room."

Oh, God. The things he would hear there. The things he would *see*.

"I don't understand," I said. "I thought you already had the evidence to indict. I thought the discovery or whatever it's called was so Calvin's lawyers could prepare."

"Nina, we need more than just part ownership in a Brooklyn safe house and a sighting outside," Matthew said. "But just between us, the investigation sort of hit a dead end a few weeks ago. That's until my tail found out about—you know what? Never mind. The point is, we've been waiting for this, and we need it."

Something else he probably wasn't supposed to tell me. And yet, I was glad he did as a single, guilty thought rang through my mind: *He doesn't know.*

Maybe he never would.

"Something on your mind?"

I blinked. "What?" Lord, how did he always manage to do that? "No."

Matthew peered at me a moment more. "You sure?"

I considered coming clean. But then, he had explicitly said not to, hadn't he? I had to figure this out on my own.

"I'm all right," I said as another plan fell into place. One I hadn't even realized I was contemplating with Coral until just this minute. "I can make that work."

"It's just for the fall, now that we know the trial date."

I looked up with surprise. "It's been set?"

Now it was Matthew's turn to look surprised. "You didn't know?" He sighed. "Yeah. The judge wasn't willing to give us another extension beyond that. Sixty days, and we head straight to trial, whether we have what we need or not. Which is why I'm here, obviously. Not just to…" He worried his jaw, clearly mulling over something. "Look, you wouldn't happen to know who a Kate Csaszar is, would you?"

I balked. "Now you'll take information from me?"

"Just answer the question, please."

But I shook my head. "I'm sorry, no. I've never heard the name before."

He studied me for a moment, then seemed almost relieved. But he didn't tell me why he was asking.

"No one else I talk to back there knew her either," he said. "So I'm back at square one."

"Did Caitlyn?" I asked before I could stop myself.

"I didn't ask," he said evenly. "I was too busy trying to talk to her husband, who had no clue."

"Well, that's too bad. She's the biggest gossip in New York. She probably knows something."

But Matthew just sighed and shook his head. I couldn't lie. I was pleased he didn't want to interact more with Caitlyn.

"Nina, bottom line: we need that surveillance. I'm sorry, but it's our only other shot before the trial starts."

The despondency in his voice was clear, and it affected me too. I wasn't used to Matthew like this. Here was a man so full of swagger, so usually confident, that generally he seemed like he would take on the world rather than admit defeat.

That was when I knew I'd do anything to prevent it. Even sacrifice myself.

I took a deep breath.

"There's a company," I said. "An LLC."

Matthew frowned and shook his head vigorously. "Nina, I told you, I can't hear any of this from you—"

"You can pretend you heard me mention it to Jane or someone else," I rattled on, no longer caring what he said. "It's called Pantheon."

Matthew froze. "How—how did you know about that?"

Now it was my turn to be shy. "I just do. I know it's registered anonymously in Delaware. I don't know everyone who owns it, but"—I swallowed, weighing my words carefully—"Matthew, one of them is Calvin."

Perhaps I should have told him the rest right then. But when I opened my mouth to do it, he just shook his head vigorously.

"That's enough, that's enough," he said. "I appreciate what you're doing, Nina, but that's all you should say."

"But I—"

"I already knew about Pantheon, doll. And I figured as much that

Calvin was one of the owners. We're trying to prove it right now, which is harder than it sounds."

"But what about—"

"Nina, *stop*." His rebuke was short and curt. It sliced through my attempt to speak like a machete. "I told you. I have to account for every source of information I have. I probably shouldn't have even asked you about this Kate character. If I report that you told me this information in confidence, I have to explain the nature of our…relationship…" He looked at me sadly, almost as if that was exactly what he wanted to do. "But if I do that, I'll almost certainly get tossed off the case, and there is no one else who can pursue it. We literally only just brought my boss in on this, and it's been almost a year. Do you understand what I'm saying here?"

I did. Of course I did. We had been over it so many times.

I closed my eyes, and for a moment, I was back in that office, so long ago. I was looking at the papers, staring at my signature. Watching the chains of this life wrap around me in an iron cocoon.

Matthew was certain this was the only way for any of us—that meant Olivia *and* me—to be free of this captor. I'd have to trust him.

I swallowed. "All right. I won't say anything more."

Matthew stood there for a moment, rubbing his chin while he thought. "Nina, I—"

"What?" I interrupted.

He looked mournful. Sorrowful. "I know I don't have a right to ask you this. But can you…if I got you something, is there any way you could access your hus—Calv—Gardner's cell?" He stumbled over Calvin's name and title like they put a bad taste in his mouth, practically spitting at the end. "It would be a SIM card, like you put in your phone. Do you think you could manage it?"

I opened my mouth to say no. But the need written clearly across Matthew's face stopped me.

"Yes," I said. "I can."

"And then you'll get out of town? Unless you want me listening in on you…"

"Won't they know?" I wondered quietly. "That I'm leaving because of this. Won't they?"

Matthew's jaw tightened. "Not if you do it right. I thought you said that you and your husband barely saw each other as it is."

The defensive note hurt.

"We didn't," I reiterated carefully. "Before he was confined to the state, he was barely home."

"So, maybe your marriage soured a bit with the sudden constant contact," Matthew volunteered acidly. "You might decide to take Olivia to school and stay for a week or two yourself. I don't know. Go to a spa or whatever ladies like you do in the mountains."

I snorted before I could help it. He had no idea how right he was.

"I could go back to school." I said it before I really thought it. But as soon as it was out, I realized it had been circulating for days. Maybe weeks. Maybe even months.

More, I'd told Jane.

What do you want? she had asked.

It was a question I hadn't even dared ask myself for ten years—since I had left Wellesley, come back to New York, and walked straight into the clutches of the man who now owned me.

But he wouldn't for long.

And I needed to reclaim something of myself again. Now…before it was too late.

I looked up. "Do you think that's ridiculous? I never went back, you know. After I had Olivia."

Matthew didn't look surprised.

"I'd be a thirty-year-old junior," I joked. "Hilarious. They'd all think I was their professor."

"I think it's a fuckin' great idea," Matthew said softly. "And if it gets you out of New York…"

He didn't finish the sentence, but I knew what he meant. *All the better.* Though being four hours from him, from the possibility of him… That sounded like torture.

"Yes," I said. "Well. We'll see. How long is it for?"

"Two weeks."

"And will you continue after that?"

Matthew shrugged. "If needed. I can't speak for the NYPD side—unofficially, they do all sorts of surveillance, even if they can't promise everything will be removed; just that it won't be used in court."

I ground my teeth. "And you *really* don't think it will be suspicious if I suddenly leave?"

Matthew shoved a hand back through his thick, dark hair. "I don't —fuck, Nina, even if this tips them off, I just—" He shook his head ruefully. "Would you believe me if I said the idea of one of them spooks seeing you naked makes me want to commit murder myself?"

"I don't understand," I burst out. "This is ridiculous. You told me I had to stay in my marriage to keep myself safe, and so I have, and now you're telling me to leave, but—"

"I said you had to stay married to him, not stay *with* him," Matthew snapped.

"So it's *my* fault I stayed in my own home? Is that what you're saying?"

"What? No. *Fuck*!" Again, his hand shoved through his hair, leaving it standing up slightly in the back. Disturbing his normally impeccable veneer. "Look, I can't pretend it's easy to send you back there. It kills me, and you know it! But this—all this—will get you out of it in the end. If—if that's still what you want."

"Of course it's what I want!" I was practically shouting, now. "But *I*'m not the one making snide jealous comments, Matthew. And I'm not pretending there's a happy ending for us at the end of this either."

"Who's pretending, huh? I never said anything like that."

"I. Know," I gritted out. "Believe me, I know. What do you want me to say here?"

Matthew's jaw quivered. His deep eyes tracked up and down my body once, twice, maybe more. He opened and closed his mouth several times, like he was rehearsing arguments that bubbled to the surface only to be tamped down again.

"Seriously, doll," he said, more softly now. "What do you want *me* to say?"

The air between us crackled. I had never wanted to touch him more, but at the same time, my chest was heavy with overwhelming sadness. This is how it would always be. No one would come out of this anything but alone.

He was doing his best.

That was all I could ask of him.

"Nothing," I said as my heart broke all over again. "Nothing at all."

He closed his eyes and exhaled through his nose. Then he opened his mouth to speak.

"Fine," he said. "I won't."

And then he kissed me.

CHAPTER TWENTY

O nce again, I kissed him back. I'd always kiss him back; I knew that now. Kissing Matthew was as natural to me as breathing. I couldn't touch him and not respond. Just like I couldn't be around him and not love him.

Even so, this was different.

Yes, it had been two months since our meeting at the Grace. Close to a month before that, a similar rendezvous. But this—raw, urgent, unstoppable—in the middle of the woods, where no one would find us and at the same time, anyone could. Somehow, it was completely different.

"I can't," he said in between kisses as we stumbled through the dirt and into the solid trunk of my favorite old oak. "Goddammit, Nina, I can't fucking stop."

"I know. Oh, *God*, I know." My words were whimpers in between starving lunges for his lips, his cheeks, any part of him I could find. It really did feel like, in this moment, I needed him to breathe.

"Wanting you. Loving you. Needing you." His teeth scraped under my jaw like he was trying to consume me. "Do you understand? It's ruining me."

I winced, even as my fingers curled into the slightly damp thickets

222 THE PERFECT WOMAN

of his hair. Oh, I understood that too. True, I was ruined in too many ways to count long before I met him. But since that fateful night, I'd become utterly shattered. I didn't recognize myself anymore.

I was no longer Nina Evelyn Astor de Vries Gardner. In his arms, I was a phantom being, somehow truer than anyone I had ever been, but at the same time, nameless.

I existed simply for this.

His hands slipped past the waistband of my breeches, taking harsh handfuls of flesh as he twisted us around and backed me up against the tree.

"Fuck," he muttered as he yanked at the buttons and fly. "Get this off. Get everything off."

"We shouldn't," I whispered even as I helped him, pulling hard enough that I feared I might rip the zipper.

"We must," Matthew argued back with a groan as his hands found bare skin.

He sank to his knees there on the forest floor, bringing my pants with him until they were piled atop my riding boots. His palms slid up and down my thighs while he pressed his lips to the smooth skin of each and inhaled deeply. The cross and the saint hanging from the chain around his neck clinked lightly.

The first time he had ever done this to me, we were high above the city, protected by the penthouse at the Grace. Since then, a few more times—once at his home, twice more at the Grace. But somehow, it was here, that I was truly in awe.

A man like this.

On his knees.

Like a gesture of prayer. A gesture of worship.

For me.

If I hadn't been positively enraptured by the sight, I wouldn't have believed it.

And then, as his tongue flickered between my thighs, I didn't have time to consider beliefs at all. Desire shot through me like an arrow. I fell back against the old oak, mindless of the bark against my back. Pinioned between the tree and Matthew, I was locked upright while he continued with his work. My fingers twisted through his thick black locks, and I pulled and moaned while he slipped one finger inside me, followed by another.

"Christ, baby"—his voice vibrated against the most sensitive part of me—"you're soaked."

His frank observation only made me that much more heated.

One day, I thought, *I will worship you like you worship me.*

Unlike anything else, I was certain I was up to the task. It felt like the only thing I was put on this earth to do at all.

"Mrs. Gardner?"

We both froze. Matthew stopped his work, and I suddenly felt like the wind had been completely knocked out of me.

From his knees, Matthew looked up at me and mouthed, "Who the fuck is that?"

I twisted so I was looking around the trunk to where Kellan sat atop one of the horses on a trail not twenty feet away. "Oh, hello, Kellan," I called in a voice just slightly too strained to sound credible.

"Mrs. Gardner?" he called again from the other side of the grove. "Are you all right?"

From his knees, Matthew grinned lasciviously at me. His green eyes twinkled from where he was resting his chin just below my navel. I had never wanted to slap him or kiss him more.

Then, he shocked me even more by slipping his hand between my legs again.

"I—yes," I creaked over my shoulder. "Just—just taking a moment to myself."

"Are you stuck, Mrs. Gardner? There's a bog over there that's deadly."

The finger tickled my delicate entrance.

I tipped my head up. "I'm *fine,* Kellan. Thank you!"

"I expect Ms. Olivia will come by to see Sunshine soon, don't you think?"

Matthew's shoulders vibrated with mirth, but he didn't stop. Two fingers slipped completely back in, joined again by his mouth just two inches or so higher.

"Yes!" I shouted.

There was silence over my shoulder as I started to shake. Matthew's other hand dug into my thigh to keep me still.

"Oh my God," I breathed lightly. "Oh my *God*."

"I'll just head back to the stables and get Sunshine ready, then, Mrs. Gardner," Kellan finally called out. "You come on soon."

The finger inside me curved. Matthew's lips sucked. I came. My entire body began to shake, tremble. Intensely, violently, yet imperceptible and silent. Thank God Kellan was half-blind. I was a leaf in the wind, fully at the mercy of the black-haired devil between my legs. And completely and totally in heaven.

I barely registered the sound of the horse and rider receding into the woods as I gradually drifted back down from my impenetrable high. Matthew's breath was warm against my thigh until suddenly it was gone, and just as suddenly, I was flipped around to hold tight to the tree and a pair of impossibly strong hands yanked my hips back.

"Matthew!" I hissed as I clawed at the bark. "Kellan—"

"Is gone," he cut me off, then thrust inside me in one quick, merciless movement. "Fuuuuuuuuck."

His voice was a rumble of desire against my neck. He pulled my hair to one side, burying his nose in it and inhaling deeply. Then he licked my neck, a long, luxurious swipe like I was something succulent, a fruit, a treat, fastened his mouth under my jaw, and sucked. Hard.

The effect was immediate. The desire that had burned through me so quickly before was raging once again as he moved.

"Do you remember?" he muttered as one hand drifted over my bottom, a thumb playing lightly over the other, more forbidden opening there. "That first night? Right here?"

Did I remember? I had practically begged him for it that night. I still didn't know what had come over me. In my mind, we had only the one night. I had never done anything like that before, and I had known without a doubt that I had wanted this man in every way possible, thinking I'd never have the chance again.

Just like I had felt every time since.

"You were so tight," Matthew murmured as he surged forward, again and again. "So fucking tight."

His thumb pressed, penetrated slightly. My chin tipped toward the sky as I arched back toward him. Lord, there was nothing like this. He was so big, I was so ready, and together we were...

"Perfect," Matthew rumbled again. He began to quicken his pace. He took hold of my hips even tighter, then moved one hand around to find my clit again. "Can you? Right here for me, baby? Will you let go so I can feel it?"

My body began to shake. I was surrounded by friction—Matthew inside me, his hand on my clit, the other on my backside. Teeth on my neck, the tree under my cheek. A moan escaped me, a siren from the depths of my soul. Matthew plunged forward and bit my skin. The hand between my legs pinched every so lightly. And I fell apart. *We* fell apart. Together, animals in nature. Lovers in heaven.

If only, my addled brain thought as I slowly returned to consciousness, *we belonged there.*

I sagged into the tree, barely registering Matthew's slow return to normal breathing, then his careful movements to put us both back together. When at last he had pulled my breeches back into place, then turned me gently to fasten them, I was already crying. Two silent streams of tears fell down my cheeks all over again.

The same emotions I felt were echoed all over his stark, beautiful face.

Love.

Anger.

Desperation.

Shame.

Matthew slipped a warm hand around my neck and pulled me close, tucking my chin into his chest so he could stroke my hair.

"Shh, baby. I know. I know."

"I just—why can't—how could—"

The words were choked between sudden violent sobs. Matthew rocked me back and forth, soothing my pain and perhaps his own too.

And after all, this was likely it. I already knew there was no way I could stay through the weekend. I needed to go home. Gather my things and Olivia's. Find some way to convince my husband I needed to leave for a few weeks without looking suspicious.

Once I was gone, there would be no reason to see Matthew again. He would be in New York. I would be...wherever I was.

But not with him.

And so the questions remained—though neither of us said them aloud as we clung to each other, hidden in the forest.

How could something so wrong feel so utterly right?

How could the universe be so cruel as to keep us apart?

———

WE WALKED BACK SLOWLY, hand in hand through the trees, then dropping them eventually as we came into sight of the house.

"I think we're going to go home tonight," I said quietly. "I—it's for the best."

Matthew looked like he wanted to argue, but didn't. He knew I was right. There were arrangements to be made. He needed to do his work. I needed to figure things out.

The house loomed before us, the driveway containing a few more cars than when we left. Yes, it was definitely time to leave.

I opened my mouth to say as much, but before I could, something else caught my eye. Something absolutely catastrophic.

"What is it, doll?" Matthew asked. "Nina, what's wrong?"

I turned away, closed my eyes, and took a moment to smooth on the implacable mask I had been trained to wear since birth. Then I turned back and fixed my expression to a hard scowl. Matthew looked startled.

"What the hell?" he murmured.

I continued to scowl, not even worrying about the frown lines undoubtedly appearing because of it.

"I'm sorry," I said, between my teeth as if I were completely angry. "I'm not upset with you. But my husband just pulled up, and if I don't look angry to see you...well, it's going to be..."

"Nina?"

Matthew's green eyes flew wide open with sudden comprehension. "Shit."

He shoved his hat back on, effectively shading his expression until he was able to control it. Then we both turned around to face my husband.

Calvin stood in the driveway, looking sweaty and rumpled from what must have been a long drive here from Manhattan. He had emerged from one of several cars we paid a fortune to store but hardly used.

"What the hell is he doing here?" Calvin demanded. He slammed the Mercedes door shut and strode across the driveway, kicking up bits of gravel as he went.

"That's exactly what I was asking Mr. Zola," I said with as much disdain as I could muster. "I just finished a ride to discover that he was here. Snooping around our family business."

"I am an invited guest with a right to basic conversation," Matthew said casually. "Your cousins and I go back a bit, if you recall. I was invited for the weekend. I apologize, Mr. Gardner. I'll just get my things and be on my way."

He nodded briefly at me, then at Calvin.

"That fucking wop rat," he seethed as he watched him disappear into the house.

"What's wrong?" I asked, unsure if I wanted to hear the answer.

Calvin was still watching the now-closed doors. "He's been asking around about—you know what, don't worry about it. He's just a cockroach, nothing more."

"Was it—" I caught myself before I mentioned the strange woman Matthew had named earlier. "Did he find anything?"

Calvin just shook his head. "Don't bother, princess. I know you don't care about me, just your own precious neck. No one has connected anything back to you, so far as I can tell."

The tension around my chest lightened. Some. Something else told me it was only a matter of time.

"Maybe…" I started, but then, another possibility occurred to me. "Maybe I should go north, then. Tie things up. They'll be watching you, but not me, I think. I could take Olivia to school. Maybe get away for a bit myself. Actually, I was considering taking a class. Maybe even work on finishing my degree, you know—"

"Nina, will you just stop babbling?" Calvin snapped. "Honestly, I don't have time for this. I'm under investigation."

I stared at the ground, waiting for the anger in my face to fall away again. "I only meant I could check on the other houses. Facilitate their sale, if that's what you need."

"I—all right, fine. Sure, yes, I'll give you a list. No sales though. Just contingency plans." He was obviously happy to have me out from underfoot for some reason. Perhaps Matthew's attempt to bug the house was a good one after all.

"You said the…papers…were done a long time ago, right?" I asked. "You said you weren't involved anymore. Is that—is it true?"

Calvin's eye gleamed. "Yes. Yes, that's right."

Then why don't I believe you? I wanted to say.

Before I could say anything else, Matthew, followed by Jane, emerged from the house. He was carrying his overnight bag and had replaced his swim shorts and open shirt with a smarter outfit of light gray pants and a white Oxford shirt, rolled up at the cuffs. His straw fedora was still in place, but he had on his sunglasses again, likely to mask his eyes better than I was able to manage.

"Do whatever you want," Calvin was saying. "As long as it takes heat off me, I'm all for it. It's about time you started contributing to this goddamn mess anyway instead of being so fucking useless."

I trained my stare carefully on the ground, but the sudden fire on Matthew's face was evident even in my peripheral vision as he and Jane approached.

"Nina?" Jane called. "Zola just said he's leaving, do you know why —oh!" She caught sight of Calvin and stopped short. "What are you doing here?"

Calvin turned, his face flushed. "This is *my* family's house. Which you maneuvered your way into less than a year ago, thanks."

Jane's bright red mouth dropped. "Ex*cuse* me?"

"Calvin!" I cut in. "Really, that's inappro—"

"Zola is a dear friend of mine and Eric's," Jane cut right back. "Who, if you don't remember, has been a part of this family his entire life, without selling anyone out, by the way!"

"Jane." Matthew rubbed his face. He obviously didn't want her saying anything to Calvin right now.

"For the last damn time!" Calvin blustered. "I did *not* sell Eric out to the SEC!"

"Sure, sure," Jane retorted. "You just keep saying that, and I'll keep forgetting it." She turned to me. "And you? Are you all right? I'm almost afraid to leave you alone with this one." She jerked her head at Calvin.

I stiffened. Could she know? No, no one knew. But Matthew stiffened too. I avoided his gaze, penetrating once again through his sunglasses.

"Jane, honestly," I scoffed as disdainfully as I could manage. "What are you thinking? This is my husband, not a common thief."

Calvin's smirk was wide enough that it made his chin wobble. Jane peered between us, and Matthew's mouth was suddenly pressed into a tight line.

"I was just talking about our change of plans as well," I said. "Calvin clearly came to make peace with Eric, and so perhaps it would be better if Olivia and I offered them some privacy, so to speak—"

"Nina, come *on*," Calvin interrupted. "What are you blathering on about?"

I had actually been babbling on purpose to give Jane and Matthew both time to get their own expressions together. But Calvin's terse interjection clarified something else.

"I was just telling Calvin that Olivia and I need to get back to the city," I said, the words tumbling out of my mouth like a waterfall. "I've decided to go back to school this fall, and the term begins after Labor Day."

I had no idea if anything I said was true or even possible, but I would do whatever I could to make it so. In that moment, I had decided, without a doubt, that I would never spend another night in the same house as this man if I could possibly help it. Matthew had given me an opening. I was shoving my way through it.

Jane's mouth fell open again, this time with genuine shock. Matthew's brows rose over his glasses, but he didn't say anything. Calvin looked blindsided, but also kept quiet. The only thing my

husband liked less than my disobedience, of course, was being embarrassed in front of others.

I turned to Calvin. "You were amazingly supportive. I so appreciate
it."

He melted, taken in by the sudden praise. "Yes, well." He reached
out and drew a knuckle down my arm. "Labor Day isn't for another
week and a half. Perhaps you could at least stay the weekend, then,
princess."

On his other side, Matthew started at the use of the nickname. The
one I had snapped at him multiple times *never* to use.

Well. Now he knew why. In part, anyway.

His fists clenched tightly, and his forearms were a sudden twist of
muscle.

I stepped away from Calvin's touch as carefully as I could. "I'm
afraid we have a lot to do, and we need to get up to Boston soon."

"Boston?" Jane repeated, now visibly excited.

"You're going all the way to Boston?" Calvin echoed.

I nodded, ignoring my husband's stunned look. "Yes. When I was
at school, I was at Wellesley. It doesn't make sense to start somewhere
else. Not when I only have a few semesters to finish." I shrugged.
"There will be online options in the spring, I'm sure, but for the fall, I'll
need to be there."

"Do you have a place to stay?" Jane pressed on, suddenly looking
excited. "Because if you don't, you should visit my friends, Skylar and
Brandon. You remember them from our wedding, and I know they'd
love to have you and Liv, and—"

"Oh, I don't know…"

"I could come with!" She grinned. "I love an excuse to see my
bestie. Stay this weekend, and then next we'll make a weekend of it
when you have to take Olivia back to school."

Matthew's face was curiously unreadable. I only felt the walls
closing in. It was becoming more apparent my grand plan to escape
would have to wait a few more days.

I turned back to Jane. "I—I'll think about it. I'm sure it would be
nice to meet someone there."

"I'll call her. She'll want you to stay, I'm sure of it. They are the best." Jane was already pulling out her phone, and a moment later, had sent a brief text. "See, it's done. No going back now."

I opened my mouth to argue, but before I could, Matthew cut in. "Jane."

We all turned to him. Calvin's face reddened all over again, as if he had forgotten Matthew had witnessed the entire exchange, and now was furious at himself for allowing it.

"I should go," Matthew said. "Mr. Gardner has a right to be here, and I don't want to make things awkward between anyone."

He leaned in to deliver a quick kiss to her cheek, and envy stabbed my gut. I wrapped my fingers together and kept my gaze fixed on the gravel, counting the pieces until Matthew and Jane were finished.

"I'll call soon for drinks," he called after her as she disappeared back into the house. Then he turned and tipped his hat at Calvin, who sneered visibly. "And, Mr. Gardner. I'll see you in court."

At the word "court," Calvin's face bloomed a sudden, virulent crimson. He looked like he wanted to punch a hole through one of the car doors with a hammy fist. Before I could stop myself, I flinched. I knew that look well. Very well.

"It was nice to see you again," Matthew interrupted, holding his hand out to me for a polite shake.

Cautiously, I took it, only then feeling the sharp edge of a metal chip sliding between my fingers.

"Everything okay, Mrs. Gardner?" Matthew asked quietly.

I flared, taking my hand back and shoving it into my pocket with the chip. That was all I needed—the slightest bit of concern would turn Calvin into a rage later, if that wasn't already in the cards.

"It will be once you and your mangy little car are off our property, Mr. Zola," I said loudly. And as cruelly as I could manage.

Behind me, Calvin snorted. "I need a drink. Nina. Inside. You'll be at least somewhat social for the *full weekend* before you and Olivia abandon me again."

"Of course," I said. "I need to change, though. Would you like me to take your things up to our room?"

"Fine, sure."

Calvin tossed his phone and everything else at me like I was nothing better than a bellhop. I turned to follow him, feeling like my heart was being torn out of my chest behind me. But as Calvin disappeared up the steps and into the house, I chanced one last look over my shoulder.

Matthew still stood behind his open car door, watching me carefully as I walked away. He had removed his shades, and his gaze was now transparent, green eyes as wide and fathomless as the ocean behind me. Wide. Open. Full of more love than I'd ever seen in my entire life.

As he backed toward his car—the beat-up Accord I'd seen parked outside his house—I pressed my fingers to my mouth and released them, a small gesture of the kiss I so wanted to give.

Matthew didn't respond, too aware of the faces potentially hidden behind the reflective window panes. But his expression didn't shift, and I soaked in that love for one last second before he left.

INTERLUDE II
AUGUST 2018

Matthew

"Come on, you can do it. Throw me the ball, Sof."

I squatted down like a catcher, held out my hands, and pretended to brace myself for the plastic Wiffle ball my four-year-old niece was holding.

But instead of throwing it the ten feet or so across the tiny yard we shared with the other brick houses around our block, Sofia just screwed up her face and began to cry.

My arms dropped. "Shit." I jogged to Sofia and squatted down again, this time to pull the little girl into my arms. "Sofia, honey. What is it? What's wrong?"

"I c-can't *do it!*" she howled.

"Can't do what, Sof?"

"Throw the *ball.*"

I bit back a smile. Like most of the women in my family, Sofia already had a talent for speaking in italics and making a man feel like an idiot in the process.

"What? Of course you can," I crooned as I stroked flyaway hairs from her face. "You nearly broke one of my windows yesterday. That's why we're playing with this sturdy thing instead of my baseball." I tossed the whiffle ball up in the air and caught it easily. "Why don't you think you can throw it, Sof?"

"Because."

"Because why, monkey?"

"Be*cause*!" she shouted. "Because of what those *boys* said to me!"

I cocked my head. She and her mother had just gotten back from Mass, which could only mean one thing. Her cousins had been acting like assholes again. "You mean Tommy and Pete?"

A big, pea-shaped tear welled out of one eye, then slid over Sofia's chubby red cheek. She brushed it away with a thick fist. "Those *boys*," she spat, like the word intimated some terrible creatures that lived in a cave.

I couldn't really fault her there. My nephews were basically gremlins.

"They said," she huffed, "they said"—another hiccup—"they said I throw like a *girl!*"

And like she had just purged some terrible admission, a torrent of tears spilled forth, which she automatically shoved angrily out of her face. Yeah, Sof was definitely a member of the Zola tribe, if for no other reason than her hot temper and stubborn charm. She might have been four, but she didn't like crying any more than the rest of us.

I didn't dwell too long on why that might be.

"Hey," I said, pushing her hand away. "You wanna know the truth, kiddo? They're just jealous."

She blinked, her tiny forehead still wrinkled with a frown. "How do you know, *Zio*. You're a boy too."

I smacked my hand against my heart, like she had just shot me through with an arrow.

She giggled. Progress.

"I know *because* I'm a boy, Sof," I told her.

She eyed me suspiciously, like she was trying to see if I was messing with her too. "*Zio*, don't trap-uh-nize me."

It took me a second to figure out what she meant, but in the end, I couldn't hold back a laugh. Christ, the things this kid learned from her mother.

"Sof," I said, still chuckling while she scowled. "I swear to God, cutie, I would *never* patronize you."

She stuck her chin out. "That's not what Mommy says. She says you trap-uh-nize everyone."

I swallowed back another laugh, straightened my face, and looked her in the eye. "Listen," I said solemnly. "Girls have secret superpowers And every man knows it, deep down in his guts. That's why they're all scared of you, Sof."

Her eyes blinked, wide and dark. "But I don't *want* them to be scared of me, *Zio*."

I cocked my head. "Why not, baby girl? You don't want to be the big bad Sofia?"

She shook her head, curls bouncing. "No. I just want to play ball too."

I sighed. Wasn't that the truth? Deep down, all anyone really wanted was to play ball with everyone else. Power, prestige. Teasing, yelling. It was all just a cover-up for that desire, deep down, to be close to others.

"Well, then," I said. "We just need to make you the best ball player there is, cutie. And if those hooligans say you play ball like a girl, you can just say, 'That's right. You jealous, clown boys?'"

"Mattie!"

We both turned to find Frankie on the back porch, a scowl on her face, hands on her hips.

"Sofia," she called. "We do not call names."

Sofia blinked, suddenly the picture of innocence. "I didn't, Mama. That was *Zio*."

"Oh, I know," Frankie said. "That goes for him too. Now, come on in for lunch. Mattie, Derek's here for you."

Sofia and I collected her ball and climbed the steps back up to the deck, where Frankie had set out a plate of sandwiches for Derek and me.

"You don't want to join us?" I asked before she shepherded Sofia inside.

Frankie's gaze flickered to Derek, then back at me. "No, you guys need to work. We'll just get in the way." And before I could argue, she closed the sliding glass door and disappeared inside.

I turned to Derek, who was watching her. He sighed.

"I take it your last date didn't go so well," I said as I picked up a sandwich.

Derek had been casually seeing my sister for a few months now with my blessing. To be honest, I didn't think Frankie could do much better, and Sofia needed a man in her life besides her good-for-nothing uncle.

"Eh." Derek shrugged. "We had a nice time, but it's not going anywhere."

I frowned. "What do you mean? I thought things were all right. You took her to a Mets game, right?"

"I thought we were having a good time, but then someone called. And, I don't know, she changed." He shrugged. "It was pretty clear her attentions were occupied somewhere else."

I frowned. I hadn't heard anything about this, but my sister wasn't exactly open about her personal life with me either. She hadn't even told me she was pregnant with Sofia until she was too far along to hide it anymore.

Derek didn't expound any more on the situation, and I wasn't one to meddle.

"Well, sorry, man," I said. "I would have liked to see things work out."

He took a bite of his food, closed his eyes with pleasure as he chewed, then swallowed. "Me too. She makes a damn good sandwich."

I snorted. That right there told me these two weren't a good match. Frankie was as good a cook as anyone raised by our grandmother, but she was the type of woman who didn't like to be valued based on that sort of thing. If I'd heard "I'm no man's maid" once, I'd heard it a hundred damn times.

"Anyway, I'm sorry to bother you on a Sunday," Derek said, pulling out his phone. "I know you've been pulling extra hours getting ready for trial. But I thought you'd want to see this."

I beckoned for the phone. "Don't worry about that. You know

we've been stuck for a while. Pray to fuckin' God something turns up with the bugs on Gardner's apartment, because otherwise, we're going to lose on appeals."

"Well, check this out."

Derek pressed play, and a blurry video began on the screen. It was on some nondescript street in an equally nondescript neighborhood that literally could have been any New England city.

A car pulled up to the curb—a big black Escalade that looked very out of place in the neighborhood. A woman exited the passenger side, purse looped over her slim wrist.

"What the fuck is this?" I demanded.

"It's not what," he said, "but who."

In my gut, I knew who it was. But it still felt like I'd been punched when the woman turned, and her familiar, perfect elegance stared back at me through the screen.

"Jesus," I breathed. "Nina?"

Derek said nothing. He didn't officially *know* about my connection with Nina Gardner, but of course had his suspicions, which he'd voiced before.

Nina walked across the sidewalk, looking nervously in both directions as she approached a chain-link fence in front of one of the peeling rowhouses. Derek and I both watched her pass through the gate, up the steps, and knock on the door. A few seconds later, the door opened. It looked as though whoever was on the other side invited her in, but she shook her head.

"Good girl," I murmured, ignoring Derek's inquisitive look. The idea of Nina disappearing inside a house like this made me want to jump through the screen and yank her out of there.

The door closed, but Nina waited on the porch, moving back and forth from heel to heel while she peered around the neighborhood. A few minutes later, the door opened, and this time a man exited to stand next to her on the porch. He was tall with graying hair and a mustache, and wore a pair of old jeans and a t-shirt that I could tell was badly stained under the arms even from this far away.

"Who is that?" I asked.

"*That*," Derek said. "Is Ben Vamos."

"The guy you found on the census?"

Derek nodded. "Yeah, we got another break, Zo. Some of the Newark department stepped up to help. Turns out Ben Vamos is a known entity around there. Slumlord, low-level crack dealer too. This video is theirs. Weird story, actually. Hungarian immigrant, but he grew up running for the Russian mob here and there before he started his own enterprise. In 1990, right before the census count, his wife was killed during a raid when his relationship with the Russians went south. She had a daughter from her previous marriage."

"Little Katarina Csaszar, whoever she is," I said, following along.

"That's right," Derek said. "According to the Newark boys, he brought Sara Berto, his wife's cousin, over from Hungary to help with the girl. They think Károly Kertész—otherwise known as Calvin Gardner—was Sara's cousin but he was already here. They all moved into Ben's house like some Hungarian Brady Bunch."

"Here's the story…" I added, but Derek just kept going.

"Ben got Calvin wrapped into his business. Small-time shit, mostly. Meth deals, maybe a car jack here and there. Then, from what I can tell, Ben got lucky. Another relative died of cancer and left him everything he had, which included a shitty house in Pompton Lakes, plus the remains of a hefty settlement from Dupont."

I raised a brow. "From the chemical spill?"

Derek nodded. "Looks that way."

I turned back to the video, which now showed Nina chatting with the man. As Vamos chain-smoked two cigarettes in less than three minutes, she kept pushing a nonexistent piece of hair behind one ear. Though I couldn't hear the conversation, it was clear she was uncomfortable. I didn't blame her. He was the last person I'd ever expect to be standing next to someone like Nina, much less someone she would seek out.

"So what happened to the money?" I asked, wishing I could hear the conversation. Or maybe not. From this perspective, I could only see the back of Nina's head, but Vamos was leering openly at her. I didn't like it. At all.

"He took that money and started investing it in real estate," Derek said. "He owns most of that block right there, and loads like it all over

New Jersey. He's a slumlord, Zo. One that makes a nice chunk of change."

I stifled a growl. The mustachioed gorilla had just stroked Nina's arm. In the video, Nina laughed nervously. She tried to step back from Vamos, but every time, he kept taking steps into her personal space. It was just a video, but I wanted to punch him in the face anyway. *Leave her the fuck alone.*

"Any family left?" I asked. "Sara, maybe?"

Derek shook his head. "Sara went back to Hungary, remember? The Newark guys think she did take Katarina with her. No records of their return."

I grimaced. "So Calvin names a woman on the other side of the fuckin' world as his 'known person.' Go fuckin' figure."

Derek nodded. "Yeah. It looks like that might be the case. But maybe it doesn't matter. Because look."

I stared at the video as Nina reluctantly shook Vamos's hand, then slid around him on the porch. He didn't leave her much room, forcing her to press her body against his greasy one in order to leave. He clearly enjoyed making her uncomfortable.

"Fuck," I muttered. Watching this was torture.

Nina exited the property and got back into the Escalade, then drove away. Vamos remained on the porch, taking his sweet time as he smoked another cigarette, looking up and down the sidewalk until it was finished. And then, finally, he disappeared back into the house.

The video ended. For the first time, I wondered if I had made a mistake in not letting her tell me what she knew about her husband's dealings. I had assumed that she was mostly in the dark, considering how estranged they were most of the time. But on top of that, anything I discovered through her would have been grounds for my potential disbarment. So really, it *was* better that I was discovering it this way.

It didn't make it any easier to take, though.

"He did all that off a settlement?" I asked finally. "The property, everything?"

Derek looked at me like I was an idiot. "Zo, come on."

"Okay, so what, a silent partner?"

Derek nodded. "We tracked it down. Most of his properties are owned jointly between him and an LLC that's registered in Delaware."

I looked up. "Don't fuck with me. It cannot be that easy."

Derek nodded, filling the gaps. "No jokes, my friend. Ben Vamos and Pantheon co-own about twenty houses in the New England area. Could be more. We got guys in Connecticut, Jersey, and Massachusetts now helping to track them down. Starting with this one where your girl paid a little visit."

"Then why wasn't Calvin there?" I demanded. "Why the fuck would *she* be there instead?"

Derek just looked sorry for me, like I was a lost puppy and he wanted to pat my head.

"I'm sorry, Zo," he said. "I really am. But you gotta face it: your girl's involved. I think she needs a bug. And probably a tail on her too."

Dread filled the pit in my stomach. Like I'd been punched before and now someone had filled that hole with cement.

"All right," I said, my mouth feeling wooden. "I'll get the warrant tomorrow." I couldn't stop staring at the video, now frozen back on a frame of the Escalade, Nina's head silhouetted through the window. Then, another thought occurred to me. "She, ah, she mentioned she's going to Boston. Taking her daughter up to school there, and she's planning to take some classes at Wellesley herself. Stay up there for a while."

Derek's eyes opened wide. *"What?* Shit. Zola, we won't be able to plant anything if she leaves the city. That's way beyond our jurisdiction."

"I know."

I worried my mouth, then pressed play on the video. I needed to see this again. And again and again if necessary in order to do what needed to be done.

"I—I can get it planted," I said slowly. I kept my eyes trained on the video, hoping to God Derek wouldn't understand exactly *how* I could make that happen. "I can do a lot more than that. If you want. She leaves on Wednesday, and she, um, she likes me."

Derek gave me a long look that I chose not to address.

"She'll tell me what we want to know," I kept on. "She'll—she'll let me get close. All the way to Boston, even. If that's what we want." I shrugged. "No one has to know."

I shouldn't have doubted my partner. When I looked up again, full comprehension shone in his eyes. But to my relief, there was no judgment there. Maybe some pity. After all, what I was suggesting wasn't strictly legal, though it was by no means uncommon. It was more that he understood the personal cost of it.

"All right," Derek said, standing up. "I'm going to get a glass of water."

And give you a second to come to terms with this. He didn't say it out loud. He didn't have to.

He went inside, and I was left there with the video. I watched again as Nina shied from Vamos's greasy touch. As she spoke to him with awkward familiarity.

"Christ, doll," I murmured as she sidled past him once more. "What the hell have you gotten yourself into?"

III

CHIAROSCURO

THEN

CHAPTER TWENTY-ONE

MAY 2009

"This looks amazing."

Nina smiled as she and Caitlyn both surveyed the lavish spread in front of them. The long dining room table was still mostly empty, but one end was jammed with Nina's favorite foods she had enjoyed in Florence: *penne strascicate*, a platter of grilled peppers and other vegetables, fried artichokes, and a rare, aged Wagyu steak sliced into thin ribbons on a cutting board. It was a bit much for a lunch for two twenty-one-year-olds, but she was in the mood for things she hadn't had the heart or stomach for in fully a year.

After all, it was almost time to celebrate.

"It really does look splendid, Marguerite," Nina told the cook. "Thank you so much. I know I made things difficult with the recipes."

Marguerite merely beamed in response, then stepped back to wait for other instructions.

"It's been *ages* since you've hosted me for lunch, you know," Caitlyn babbled on. "I was beginning to think you had forgotten about all of us, tucked in your own world here with the baby. Madison said you even skipped spring fittings in Paris."

Nina shrugged. She couldn't care less about her couture wardrobe anymore, nor any of the silly girls who once made the semi-annual trips with her. "It's an easy world to be tucked into. And I don't mind doing it."

"Isn't that what the nanny is for, though? Honestly, N, I really don't understand why you don't just leave the baby at home with people you hired to take care of her."

"I didn't actually hire her. That was Calvin's doing."

Caitlyn watched with barely conceded disdain as Nina took Olivia out of the pram and cradled her against her silk-covered shoulder. Her Prada blouse would have to be laundered immediately, if it could be saved at all from the horrors of spit-up. There were worst things.

"What do you think, darling?" she cooed to Olivia. "Should Mama let other people raise you?"

"Oh, N. I didn't mean it like that."

But Nina was too happy to have company and good food to be annoyed for long. This meal, after all, was supposed to be an olive branch of sorts. And it was true—she had neglected Caitlyn and many others over the past few months.

She couldn't really explain why, exactly, she wanted to remain alone with the baby. Call it a mother's sixth sense. Maybe it was just hysteria. But for whatever reason, she always felt like something genuinely might happen to her daughter if she weren't right by her side.

The baby cooed, her temper settled by the simple embrace. Olivia's eyes, a dark, deep brown compared to Nina's gray, twinkled brighter than the chandelier above them, and for a moment, Nina was looking at her child's father. Her *real* father.

Peppe. With any luck, she'd see him soon.

"Please don't wait for me," she said to Caitlyn. "I'm sorry, I just have to feed Livy—otherwise I won't be able to take more than two bites." She turned. "Marguerite, can you bring some wine for Caitlyn, please? The *Poliziano*, please."

Marguerite bobbed, then left to retrieve the wine. While Caitlyn began dishing herself up, Nina pulled an earlier prepared bottle from the custom Celine bag at her feet, a gift from her mother when she had returned from the spring season in Paris. It was a little odd to be using a one-of-a-kind handbag to store diapers and bottles, but Nina had to admit, she quite liked it.

"What?" she asked Caitlyn, who was making a surprised face at the paraphernalia. "I *am* her mother. And for the record, while I do have help, I like doing this."

Seven months into the job now, it still felt strange to say it. Strange, and yet completely normal. She *was* her mother. As completely and more emphatically than Nina had ever been...anything.

"I'm just shocked," Caitlyn said, nodding at the bottle. "Calvin seemed to think you were going to nurse her forever."

Nina frowned as Olivia pushed the bottle away, as she often did. "I still pump, but I'm trying to get her used to the bottle for the times when I do leave her with someone else." Then, something else occurred to her. "You talk to Calvin about breastfeeding?"

"I—no. We just ran into each other at a lunch or something." Caitlyn waved a hand through the air like she was batting away a fly, then spooned some vegetables onto her plate. "He happened to mention it."

Nina blinked, then focused on trying to get Olivia to take the bottle again. She still generally didn't care for it when her mother was readily available.

"People act like six or seven months is an eternity," she said. "Many women do this for years, you know."

Caitlyn snorted. "Good lord, could you imagine a toddler walking up to you and asking for it like a box of crayons or something?"

Nina shrugged. Perhaps a year ago she might have snarked at the notion, but these days, she felt more and more that no one was in the position to judge what a mother did for her child.

Nina didn't mention how many times Calvin also commented jealously on the state of her breasts. She didn't understand why. Aside from the fact that they were small, never anything to write home about, it wasn't like he had ever touched them anyway. Or ever would.

One month, Peppe. I'm coming.

In just one more month, this miserable year of marriage she and Calvin had promised each other would be over. She would move on, and her first order of business after the imminent divorce was going to

Florence and introducing Giuseppe to his daughter. She hadn't yet gotten up the nerve to contact her former lover, but that was neither here nor there. The tickets were purchased. The summer villa rented.

After that…who knew?

"Come on, darling," she cooed to Olivia. "Take the bottle so Mama can have a bite with her friend."

But it was no use. Olivia batted and pawed at Nina's shirt, shoving the rubber nipple away until finally, Nina conceded.

"I'll be right back," she said to her friend. "It won't take more than twenty minutes, and then I can put her down."

"Oh, you don't have to leave," Caitlyn said, waving her fork around. "Trust me, ever since Kayla 'breast is best' Cartwright had hers last March, she's been whipping it out all over the place. Central Park, Bergdorf's, you name it. Half of New York could probably sketch her nipple from memory."

Nina hid a smile. While she was so far the youngest of her own cohort to have children, it didn't surprise her that there would be a few of the older ones—new money, mostly—to embrace what they saw as more "natural" methods of childrearing. She, however, generally fed her daughter alone, lest she risk the shame of her husband or the prying eyes of staff. She honestly couldn't imagine nursing Olivia in public. But then again, there were a lot of things she couldn't imagine doing these days.

And it really had been a long time since she had seen her friend.

"All right," she said, almost nervous as she unbuttoned her blouse. "I will."

"Good job, N. Live a little," Caitlyn joked even as Olivia craned her head eagerly.

"*What* are you doing?"

Both girls whirled around, and Nina yanked her shirt closed.

"Oh, hello," she said as Calvin entered the room. "I thought you were traveling again this week. I wasn't expecting you until tomorr— Mother? *Grand*mother?"

"Hello, Nina."

Calvin stepped aside to reveal Violet, as addled as ever by the effects of Valium and likely a Bloody Mary within the hour, followed by the petite, imperious, and extremely sober Celeste de Vries, who peered around the yawning dining room as though she were inspecting a starving artist's garret apartment. This, of course, was the bigger surprise. Celeste de Vries didn't visit other people. They came to her.

"I see you haven't done much to the place," she remarked dryly as she walked in. "I had expected more of you, Nina. My cousin had such terrible taste in wallpaper."

"She really did," agreed Violet as she examined the teal jacquard. "God, look at it. It must have been done when *I* was a child." She turned brightly, if slightly vacantly, to her daughter. "Hello, darling! I was at Mother's when your *lovely* husband paid us a house call. We decided to return the favor."

She smiled, revealing a row of bright white caps, but the expression didn't reach her eyes. Nina rocked Olivia, who was starting to fuss again.

"I—I'm sorry. I, I've been busy. As you must remember." Nina gulped, not knowing exactly what else to say. What did she really care about wallpaper at the moment? She had a baby to take care of, and it was only now, seven months into the job, that she was starting to feel a little like she was getting the hang of it.

But the entire situation was odd. Her mother barely remembered she existed on the best of days, and her grandmother called people to her, not the other way around. What on earth was going on?

She didn't have time to find out. As if to reinforce her mother's point, Olivia gave a great yowl. Caitlyn smiled at her plate while Nina pushed back from the table.

"I'll only be a moment. I just need to feed Livy," she said as she stood up. "Marguerite made more than enough if you would like to join us."

But Celeste's voice stopped her before she could make her exit.

"Nina."

How could a single word carry so much force? And yet, Nina couldn't ignore its pull. Not from the one person whose opinion she had ever cared for. She never understood how she could be so terrified by Celeste and yet desperately admire her at the same time.

"Cook, for God's sake, get the nurse," Calvin snapped just as Marguerite reentered the room with the wine.

Her eyes widened as she caught sight of the other visitors, and wordlessly, she bobbed and dashed off in the direction of the nursery.

Nina frowned. "Calvin, was that really necessary?"

Her husband's pale, shiny face gleamed with resentment. "I think it was. Otherwise what am I paying her for?"

"What are *you* paying her for?" Nina echoed softly.

Despite the fact that Calvin's face turned roughly the color of an eggplant, she couldn't help herself. It was the little things like that which had, frankly, come to drive her crazy over the last year. Calvin seemed to have forgotten the terms of this arrangement. He had forgotten whose fortune really paid for this lifestyle.

Or maybe, Nina thought as she tried not to shy from his insipid glare, he hadn't forgotten at all. Perhaps he had just begun to hate her for it instead.

Denial was a powerful, powerful thing.

Nina swallowed and turned to her grandmother. "I'll only be a moment," she said as Olivia continued to squall, tiny arms flailing.

"That won't be necessary." Celeste beckoned to the nurse, who had just appeared in the room behind Marguerite. "You there."

"Her name is Greta," Nina put in, only to receive sharp glances from both Celeste and Calvin.

"Take the child," Celeste spoke louder, her voice dripping with disdain, as though Olivia's cries were personal insults toward her. "I assume you have formula and anything else you might require in the nursery. Please feed the child and bring her back when she is less…obtrusive."

Nina's mouth dropped. "Grandmother, perhaps you misunderstand. I'm still nursing. She won't take a bottle, so I need to breastfeed her—"

"Nina."

Celeste's voice was a gavel on the heavy wood dining table, the judgement clear. The de Vrieses were masters of propriety on the outside, scheming and vengeful underneath. Denoted under Nina's name was a clear message: we do not talk about such things in polite company.

Violet chuckled, her rings clinking lightly on the wineglass she had already helped herself to from the table.

"She did the same to me," she whispered conspiratorially as she came to look at her granddaughter. Almost happily, as if *finally* she could pass on the misery of being Celeste de Vries's daughter to someone else. Her wine sloshed over the rim of her glass, narrowly missing the baby's head.

Nina clutched Olivia closer, and the baby whimpered and burrowed into the silk, looking for a breast.

"Good God, Nina," hissed Calvin from the other side of the table, where he had taken Nina's seat and was already serving himself a full plate. "Don't embarrass us."

Next to him, Caitlyn's eyes glimmered with sympathy. Or maybe it was pity.

Nina opened her mouth to argue. To put her foot down. But before she could, the child was lifted from her arms, the Celine bag picked up from the floor. Olivia immediately started screaming.

"Please remove her before I grow deaf," Celeste snapped at Greta, who left the room with a *very* unhappy baby.

Everyone sat silently while Marguerite scurried around setting three extra plates. Once Olivia's cries were no longer audible, the rest of the party relaxed, though Nina could only stare at her plate, biting back tears and the instinct to sprint after her child.

"Thank you, no," Celeste said when Marguerite tried to pour her a bit of wine. "But perhaps a glass of Perrier..."

"I'll get it." Calvin sprang up from the table, faster than the lap dog Nina thought he was imitating admirably. "Give you, er, a moment to talk."

He and Marguerite both left the room in a hurry.

Caitlyn put her napkin on the table as if to leave as well. "Should I..."

"No, no, don't be silly," Violet chided her. "You're practically one of the family. Mother, look at all this new blonde in her hair. Caitlyn and Nina could be twins!"

Caitlyn preened, as though the thought made her shine a bit brighter, though Celeste remained as steely as ever.

Still irritated by what had happened with Olivia, Nina was too busy noticing Celeste's less-than-immaculate appearance to reply. It wasn't like her grandmother to refuse a glass of wine. Her Hermés scarf, her hair, her nails—that was all in order. But something about Celeste didn't quite look her normally polished self.

"Grandmother," Nina said. "Are you quite well?"

"Quite," Celeste responded, perhaps a little too sharply. "Are *you*?"

Her gray eyes glinted as she cast up and down Nina's body, clearly looking for remnants of Olivia—a bit of spit-up, maybe a stain or two. No luck. Not this time, anyway.

"I couldn't believe it," Celeste continued, "when your husband mentioned you were still doing...*that*"—she waved a disdainful hand in the direction Olivia had gone—"after more than six months. You're depriving that child of solid food, Nina."

Nina reared, dander raised all over again. "Grandmother, the doctors say Olivia will need milk or formula as her primary food source until she is at least one."

"Then formula it should be. You were raised on it, as was your mother. I won't have you ruining your looks just for the sake of your child whose needs can be met otherwise. This family has appearances to keep up, girl."

And there it was. The outright decree that first and foremost, the purpose of the de Vries women was to look pretty and act properly.

"So, of course, when your husband mentioned your *habit*, we came straight over," Celeste concluded.

Nina nearly choked on her bite of salad. "Calvin reported me to you for feeding my own daughter?"

Violet snorted in a most unladylike way, but quickly covered it before she caught too much of her mother's ire. "Goodness, no. He came because he wanted more of Mother's money. Another ten million dollars at least, he said."

Nina's mouth opened and closed several times. "He wanted *what*?"

Caitlyn studied her plate, rearranging her vegetables in row after row. Violet snickered behind her wineglass.

Celeste, however, merely arched a silver brow. "You didn't know?"

"Didn't know what?" Nina asked. "About today's request? Or that they amounted to that much?"

"About the *multiple* monetary requests your husband has made over the past year." Celeste tipped her head. "After the gift *you* made from your own trust, I assumed you were aware of the others. Now that he has exhausted the allowances the board gave him from *your* fund, he has come to me."

Nina shook her head vigorously as she took a long drink of water. "No, I—no, Grandmother, I assure you I did *not* know."

"What is this business he's doing, Nina?" Violet wondered. "It was very strange the way he appeared. He was sweating all over Garrett when he came into the parlor to talk to Mother, but when he saw me there, he didn't want to say." She tossed back a bit more of her wine and giggled lightly to herself. "It took us ages to get anything out of him."

Celeste rolled her eyes while Caitlyn hid a smile behind her napkin.

"His business, Nina," Celeste said. "What is it?"

Nina sighed. Most of the time her mother's semi-permanent state of minor intoxication was only slightly annoying. Right now, though, Nina wanted to shove her back into the elevator.

"I—it's a real estate venture, I believe," she said, stumbling slightly.

"Yes, I know that. But I failed to see how anything in the business proposal he submitted last year explains a need for the kind of additional funding he wants. Do you know what it is?"

"It's—I—" Nina's cheeks reddened. She really knew very little about what Calvin was doing with their money beyond his claims of "flipping properties," largely because she simply didn't care. "He needed something to do, Grandmother. How is this any different from Mother's charities, or even my father's ventures?"

Violet coughed into her drink. "Your *father*?" she asked. "Are you really comparing your husband of less than a year to a man I've been married to for more than twenty-five?"

"Well, at least Calvin is here," Nina snapped, hardly believing that she was defending him. Still, her parents' so-called marriage was a joke, and everyone knew it.

He'll be gone in a month! she wanted to shout. *You don't need to worry about this anymore!* But of course, no one in this room knew of the arrangement. No one ever could know.

"Nina Evelyn Astor de Vries *Gardner*," pronounced Celeste, emphasizing the final name as if to remind Nina that she was not technically part of the de Vries family any longer. "Do you mean to tell me that this family has funneled nearly ten million dollars to your husband, and you have no clue what he has done with it?"

It was a trinket compared to her family's vast fortune, but the reality was that there was only one way he could have gotten twice what she had conceded, by somehow forging her signature on the request to the board.

"I—I—I—" she stuttered, only reinforcing her grandmother's impression of her idiocy.

"Nina's right, it *is* real estate," Caitlyn's cheery voice interrupted the detente, causing everyone at the table to swivel toward her. She blinked, looking around at her sudden audience. "Calvin and I ran into each other at lunch last week, and I—well, he told me a bit about it. Would you...like me to share?"

"Please," said Celeste with a sharp look at Nina. "Since Nina is apparently too caught up with rattles to pay any attention."

Caitlyn swallowed heavily. "Well, um, it's this project he's doing. He buys in outlying areas around New York. Towns that are starting the upswing as commuter areas, but where the market hasn't quite followed yet. Basically, he's flipping properties that have turned commercial, but he's using his, um, knowledge of the area to do it."

"Why wouldn't he just do it all in one part of town?" Celeste wondered. "How can he manage property all over New York? And now I gather this has already expanded into the greater New England area. Isn't that spreading himself a bit thin? He'll need a different accountant for every state."

"Um, I think it's diversifying, he said?" Caitlyn stumbled around the language, ending her sentences as questions. "Better than putting all his eggs in one basket?"

Nina studied her friend, who did not meet her eye. It must have been quite a lunch she had had with Calvin. Particularly since she didn't think to mention it to her.

Celeste also seemed to think so. She turned to Nina. "I expect you to learn more about this before the family gets further involved. I will not write another check or approve any other requests from your trust until we see a full business plan."

"But, Grandmother—"

Celeste only held up her palm. "That's final. I'll not speak any more about money. It's crude over lunch."

"I couldn't agree more." Calvin's voice boomed as he strode back into the room and deposited a chilled bottle of Perrier next to Celeste, then made a big show of pouring it into her water glass.

Celeste's lip curled as she watched, almost as though she were disgusted by the idea of touching the water after Calvin had.

"Thank you," she said when he finished, though Nina doubted she meant it.

It didn't matter. She had no intention of writing any kind of business plan with Calvin anyway. *One more month*, she thought as she reached for the middle of the table to serve herself some pasta. The ten million could be written off as a divorce payoff. Ending marriages had certainly cost other family members more. Like exile, for one.

Nina sighed. She wasn't sure taking a break from her family would qualify anymore as a punishment.

"Pasta, princess? Really?"

Everyone turned toward Calvin, who was busily forking several pieces of bloody steak onto his plate. Not for the first time, Nina wondered again how a human being with so many resources could always look so ill-fitted to...everything. The arms of his navy jacket pulled around the shoulders, and because he had forgotten to unbutton it at the waist before sitting down, it also tugged oddly around his stomach and the sides. Nina wondered if he was aware that his pants were black and therefore mismatched.

Incredible, she mused. In the last year, she had watched Calvin jump into the trappings of her family's wealth and circle with all the grace of a cow diving into a duck pond. He had acquired all the visual things he perceived as hallmarks of the upper class: the stodgy driver, the ugly heirloom furnishings, the tailor who had last serviced Nina's *grandfather* in the early eighties. And still the man managed to make ten-thousand-dollar custom suits look like polyblend discount rack fare.

"What's wrong with pasta?" she asked through her teeth.

"What *isn't* wrong with it?" Violet babbled, then laughed to herself before taking another gulp of wine. Her plate was completely empty.

Calvin added two more pieces of steak to the mountain he'd already gathered. "That depends. Are you trying to turn back into a refrigerator?"

Violet cringed. Celeste's face didn't move.

"Cal," Caitlyn said, who somehow managed to be friendlier with one syllable than Nina ever could. "It's just a bit of pasta. Plus, Nina and I had spinning this morning. Trust me, she earned it."

"What she *earned* is the right to get rid of those last few pounds," Calvin grumbled. "You heard your grandmother. You have to watch your appearance as a part of this family."

Nina didn't even bother reminding him or anyone else at the table that she was somehow thinner now than she had been before the baby. Depression, she suspected. Not to mention the constant desire to escape her house had her walking all of Central Park with the stroller almost daily.

But the truth was, this had nothing to do with her weight and everything to do with the fact that she still had not, as of yet, allowed Calvin to touch her. The fact that he continued to stumble sporadically into her bedroom in the middle of the night, drunken and irritable after trying to woo prospective "clients" (or so he said) was an entirely different issue and not one she really wanted to take on.

Instead, she reached for the plate with the stubborn set of her jaw as if she were thirteen, not twenty-one. "I'll only have a little."

"Nina," Celeste said just as her granddaughter was reaching for the pasta. "Have the salad. It's nearly summer, and you can't go to the Hamptons looking like that."

Reluctantly, Nina dropped the platter and left it in the center of the table.

"What inspired this feast, N?" Caitlyn asked in an overly friendly voice, clearly trying to break the ice.

"Oh, I don't know," Nina said as she forked a few pieces of escarole. "Memories, I suppose."

Calvin snorted before shoving enough penne into his mouth that the sauce dribbled over his lip. He looked like a sloppy vampire.

"Memories of what?" he asked, mouth full.

"Probably of Italy," Violet tittered. "It *is* Italian food, isn't it?"

Calvin tensed, but didn't reply as he chewed. Celeste's steely expression turned back on Nina.

Maybe it was the plate of plain lettuce that had somehow replaced the rest of her meal, but Nina suddenly felt emboldened. "Yes, I was thinking of visiting again this June. I miss it."

"Oh!" Caitlyn replied. "For your anniversary? What a lovely idea. Are you going to show Calvin your Florence?"

Nina just took another bite of lettuce, wishing bitterly it were the fried artichokes. Calvin stopped sawing his beef; then too carefully, he made a production of unfolding his napkin and proceeding to tuck it into his too-tight collar.

"That will depend," he said just before shoving another piece of bloody steak into his mouth.

"Depend on what?" Nina asked.

"Celeste, I wonder, has anyone heard from Eric lately?" Calvin asked over her question. "Some of my associates have been wondering about him."

"Ooooh, no, no, no," Violet murmured into her wine.

What associates? Nina wondered. So far as she knew, Calvin rented a one-room office space off Wall Street.

Celeste seemed to have the same question on her mind.

Caitlyn perked up, but Nina shook her head. She knew what was coming. This had been a particularly sore subject for her family. Calvin had continued to pepper her family about Eric's whereabouts over the past year, and every time, he received escalating responses of the same sort: No, and it wasn't any of his business.

She didn't know why Calvin was so intent on contacting her errant cousin, but at this point, Nina had no desire to find him either. Yes, she missed the boy who had for all intents and purposes been a brother to her. Yes, she had wondered where he was and if he was all right. But at this point, his continued absence—treating her in particular like she was the same as the rest of their horrid family—was too painful to forgive.

"I have." Celeste surprised everyone before taking a measured sip of her sparkling water.

Everyone turned to her in shock.

"You have?" Violet asked. "Mother, why didn't you say?"

"Where is he?" Nina couldn't help herself. "Is he all right?" Apparently she cared enough to know that much.

"A contact at Dartmouth informed me the boy is moving to Cambridge. He was in Hanover this week requesting recommendations from his professors."

"But...why? Where is he planning to go?" Nina hated herself for the eagerness.

But Cambridge was outside of Boston. Only minutes from Wellesley, the school she had attended until just last year.

"Apparently he's planning to apply to law school in the fall," Celeste said wearily, as though the very thought of it tired her out. "So said Charlie Reynolds, at any rate."

Charles Reynolds was the president of Dartmouth College.

"Another stage of his rebellion, I suppose," Violet said as she delicately picked at a bit of her own penne. "This after spending the year backpacking across God knows where in South Asia, right, Mother?"

Nina gaped. She had heard no word about that trip either.

"If attending Harvard is the boy's worst rebellion, he's welcome to it," Celeste replied curtly. "And if it makes him the man he needs to be in order to run this company, so much the better. His father did the same thing, you know, right down to marrying a girl raised in a hovel."

A quiet descended over the table. Jacob de Vries, Eric's father and Nina's uncle, had died in a terrible sailing accident when Nina was only a small child, and since then, Heather, Eric's mother, had remarried and generally stayed away from the family. Nina cringed, having heard comments like these her entire life. It made sense, now, why the vitriol toward Penny, Eric's deceased fiancée of a similar background, had been intense enough to drive the poor girl to her death. Celeste had simply seen it as history repeating itself and acted accordingly.

Nina cast a glance at Calvin chewing a large bite of steak with an open mouth. Not for the first time, she wondered if she hadn't traded for the worse end of the bargain in her attempt to avoid her grandmother's judgment.

"Do you—" Calvin cleared his throat awkwardly as Celeste's gaze cut across the table. "Do you really think that's best? Given his defection from the family. After all, Nina is right her—"

"A donation to the law school has already been made," Celeste interrupted tersely. "And when he's ready, we'll bring him back into the fold. He'll come home. They always do."

Nina didn't know how to feel. She was certain that Calvin's unlikely defense of her had nothing to do with his affections. All signs pointed to him hating her. More now than ever. On the other hand, she also couldn't help feeling the prodigal son narrative was a little over-wrought when she was, in fact, sitting right here.

Sometimes she wished Eric wouldn't return at all. Partly because she was still angry at him, but partly because in some ways, she envied his journey for independence. If only he had invited her to come with him.

Still, Boston…

"You know, I was thinking of going back to school," she said casually, like she was suggesting a haircut, despite the fact that it had only just occurred to her.

When she looked up, she found Calvin and Caitlyn staring at her with open mouths.

"What?" Calvin demanded.

"School?" Caitlyn glanced over Nina, like she had somehow dripped red sauce over her white blouse without realizing it. "Really, N?"

Celeste and Violet did not speak.

Yes, she knew it was somewhat pathetic, tailing after Eric like a lost puppy. But suddenly, the idea sounded almost as good as going to Italy. Now that she was thinking about it, she did in fact see a clear path for herself and the baby after the divorce. And it was in Boston, not New York.

She could finish school.

Find the one family member she had ever truly cared about.

Make a real life for herself and her daughter outside this godforsaken city. This ridiculous family and its ridiculous rules.

"And just how do I figure into this plan of yours?" Calvin broke through her thoughts darkly. "Or have you forgotten again that you're a married woman?"

Nina looked up to find all four faces surrounding the table peering at her like a mismatched group of theater masks. Of course. No, she shouldn't be thinking about her impending escape yet. She owed Calvin at least some saved face, she supposed.

"Oh, er... Well, you could do your business anywhere," she scrambled. "You travel so much anyway, and I'm sure there are 'properties' worth purchasing in New England too, don't you think?"

Calvin's eyes bugged at the word "properties." Caitlyn and Violet looked awkwardly between the two of them, but didn't say anything as they both took heavy gulps of their wine. Celeste continued to peer at Calvin, awaiting his response with the patience of an executioner.

Calvin opened and closed his mouth several times, revealing more half-chewed steak swimming around his tongue. Finally, he swallowed, then picked up his knife again, wielding it almost like a weapon.

"I think," he said in an even voice that was meant to sound intimidating, but instead appeared more pedantic, "that *we* will have to talk about these plans later. And, Nina?"

She blinked. She had already been looking at him. Why did the idiot have to say her name like that, beckoning her attention like she was an errant child?

"Yes, Calvin?" she said as sweetly as she could manage.

"We *will* talk about it."

Caitlyn cringed. Violet and Celeste remained perfectly still.

But Nina refused to look away.

"Of course, Calvin," she said. "We will."

And then she helped herself to a large serving of pasta.

CHAPTER TWENTY-TWO

JUNE 2009

O utside the thick oak door of what was now Calvin's home office, Nina took a deep breath. Nervously she clicked her heels together, like she was Dorothy in the *Wizard of Oz*.

There's no place like home. All she needed was a quick signature, and she could go there at last.

Everything was set up.

She had purchased a house in Newton, a suburb just west of Boston. Re-enrolled at Wellesley for the fall. Even sent a letter to Eric at his last known address there, though that had been returned again. No matter. He would be back, and in the meantime, Nina was making a life for herself on her own.

She fingered the thick manila envelope. This was the last piece of the puzzle.

Since the awkward luncheon with her family and Caitlyn, Calvin had been suspiciously quiet. There had been no more awkward appearances in her suite at odd hours, no more shouting matches or veiled statements. Celeste too had mentioned his requests for more money had subsided. Even his threat to "talk" about her plans for school had gone untested. It was almost as though he had been avoiding her and everyone else.

But no more.

Today was their anniversary. It had been one year exactly since she stood in that dusty church and lied in front of God and all those people when she had promised Calvin Gardner her life and love. Divorce wouldn't be pretty, but it was inevitable. Plenty of people didn't make it past their first year. Embarrassing, but not a scandal.

And it was, finally, time.

"It will be all right," she said to herself. "It will be all right."

"Nina?"

The door flew open, and Calvin's squat, sweaty body filled the frame, face glistening with sweat and stress. Behind him, a mess of papers was shoveled atop his desk next to two open laptops and a fair amount of clutter.

"What in God's name were you muttering about out there?" he demanded. "Were you spying on me? Listening through the door?"

Nina frowned, taking a step back. "What? No, of course not."

Calvin scowled, then yanked absently at the fat yellow tie swinging around his thick neck and whirled back inside. "Well, then. What do you want?"

Nina swallowed and gripped the manila envelope in her hands. How had it come to this? One year ago, he had been so kind to her... now his voice dripped contempt. So much derision. And for what? What had she ever done to deserve it?

She took a deep breath. "I—do you have a moment?"

Calvin scowled harder. "Fine. If you have to, come in."

He returned to his desk in a huff, and Nina cautiously let herself inside the room. It was musty and dank, like too many people had been perspiring close together around the desk. There were several bowls encrusted with food residue piled on a coffee table along with a few other used coffee cups. Some of the windows looking out to Ninety-Second Avenue even bore bits of condensation along the edges.

"Been burning the candle at both ends?" Nina did her best to strike a conversational tone, trying not to linger too long on any one part of the mess.

"Understatement of the century." The desk chair creaked loudly as Calvin flopped into it, and he immediately started clicking on the computer. "Can we get on with this? I'm expecting a phone call in a few minutes."

"Okay. Well, this shouldn't take long. I hope."

Nina approached the desk, but before she could offer the manila envelope, something else caught her eye lying amidst the clutter.

"What's this?" she asked, picking up a small gold, or maybe brass, coin from a dish containing other loose staples and paper clips.

The gold was chipped, grimy, and tarnished to the point where the letters—which looked like Latin—were mostly obscured along with the two-faced man on the front. It looked a lot like the ancient coins she had seen in some of the archaeological museums in Rome. Nina frowned. Something else about the coin was familiar, but she couldn't quite say what. For some reason, it made her think of her uncle, Eric's father. But that was ridiculous—Uncle Jacob had died when they were children. Nina had not even been nine. She barely remembered him as it was.

"Why?" Calvin asked, a little too quickly. "Do you know anything about it?" He sounded eager, for once, to hear what she had to say.

Nina looked up, about to tell him everything she was thinking. But the unfiltered greed smeared over his sweaty face made her stop.

"No," she said. "I don't. What is it?"

He squinted, causing the wrinkles that were showing more and more around his eyes to deepen. "It's a coin," he said. "Have you been able to find Eric? It's important."

More confusion. "No. I keep telling you, he's not returning anyone's calls or messages." She didn't mention the letter that had come back.

"Did he ever introduce you to any of his friends? The ones he made in college?"

Nina frowned. "Not many, no. He wasn't particularly interested in coming home in college, so we never really met his cohort…"

"No one? John Carson, Jude Letour? Michael Faber? Any of them ring a bell?"

Mutely, Nina shook her head.

Calvin swore profusely, picked up the coin, and hurled it across the room, where it hit the mahogany wainscoting with a clink, then fell noiselessly to the rug.

"Why? What's this all about?" Nina asked. "Does it have something to do with that dirty coin?"

Calvin sneered. "God, you're so clueless, you know that? That 'dirty coin' is more valuable than this entire apartment." He crossed the room and retrieved the coin from the ground, cradling it in his palm like it really was the treasure he claimed. "Can I ask you something? And will you be completely honest?"

Nina paused. This felt like a trap. "I..."

"Is there something about me specifically that says 'not like you'?"

Nina cocked her head, unsure what to make of the question. The sudden show of vulnerability was unlike anything she'd ever heard from her "husband." "I don't know what you mean. Not like me personally? Or not like...what?"

"Not like you." Calvin wagged one hand up and down, pointing at her general being. "All of you. The ones with ten houses and thousands of trust funds. The ones who own chalets in the Swiss Alps and private islands in the Caribbean. The ones who think ten million is chump change and have for three hundred years."

Nina considered. She didn't know how she could pick the other two girls with trust funds out of her orientation group at Wellesley, but she knew them immediately, just as they had known her. Nor could she explain the exact ways in which, beyond his ill-fitting clothes, Calvin stood out no matter what at every social gathering, every casual salon, every cocktail party.

It was a thousand things and none at all. But always there, nonetheless.

Still, she knew she couldn't speak the truth: if fitting into the world of generational wealth was Calvin's goal, he should give it up now. Some were better at it than others, but her husband was certainly not one of them. And by now, she knew he never would be.

"I grew up with nothing," he said before swiping the bottle of gin off his desk and pouring a large quantity into what looked like a used coffee cup. "Did you know that?"

Nina was quiet. She had known he hadn't grown up in luxury, of course. But not nothing.

"My father was Hungarian. He was actually imprisoned during the Cold War uprising and then fled the country after it failed. He made it to New Jersey and ended up in New Brunswick, where he met my mother."

Nina remained quiet. Calvin had never spoken about his family before. She wondered now why she had never thought to ask.

"And then he died right after I was born," he continued. "Cancer. Weak son of a bitch. My mother barely spoke English and worked as a housecleaner. We shared a townhouse with two other families scraping by. She was a whore, though. Pulled up her skirt for any man who would help with the rent. And when the last one got her hooked on crack, she started doing it professionally too. Like I said, a fuckin' whore."

Nina closed her eyes, not wanting to hear any more or imagine what kind of life would make a man talk about his own mother like that. Even she had more respect for Violet than this, and she wasn't exactly mother of the year.

Calvin poured another heavy dollop of gin into his cup and tossed it all back in one go. "I left when I was sixteen. Moved around from house to house, doing whatever I could to make enough to get out on my own. Because I swore I'd never end up like that again. Hungry and cold and poor as shit. I'd be the man my father never could be, if it was the last thing I did." He worried his jaw as he picked up the coin and turned it back and forth in the light. "Do you know what the Janus society is?"

The name prickled in the back of her mind, but she couldn't have said why. "No. What is it?"

"It's a secret. Kept by the only people who really fucking matter in this world. But no matter what I try, no matter what I do, they won't let me in."

"And Eric is...a part of it?" Nina ventured.

His eyes flashed. "So you do know what it is."

For some reason, Nina took a step back. "I just put two and two together. You've never stopped asking about him, despite the fact you've never met."

"Don't make assumptions you can't back up, princess." A vein at Calvin's temple began to throb. He tossed back another large gulp of liquor. "It doesn't matter now. The trick with these assholes is that you find a way to make them need you. And they'll need me soon enough. I'm making fucking sure of it."

He tossed the coin back onto a stack of papers, then turned around to dig through the liquor cabinet for another bottle.

"What are these?" she asked as she looked more closely at the papers and documents strewn across the desk.

They were forms, mostly. Some laminated cards or what looked like passports. And other documents bearing vaguely Eastern European names under official U.S. and Canadian seals. Many of the names were repeated on multiple documents, and nearly all of them requiring addresses used the same four or five residences in different areas of New Jersey, Brooklyn, and Staten Island.

"Calvin, these are immigration documents." Nina started paging through them. "Passports. Visas. Driver's licenses. What is all this? Why do so many have the same addresses?"

She flipped another paper over—the front page of a title, also bearing the same address.

She looked up. "Is this one of the houses you bought with my money?"

Calvin snatched the papers from her. "*Your* money?" he snapped. "I thought it was a gift for *me*. That would make it mine now, wouldn't it?"

"These are fake. Even I can see that. Just what do you think you're getting away with?" She shook one of the passports at him. "What is this?"

"Nothing," Calvin snapped as he grabbed it out of her hand. "Did I ask you to nose around my things?"

"It's not nothing. What have you gotten involved in?"

"God. You really are such a fucking princess, you know that?" he spat. "Who do you think makes the world you live in so goddamn perfect, Nina? Who do you think cleans your tower in the clouds and makes your food and takes care of your children, huh?"

Nina backed away. "You're drunk. Maybe we should continue this tomor—"

"People enter this country illegally every fucking day," he rattled on as he walked around the desk. "And you know what? If they didn't, the world as we know it wouldn't exist. People like you *need* people like me to make sure you get your Marguerites and your Consuelas to cook your meals and clean your house and raise your damn kids. So why shouldn't I make a buck out of it, huh? *Why not,* when my own fucking mother couldn't in the same goddamn position?"

Suddenly, Nina found herself backed up against the row of book-shelves that filled one corner of the room. She stared at Calvin as if he were a stranger. Indeed, he felt like one.

But, she thought, *it's all over now.* If he wanted to run some kind of immigration fraud ring without her, he was welcome to it.

She just wanted to be done with it.

As if he read her mind, Calvin's bitter gaze shifted to the manila envelope lying haphazardly on the desk.

"What the hell is that?" he asked, eyeing the package like it was liable to attack.

Nina took a deep breath and pushed off the bookshelves to step nimbly around him. She didn't know why she was so nervous.

"Papers," she said. "The divorce papers."

Calvin's head turned so quickly, his jowls shook slightly under his weak chin. "What?"

"Well, um, it's been a year. And we said—"

"I know what we said." He picked up the papers and tapped them on the edge of the desk like he was getting ready to swat a fly. "Don't waste any time, do you?"

Nina's stomach squeezed. "Calvin, please."

"Am I so abhorrent?" He gently waved the envelope through the air like he was fanning away his own terrible stench. "You're that eager to be rid of me that you had to do this on our anniversary?"

"Well, it's not like it's something special," Nina protested before she could help herself.

The mug in his hand flew across the room and shattered against the opposite wall with a smash. Nina followed its progression, then wrapped her arms around her stomach as she turned back to Calvin, genuinely afraid of what she might see.

"That," he said, "wasn't very nice. Considering everything I've done for you."

"Maybe then. But now—"

"But what, princess?"

"But now you—you despise me." Nina's chin quivered as she spoke, and she hated how much just acknowledging the fact upset her. "You've made that clear since the baby arrived. Neither of us mean anything to you. Aside from that...I think the ten million dollars you've taken from me and my family is pretty enough payment."

Calvin flared. Nina shook her head. She had never wanted this to be painful or hurtful.

Control, Nina, she could practically hear her grandmother intoning. *Always maintain control.*

"Calvin," she tried again once she had flattened her tone. "Please. Let's not pretend this was ever something it wasn't. We were an arrangement from the beginning. You kindly offered me a way to keep my family's name intact. I provided a means for you to get this"—Nina waved her hand around the mess on the desk—"whatever this is, started. Let's call it even and move on. Just so you know, I requested my lawyer double the settlement. You'll receive twice what we originally said."

It was a lot. Not the additional ten million he had requested last month, but more than enough for him to have what he had just said he wanted: never to have to suffer the way his parents did. If he did things right, he'd never want for money again.

Calvin dropped the divorce papers back on the desk, and they both stared at them for several moments.

When he looked up, his cruel eyes shone. "No."

Nina's jaw dropped. "*No?*"

Calvin stood and readjusted his belt. "No, princess, I don't think so. The answer is no."

A sinking sensation lodged in Nina's belly. Surprise, followed by a hanging weight of dread. "What—what do you mean? How can you say that? We—we had an agreement."

But Calvin only crossed his meaty arms. "Agreements can change."

Nina felt her mouth go dry.

"I'm glad *you* got whatever you wanted from this arrangement, princess, but I'm afraid I didn't. Not by a fucking long shot. This isn't happening."

"Yes, it is!" she cried, all vestiges of control gone for good. "I've, well, I've already made plans. I'm taking Olivia to Massachusetts with me, where I'll finish school, like I said. I bought a house. I'll get a car."

"You're not listening, Nina. You're not going anywhere."

"I *am!*" She was shouting now, hating the way her face heated up with rage. Emotion. "I already have the plane ticket, the house, everything. It's settled!"

"A plane ticket?" He perked up. "To Boston?"

Nina cowered, realizing how much of the game she had actually given away. "I—no. It's for...Florence, actually. I'm taking Olivia. I decided. Oh, Calvin, I'm sorry, but I want Olivia to know who her father really is. I want him to know about her. We'll keep it quiet, I promise. I'm sure Grandmother will do whatever it takes to keep everyone's names out of the press. But then...Calvin, I don't want to stay in New York anymore." A tear ran down her cheek. She had never known how much she felt that way until just this moment. "You said you needed to make your own life? Well, I do too. And I'm not looking for your permission."

"Well, that's too bad, because you don't fucking have it!"

He grabbed the papers off the desk and hurled them away. They erupted midair in a sharp plume of white before scattering across the floor in listless piles. Calvin's barrel chest heaved, sweat seeping from under his arms.

"You see, I know something else you don't," he said with a cruel curl of his upper lip. "Your old grandma? She's sick. She hasn't told anyone else about it, but I heard her say something to her butler about her meds. Zofran. Know what that's for?"

Mutely, Nina shook her head.

"Cancer, babe. To help with the nausea from the chemo." Calvin nodded, like it was good news. "She's terminal, babe. She's about to kick the bucket, hard. Now, it might take two years, or it might take ten, but one day old granny is going to be out of the picture. And with your cousin jumped ship, that leaves one heir left."

Nina swallowed. "You mean me?"

Calvin stepped closer and pulled a lock of hair away from her ear so that as he spoke, his hot breath pooled around her earlobe.

"Did you really think I was going to miss out on my share of seventeen billion dollars? Time to face facts, princess. You're stuck with me. For life."

For a moment, Nina thought Calvin might charge at her. But instead, he turned around, riffled through a few other papers on the desk, then turned back with one particular document and shoved it at her.

"You're going to stay here. You're going to be my wife. And you're going to support my business until I get whatever the fuck I want and become one of *you*. Because if you don't, I'll drag you down to my level, Nina. Starting with that."

He shoved the papers at her again, and Nina took them. As she paged through, an eerie chill descended over her shoulders like an invisible cape. Or maybe just a cage.

It looked like a deed to one of the houses listed on so many of those applications.

"What...what is this?"

"It's a mortgage," he said. "Five, actually." His face turned sour. "Opened in the name of a corporation that *you* happen to own. The goddamn banks see my name, and they think I'm no one. They hear the name 'de Vries,' and suddenly every damn door is wide open."

She flipped through the papers. On the front was a name: Pantheon, LLC. A company, apparently located in Delaware. But on every page that required initials or the full name of a representative, her name was written in.

She set the papers down. "These aren't mine."

"Tell that to a judge. I'm pretty sure that's your signature."

"But...but..." Nina shook her head. "But I had nothing to do with this. What did you do, forge these?"

"You should really make your mark something more notable, princess. This was embarrassingly easy."

Nina felt like her lungs were freezing. She couldn't breathe. "Calvin, I have nothing to do with this!"

"And yet," Calvin said, grinding his teeth into a sly, bone-chilling smile that spread his face like fingers in bread dough, "you do." He tapped a thick finger next to her name, which was far too legible in her neat, polished script. "Right there. If I get caught, you'll be liable. They'll connect you to the whole scheme. Smart, isn't it?"

"But how—don't you have to be present to purchase property?" She knew this only because she had just done it herself.

Calvin grinned, his teeth like razors. "You were. Don't you remember?"

Nina swallowed. She didn't understand how, but somehow, he had managed to buy five houses around what looked like Brooklyn under her name, without her being present. There was only one explanation—someone was faking her identity. Someone Calvin knew. Someone the powers than be would have believed was her as well.

As she looked around the office, she realized how easy it would have been for her husband to orchestrate such a thing. Since he was apparently trafficking in forged identifications, it wouldn't have been hard to recreate hers.

"No," she said. "*No.* I'm leaving. I'm talking to Grandmother. She'll fix it—she'll fix everything, and she will take care of you, just like she does everything. You just st-stay away from me. You can't do this. You can't do any of this!"

She turned to go, but his voice yanked her back.

"I think you have that wrong," Calvin said. "Your grandmother doesn't take care of her family. She takes care of the people she thinks hurt it." He tipped his head. "I always wondered what her husband did to piss her off. And wasn't your uncle a bit of a black sheep too before he died? I never found a sailing accident all that convincing, to be honest."

Nina's mind raced. This was preposterous. Her grandfather had passed years before her birth, and her uncle Jacob when she was just a girl. She had never questioned their deaths or what had happened… but could there be any truth to what Calvin suggested? She hated that she was even considering it.

"And then," Calvin continued, "there's the case of your cousin's fiancée."

Nina froze near the door, the bloody images she had seen of Eric's love lying in a bathtub flashing through her mind. Maybe she had been afraid of that all along.

"I have wondered," Calvin continued, his voice cutting through the room like a knife through butter. "If she was pregnant too. Would have been awfully inconvenient for the golden heir to knock up the Greek girl at twenty-two."

Nina felt her skin begin to crawl. It was like he was speaking her greatest fears out loud.

"And if that's what she would do to her, think what she would do if she knew her only great-grandchild was the bastard of a washed-up professor."

"No," Nina whispered, more weakly now. "I'm leaving. You…I have to."

"Go on," Calvin sneered, his oppressive bulk emanated heat just behind her. "Just know if you do, you're signing your own arrest warrant too. No one will believe you, Nina. That's your signature. Every single notary will swear you were there under oath. Do you really think dear old Granny is going to defend you against that? If you really think she'll embrace you after the inevitable field day the papers will have at your expense, you're even more naive than you look." He leaned close so his belly touched the small of her back, and his thick lips brushed her ear. "She doesn't care about you, Nina. None of them do."

Nina had to grab the edge of a shelf near the door to keep from falling. For a moment, she saw her grandmother in the front row at her wedding. Watching the ceremony not with love or wonder or pride.

Nor with concern or care, the way one might expect from a loved one. Disappointment, she had seen instead. And after she had allowed Calvin to kiss her and seal the rites: disgust.

"How could you?" she whispered as she slowly turned back. The deed shook in her hand. "You're stealing my life."

Calvin surveyed her for a moment, then scoffed when he spotted two large tears welling up and falling down Nina's cheek.

"I'll make you a deal, princess," he said. He pointed at a large stack of papers on the other side of the desk. "See those over there? Those are the deeds to every piece of property that pretty ten million bought over the last year. And to save you time, Pantheon's name is on all of them, along with your ridiculous little scribble."

Nina felt her heart turning to concrete. Not the kind that held steady. The kind that crumbled under fire.

"A deal," she said. It was hard to breathe. It felt like someone had punched her in the stomach. "What kind of deal?"

Calvin came close again, then slipped one sausage-shaped finger under her chin and tipped it up so he could look at her.

"You get me in with Eric's people. With *your* people. You sell it to them; you make them learn that I fucking belong at the top of the world with all the rest of you upper-crust assholes. You make me a true power player, and I'll take your name off those deeds when the day comes that I don't need you. You bring me new partners, the kind I *really* want to go to bed with…and I'll stop trying to get into yours." He eyed her body with unmasked lust. "Or maybe I won't. I think it's long past time I asserted my *other* marital rights."

So this is what hopelessness feels like, Nina thought vaguely as she experienced the strange sensation of her body starting to shut down. The concrete in her head began to spread through her chest and limbs as Calvin's fingers roved down her body. It would be so easy to let him take what he wanted, she realized, as they took hold of her backside, her shoulder, slipped between her legs.

But she couldn't give him that. She couldn't give him everything.

"Get *off* me!" Nina erupted, a whirl of motion as she slapped his hands away. "*Don't you touch me!*"

She dodged out of reach, finding the door only to be yanked backward and caged against the shelves.

"You think you're so much better than me, don't you, *princess*?" Calvin said nastily as he shoved her back. "Do you have any idea what they say about you? That you're nothing but a spoiled child who couldn't even make it through college without going back to her grandma's money. They say you're an idiot who doesn't care about anything but clothes and jewelry. Not even your own daughter."

Suddenly, Nina's voice was steel. "You touch me again, I swear to God, I will scream loud enough that every person in this building will call the police, Calvin. I'll cry rape. I don't care if I go to jail too. I'll tell them what you did, and I'll use every cent of my money to bury you."

The utter virility of her words surprised even her. She honestly didn't know she had it in her.

But to her surprise, Calvin smiled.

"What money?" he asked softly. "Don't you understand? You have nothing that truly belongs to you. Your credit cards belong to your family. Your trust, your allowance, your home—all from them are trussed up tighter than a fucking roasted chicken. And, as we've already discussed, your family won't have a thing to fucking do with you if you disgrace them. You and your little *bastard* would be gum on the bottom of their shoes."

Nina suddenly couldn't breathe. She wrapped her hands around her neck, as if to force air in and out of her windpipe. "No." Her voice was a breath. Barely a whimper.

"And there's one more reason I know you won't leave, princess," he continued, then licked his bottom lip, like a predator about to pounce.

"Why—why is that?"

"Because if you take one step out of this apartment, you'll leave that baby of yours alone. Maybe not right away, but one day, you will. And I don't think you'll like where she ends up."

A chill sprinted up Nina's spine. "Excuse me?"

Calvin tapped his lip, like he was thinking of something else. "You know, come to think of it…some people would pay a pretty penny for a little girl like her. All I'd have to do is draw up the papers."

The lump in Nina's throat turned to a rock. "Y-you wouldn't."

He leaned in so his rubbery lips touched her ear again. "Try me."

"*STOP!*" Nina's shriek came from deeper in her soul than anything ever had.

Calvin reared. His face turned the color of a ripe tomato, and then, without warning, his hand whipped through the air and found her cheek with a loud slap that sent her ears ringing.

"Stupid fucking cunt!" he growled, then grabbed her collar and rammed her against the bookshelves hard enough that the wood ridges jammed painfully into her back. He slammed her again, this time hard enough that his absurdly large wedding ring, with five separate diamonds set into the thick gold, sliced into her cheek.

But Nina didn't give him what he wanted. Instead, she held herself as tall as possible against the onslaught. The knuckles meeting her jaw with a particularly vicious backhand. The hard wood corners of the shelves ramming into her hips, her shoulders, her head, again and again.

It could be worse, said some strangely placid voice in the back of her mind. *He could use actual fists. He could use his feet.*

He could rape you too.

And what would Grandmother say to that?

She'd probably ask what you were wearing to deserve it.

At last, when he had tossed her around the room enough that sweat had dampened the center of his shirt and his breathing was curiously postcoital, he released her into the corner, trapped against the shelves.

Nina slowly worried her jaw and touched her nose gingerly. It didn't seem broken, but she honestly wasn't sure. There was a steady trickle of blood falling over her lip.

"Still don't want to fuck me, princess?" Calvin sneered. "Sure it's not the lesser of two evils?"

Nina had never been more sure about anything in her life.

She stared at the papers on the desk. The bars of her new prison. Calvin was right. There would be no one there to save her from this. She had created this cage for herself. But she'd be damned if she'd risk making another one too.

"Yes," she said quietly. "I am."

Calvin spat. "Have it your way. But don't cross me. Consider yourself warned."

Beyond the door, there was a distant wail of a child. Olivia, seeking Nina's attention. Both Nina and Calvin perked at the sound, but neither moved. Calvin because he didn't care. Nina because she cared too much.

"Greta will get her," Nina said, hating that she had to concede even that. But there was no way she could show her face to the household staff now. There was no way she could show any of this to anyone. Calvin had made that very, very clear.

"Well, princess? What'll it be?"

And with that, her heart hardened completely.

"All right," she said quietly. "But if you want me to be your representative, so to speak, I have a few requirements too. For one, you need to keep your hands off my face. No one will trust a woman with a black eye or a broken nose." She bared her bloodied teeth in the kind of smile needed to charm women at luncheons and the men they married. "You want to be like us, Calvin? Here's your first lesson: keep your brutality behind closed doors where it belongs. Keep it away from where people can actually see it."

He looked like he wanted to hit her again. Like he wanted to break her nose for real, maybe knock out a few teeth too. But to her surprise, he nodded.

"Anything else?" he asked.

Nina sucked in a breath, forcing herself not to flinch at the sharp pain in her side that accompanied it. "Yes," she said. "They also keep their children out of it. Olivia *never* sees any of this. And you keep your fucking hands off her. Forever."

Calvin was quiet for another long moment. Then, eventually, he stuck out his hand, like a sick parody of the deal they had made together one year earlier. Feeling like she was about to vomit, Nina slowly returned the handshake, fighting a revulsive shudder at the feel of his sweaty palm pressed against hers.

"Done."

CHAPTER TWENTY-THREE

Nina stayed in her bedroom with the baby for over a week while the cuts and bruises on her face healed. The others on her back would be there much longer, and given how painful it was to breathe, she was fairly sure she had a few cracked ribs that might take even longer.

The staff left her food by the door—Calvin had told them she and the baby had some terrible virus and were contagious. No one argued, because no one argued in houses like theirs. All staff employed by de Vrieses signed NDAs, and even then, their generous salaries would have ensured their loyalty regardless.

Loyalty to whom, though?

She spent the days watching Olivia with a fascination that now bordered on obsession. She had never noticed, for instance, the exact length of the shadow cast by her daughter's eyelashes when she slept. Or the perfect, tiny dimple at the end of her perfect nose.

She was still small for her age, and slightly behind developmentally, though the doctors assured her that was normal for a preemie. She still spent most of her time on her back and tummy, only just able to roll herself over and back.

She fed her formula, which she seemed to like, since what little milk Nina had left could not possibly sustain the child. It was just after each feeding, though, that Nina fell most in love with her daughter, when they would lie on the big bed together as the sun dipped beyond the New York City skyline, and Nina watched sweet baby dreams play across Olivia's face as she drifted off to sleep.

And then, when Olivia slept, Nina would lie on her bed, cradling her face and arms as she stared up at the box beam ceiling of the hat box of a room. Once she'd had so many plans for the place, but now she couldn't care less. A prison was a prison, whether it was covered in chintz or bars. She waited for the throbbing pain under her shoulder to subside a bit more. For the knot on the back of her head to ache a little less.

And while she waited, she forced herself to let go of the life she thought she might have. And another started to take shape in its place.

She saw that she would no longer dedicate her time to school, but to social events. That she would return to the fold of parties and luncheons with her husband on her arm, his ticket into navigating the world of New York high society.

She saw that she would have to hire round-the-clock help for Olivia until the time came when she could safely send the girl to boarding school, away from this madness. Away from the farce.

She saw that like her parents, she would barely know her daughter. And that it was in Olivia's best interest for that to be the case.

She saw that she would never be free unless she could become as much of a monster as her husband was to get rid of him.

And where, really, was the freedom in that?

On the eighth day, sometime in the early morning hours, Nina rose from the bed and found her face was clear in the mirror over her vanity. In the mirror's reflection, Olivia still lay sleeping on the bed. Nina stared at her limp, bedraggled hair, at the shadows under her eyes, and could hardly recognize the woman she saw. Even when she was pregnant, she had looked more like herself. Now she was a battered ghost. Fitting, considering she was having a hard time figuring out what to live for.

She trudged into her closet to find some clothes that weren't grubby loungewear, but stopped when her eyes fell on the shoebox shoved on a shelf in the far corner. She stood up on her tiptoes to pull it down, then sank to the floor of the closet and began sifting through the dozens of love letters Giuseppe had passed her over the months of their affair. Letters full of praise, adoration, love. Emotions she'd never received from anyone before him—not friends, not family. No one.

When she had read through them all and shed more than a few tears, she was surrounded by crumpled pieces of cardstock, but the horrific weight in her chest had lifted slightly. Maybe there was one person in the world who would care enough to help in this dire situation. Maybe there was one last refuge to seek.

She padded out of the closet and checked the clock on her nightstand. It would be only one o'clock in Florence now. Giuseppe would be coming home for lunch before teaching an evening class with the summer term students. She could see him now, sitting on the balcony of his apartment, enjoying a *panino*, perhaps, or a bowl of leftover pasta reheated with a splash of cream and ribbons of fresh basil, followed by an espresso.

Without thinking twice, she grabbed her cell phone from the vanity and sank into the seat as she dialed the number she had memorized long ago. The call went to an automated Italian message indicating the box was full. Nina drew up her contacts and found the number he had told her never to use unless it was a true emergency.

She believed this qualified.

"*Pronto.*" The female voice that answered sounded old, tired. A little bit clogged, like a sink.

The housekeeper, Nina guessed. Or perhaps his mother, whom she knew lived with him and his family.

"Excuse me," Nina said in her awkward Italian. "Is Professor Bianchi available? I'm..." She paused for a moment, searching for a reason she might be calling. "I'm from the university. We need—"

"Lord, you people can't stop!" the woman interjected. "My poor son has been dead two days, and all you can think about is clearing his office!" The woman's voice descended into a babble of tears and coarse language.

Nina, however, couldn't concentrate long enough to decipher any of it. The only word that lingered rang like a bell inside her head.

Morto.

Dead.

Giuseppe was…dead?

"*Scusi, scusi, signora,*" she finally managed in a voice that sounded as hollow as she felt. "I am so sorry. I didn't—I didn't know. Please give my condolences to the family."

She hung up before the woman could reply, then sank to the blush-colored carpet, hugging her knees to her chest, and suddenly rocking back and forth like a child in the middle of her room.

Peppe was dead. *Dead.* How could this have happened?

How do you think, princess? This time it was Calvin's sneer that filled her mind.

She took her phone and frantically punched in a search. A death notice appeared immediately—Giuseppe was a respected member of the art intelligentsia in Florence. His death would have been reported immediately, and it was.

Heart failure, said the papers. Suddenly in his home. Services to be announced.

She stared at the words, feeling somehow they too weren't real. Peppe ran three miles every day. His health was better than most people her age, let alone a man in his early forties. And yet, he was dead…

What did you really think was going to happen, princess?

Again, Penny's tragic death passed through her mind.

No. It couldn't have been.

And yet…Grandmother had known about Peppe. She had made that clear at Christmas, hadn't she? And then there was the way her eyes had drifted over the Italian feast Nina had requested. The veiled disappointment when she glanced at Olivia.

It wouldn't have taken much for her to learn that Nina was planning to visit Florence. Just like it wouldn't have taken much for her to do the unthinkable…again.

Fear skittered up Nina's arms and legs in a way it hadn't in days. Her bones felt heavy, as if the knowledge of her family's cold-blooded tendencies, along with her husband's, were sinking into her, all the way through. She felt drowned by the sudden knowledge.

Calvin was right. Nothing. She was nothing. She had nothing. And she never, ever would.

A gurgle sounded behind her. An absolutely unadulterated sound of joy, a tiny baby's giggle.

Feeling like a ghost, Nina got up and walked to the bed.

Olivia was sitting up. In the middle of the bed, she was sitting straight, having pushed herself up at last, chest forward. Wobbling slightly, but proud nonetheless. Her dark eyes met her mother's and twinkled with utter possibility. So full of her father's light.

Nina choked back a sob.

Olivia held out her hands.

Nina rushed across the mattress and rained kisses over Olivia's downy head.

"Oh, my sweet girl, my love, my darling," she murmured nothings while Olivia squealed with joy. "You sat up! You did it, lovey, you did it!"

The two rocked together on the bed for several minutes, maybe an hour before Olivia made it clear it was time for something to eat. After that, they would have a bath. Cleanse the week of sadness and filth off themselves. Find a way to figure the rest of their lives out together.

When Nina finally left her bedroom, daughter in her arms, it was with the resigned awareness that she was beginning a new life, but also sustaining another. Maybe she would have nothing, but she would make damn sure her daughter had everything.

She straightened her back. She opened the door. And she didn't look back.

NOW

CHAPTER TWENTY-FOUR

SEPTEMBER 2018

Nina

"Mama? When are we going to go?"

I checked my watch, then peered down Tenth Avenue, looking for any sign of my late cousin-in-law. It was eight o'clock in the morning, the sun was shining steadily on us from the East River, and the city seemed to be buzzing with the same energy I'd felt for the last week and a half.

"Soon," I told Olivia, though I felt jittery myself.

The last time I had felt this excited was when I was nineteen and about to board a plane to Italy for the year. It wasn't the first time I had left New York anymore than this was. It wasn't even the first time I had been to Europe, or even Italy. But it was the first time I had gone there for *myself*, and that made all the difference.

This time I was only traveling four hours north to Boston, but it might as well have been across the ocean for how it made me feel. After three sleepless nights on Long Island—I could never sleep when I had to share a suite with my husband—we had all three returned to New York, and Olivia and I had prepared not just one but *two* sets of belongings for the school year in Massachusetts.

Calvin, of course, hadn't been particularly happy with my decision to leave—or at least, he hadn't been very happy with my decision to surprise him with it in front of all those people, which I'd paid for that night behind our bedroom doors. The bruise on my back was only just starting to fade, and there still was a knot on the back of my head. I didn't care. It was worth it.

More surprising, however, was the fact that once he had rid himself of that aggression, Calvin didn't argue anymore with the proposal. Unlike the last time I suggested returning to school, he actually seemed a bit relieved I wouldn't be around. It was one thing to force a marriage when he was traveling nearly all the time. It was another completely when we essentially had a court order to cohabitate.

I fingered the list of addresses I needed to inspect before term started. I still didn't understand why a property manager couldn't take care of it, but I supposed stranger still were the three envelopes in my purse from Calvin to the tenants. Notices of eviction, he said, upon termination of their leases. He was getting out of the hospitality game for good, before anyone could freeze *all* our assets.

"Do you think Auntie Jane is going to get here soon?"

I smiled at the familiar moniker. Olivia was fairly in love with Jane these days, and I couldn't fault her for it. I quite liked her myself.

Except, of course, when she was late.

"Hopefully," I said, checking my watch again. "I did tell her eight. I don't particularly want to get stuck in traffic getting into Boston."

"Hey! I'm here, I'm here! I'm so sorry I'm late!"

Olivia and I turned around to find Jane scurrying down the street, a small, bespectacled tornado of black. She was dressed in a simple black jumpsuit fitting for the hot weather, but between her red cat-eyed glasses, the teal and purple streaks in the back of her hair, and the studded leather bracelets around one wrist, she looked a far cry from the wife of one of New York's wealthiest businessmen.

As it did whenever I saw her, envy struck into my stomach. Not at her clothes, per se, but at her unabashed sense of self. Jane was never anything but exactly who she wanted to be.

"Hey, kiddo!" She leaned down and kissed Olivia on the top of the head before moving to kiss my cheek as well. Real kisses, not the ones that only touched the air. "I'm sorry, but did you grow since Saturday?"

Olivia giggled shyly. "You're silly, Auntie Jane."

"You can ask her to stop calling you that if you like," I said. "If it's too familiar, I mean."

"Are you kidding?" Jane grinned at Olivia. "I have a million aunties back in Chicago. I'm psyched I finally get to be one too." She shrugged. "I was tailor-made for the weirdo aunt role anyway. I will *own* the auntie business."

Again, Olivia giggled. Even I couldn't manage to hide my smile. Jane wasn't exactly wrong about her eccentricities.

"Is this *your* car?" Jane asked, turning to face the sensible car parked in front of us on the curb.

All three of us turned to face the sage green Volvo I'd purchased earlier this week. Calvin had ridiculed me endlessly for choosing what he called the most boring car on the planet. But I quite liked the little coupe. It was small and practical and safe, with the added benefit of not drawing every eye within a hundred feet the way the rest of my family's vehicles always did. No gleaming chrome mascot leaping off the nose or ridiculously tinted windows that made everyone stare when you passed anyway. And best of all, no driver.

"Don't you like it?" I asked, suddenly uncertain. "I thought it was sweet. Not too flashy."

Jane just blinked back at me with something resembling pride, I thought. "I think you might be the *real* black sheep in your family, Nina."

I snorted before I could help myself. "I think you have me confused with your husband, Jane. I'm not the one who ran off for ten years."

"Before coming right back to the fold and accepting his wads of cash? Please. Eric's about as rebellious now as a minivan, in his custom suits and board meetings." She shook her head. "He was a square in law school, and he's a square now. It's just that your family's square happens to be a couture one."

"Is he a square everywhere?"

I wasn't *trying* to be suggestive, but it just came out. I didn't miss the way Jane and Eric looked at each other when they thought no one was watching. And I had a feeling it took a bit more than our family's money to keep someone like Jane happy.

"Well. maybe not *everywhere*." She shrugged happily, like she was recounting some secret to herself. "He may or may not join us next week if he can get out of some meetings. What can I say? The man is obsessed with me."

Jane's eyes danced mischievously as she reached one hand behind her ear to flip her glasses suggestively off her nose several times, making Olivia giggle again.

"As I was saying," she continued. "I may be relatively new in town, but in the de Vries family, I'd wager a Volvo *definitely* qualifies as a solid rebellion. You're the only one of those goobers, my dear husband included, who doesn't want a bit of flash in their lives. And I freaking love it."

"Hurray!" Olivia cheered. "Mama's a rebel!"

"Well, whatever I am, it's settled now."

My cheeks pink as I unlocked the trunk of the car to reveal the small bags for Olivia and me while we stayed the few days with Jane's friends before school began. The rest of Olivia's things were being sent directly to her school. But I found I wasn't attached enough to mine to bring anything beyond the few necessities I had packed. What use would I have for yards of couture when I was sitting in a crowded classroom?

"Just put your bag in the back here, and we'll be on our—"

"Hey, Jane! Nina! *Elefantessa!*"

The three of us turned to see the last figure I expected to see striding down Fifty-Eighth Street: Matthew looked as fine as this late summer day in a pair of slim blue pants, a white shirt with the shirtsleeves rolled up in the heat, and a matching blue jacket draped over a small duffel bag and a briefcase. His black tie flapped over his shoulder as he walked, and he had to clap his fedora to his head to keep it from blowing away in the wind. But the sun gleamed off his aviators and bright smile alike.

It honestly felt like my heart stopped right there on the street. What in God's name was he doing?

"Well, this is a sight for sore eyes," he greeted us as he came close enough to deliver a warm kiss to Jane's cheek. "The three most beautiful women in New York, waiting on a sidewalk just for me."

"Hey, Zola," Jane replied as she returned his kiss.

Like always, a brief arrow of jealousy skewered me at their intimacy, even though I knew Jane was entirely devoted to Eric. But when Matthew took off his hat and darted a kiss to my cheek in the same, casual way, the jealousy turned to something else entirely and sent shivers to my toes despite the heat. It sizzled in my belly long after he had offered the same to Olivia.

"Hey, sweetheart," he said. "Don't tell me you don't recognize me without the pool."

Olivia shook her head shyly and nudged against my hip. Matthew winked at her and grinned again.

"Why are you here?" I demanded, unable to stop myself again.

He looked up and removed his sunglasses so that his dark green eyes could sparkle along with the rest of him. I bristled, even as my heart beat a bit faster. Good lord, would he *always* have this effect on me? I didn't even have to pretend to be annoyed with him—his cocky presence made that easy enough.

"Hello to you too, duchess," Matthew said mildly. "I'm sorry to crash the party, but Jane said I could hitch a ride with you all to Boston."

I turned to Jane, who shrugged, as if she hadn't just last week been asking me about a connection between me and Matthew.

"I told Zola he could avoid the bus," she confirmed. "Turns out Brandon got tickets to the Sox-Yankees game this weekend."

"We've been planning this for months," Matthew added.

I looked back and forth between them, amazed that neither of them seemed the slightest bit perturbed by the obvious line being crossed here. Hadn't Jane been a lawyer too before moving here? Hadn't Matthew and I *just* established that we needed to stay as far away from each other as possible.

"Jane," I said once I was able to control my features again. "Would you mind helping Olivia into the back seat, please? Matthew, might I have a word?"

"Come on, kiddo." Jane turned to Olivia and began shuttling her into the car. "Let's let the grownups fight for a second."

"What?" Olivia asked as she crawled in. "Why would Mama and Matthew fight? I thought they were friends?"

"They fight *because* they're friends, love bug," Jane said. "Some of us are weird like that."

Olivia glanced curiously between me and Matthew before Jane closed the door. I stepped behind the open trunk, which helpfully hid Matthew and me from view once he followed.

"You shouldn't be here," I said quietly.

"You shouldn't look so beautiful."

I looked up and huffed. "I'm serious."

"So am I."

I sighed. "Matthew…"

His smirk disappeared. "Look, it's just a weird coincidence, all right? Brandon and I have been friends a long time. We always go to this game together. We really have had these tickets for months. And don't worry, I got a hotel near Fenway, so I'll be nowhere near you guys, all right?"

I tipped my head. "You must think I'm an absolute idiot."

At that, his mouth turned slightly grim. "I think you are a lot of things, doll. An idiot is *definitely* not one of them."

We stared at each other for a solid minute, trying very hard to stay angry. It was difficult, though, with the way his eyes continued to drop to my lips, and the way I couldn't stop noticing the perfect, stubbled line of his jaw.

Matthew's mouth twitched. He knew exactly what I was thinking. I exhaled, and all the tension wrapped in my shoulders seemed to go with it. I couldn't stay angry when he was looking at me like that, green eyes wide and guileless.

I tried again. "You're the one who keeps saying we need to stay apart, Matthew. If you need to get to Boston quickly, I'm happy to get you on the next flight out of Newark. You'll beat us there, and it will be much more comfortable than sitting in the back seat with my nine-year-old."

"Nina, come on. I'm already here. I'm not going to jump you in the car in front of Jane and Olivia. Much as I might like to, anyway."

"Matthew!"

He chuckled. It was infuriating.

"Are we walking a shady line here?" he asked. "Maybe, yeah. But I'm not breaking any laws sitting in a car, Nina. It's not my fault we run in the same social circles. Now, can I please sit in the back of your"—he balked as he turned to the car—"holy shit, is that a *Volvo*?"

I rolled my eyes. Good lord, not this again. At this rate, we'd never get out of the city.

"Get in," I said. "Let's just get this over with."

"Besides, doll," Matthew added with another cheeky grin. "Who's going to know? Outside this city, we're free."

He closed the trunk and sauntered around the car to get into the passenger side. I stood in the back for a moment before I got in too, thinking to myself how I wished those words could be true.

———

PERHAPS I SHOULDN'T HAVE WORRIED. The four-hour drive north was quiet, mostly filled with Jane and Matthew's chatter, especially after we stopped midway and I traded seats with Matthew, allowing him to chat with Jane while she drove, since she knew the way to her friends' house. Olivia kept herself firmly shoved in the corner, too well trained at this point to do something so untoward as lean on her mother's shoulder the few times she grew sleepy. It was my fault, of course. How could she know how to snuggle with anyone when I had been teaching her for so long to be purely independent?

"I'm staying right by Fenway," Matthew said as we neared the city. "You can just drop me at one of the green line stops near Sky and Brandon's. I'll meet him at the game tomorrow."

Jane, however, just gave Matthew one of her trademark withering stares. "I'm sorry, have you met our friends? Do you think *they* would be all right with that? Just keep your ass in your seat, bucko. You're at least coming home for dinner."

Matthew turned toward me and raised his shoulders, as if to say *I tried, doll.* I sighed and tried again.

"Really," I said as Jane turned off the main freeway just west of Boston. "Are you sure it won't be strange, Livy and me staying with your friends? We really can get a hotel for the weekend."

Jane shook her head vigorously. "Oh, no, they *love* to host. Not huge parties or anything, so don't worry. But close friends and family? The more the merrier. This time of year, they usually have Skylar's half brother and sister with them too, plus their own kids, so Liv will have some playmates too."

I blinked. While I was sure that Olivia had friends at school—she had mentioned a few—I had never really seen her play with other children casually at home. I realized with a pang of guilt I had no idea what that would look like for her.

"Hmm," I said. "I don't know. I feel bad about imposing on people I've never met."

Jane snorted. "Nina, I hate to break it to you, but you're not getting out of this either. Skylar is like a sister to me *and* Eric, and we asked her to help you get settled. I'm afraid you're stuck with her now, because my best friend is equal parts stubborn *and* loyal."

Matthew chuckled. "That's putting it lightly."

Catching my skeptical gaze in the rearview mirror, Jane just grinned. "Relax, Nina," she said as she turned onto a familiar offramp that suddenly made me feel eighteen again. "Once you're friends with the Sterlings, it's for life. There is no safer place in Boston for you or Liv. I promise."

I straightened at the word "safer." Why would she think I needed that in particular? Why didn't I want to admit it?

I ignored the glances Matthew gave me over his shoulder too. The last thing we needed was for his odd radar about my safety to go up again.

"Where are we, Mama?" Olivia piped up, saving everyone from the strange awkwardness that had almost descended.

Matthew turned fully around in his seat to flash his bright grin at Olivia. "Hey, kiddo, you're awake. This is Brookline."

Olivia eyed him right back with an iciness I regretfully recognized as my own. I sighed. I had hoped that in living away from me, she would have forgone that particular trait. I'd hoped it was learned, not inherited.

"Brooklyn?" she wondered. "You mean we've been driving for hours and we're still in New York?"

Matthew's deep green eyes flickered playfully in the mirror. "No, sweetheart, Brook*line*. It's a suburb of Boston. Some friends of mine live here."

When he called her "sweetheart"—foreign to someone certainly no more accustomed to such endearments as I was when I met him—Olivia started toying with one braid. I watched curiously as the corner of my daughter's mouth twitched once she knew Matthew wasn't looking at her anymore.

The ice was thawing. I knew the signs. She liked Matthew. She liked him very much.

"Brookline," she murmured to herself, over and over again. "Sweetheart."

Ten minutes later, we pulled up to a solid iron gate barring entrance to a large property surrounded by stone walls. Jane wasn't joking when she said this was one of the safest places we could possibly be. The Sterlings' property was a veritable fortress in the middle of Boston.

"Hey, it's Jane here with a bunch from New York," Jane spoke into the intercom clearly manned by some kind of security center inside the compound. She also waved at the cameras pointed at the car.

"They had some issues with security when they first got together," Matthew murmured as the gates opened for us almost immediately. "Brandon is pretty protective over his family."

I nodded. "Well, yes. He would have to be, wouldn't he?"

"What do you mean?"

"Wealth makes you a target," I said with a shrug. "It can be quite a burden, you know."

Matthew snorted. "Yeah, I'm sure it's terrible to have all those millions and billions you have."

It was hard to explain to those who didn't live it. I had had security on and off since I was born, depending on the family's visibility and what kinds of threats we were receiving. There were several years during my adolescence when multiple stalkers meant I needed twenty-four-hour bodyguards.

"No, she's right," Jane put in a little too sharply.

Her gaze flickered back to mine through the mirror with the same kind of knowing, though hers was threaded with more than a little residual terror. Of course, she'd experienced the realities of that targeting in the worst possible way only a short time ago. She had jumped right into the frying pan, whereas I had built up a tolerance against the sizzle all my life.

Matthew stayed quiet for the rest of the short drive to the house at the end of the maple-lined driveway. It wasn't nearly as large as the Long Island compound, but still big enough to contain two separate guesthouses at the far end of several acres, a small orchard, and a huge meadow surrounded by other bright green trees that seemed perfect for climbing. One of them even had a tree house in it.

But I was too busy meditating on the previous conversation to appreciate Olivia's apparent excitement about her new surroundings.

The note of accusation in Matthew's voice was still ringing through my ears.

"I didn't choose this life," I said quietly.

Matthew turned back again, and his glance flickered to my wedding rings, then back up again. "Didn't you?"

We stared at each other hard. But before I could answer, the car pulled to a stop.

"Come on, doll," Matthew said quietly as Jane and Olivia scrambled out of the car. He glanced around, then reached a lightning-quick hand back to squeeze my knee before retracting it. "Meet some good people. You deserve a few more of them in your life."

CHAPTER TWENTY-FIVE

I had met the Sterlings a few other times. Close friends of Jane and Eric, both Brandon and Skylar were in their wedding last year, and Skylar, as matron of honor, had treated the entire bridal party, including me, to a trip to London for Jane's bachelorette party. I didn't know her well, but I did recall her being kind, genuine, and straight-forward in the best possible way.

The two of them were standing outside the large white colonial farmhouse when we emerged from the car at the end of the gravel drive, but it wasn't in welcome. Instead, it sounded more like they had escaped the house to have an argument. Skylar's small, tomato-red head was swinging angrily as she gesticulated wildly at her husband's towering form. He simply crossed and uncrossed his arms grumpily.

"Brandon, this is insane," she was saying. "I do not need a bunch of random women performing spa treatments on me for an entire day while you and Zola are at the game. Please just call the salon back and cancel. It's too much. Way, way too much!"

Brandon's face screwed up with frustration while he ripped a mangy Red Sox cap from his head and shoved it back on again. "Girls like that kind of crap, Red."

"That's a massive generalization," Skylar snapped back. "Just because

I have a vagina doesn't mean I'm genetically predisposed to cosmetic pampering. Are you trying to say I need a little work done? Is that it?"

"Jesus Christ, Skylar, *no!* I just—fuck!"

"Can you tell she's a lawyer?" Matthew said into my ear. "Better than Brandon was, and that's saying something."

I chuckled. "If I couldn't before, I would now."

"He hasn't even gotten started," Matthew replied. "It's pretty funny once they get going."

I peered at him sideways. "It takes one to know one, I suppose."

For that, I received a generous wink that made warmth pool in my belly.

"Oh, for Christ's sake, Skylar," Brandon grumbled. "It's *nice.* Jane likes this stuff. Eric told me."

"Jane likes the black nail polish she gets at CVS, not the medieval caste system exemplified by the modern nail boutique."

"I do like CVS," Jane said, only to receive a blue-eyed glare from Brandon. "What? I do. But, Sky, there are plenty of salons where—"

"And I don't want to have to negotiate an entire day around a bunch of weird staff who are forced to be nice to us because of your big wallet, Brandon," Skylar rattled on like Jane hadn't even spoken. "Seriously. It's really nice, but I just want some alone time with my friends. It's not that complicated!"

"Am I missing something?" I asked Matthew. "Is she angry because he surprised her with some estheticians?"

A knowing half-smile reappeared. "Skylar's got issues with money. It drives her crazy when Brandon does extravagant shit for her. And it drives him crazy when she won't take it."

I frowned. "Aren't they married? Or was there a very strict prenuptial agreement?"

"Oh, there was a prenup, all right. And a postnup too after she got her firm started and his lab took off. Skylar wrote them both." He chuckled. "Brandon keeps tearing them up, and she keeps writing them all over again."

"Maybe that's the secret to longevity," I joked.

"What, never finishing the damn thing?"

"No," I said. "Never taking each other for granted."

"Fine!" Brandon shouted, a thick Boston accent emerging along with the rising volume. "Stubborn woman, *fine*. You wanna stay here and write briefs and babysit instead of having your nails done with your girls, be my guest. But Mattie and I are *not* leaving if it goes to extra innings this time, Red. I mean it." He took a deep breath to rearrange his features, then turned to face us. "Hi. Sorry about that. I love my wife, but she is damn near impossible sometimes."

"Brandon!"

"Red."

I couldn't see the look he gave her over his shoulder, but Skylar suddenly turned as scarlet as her nickname and resolutely shut her mouth. Jane started giggling where she stood next to her friend.

When Brandon turned back to smile at me, Matthew, and Olivia, I couldn't help but smile back. The man actually could have fit right in with my family—he was very tall, with wavy blond hair that flopped over his ears and a pair of the most penetrating blue eyes I'd ever seen. But unlike my icy family, his expression was open, kind, and full of humility and humor.

"Nina, right?"

I accepted a kiss on the cheek, ignoring the way Matthew watched the entire exchange carefully.

"Yes," I said. "Lovely to see you again, Brandon."

"You too. Welcome."

"Daddy?"

A little red-haired girl who couldn't have been more than four or five appeared at the door holding some kind of stuffed creature with a large horn sticking out of its nose.

"Hey, Pea," Brandon said. "Come on down and meet our guests."

"Yeah," Matthew said as the girl skipped down the steps. "I'm a guest this weekend, Jenny. Did you hear that? Tell your narwhal there."

As all children, the little girl seemed to fall almost immediately under Matthew's spell as she skipped down the steps and immediately into his arms.

"You're not a guest," she said as he swung her up for a bear hug. "You're just Uncle Zola."

"Dang, I guess you're right. I better pay the piper. Put her there, slugger."

Matthew offered his chin to the tiny girl, who giggled, then touched her fist lightly to his stubbled jaw. He promptly stumbled backward as if punched, causing Jenny to laugh hysterically.

A hand touched my hip. I looked down to find Olivia drawn close, one hand curled into the silk while she watched Matthew and Jenny's antics intently. By the time they had finished, even Skylar was smiling again. Children's joy is infectious.

Finally, Matthew set Jenny back on the ground and acted like he needed to catch his breath. The little girl returned to her parents and peered at me and Olivia with a pair of intense blue eyes that matched her father's.

"Who are they, Daddy?" she asked.

"Remember I told you we invited some friends for the weekend? This is Nina and her daughter, Oliva. Can you say hello?"

Jenny turned toward us and waved a tiny hand. "Hello."

I bent down so I was face to face with her and offered a smile. "Hello, Jenny. My name is Nina, and this is Olivia. We're related to your uncle Eric. It's very nice to meet you."

"You look sad," she told me, blue eyes guileless. "Do you need a hug?"

It was a harmless question, but one that took me off guard nonetheless. "I—how kind of you," I said. "But I think I'm—"

"She's *my* mama," Olivia cut in suddenly, with a sharp voice that surprised even me. "If she needs a hug, *I'll* be the one to give it to her."

She turned, swallowed thickly, and then, before I could stop her, threw her arms around my neck so tightly I could barely breathe. And yet I found I wouldn't have removed them for the world.

Something inside me uncoiled. I closed my eyes for a moment, clasping my daughter's head to my shoulder and breathing in her sweet, nameless scent she had had since she came into the world. Oh, I had forgotten that lovely smell. A bit sweaty, warm, but somehow full of life. Love, really. That's what it smelled like. A unique kind of love that only belonged to her.

Over her shoulder, I found Matthew staring at us, his brow furrowed with need. He cleared his throat and looked away, but not before I saw a wet shimmer over his deep green eyes.

"Thank you, darling," I whispered, then let my daughter go and stood up.

Brandon and Skylar were just chatting with their daughter, clearly used to this sort of display of affection. Jane, however, was watching me with understanding as I stood and brushed the creases out of my skirt.

"Why don't you and Jane show Nina the cottage?" Brandon said. "Zola and I can wrangle the kids inside. I don't want to leave Luis with the other two for too long." Behind him sounded a loud yowl of a much younger child, and immediately, Brandon took off into the house.

"Go on," I urged Olivia. "You'll have more fun with the other children."

She blinked up at me solemnly but obediently detached herself from my skirt. For a moment, I almost called her back but decided against it. It was better for her not to get too attached, this close to her departure for school. Or maybe it was just better for me.

CHAPTER TWENTY-SIX

"How many children do you actually have?" I asked Skylar as we turned down a path through the property that led toward two small cottages at the perimeter.

"Oh, it's a houseful right now," Skylar said. "We adopted Luis last year, and right now my sister and brother are staying with us before they go back to Andover too." She brightened. "They might know Olivia, actually. Jane mentioned she goes to the same school."

I brightened. "Oh! That's a pleasant surprise."

Skylar nodded. "They'll make her feel at home."

Jane and I followed her down a path through a grove of large oak trees that provided a lush, welcome canopy of green in the late summer heat.

"That's Brandon's lab," Skylar said, nodding toward the nearer cottage that looked like it was under construction. "It's almost finished, but they have workable space in the basement right now."

She didn't expand on what I knew a bit from local gossip—that Brandon Sterling was something of a renaissance man. Having made his fortune in the market, he had switched to law later, and then, after meeting his wife, had switched to some kind of engineering or research.

"And this," Skylar said as we approached the door of the second cottage, "is for you."

She let us into the small house that included a kitchen, living and dining rooms, and two doors that opened into two guest bedrooms connected by the small bath. It wasn't by any means large, but at first glance I could see that while comfortable, all the white and wood farm-house furnishings were of the highest quality. Everything had been done in bright whites, sage greens, and warm cream, the kind of colors that made you feel like you were wrapped in a blanket on a freshly cut lawn in the middle of summer.

"It's lovely," I said honestly. "Very homelike."

"It's yours and Olivia's for as long as you need," Skylar said.

I turned from peeking into the bathroom. "What? Oh, that's really not necessary. We are only here the weekend before I get settled in my own house."

"You bought a house in Boston already?" Jane asked.

I shook my head. "Um, no, I bought it a long time ago. I used to have a property manager deal with it and rent it out sometimes, but not for years now."

"Oh." Jane traded looks with Skylar. The two of them seemed to share some kind of telepathic communication, because Skylar closed the door behind her and walked to the kitchen to pull out a bottle of wine from the refrigerator.

"Shouldn't we...get back to the children?" I asked, even as Jane was taking a seat at the counter.

"They'll be fine," she said, pushing the other barstool toward me with the sole of her foot. "Sit. It's five o'clock somewhere."

Skylar poured all three of us glasses of a lovely, fresh pinot grigio, and we sat companionably sipping before Jane darted another look to Skylar.

Skylar opened her mouth to say something, but before she could, there was a knock on the door. We all turned to find Brandon entering the cottage, looking a far cry from the frustrated lion he'd resembled early. Right now, he looked downright contrite peering under the bill of his Red Sox cap.

"Hey, Red," he said before nodding. "I—can I have a minute?"

Skylar straightened behind the counter. "Um…"

"Actually, I can just say it here. I'm sorry about the spa crap, baby. I didn't mean to make a big thing. Do you forgive me?"

Immediately, Skylar softened and moved quickly across the room to wrap her arms around her husband's torso. "I'm sorry too for over-reacting. I know you were just trying to do something nice for us, but honestly, Jane and I just wanted some time with Nina to ourselves without any strangers around. Forgiven?"

Brandon smiled, and the light he shined toward his wife seemed to brighten the entire small cottage.

"Forgiven," he repeated. "Especially later."

He slipped his arm around her waist, then lifted her up to his eye level. They exchange a short but somehow still passionate kiss, then smiled at each other, lost for a moment in their small bubble.

I took a long sip of wine. That was it? I honestly wasn't sure I'd ever seen a couple approach each other with that kind of blatant affec-tion and straight humility after an argument. But it was clear that there was a lot more love than anything else in the Sterlings' marriage. These were two people, however strong-minded, who had somehow managed to make it work.

"Let me guess, Nina," Brandon said once he was finished making up with Skylar. "Matthew's digging you out of a nasty legal mess too?"

Jane and Skylar both chuckled with him at some inside joke.

I frowned. "Did I miss something?"

"You'll find Zola is something of a white knight around here, Nina," Jane said.

I cocked my head. "Because of how he helped you and Eric? Is that how you all became friends?"

"Ohhhh, no," Jane said. "He's been saving this group's ass for much longer than that, starting with these two."

"What do you mean?" I wondered.

"Oh!" Brandon turned to me. "Then you don't know."

I frowned. "I don't know what?"

Skylar smiled grimly. "Trust me, we have tried to give him so much more than Fenway tickets for what he did. Ironic, really, considering he thinks he's such a schmuck." She shook her head. "Couldn't be more wrong."

"Well, he did hit on you *and* Jane at various points, Red," Brandon put in.

"Oh my *God*," Jane said. "Are you and Eric *ever* going to get over that?"

"Probably not," Brandon conceded with another grin.

Skylar elbowed him in the gut. "Please, he's one of your best friends now. And as I've said about a *million* times in the last six years, it was like kissing my brother."

She proceeded to tell me an incredible story about her father's gambling addiction and Matthew's hand in keeping her and her family safe from a small mafia ring in Brooklyn that had, at one point, actually kidnapped Skylar, igniting a media frenzy around the Sterlings that had only gotten worse during Brandon's brief flirtation with politics.

My mouth fell open as I listened to all the ways that Matthew, with his good, strong core, had saved people that the rest of the world would probably assume could save themselves. The rich liked to believe that all their money could control the world and solve every problem. But it was humbling, really, to discover what a trap it could also be. Matthew offered them all a way to believe in good people again.

He really was their savior. Their white knight.

And maybe, in another world, he could have been mine too.

"That's why we moved here, out of the city," Brandon said when she was finished. "Better security, more privacy. We wanted to make a sanctuary for ourselves, but also for anyone else in our family who needed it."

His words spoke to my soul. "How private is this, really?"

Brandon grinned. "As private as it gets."

"Brandon runs an electronics lab right now that got a big government contract last year for spyware detection," Skylar said proudly. "He tests everything out here.

"Well, it is one reason we don't cut down the oaks," she said frankly. "Even though it *would* be nice for the kids to have a little more grass to run around on."

"Why, so press can fly their drones over to spy on us again?" Brandon spat. "I don't fuckin' think so, Red. Not with my wife. Not with my kids."

I couldn't help but admire his fierce protectiveness over his family. I had grown up in another protective family, but one that was more interested in its own preservation than the actual people within it.

What would it be like for someone, anyone, to stand up for my safety in that way?

What a gift, was all I could think.

Skylar seemed to know it too. She wrapped an arm around her husband's waist and tugged on his shirt to pull his attention down to her. Brandon obeyed, and his gaze immediately softened as he leaned over to press his lips to hers.

"Do you love me yet, Red?" he murmured without a care in the world. Like I wasn't even there.

Skylar's upturned face shone with love and happiness. Nothing masked. Nothing hidden.

"Always," she whispered before Brandon kissed her once more with a hum, then let her go.

"That's lovely Matthew is so kind to you all," I said quietly, suddenly missing Matthew's touch more than I ever had.

"Well, he's not exactly terrible to you, is he?" Jane asked.

I looked up. "I think you're forgetting that he's currently investigating my husband for trafficking."

An awkward silence descended through the cottage. Jane looked wounded. Skylar darted a glance at Brandon, who nodded covertly.

"I'll give you ladies some space," he said. "Zola's alone with the girls, poor bastard. They probably have him made up like Debbie Harry by now."

Jane snorted. "Oh, I'd love to see that."

"He won't care. Little girls love Matthew, and he's so good with children," I said.

"Is that so?" Jane asked. "And...you know this because...?"

I flushed, immediately realizing what I had potentially given away. I cleared my throat. "Oh, um, at the white party. He was very kind to Olivia in the pool, remember?"

Skylar studied me. "Go on, babe," she said to her husband. "We'll be back in a little bit."

Brandon left, and once we could no longer hear his heavy footsteps outside, both Skylar and Jane turned to me.

"Can I ask you something point blank?" Jane said. "Just between us."

I frowned. "Okay..."

"Is Calvin guilty of any of the charges against him?"

I started, shocked that they would even ask me, particularly considering whom the third houseguest was. But as I looked between Jane's and Skylar's equally penetrating gazes, I found I didn't want to hold back. These were not women who messed around. No pretense. No fakeness. Just genuine, unadulterated concern, but the kind that was unflinchingly honest.

"I don't know," I said honestly. "That's the truth. But at one point when we first met...yes. Yes, he was involved with something along these lines. I also know that he tried for many years to become a part of that Janus organization—the one headed by John Carson. Since his death, though, I really don't know about anything else."

"Is he a good husband to you?" asked Jane.

I still couldn't look away. "No. No, he is not."

I had expected it to feel terrible. Expected guilt, dread, panic to consume me. But instead, the heavy weight that always seemed to be sitting on my chest dispersed a bit. I felt lighter just for speaking my truth out loud.

Jane glanced at Skylar, who nodded slightly.

"I thought that might be the case," Jane said. "Look, Nina...I hope you're not mad, but I did talk to Skylar about some of this stuff."

"What? Why?" I reared back in my seat. "Jane, why would you do that?"

"Because I'm a divorce lawyer," Skylar said.

"Correction: my best friend is a shark," Jane cut in. "I'm sorry for talking, Nina, but you can trust Sky. I promise."

"You can give me a dollar if it makes you feel better," Skylar said. "Then I'm legally disallowed from talking about your life with anyone. And if you're living in Massachusetts for a while, you might want to consider establishing residency regardless. That way I can represent you in court, of course."

I frowned. "Why is that?"

"There are a lot of similarities. But one of the big ones is alimony. New York requires a ten-year marriage to provide alimony for up to six years after, whereas in Massachusetts, it's only four. But it's not just that. Brandon and I can help in other ways."

"Look," Jane said. "I won't claim to know everything about your situation with the moldy cheese wheel you're married to. But real talk: something has never seemed right between you two. I knew for sure after I saw this." She pointed her finger at the now mostly faded bruise peeking out from under my linen shirt. "If you...if you need help... getting out...Sky and I both wanted to offer our assistance, however we could."

I frowned down at the bruise, then back up at them. "I'm sorry, but you're mistaken. This is just—"

"A fall down the stairs?" Jane asked.

Skylar just remained silent.

"Okay," I said slowly. "Help. What—what does that mean, exactly?"

"Well, for a start, we have this place for you and Olivia if you need a place to stay safely," Skylar said. "You already know about the security. This isn't some place your husband could find you. Not if you didn't want him to."

I was quiet for a moment. Then, "You do know I have access to quite enough funds to secure a divorce if I wanted, don't you?" I asked.

"Money doesn't always buy trust," she replied frankly. "I think you know that too."

I arched a brow. "Eric might be the official owner of the family billions, but I have my own money. Or will, once the will advances past probate. Grandmother made sure of that." I shook my head. "I appreciate the offer, Skylar, but it really isn't necessary. It's also predicated on the assumption that I want to get divorced in the first place."

"Don't you?" Jane asked. "You just moved out of state when Calvin can't leave."

I shrugged. "I wanted to finish my degree and be closer to Olivia."

"What about the fact that you're in love with Matthew Zola?" Jane said.

Her bluntness was a cleaver.

"I—I'm *sorry*?" I choked.

"And the fact that he's head over heels in love with you," Skylar added.

"You could tell?" Jane asked her, sounding amused.

Skylar rolled her eyes at Jane. "Only the second he got out of the car, Janey. Brandon always teases him when they play cards, you know. Worst poker face ever."

"Well," Jane said, "I knew about him the second you two ran into each other at my apartment last spring. And I suspected about you when I saw you two at the Met Gala in May. But honestly? I didn't really know until last week, when your mother mentioned you hadn't worn a bikini since having Olivia."

Mother. I knew she'd make a thing of that. Jane looked eager, like she thought the revelations might provoke something, but still I remained silent. Matthew might not have a poker face, but I'd learned that trick from birth.

Jane sighed. "Look, Nina. Normally, I wouldn't push like this. But for a few days last January, you were there for me when no one else was. You and Olivia stayed in my house. You made sure I was all right when Eric was gone. You saw what needed to be done, and you cared enough to do it."

I worried my fingers together. I didn't say that time was also when I had first met Matthew or mention the shame and guilt I felt because of it. But she was right about one thing. In the last year or more, I had come to care about Jane and Eric, as a couple and not just for my cousin's sake. I had never said out loud how much Eric's return had meant. That after the dust had settled, and especially after he and Jane were put through the traumas of the spring, I had realized just how much both of them meant to me.

Family. Real family.

It was a gift, not something to be stonewalled.

"Okay," I said in a voice even I could hardly hear. "Yes. I do love him. Very—very much."

Skylar and Jane both beamed with satisfaction. But each word caused a fissure in my heart.

"But...that doesn't really matter," I continued. "Because we both know it won't work in the end."

Oh, it did hurt to admit it out loud. To have witnesses to my tragedy. But for some reason, I thought Jane and Skylar in particular could understand. After seeing them both with their spouses, it was clear they knew what it meant to meet the soul of your heart. They could imagine what it meant to have it ripped away too.

I proceeded to explain exactly why Matthew and I both understood our relationship was destined for failure. Skylar and Jane both looked like they wanted to argue several times, but by the end, both wore twin resigned expressions that told me they had come to the same conclusions.

Skylar's large green eyes shone with pity. Jane, however, wasn't done.

"Okay," she said. "Matthew aside...what about your marriage? Just because you can't ride into the sunset with a dashing Italian doesn't mean you should stay in a loveless marriage."

"I agree," Skylar rejoined. "Not that you need my opinions neces-sarily, but I do."

I bit my lip, wondering for a moment if I should tell them just why I had no real choice in the matter. At least not until the trial was over.

But before I could speak, Jane reached out a hand and covered mine. The simple touch shook me to the core.

Matthew had once done the same, in the exact same way, the first night we met. He had been actively trying to charm me at the bar that night, but it wasn't until his pretenses dropped and true compassion emerged that I had known I had no chance of fighting the inevitable.

Do you know how long it's been since someone held my hand? I had asked.

Jane's gesture too was simply out of friendship. And it touched me nearly as deeply.

"You did what needed to be done," she repeated. "So this is me doing what needs to be done for you. Nina, please hear this, from the bottom of my heart. You deserve to be happy."

My lower lip began to tremble, and so, before I lost things completely, I pulled my hand back and buried my face in my palms. What was happening to me? When had I become so transparent?

Even more, when had I stopped caring?

Since him.

It was true. Knowing Matthew had changed everything. Even if he wasn't the path toward that happiness, like Jane, he had come to make me believe I deserved it too.

When that might happen, I still didn't know. But I determined to find it somehow.

"Thank you," I said. "I have a lot to think about. And I promise you, I will."

———

"THANK you so much for the use of the cottage," I told Skylar again when we were on our way back to the main house. I had considered offering to stay at a hotel, but found I actually wanted to accept the Sterlings' hospitality. "I'll try not to infringe on you for too long. I'm going to visit my house in Newton tomorrow, so hopefully I can be out of your hair by the end of the weekend."

Skylar shook her head. "It's no trouble at all, really. I meant what I said. Stay as long as you like."

I shook my head, still shocked by how extraordinarily open she was. The richest people I knew didn't like opening their homes, which were large enough that several families could live in them for days without seeing each other, for more than a day or two, even to good friends. It was hard to imagine having friends as loyal as Brandon and Skylar, Eric and Jane, and Matthew all seemed to be to each other. I was coming to realize that the relationships I'd worked so hard to maintain most of my life were nothing but mirages. I couldn't trust any of them to be real.

As if she read my mind, Skylar set a friendly hand on my shoulder.

"I know it's a complicated situation," she said. "But you can trust us. I promise."

I nodded. "I can see that. Thank you."

"Come on," Skylar said. "I'm not an amazing cook, but I can rustle us up some tea and a snack if you want."

We entered the house and rounded the corner into the kitchen, but only to discover the adjoining solarium already occupied. A laptop computer was perched on a coffee table between the two oversized armchairs, playing some sort of Disney movie on low volume. The armchairs, however, were completely full of people, all fast asleep. Brandon and Matthew were slumped into the oversized cushions, legs splayed on the ottomans. Meanwhile, Jenny was splayed over her father's big body, and my own daughter was curled under one of Matthew's arms.

"What do you suppose happened here?" I murmured.

Skylar checked her watch. "Well, I can tell you this isn't exactly out of the ordinary for the average Saturday afternoon. Luis is still napping, which means upstairs is off-limits. My guess is the girls wanted to watch a movie but also needed a snack, so everyone crammed here...and fell asleep to *Frozen*." She nodded at the screen. "I don't know about yours, but mine is obsessed with Anna."

I blinked at the animated characters flitting across the small screen. I was ashamed to admit I had no idea whether or not Olivia liked this film. I honestly didn't know anything about her current tastes.

At any rate, I was too entranced by the sight before me to answer. Matthew's arm was wrapped protectively around Olivia's shoulders, and my daughter was curled up like a shell into his side, nose buried into his strong chest. Her mouth was slightly open in a deep sleep, but it was really the way one hand still clenched a bit of his shirt that made my heart squeeze. I'd never seen her hold tight to anyone like that— not any of the nannies. Certainly not Calvin. And not me—not since she was a babe.

A small sigh escaped her lips, and Matthew stirred slightly. His eyes blinked open sleepily, then sharpened when he caught me watching. A crooked smile appeared.

"Hey, doll," he mouthed silently.

I couldn't help the blush. Or the smile.

"Nina, do you want that tea?" Skylar asked from where she was now rustling in the kitchen, back to us.

"Er, yes, please," I said.

Matthew's eyes flickered toward her, then back to me before he stretched his other hand over the side of the chair and snagged mine. He softly pressed his lips into my palm. I shivered through a silent sigh, fighting the urge to wrap my arms around them both. What other chance would I have to hold them both together?

My loves.

Then Olivia stirred. I pulled my hand back. Matthew's eyes darkened, but he didn't argue. Instead, he kept his arm wrapped securely around my daughter and held her close until she settled once more. My heart squeezed along with them.

From happiness. From love.

And yes, from sorrow.

CHAPTER TWENTY-SEVEN

"Going somewhere, doll?"

At seven o'clock the next morning, I was unlocking the door to the Volvo, prepared to run my errands for the day. Jane had already assured me that she would watch Olivia while I was gone. The kids were only just waking up, but I wanted to get everything out of the way in one go. I only had a few more days left with my daughter before we had to bring her and the older kids to school.

I whirled around, nearly spilling the coffee Brandon had offered all over my crisp Yves St. Laurent blouse and pencil skirt.

"Matthew!" I cried, pressed a hand to my heart. "Oh, you scared me. What are you doing here?"

He looked a far sight from the polished, besuited lawyer I usually remembered, instead dressed in much more average weekend fare of worn jeans and a white t-shirt, over which his necklace bearing the cross and saint's medallion gleamed. His sleek hair was pleasantly rumpled, and he had a night's worth of black stubble shadowing the sharp lines of his jaw as he shuffled toward me, still barefoot.

I had seen him once before like this, when I had appeared at his house after John Carson's death, beset with terror and need. He had answered the door in nearly the same uniform, smudged with grease and dirt after a day of working around his house. He looked, for lack of a better word, utterly common. And completely delicious.

I had wasted no time in tackling him right there on his doorstep, and right now, in the bright morning sunlight, I wanted to do the same. Did he know how the cheap cotton clung perfectly to his biceps? Did he have any idea the way the denim perfectly outlined the long, elegant muscles of his thighs? God help me if he turned around. In jeans, the man's backside would give any Roman statue a run for its money.

I tightened my grip on my coffee mug, conscious that if I didn't, I was just as likely to drop it.

"You stayed," I said. "I—I thought you were getting a hotel."

The previous night had ended with a raucous dinner in the main house with the children playing games upstairs until bedtime while I had spent most of the evening alternating between the joy of lingering around a table for hours with people I actually liked and reminding myself not to do what came most naturally when Matthew was around. We had not sat next to each other, instead wisely taking places at opposite sides of the Sterlings' patio table. But I could feel his eyes watching me over his wineglass. And every time he passed me on his way in and out of the house, when the combination of paper, cologne, and wine would waft by, I'd have to squeeze my legs together and grip the table to keep myself from following.

And so, once we found Olivia passed out on one of the bunkbeds in Jenny's room, I went to bed early myself, praying that when I woke the next morning, the temptation would have vanished along with my fatiguing resistance.

No such luck.

Matthew shrugged as he set a hand atop my car, half caging me against it as he took a sip of my coffee. "You try convincing Skylar out of hosting her friends. Besides, the beds here are more comfortable than the Holiday Inn."

I might have thought it a poor excuse if I didn't know myself now how insistent the Sterlings were when it came to hospitality.

"But you're going to the game with Brandon today?"

Matthew's eyes narrowed slightly over the rim of the mug, but he nodded. "Yep. Game starts at one."

"No confession today?" I asked. "Or Mass tomorrow?"

One side of that delicious mouth hooked in a half-grin. "Ah, no. Not this weekend. Why, you want to come repent with me?"

I almost asked "For what?" But I wasn't sure I'd be able to handle the answer.

"You're looking awful nice for early on a Saturday, duchess," Matthew remarked. "Where are you hurrying off to? Got a hot brunch date?"

I snorted. "Hardly." Was that jealousy threaded through the joke? "I'm going to run some school errands for Olivia, and then I need to meet the tenants of my property in Newton."

His eyes brightened. "You have a house in Newton?"

I nodded. "Yes. I purchased it just after Olivia was born. I thought then I might go back to college, but…" I shook my head. "It, um, didn't work out."

Sympathy crossed Matthew's handsome face, but surprisingly, he didn't press. On that, anyway. "So the house. You're planning to live there, then?"

"I might." I fingered the edge of the car door, suddenly wanting to get in and escape this theory. I had wanted to leave New York for years, but when I spoke to Matthew about the possibility, it came with a stab of pain.

"And you're not going anywhere else this morning? Just errands and house hunting?"

Something about his tone cut. Just slightly. "Why are you asking me all these questions?"

I could tell he wanted to offer a quick rejoinder. Probably answer my question with another question, as he so often did. Cross-examine me until my head was spinning with irritation and confusion, until I'd tell him whatever it was he thought he wanted to hear.

But instead, he just shook his head with a rueful smile. "Just plain curiosity, doll."

He glanced behind him toward the windows of the house, perhaps to check for adolescent spies of some sort. "I'll see you tonight, sweet-heart. Or tomorrow, if you're asleep when we get back. Don't wait up."

He darted a quick kiss to my cheek, then started back to the house.

"Wait, what?" As his words sank in, I called out, bewildered, "I thought you were going back to New York after the game tonight."

Matthew turned back and flashed another grin. "Didn't they tell you? It's a Yankees–Red Sox doubleheader on Wednesday, and I'm due some vacation time. I'm staying a bit longer." He winked. "So, I guess you're stuck with me for a few days, doll. I'll try not to get in your way."

I stood there, unable to move as he reentered, waiting for my head to stop pounding at the notion that I'd get an entire week of this torture. An entire week of Matthew and his unintentional charm offensive.

I couldn't decide if it made me happy or terrified.

Likely some of both.

———

IT WAS past one by the time I finished the majority of my errands and got back to Boston, where I picked up a sandwich for lunch on my drive back into Newton. It had been a while since I'd visited Boston—ten years, in fact—but other than a few new stores here and there and a greater prevalence of Starbucks, the area hadn't changed much. Still the same large houses lining the sloping streets toward Boston College, another area school. Still the tree-lined streets and neatly paved side-walks only occasionally littered with children's bikes or chalk drawings.

When I'd originally bought a house in this neighborhood, I'd done it with children in mind. Once, I'd had the idea of sending Olivia to a public school instead of a prep school like the ones I'd attended, and Newton had some of the best in the area. I certainly hadn't imagined sending her hours away at the tender age of five. It troubled me still to think of the day I left her in that classroom, watched as she had stood in the window, arms wrapped tightly around her waist until the large front doors of the academy had closed behind me.

Maybe that was the reason I'd chosen Andover, a boarding school outside of Boston, instead of something closer, like Girard or Rumsey. Maybe a part of me had never completely given up on this move, leaving a clear route when I was ready to leave that life and pursue another. One where I could meaningfully be reunited with my daughter at last.

I parked the car outside the classic colonial with the bright white shingles and Tuscan columns framing a black door. At first, it looked the same. I had originally fallen in love with its farmhouse appeal, with the yawning backyard, the willow that shaded a small creek at the far corner, and the large deck where I imagined rocking Olivia to sleep under the stars I never saw in New York. I remembered thinking it would be a cozy place to live when the New England snows hit, with its multiple fireplaces and large chef's kitchen. I had wanted to learn to cook. Maybe even one day get married to someone I actually loved and have a real family.

For a moment, I could see Matthew's face peeking through the windowpanes, eager to greet me as I returned home. Quickly, I shook away that particular vision. Even if our future hadn't been doomed, this was not the place for him. My love was a New York native, through and through, as much for his family as for his job and the home he had already bought for himself.

Pipe dreams, all of it. Time to let them go and find a way to make my own happen without him.

Too depressed and saddened to bother with this house, for years I had allowed Calvin to take care of it via his own property management firm. A mistake, I now knew, but one I could rectify. A simple call informed me that as of last year, they no longer managed the house, and as far as they knew, it had been vacant since the previous tenants left a few years earlier.

My heart sank as I got out of the car. Neglect of my sweet, beautiful house was everywhere. The windows were filthy after a year without washing. The bushes and trees badly needed pruning, and the grass was overgrown and gone to seed where other parts of the yard hadn't been completely torn out. The paint was peeling, more gray than white near the foundation, and the gutters on the left side were cracked and overfilling with debris.

Vacant, I had expected. In minor disrepair, perhaps. But this utterly broke my heart.

"You there! Hello?"

I turned to find an elderly woman with tight pin curls and pale, wrinkled skin hurrying across the street toward me. Her finger was already pointed toward me, and she had that way about her I knew well—a woman of relative means who assumed her opinion was more important than most.

"Do you know the people that live here?" she demanded as she huffed to the sidewalk where I stood.

I frowned back at the house, baffled. "There are people who live here?"

"Yes," blustered the woman. "They moved in four months ago, and I have to say, they are the *worst* neighbors we've ever seen. It's bad enough the house ended up a rental, since that damages the neighborhood enough, you know. But then it sat empty for a year, begging for vagrants and whatnot until *these* people moved in. And since then, it's been nonstop. People in and out at all hours of the night. Horrid sounds, screeching cars." She made a sound in the back of her throat that conveyed her clear disgust. "Are you here to do something about it?"

I wanted to ask what she thought I could possibly do by myself, but instead found myself straightening to my full height of five feet, nine inches, plus the added three from my heels, and smiled.

"Yes," I said. "I'm the owner. And you have my word I'll take care of the problem myself."

The lady nodded, but not without looking me up and down, as if to assure herself I was what I said I was. I could feel her eyes catch on my elegant Chopard watch and the demure double-strand of pearls I had put on this morning. She relaxed.

"Good," she said. "You see you do."

"Thank you," I told her. I paused, then reached into my purse for my phone. "Might you have a phone number where I could reach you? Or perhaps you would like mine in case you notice anything else questionable? You seem to have quite the keen eye."

She was eager to offer her number. Flattery goes a long way, as I'd learned from my grandmother. So did unblinking eye contact and long, unabashed silences. By the time the woman finished entering her number into my phone, she was much less inclined to be snappish.

"I'll be in touch," she said, handing it back to me as I fixed her with a direct stare. "I—thank you for your attention."

She crossed the street and scurried back into her own house without much of another word. I turned back to my house. Well, well. This was a development. With a sudden knot of anxiety in my stomach, I walked up the path to the front door and knocked.

For a moment, I didn't think anyone would answer. Then footsteps sounded behind the door.

"Who is it?"

I stood awkwardly outside the house, keenly aware that I could be seen through the peephole. "My name is Nina de Vries," I called out. "I own this house."

There was a silence. Then the door unlocked and opened, revealing a young woman with mangy, mouse-brown hair and tired-looking pale skin.

"You is who?" she asked in a thick accent I couldn't quite recognize, but which sounded vaguely Eastern European. Her light blue eyes were glassy and unfocused, and she wore nothing but a dirty nightdress with bare feet.

I frowned. "Nina de Vries." I offered my maiden name because, as I understood it, that was still on the deed. I had used it before the social security office changed my name for good. "I'm the owner."

Her glazed eyes drifted up and down, taking in my prim white clothes. "No, no. You is not who comes. Where is Miss Gardner?"

I frowned. "Do you mean *Mrs.* Gardner? That would be me. De Vries is my maiden name." I craned my head, trying to look over her shoulder. "Who are you and what are you doing in my house?"

"No, no, you is not Mrs. Gardner. She is shorter. Kate, sometimes, he calls her."

I took a step back and checked the address nailed to the house, just in case I had lost my mind completely and knocked on the wrong door. No, 2251 E. Chestnut Drive. This was correct.

"I'm sorry," I said. "I don't know any Kate. I am *Nina* Gardner, and I'm the actual owner of the house. Here, I can show you the deed." I pulled out my phone, quickly swiping to a file storage app. "Are you the current tenant, or—"

"No, no, no, you come back later with Kate. We talk to her."

"Glória! *Menj el az ajtótól!*"

The girl's eyes widened, and she immediately scurried away from the door, leaving me with a clear view into the sitting room, where four or five women were congregated on sleeping mats and a few threadbare sofas. Before I could get a better look, the door was filled again, this time by a short, barrel-chested man in a worn blue polo shirt and faded jeans. His gray hair ringed an otherwise bald head, and in the middle of his flushed, frown-lined face was a nose the color of cherries.

"Who are you?" he barked in a similarly accented voice, though his wasn't nearly as thick as the woman's. "What do you want?"

I frowned. "Well, I was just telling that young woman that I'm the owner of this house. I wasn't aware there were tenants in it right now. I'd like to see your lease, if you have it."

"Owner? No, you're not the owner."

I sighed impatiently. "Actually, sir, I am. I'd also like to take a look around to assess the state of the house and property. It looks like it's been neglected severely while I've been away—"

"You are not allowed to be here," the man snapped. "Twenty-four hours' notice. Massachusetts state law."

He started to shut the door in my face, and against my better judgement, I pressed both hands against it to keep it from shutting entirely.

"Excuse me!" I demanded. "That law only applies to legal tenants, and as far as *I* know, this house hasn't been rented at all."

"You are Mrs. Gardner?" he asked.

I nodded, then whipped out my wallet and flashed my driver's license at him. "My name is Nina de Vries *Gardner*, yes."

He looked at the ID, then back at me. "You need to enter? Twenty-four hours. Now, go away."

But just as the door was closing, the man stepped aside, revealing one of the girls on the couch. She looked at me with a wide-eyed look that could only mean one thing: *Help*.

"Who is in here?" I asked, pushing the door back open. "And may I ask how many people you have on the premises? The property is only zoned for five residents."

I was making things up as I spoke. Anything to open the door. Anything to see a bit more, to help that poor girl or anyone else here who might need it.

"Lady," said the man. "I don't know who you think you are, but you're going to want to leave. Now." He pulled up his shirt and revealed the butt end of a revolver that had been wedged between a furry belly and his jeans.

I stepped back as though I'd actually been pushed. "Oh. Oh, yes. I —I suppose I should."

"And tell Calvin we deal with him only, you got that? No more blondes. *No more*. You got that?"

Flustered, I nodded. "Yes. Yes, I understand."

The door slammed shut, and somehow I made my way back to my car, shaken through to my bones. Somehow, I got back in to the driver's seat, and though I knew I should leave immediately, I still took my time, checking my mirrors, readjusting the back of my seat. I looked a few times toward the house, feeling like someone was watching me through the tatty curtains, but nothing moved.

Who was the man, and how did he know my husband? Not to mention another blonde?

I pulled out my phone, drifting my thumb over the numbers 9-1-1. The blank, terrified looks of the women in that room stayed with me even when I shut my eyes. I knew that look. I had seen it in my own reflection too many times.

I also knew what came after. My cheeks tingled with the memory of those blows. My knees and elbows ached with the force of countless contact against walls, armoires, tables, chairs. If I called the police now and this man reported seeing me at the house, I didn't even want to think about what Calvin's response would be for my meddling.

Skylar's mention of privacy and security echoed in the back of my mind. She had seemed to think it was a necessity in my current situation, and for the first time, I couldn't help but agree. A part of me wanted desperately to take her up on her offer. It would be an elegant solution. But the reality too was that I was nowhere near close to being able to leave. Not now, anyway. I didn't even have a place to live.

I dropped my phone back in my purse. Good lord. What was I going to do?

———

I CONSIDERED ALL these questions as I drove around getting the last few things needed before Olivia went to school. By the time I had a car full of school supplies, weekend clothes, and anything else I could imagine she'd need, I had only come to one conclusion: until I managed to find a satisfactory home somewhere between Andover and Wellesley, I'd have to be content staying with the Sterlings. I was still pondering just what might be going on at the Newton house as I pulled the car to a stop in the Sterlings' circular driveway and stopped the engine.

"Matthew! Noooooo!"

I sprang out of the car at the sound of the loud shriek and was greeted by the sight of Matthew in the center of a ring of children, which included Olivia and Jenny, plus a dimple-cheeked boy who looked maybe two, and a couple of older children I took to be Skylar's half-siblings, Annabelle and Christoph. Matthew was holding Olivia with her arms around his waist while he twirled around and around, causing her feet to fly out behind her.

"Ahhhh!" she screamed with the kind of joy I had never heard from my daughter. Not in nine and a half years.

"Hold on, kiddo!" he cried as he whirled faster, until finally they were both out of breath.

He released her gently back to the ground, and almost immediately, he was tackled by her and the rest of the children, the smaller ones begging for their turns while the older two just seemed to enjoy the chorus of hugs and contact.

"Wait, wait, wait, you hooligans!" Matthew cried, grinning hard as he fought to free himself of all the tiny hands. "I need a break! Hold on, Liv, lemme say hi to your mom. Then the merry-go-round is back in service."

"I'll take his place!" the boy, Christoph, volunteered with a slight French accent and was almost immediately pounced on by the other kids while Matthew made his escape.

"Hey, doll," he greeted me, still out of breath as he wiped his brow.

He was red-faced and gleaming with joy. I wanted nothing more than to kiss every part of him, and maybe lick the drips of sweat from his neck.

I shivered. Oh, no. I couldn't go there. Not now.

"Having fun?" I asked.

"Sure am," he said.

"What happened to the game?" I asked, checking my watch. It was nearly five o'clock. Good lord, where had the time gone?

"Ah, it was a shitshow, if you want to know the truth. Sox won, nine to zero." He scowled adorably. "Pathetic. And now I owe Brandon a Benjamin, to top it off."

I hid a smile. I couldn't have cared less about baseball, but I enjoyed his passion. "I'm sorry to hear that."

"You were gone a while. Get everything done?"

I turned back to the children, not wanting to dive into the nightmare I'd found. "For the time being."

"So, moving in to your new digs this week, I take it."

"Not likely."

"What happened?"

I sighed. And then because I had to tell *someone*, I proceeded to fill him in on the house's strange new denizens and the man with the gun. By the time I finished, Matthew was rubbing his jaw, forehead furrowed so deeply his brows were almost touching.

"Do you have to go back?" he asked.

I shrugged. "Tomorrow, I suppose. I'll probably need to hire an attorney to serve the eviction notice. I wouldn't normally push right now, but the house is in such disrepair, and, well, it's *mine*."

"Of course it is, baby, of course," Matthew murmured, rubbing a sympathetic hand on my shoulder.

I fought the urge to collapse into him and accept his comfort for real.

"Take Brandon and Skylar up on their offer," he said. "Stay here while you figure it out."

I looked up. "You knew about that?"

Matthew shrugged. "Brandon might have mentioned it at the game. Apparently, Skylar's pretty keen on you, doll. Not that I blame her."

There was a loud whoop as Annabelle and Christoph were now taking turns spinning Jenny and Olivia around in the grass.

I sighed. "I can't think why. She barely knows me."

A finger slid under my chin, and Matthew tipped my face gently toward his. "Because she knows the goods, baby. And you're the goods."

For a moment, I almost believed him. But then the finger dropped, and I turned away, back toward the kids who had all collapsed, aside from Luis, into the green blanket of grass.

"I'll go with you," he said. "You all drop the kids off in the morning, right?"

I nodded. "Yes."

"Right. We can dig around public records. Find out what's going on with the people living there, contact the police if we need to. You don't have to do this alone, Nina."

We turned back to watch the kids again. There was something soothing about watching children simply be happy. Olivia in particular continued to shriek with unabated joy as she and Jenny whirled around together in some bastardized version of "Ring Around the Rosie."

"You know," Matthew said, breaking through my daze, "the first time I met her, I couldn't get her out of my mind. Do you remember that?"

Did I remember the moment where my brown-eyed, half-Italian daughter had looked straight into the eyes of a man carrying the same sort of blood between his veins? Did I remember the moment my heart stopped from wanting them to know each other more?

"Yes," was all I said. "Yes, I remember."

"Not just because she looks like you—stupid beautiful, of course— but because, I don't know. There was something about her that just made me feel connected." He shrugged. "Probably you. But I couldn't get the idea out of my mind. The three of us together. Maybe a couple more in the mix."

I was silent as I watched the children, concentrating on staying perfectly still lest my face give away all my raging emotions.

"What about you?" Matthew asked quietly. "Did you ever think of it? You and me? Kids? A family together?"

I could feel his gaze on me, though I didn't dare look at him. I thought of the house with its once-bright white paint. I thought of the backyard with the little stream and the deck with the rocking chair. I thought of Matthew in a large sitting room, wrestling with two children on the floor while I sat on a sofa, nursing our youngest.

"Many times," I admitted just as quietly. "Every day since we met."

And then, before he could say anything else, I turned to go inside and help Skylar with dinner. Because I knew no matter what, the look on his face would break my heart with longing. And I'd had quite enough of that for one day.

CHAPTER TWENTY-EIGHT

"I'll miss you, darling."

My hands fluttered over Olivia once more, who stood patiently as I checked her over for the fourth time since I'd announced I was leaving. We'd driven as a caravan to Andover behind Brandon and Skylar's large Yukon; Matthew and me in the car with Olivia. Skylar's siblings were the ones who attended here, albeit as middle-grade students in a completely separate wing. The Sterlings had hustled their tribe in one direction, and Matthew had stayed in the car while I escorted Olivia through check-in at her own dormitory.

She was still dressed in her casual clothes, but her uniforms were neatly folded in the assigned wardrobe beside her bed, which we had dressed in the new bedding I purchased. While Matthew took the morning to teleconference with his office from the car, we had spent the last several hours decorating her room together with some new things and others taken out of her summer storage. Ironically, Olivia seemed to be more excited to rediscover her old stuffed animals and posters after a summer apart than at the prospect of hanging new posters on her walls.

Her roommate, a sweet girl named Veronica, giggled from her bed on the other side of their shared room, where she was reading some sort of comic book.

"Don't worry," she said. "My mom did the same thing. She'll leave soon."

"Not if I can help it," I chided, suddenly overcome with the need to pull Olivia in for one more hug.

"Mom," Olivia mock-complained, though the pink in her cheeks told me she wasn't too upset.

Finally, I let her go. "Are you sure you have everything you need?"

She nodded. "Yes, and if I need anything, Ms. Hamlin's room is just down the hall. She's one of the nice dorm moms. We got lucky."

"And you like your room? You two feel safe here?"

Veronica and Olivia both nodded.

"This room's a lot nicer than last year," Olivia said. "I like the view of the cherry trees. Plus, Ronnie and I are actually friends, not like me and Janet Horner."

Veronica snorted. "Oh my gosh, ew! I feel so bad you had to room with her."

While the girls gossiped a bit more about their classmates, I peered out at the aforementioned cherry trees, whose gnarled branches were currently swathed with green. I didn't remember being this comfortable being alone at Olivia's age, but then again, over the last few days it had become increasingly obvious that Olivia's shyness had less to do with her innate personality and more with her surroundings. At Skylar's house, and later here, she was confident and chatty. It was New York that made my little girl scared.

Just one more reason to make the changes we both needed.

"Okay, then," I said reluctantly. "I suppose that's everything."

Olivia flopped down onto her bed with a grin. "Don't worry, Mama. You'll be okay."

I couldn't help but smile. "Aren't mothers the ones who are supposed to console their daughters, not the other way around?"

"Tell that to my mom," Veronica said. "She cried for a whole *hour*." She looked pointedly at Olivia. "You're lucky you're getting away with just a hug or two."

For a moment, Olivia looked like she wouldn't actually mind if I burst into tears. But then she tipped her long nose up in that steadfast de Vries manner.

I hugged her again.

"I'll be here on Friday to take you back to the Sterlings' house with Anna and Christoph," I murmured into her hair. "Maybe we'll get lucky and I'll have found a house before then."

"I like Brandon and Skylar's house," Olivia said. "I wouldn't mind staying there more."

"They do have a lot of children," I agreed.

"Oh, it's not that."

I released her and looked down. "Then what is it? Skylar's not a particularly good cook."

She shrugged in a way that was strangely and distinctly European. "It feels like a home," she said. And then, perhaps as an afterthought, "And maybe Matthew will come back."

I opened my mouth, unsure of what to say. On the one hand, I loved that my daughter and Matthew seemed to have made such a genuine connection in such a short period of time. But on the other...

"Don't worry, Mama. If Daddy asks, I won't tell him about Matthew."

My jaw dropped. "I'm sorry?"

"He wouldn't like it." Olivia's eyes darted toward her roommate, then back to me. "Because of the trial, you know."

My heart fell. My poor, poor girl, having to negotiate these power dynamics.

"So, you know?"

"That he's one of the lawyers going after Daddy?" She nodded sadly. "Yeah, I overhead him mention it to Brandon. Plus, Daddy really didn't seem to like him at Grandmamá's house."

"You don't seem to be bothered much by it," I observed.

Olivia was quiet for a minute. "Well...I don't want anything bad to happen to Daddy. But..."

"But what?" I prompted.

Her little brow furrowed. "Sometimes I think it would be okay if we didn't see him at all."

I didn't push her further. No children should be asked to condemn their parents, even if they don't know they aren't *really* their parents.

"Do you and your father talk a lot?" I wondered.

She shrugged. "Oh, no. He never calls me here. But I just thought you'd want to know I still wouldn't say anything. Just in case."

A pang of guilt knotted in my stomach. At the idea that Olivia felt as though she had to choose sides, but also at the fact that she didn't know the truth. It wasn't the first time I'd wondered what she would say if she knew who her real father was. But it was the first I'd *really* wanted to tell her for her own sake.

Instead, I gathered her close for one last hug. "I love you." I kissed her forehead. "I'll see you on Friday."

"Bye, Mama. I...I love you too."

———

MATTHEW WAS WAITING in front of the car when I returned, leaning against the door. Despite being on vacation, today he was dressed for business in a sand-colored linen suit, straw fedora tipped to one side while he read something on his phone. "Just in case," he said, though what case that might be, I didn't know.

When I approached, he hastily stowed his phone in his pocket.

"Hey, doll," he said as he removed his hat. "Everything go all right?"

I sighed. "Yes."

He didn't look convinced.

I pressed my lips together, suddenly trying not to cry. "It's always difficult to say goodbye. I miss her when she's gone."

"Why not have her come home, then? There are good schools in New York too."

"You know who my husband is, Matthew," I said quietly, though the truth was, he really didn't. Not like I did.

But he knew enough to nod his head in sympathy. "Ah. Well, maybe when you're more settled at Wellesley, huh?"

I swallowed. "Let's get going. I have a lot to do today."

He slipped into the passenger side after I unlocked the door, and for a moment, I had to steady myself as his musk swept over me. Oh, God. Was I really spending the day with Matthew, unattended?

"Don't worry," he said as if he was reading my mind. "I won't try anything, if that's what you're thinking?"

"What? Why not?"

He chuckled. "A little desperate for some action, are we, duchess?"

"Stop."

"To answer your question," he said lightly. "Because while I haven't seen any tails, and neither has any of our other surveillance, there is always the off chance that your husband is having you followed. If you think there is any reason he might."

I bit my lip. "No," I said quietly. "I would honestly be shocked if he was."

Calvin thought he owned me, plain and simple. And perhaps he did. For now.

Matthew gave me a queer look, but let the comment lie. "Be that as it may, we should still be careful. We can say pretty easily that I'm a guest of the Sterlings helping you out with the creeps in your house because I am. But that gets a little tougher if I'm caught sucking that lip the way I really fuckin' want to right now."

I wasn't so sure about that. But I also wasn't sure I cared anymore.

"Nina."

I blinked. "What?"

"Stop biting your lip and drive, baby. Otherwise people are going to start looking."

I started. There were, in fact, a few parents and teachers glancing at us curiously, obviously wondering why we were sitting in a car without moving.

"Right," I said, then started the engine and pulled out of the spot.

"You're quiet," Matthew said after another fifteen minutes, when we were back on the freeway on our way to Wellesley.

I glanced at him, then back at the road. "Am I?"

"Well, you're always quiet, but particularly right now. Not that I don't like pensive Nina, but I do wonder what she's thinking."

I paused to change lanes, ruminating on the thoughts that had been running around my mind over the last few days.

"I've been thinking," I said as the landscape raced by. "I want to tell Olivia the truth."

"The truth," Matthew said slowly. "About…"

"About her father," I said. "Her real father." I bit my lip again, thinking hard. "You're going to do your job well. I know you are. And if that's the case, I'll have some space to start a new life for the two of us. It's only right we begin it with honesty, she and I. Don't you think?"

"You don't think Calvin will have anything to say about that, even from prison?"

"He doesn't have as many rights as he thinks he does," I replied evenly. "Considering he's not even on her birth certificate."

At that, he looked genuinely surprised. "He's not? Weren't you married by that point?"

I nodded. "We were, yes. But he wasn't at the birth. My friend Caitlyn was, actually. You remember her, don't you? Caitlyn *Calvert*?"

Perhaps it was petty, but I rather enjoyed the way Matthew squirmed at the name.

"You know I do," he said with a narrow green look. "I guess I didn't realize the two of you were so close."

"Not as close as you, if I remember correctly." Outrageously, I winked, enjoying the way his jaw dropped when I did.

"Doll," he said. "Did you just make a joke at my expense?"

I chuckled. "Could do."

He grinned. I felt like the sun had just shone directly on me.

"Anyway, yes," I said. "We were close. She was my best friend back then. And was until just recently." I glanced pointedly at him. "You remember, don't you?"

"Eric's wedding? Yeah, I remember."

"I thought she was family," I said. "I'd always wanted a sister, and there were times she acted like one. But after the wedding…I guess I just realized that neither friends nor family would really do something like that."

"No," Matthew agreed. "They would not."

I shrugged. "She was never much of an influence on Olivia. Over the years, it became clear that she was in my life more because of what she could get out of it rather than because we were actually friends. We have been talking more recently, though."

Matthew frowned "You have?"

"Courtesies, mostly. But yes, from time to time she checks in." I threw him a mischievous glance. "Don't worry, she doesn't mention you."

His expression didn't change

"You deserve better."

"Better than what?"

"Better than everyone." His smile was sad. "Better than me, that's for damn sure."

There's nothing better than you, I wanted to say. But I sensed it would only be an invocation of what we both wanted, but knew we could never have.

"Olivia's father's dead, right?"

I did my best to ignore the band of guilt that squeezed my chest whenever I thought about Giuseppe's death. "Yes, he passed about a year after she was born."

"So how would you tell her, then? Or...what would you tell her?"

"I'd like to take her to Florence. She's old enough now. I could show her where I went to school. Where I met her father. Maybe I could find his family, and if they still own the olive farm, I'd take her there too." I blushed, realizing suddenly that Matthew didn't know its significance. "That, um, was where she was conceived."

To my surprise, he didn't look irritable the way so many men might when the subject of former partners arose. Most women I knew couldn't say a word about past lovers to their husbands unless they wanted a fight on their hands. I certainly didn't like hearing about Matthew's, even if I could joke about them.

Maybe it's because he doesn't care anymore, a small voice said.

"Not jealous?" I asked before I could help myself.

His dark brow rose. "It's hard to be jealous of a dead man, doll."

"But you don't like the idea."

He didn't answer right away.

"Honestly, doll? Not really."

"Why is that?"

"Because the guy sounds like he was a fuckin' asshole."

My mouth fell open. "What an incredibly inappropriate thing to say. Giuseppe was absolutely not an—an—"

"Asshole?" Matthew finished for me. He shrugged, his irreverence palpable. "He wasn't good to you. Don't expect me to like anyone like that."

I bit my lip. "I beg to differ. I thought he was very good to me, in his own way."

Matthew removed his sunglasses so he could look at me straight on. "He was married."

"So am I."

"That's different."

"Is it?"

"Yes, it is!" he said fervently. "You are trapped in a marriage with a dipshit sociopath. Your professor was just a faux intellectual with a midlife crisis, but instead of taking care of his family, he decided to prey on a nineteen-year-old girl. It's *different*."

"He loved me," I said bitterly, though even now, my resolve was cracking.

Matthew stared at me for a long time, breathing heavily.

"Yeah, well, maybe he did. I can't fault him that, the poor bastard. But, Nina, that doesn't make what he did right. And honestly? If he did love you?" Matthew shook his head, like he still wasn't quite convinced. "I'll tell you this much, it would take more than an ocean and a shitty marriage to keep me from you if I were in his place."

"No, for you, it just takes a trial."

Matthew's eyes were suddenly pools of guilt. "Brutal, baby," he said softly. "But I suppose it's fair too."

We drove for a bit longer in silence until I took the exit toward Wellesley. Matthew's accusations beat along with my heart.

"Look," he said a few minutes later. "I get it. First love…that's tough. It makes us look past all sorts of things in hindsight we should remember. No matter how bad that first love is, we never forget it, do we?"

"Like you and Sherry?"

I was being even more petty now, bringing up another lover who was firmly in the past. But for some reason the thought of the woman who had left Matthew when he was off fighting for his country bothered me more than any floozy he toyed with before we met. Caitlyn, someone I knew for a fact Matthew had never truly cared for, was one thing. It was another completely to bring up the only other woman he had truly loved.

"Don't like it either, do you?"

I bit my lip. "I hate it."

"Join the club, sweetheart. The thought of anyone besides me laying a finger on you makes me want to commit murder way too often for my personal comfort." Matthew pulled at his collar and slouched in his seat, like he wasn't quite sure he could handle his own thoughts even now. "And I'm the one who has to send the love of my life home to another man every fuckin' night."

The vitriol wasn't aimed at me, but I felt it anyway. It was impossible not to. Our reality hurt us both.

"Well, if it's any consolation, I hate it too."

His eyes dropped with shame. "Yeah. Shit, I'm sorry. I know you do." Then he looked hopeful. "But you're here now, right?"

I pulled onto campus and navigated toward one of the parking lots, but I didn't answer.

"Now who's the quiet one, doll?"

Once the car was stopped, he put his hand on my knee before I got out.

"The truth?" he asked quietly.

I looked at his hand. His palm was so broad and warm, like it belonged there, caressing my skin. I'd never wear pants again if he would touch me like this, right there, every day.

"Always," I said. "Even when it's hard."

He offered a lopsided smile. "I am jealous of him. But not as a person, because he's gone. I'm jealous because it feels wrong, somehow, that you'd go back there without me." He pressed his lips together in thought. "Technically, I'm no more Italian than Olivia. A mutt, just like she is. And I've only visited once, plus the time I was stationed in Sicily."

"You're pretty Italian to me," I said. "Given how you grew up. You speak the language and everything."

"I speak a bastardized version, just like every other kid on my block," he said. "I just..." And then he frowned. "Promise you won't go to Italy without me?"

I smiled, like he was making a joke. "Okay, I promise."

"No, really, doll. Promise. I can't really explain it, but I don't want you or Olivia there unless I can see it for myself."

My smile dropped. "Okay. I promise."

This time, I was the sad one because I had to lie. But then again, his smile was just as sad. Because I think he knew it too.

CHAPTER TWENTY-NINE

The rest of the day passed in relative peace as Matthew accompanied me first around Wellesley to register for my classes, then to meet with a real estate agent to look at a few houses for rent in the northwestern suburbs of Boston. When he wasn't purposefully trying to rile me up, Matthew was a delight. And so we continued, and I tried not to think about the fact that eventually this day would end, and we would be back to our normal of trying (and, it seemed failing) to associate with one another out of pure survival.

"It's not funny," I protested as we drove away from the realtor's office in Brookline.

I had turned down the four properties she offered. She had promised to come up with a fresh list within a few days, but I didn't have my hopes up. I was going to have to buy again, I knew it, which meant I likely wouldn't be able to move for a month at the earliest.

"It is funny. I've never seen you shop before. You're like the Queen of fuckin' England, tapping around with your pointed finger."

Matthew giggled. The man actually giggled, somehow made it look attractive, and it was at *my* expense. He propped up his hat, stuck out his nose and flopped his hand forward in the most irritating fashion as he continued his imitation.

"Tell me," he said in a fake British accent that didn't sound a thing like me, "are you *really* trying to convince me these floors are original oak when they are clearly *la*minate?"

"It was a perfectly fair question," I protested. "I won't be taken advantage of like that."

"Come on, doll. You were a little hard on her."

"Let me tell *you* something, Mr. Zola," I returned. "People see this, and they don't always see someone worth reckoning with. They see the pretty face and the blonde hair, and they assume I haven't got anything but air between my ears. And then they see the big ring and the designer purse and assume I also have a lot to take. I *have* to act like that and ask abhorrent questions that way. If I don't, I'm not given one iota of respect."

"All right, all right." Matthew patted me on the leg again—he'd been doing that a lot, I noticed—and offered a rueful grin. "I apologize, baby. But you do realize it only makes you that much more of a duchess, don't you?"

I shrugged as I turned down Chestnut Lane. "As long as it's not a princess, I can accept that. Besides..." I pulled to a stop in front of my sweet dilapidated white house. "How can I sign a lease when I have the perfect home right here already? It might be full of vagrants at the moment, but it's mine."

Matthew didn't answer. He was no longer relaxed, but sitting forward on the edge of his seat while he peered at the house, seeming to take in all of its elements and flaws.

"*This* is your perfect home?" he asked, clearly aghast.

"Well, it was ten years ago. But I could bring her back to life, I'm sure of it. God, look at that awful van." I noted the large brown thing taking up most of the driveway. "That wasn't there yesterday."

"It wasn't?" Matthew pulled out his phone and snapped a picture.

"No," I said. "So what do we do now? Call the police, do you think? Skylar checked last night. There is no lease on record for this property—"

"No, but that doesn't mean anything," Matthew cut in. "Most landlords don't record leases anyway. In most states, no one is required to file them with a government agency."

"So I'll have to ask Calvin about it, then." I stared at my hands, full of dread.

"I don't think you should do that yet."

I looked up. "Why not?"

He didn't answer, instead just stared at the house for a few moments, then sat back in his seat. "Do me a favor. Drive around the block, then park up the way we came, about five car lengths back. In the shade of the oak tree."

"Why?"

"Nina, just do it, please."

Reluctantly, I did as he said. A few minutes later we were parked on the side of the road, partially hidden under the shade cast by the oak in the front yard. Once the engine was turned off, Matthew pulled out his phone and chose the camera app as if he was going to take a picture.

"What are you doing?" I asked, making to get out of the car.

He put a hand on my arm. "Wait."

I pulled it away. "Matthew, can we please just get this over with? I have a right to see what's going on in my own house—"

"Nina, hush."

Just as I opened my mouth to argue that *he* should hush himself, the door to the house opened, and three pale girls, led by the one who had answered the door yesterday, trudged out in a line toward the van. Matthew clicked away, taking pictures of all of them. The door opened again, and they were followed by the man from yesterday.

"There he is," I said. "I'm getting out."

"Nina, you sit tight in the fuckin' car. I'm not kidding."

"Matthew, what is going on? That's the man I spoke to yesterday."

He just continued to snap photos as the party opened the van and got in. "Yeah, I figured."

"What is going on? Do you know him?"

"Do *you*?" The question was curt and cold, suddenly laced with tension.

I frowned. "What? No, I told you I have no idea who he is."

We watched the van pull out of the driveway and down the street until it was out of sight.

"Well, that's perfect," I said. "Matthew, I needed to talk to him."

"Well, you can look around right now. They aren't there, and if they're squatting, entering isn't violating any of their rights." He looked at my purse. "You have your keys?"

I went still. Something about this felt very strange. "I...yes, but—"

"Well, come on, then," he said curtly. "Let's go."

He followed my cautious steps up to the house, then watched as I slipped the key into the lock. It gave immediately. I frowned. I wasn't sure it was a good thing that even the locks hadn't been changed in ten years.

"Come on," Matthew said again as he glanced up and down the street. Then he took my hand and pulled me quickly inside.

It was even worse inside than out. My beautiful house had been completely wrecked and was now clearly functioning as some sort of drug den. We walked into a living room that had been strewn with rumpled sleeping bags. Tourniquets and syringes were strewn in a few corners along with spoons and materials I assumed were used for some sort of drug production. The walls were scraped and stained. The only furniture was an old TV in one corner cramped by two battered couches that looked like they had been pulled from a dumpster.

"Oh my God," I breathed, holding a hand to my nose to block the strange burnt stench that filled the room.

"Shit," Matthew said. He took pictures of everything we saw, then grabbed my hand and pulled me through the house.

We didn't venture upstairs, but the rest of the main floor was much the same. The kitchen was strewn with leftovers and rotting takeout.

Matthew opened a cupboard and swore loudly. "Jesus, that's a shit ton of fentanyl."

The sun room at the back of the house contained more drug paraphernalia as well as a stack of pornography in one corner.

"What *is* this place?" I wondered as we approached the back deck. "What are they doing here?"

"A safe house," Matthew said shortly.

"For what?" I stared.

He darted a dark look at me, but couldn't answer because right then there was a sound of jangling keys as the front door was unlocked.

"We have to get out of here," Matthew said, pulling me quickly toward the back of the house.

Just as the sounds of heavy feet slapped on the wood floors, we opened one of the french doors and slipped into my beautiful backyard, which was now just as overgrown and mistreated as the front.

"Stay down," Matthew whispered as he peered low through one of the windows.

I did not stay down. Instead, I looked with him, shocked again by what I saw.

"There's only one," I whispered. "Where did the others go?"

Matthew's mouth remained in a tight line as we watched the man I had spoken to yesterday slump onto one of the sofas, set his gun on the side table next to him, and reach for a warm beer that had been sitting on a dirty cooler. The woman, whom I recognized as the one who answered the door and asked for Kate, reached for one of the tourniquets and needles beside him. He snapped at her in a language I didn't recognize, then grabbed the back of her head. She jerked at first, but I watched in horror as she turned to him in a resigned fashion and started to unzip his pants.

"Let's go," Matthew said, pulling me away. "Now."

We crept around the side of the house, darted through the bushes, and into the shade of the oak tree, where we walked quickly back to the car.

"Drive," he ordered as soon as we were both in. "Now."

———

WE WERE both silent all the way back to Skylar and Brandon's, both obviously pondering what we had just seen. Matthew's shoulders remained tense and cold. His hand crept nowhere near my knee or any part of my body. It wasn't until we had parked in front of Skylar and Brandon's house and gotten out that he turned to me beside the car and spoke.

"Do you need to go anywhere else?" he asked.

I frowned. "No. We're already here. Where else would I need to go now?"

He looked disappointed. And frustrated. "Nothing else you want to check up on? Things you need to tie up before you start school next week?"

I turned to him, suddenly irritated myself. "What are you talking about?"

"I'm just asking a question."

"Why?" I asked.

Matthew tipped his head. "Why what?"

"Why the question? Why this whole day, now that I think about it? Why did you follow me everywhere? Come with me to all these errands?" I frowned. "I didn't need help with this, and it can't have been terribly interesting for you."

"Doll, you have no idea how interesting this is. I'm fuckin' fascinated right now."

I scoffed. "Tell me another. Please."

Suddenly, I was backed up against the car, with more than six feet of hot-blooded, dark-eyed prosecutor glowering over me from under the brim of his fedora.

"Nina," he growled, "do I *look* bored right now?"

I gulped. "No, but—"

"And did I say anything about wanting to be anywhere else but right here with you?"

I swallowed harder. "No, but—"

Matthew smirked. It brought out a dimple on his right cheek, and I wanted to hook my finger in the divot and kiss him. Hard.

"What are you looking for here?" I wondered. "What are you expecting?"

He shot me a bemused look. "Why? Should I be expecting anything?"

I frowned. "No, of course not. But still. This isn't adding up."

Matthew worried his jaw. He hadn't, I noticed, let me up from the car. If anything, I was trapped more tightly to the shiny metal, his knee between my legs, broad chest pressed to mine.

"You know you can tell me anything, right?" he asked.

I hesitated. Was he serious? How many times had he told me the exact opposite—*not* to say a word? "What makes you say that now?"

His eyes searched mine. "Nothing. But..."

And then, instead of finishing his statement, he kissed me. My lips fell open instinctively, and his tongue dipped in to tousle furiously with mine. Searching, somehow, just as insistently as his questions before.

"Why?" I gasped when he finally released me. I felt like I was drowning, but because he was gone, not because he was there.

Still.

"Why what, doll?" Matthew pressed the back of his hand to his mouth, like he was trying to keep whatever remnants of the kiss firmly in place.

"Why do you keep doing that?"

"Doing what?"

"Kissing me. You keep saying we shouldn't—"

"You say it too."

"Even so!" I burst out. "I'm—you're—" I shook my head. "You make me feel so weak. And I am. You're the stronger one, but you keep taking such advantage..."

He looked at me like he wanted to argue back again. I didn't blame him. We were so good at it, and it only inevitably started more fireworks. Carefully, he slipped his hands around my neck, cradling my head in his warm palms like I was some precious treasure he couldn't bear to drop.

"I'm sorry," he said softly as his thumb brushed over my cheek. "I know I shouldn't. But every time I look at you, I can't help thinking, this might be my last chance. One day soon, you'll be gone forever, and the truth is, it fuckin' guts me." He took a deep breath, then exhaled slowly. "I kiss you because I have to, Nina. I kiss you because I might never have the chance again, and if I don't take it, I'll never forgive myself."

Suddenly, he was kissing me again, with tongue and lips and his hand slipped up to wrap around my throat just tight enough that I felt secure, but not squeezed. Just as quickly, it turned into devouring.

And then, in the middle of it, he pulled away on a sharp gasp. "Fuck. *Fuck.*"

"What is it?" I asked, though my voice was somewhat hoarse from the effect of his fingers. "Matthew, p-please talk to me." I could hardly speak, I wanted him so badly.

He stared at my lips like a tiger premeditating an attack.

Do it, I found myself thinking. *Just pounce.*

But instead, his hand dropped, and he turned away. "I'm going for a walk."

I stood up. "Are you serious? You're going out *now?*"

"Yes."

"Why?"

"Because I need to cool the fuck down!"

Before I could argue further, he had clapped his hat back on, swept his jacket over his shoulder, and was striding for the gate.

"I'll be back in an hour," he called over his shoulder. "I told Skylar we'd be home for dinner. And *I'm* not a damn liar."

And with that, he left me standing in the driveway, hand to my mouth, lips throbbing, wondering just what exactly he meant by that last remark.

CHAPTER THIRTY

A t first, I thought that Matthew might miss dinner after all, but he slipped in just as Skylar was setting large, utilitarian platters of spaghetti and meatballs on the oversized farmhouse table just off the kitchen. Despite the fact that three of the five children had left for school, it was still a boisterous affair that became a reunion of sorts when Eric showed up to surprise Jane, along with Kieran Beckford and her wife, Pushpa. Kieran was another of Skylar's (and once Eric's) law partners and apparently an old friend of Brandon's too.

I, for one, mostly listened as the raucous, joyful conversation embraced the party like a merry hug. Eric in particular was fascinating to me as I witnessed a genial comfort in my cousin's bright smile and open laughter that I'd never known anyone in my family to possess. Now I could see just why he had stayed away from New York for so long, and why he and Jane continued traveling back and forth from Boston so frequently. Their friends were special. The warmth in this home was special. These were the types of people who made their family rather than accepted the lot they had been given, and the difference shined through.

So, I thought. Money didn't have to equal propriety. Manipulation.

Chill. Theoretically, I'd always known these things to be true, but I'd never really seen it. Not up close. Not like this.

At the far end of the table, I caught Matthew watching me over his wineglass while his thumb circled the edge, again and again. Most of the time, he was right in the middle of the conversation, having known nearly all of these people for years himself. But every so often, just like now, he would catch my eye and fall back into a pensive silence to match mine.

I wanted to ask him why he had run off so suddenly. Why his mood had shifted almost as soon as we had turned down my block in Newton. I wanted to ask him if that last kiss still burned on his lips the same way it did on mine.

But every time I was about to gesture that he meet me outside, he looked away or made some joke that set everyone laughing once more, and I was pushed further back into my own thoughts.

"What do you think?" Skylar asked as she returned from putting the smaller children down for bed. "It's a nice night. Nightcaps around the orchard fire?"

"Only if you can get Brandon to tell *the* story again over brandy," Pushpa said as everyone rose from the table. "Every time, he slithers out of it."

"Jesus Christ," Brandon muttered from the kitchen sink, where he was making a mess of his shirt trying to do the dishes. "Not that shit again, Pushpa."

"What?" Pushpa blinked her large eyes balefully as she moved to a cabinet and began to gather snifters for everyone, clearly comfortable with the house. "I have never had a satisfactory recounting of it, you know."

"What story is this?" I asked as I took a stack of dishes into the kitchen.

Skylar smiled as she took them. "They love to retell how Brandon tried to get me to be his mistress."

"I *never* used that word," Brandon snapped over his shoulder, hitting himself with a spray of water.

"No, you only offered to put her up in a condo a few days a week so she would be at your beck and call. Who did you think you were?

Richard Gere in *Pretty Woman*?" Kieran shot as she located a bottle of
brandy from the liquor cabinet.

"What is this, 'pile on Brandon' night?" the man himself asked.

"Well, it is fun, Mr. Lewis," Jane jeered as she carried over the
empty pasta platters.

"Leave it," Skylar said as she pulled the sprayer out of Brandon's
hand. "You're too riled up to do dishes, babe. You'll get soaked."

After they made sure their phones were synced with the children's
monitors upstairs, we followed the Sterlings out to the orchard next to
the house, then settled around a large firepit and watched while
Brandon and Matthew quickly got a nice steady blaze going in front
of us.

"I'd like to hear this story," I said as we all took seats in large rattan
chairs around the firepit on the outer edge of the orchard.

Pushpa grinned at Brandon as she clutched a blanket around her
shoulders. "See?"

Brandon rolled his eyes, but grabbed Skylar's hand as he began to
talk. "There's not much to tell. They just love hearing about how I
messed up with Skylar again and again when we first met. It's embarrassing, really. And these assholes never let me forget it."

"What did you do?" I wondered.

"Asked me to be his weekend woman," Skylar joked.

"Red!"

"Well, it's true," Skylar rejoined. "I think the way you put it was,
'nip it in the bud,' right? Complete with a wardrobe allowance and a
condo?"

Laughter erupted around the fire as Brandon's cheeks pinked, even
in the dim light. I wasn't sure I found it funny. I personally knew
several men who actually had real mistresses they treated in almost
identical ways. But having met Skylar, I couldn't imagine her ever
even considering such a proposal.

"And what did you do?" I asked.

Skylar smirked. "Called him a pig and told him to burn my file."

The laughter grew louder. Brandon, though taking it all in good
stride, didn't seem to find it quite so funny either. In fact, he looked
downright guilty as he carefully watched his wife.

"At the time, I just thought he was a womanizer," she said. "Little did I know he wasn't available. Not really."

"But he still had to have you." This time it was Matthew's voice cutting across the fire. But he wasn't looking at her. He was looking at me.

"Red."

Brandon's deep timbre cut through what remained of the jokes at his expense. Everyone quieted, and the intensity of the way he was looking at his wife brooked no room for her to look away either. No one could.

"If we're gonna tell these stories, baby," he said softly, the guttural edges of a South Boston accent creeping out with his emotion, "then we have to tell them right. We need to include the parts where I chased you through a blizzard in the middle of the night just to get your name. Or how I racked my brain for weeks about how to convince a woman like you to love a man like me, making fuckup after fuckup, sure, but never stopping because it always came down to one truth. There was no one else but you. Not from the second I laid eyes on you." He leaned over in his seat, begging his wife to look at him. "You know that, Red, don't you?"

The other couples around them leaned into each other as well. I tried not to stare as Jane whispered something into Eric's ear that made his eyes flash, even in the darkness. Nor could I help but notice the sly smile on Kieran's face as Pushpa made a secret gesture that clearly meant something between the two of them. It felt intrusive to watch any of their interactions, and so, in the end, my eyes landed on the only other unattached person in our party. And Matthew, of course, was staring right back at me.

"I know," Skylar murmured, reaching out to trace Brandon's jaw with her fingers until she traced his lips too.

All at once, the big man stood and pulled his much smaller wife up with him.

"Friends," he said. "Stay as long as you like. But my wife and I need to finish this storytelling on our own. Good night."

I watched again as they meandered back through the orchard. Skylar's laugh filtered through the trees when Brandon paused to lift her into his arms and carry her inside like she was his new bride, not his wife of five or more years.

"I think that's a night for us too," Kieran said as she and Pushpa stood and collected their glasses. "Nina, it was nice to meet you."

"And you," I called as they left. "I hope to see you again." And I meant it too.

"And then there were four," Eric said softly, reaching for Jane's hand.

He, Jane, Matthew, and I scooted our chairs closer to the fire, so the flames licked our faces and cast a corona that ringed us in the black of night.

Jane sighed, burying her face into his shoulder. "Talk some poetry to us, Eric. It's a good night for it."

Eric raised a brow. "You think, pretty girl?"

Jane's eyes closed dreamily. "I know."

Eric smiled sweetly at her, then began to recite.

> *I went out to the hazel wood,*
> *Because a fire was in my head,*
> *And cut and peeled a hazel wand,*
> *And hooked a berry to a thread;*
> *And when white moths were on the wing,*
> *And moth-like stars were flickering out,*
> *I dropped the berry in a stream*
> *And caught a little silver trout.*
>
> *When I had laid it on the floor*
> *I went to blow the fire a-flame,*
> *But something rustled on the floor,*
> *And someone called me by my name:*
> *It had become a glimmering girl*
> *With apple blossoms in her hair*
> *Who called me by my name and ran*
> *And faded through the brightening air.*
>
> *Though I am old with wandering*

Through hollow lands and hilly lands,
I will find out where she has gone,
And kiss her lips and take her hands;
And walk among long dappled grass,
And pluck till time and times are done,
The silver apples of the moon,
The golden apples of the sun.

"I didn't know you were such a poet," I said once he was finished. I was learning all sorts of things about Eric tonight.

He offered a hesitant, lopsided smile. "I'm not. That was Yeats. I was an English major at Dartmouth. Didn't you know that?"

I shook my head. There were so many things we never shared with each other after he left.

"I thought of that poem a lot when I was in New Hampshire, out by the woods. And later...after Penny died."

Everyone was quiet. Jane clearly wasn't surprised to hear about Penny, the girl Eric had planned to marry before she died when they were only twenty-two. I, however, had barely heard him speak about her.

"She's why you left New York," I said.

It wasn't a question, but Eric nodded anyway.

"The first time, just to get away from the family bullshit and take her with. And then after...yeah. Grief really messes you up," he said.

"So does family pressure," I remarked dryly.

"Well, sometimes the people we want aren't the people others think we should have," he said as he stoked the fire, causing a blast of sparks to shoot into the air "It's so common with the de Vrieses, it's practically a rite of passage."

I frowned. "Who else do you mean besides you?"

"Well, my mother, for instance. John Carson definitely didn't want my father to marry her. And neither did Grandmother, from what I hear. And then, of course, there was Penny."

"After what they did to her, I'm surprised you ever came back," I said, in spite of the years of resentment I'd felt toward him for just that.

Eric shrugged. "Penny was tough. She took it on the cheek most of the time."

"I shouldn't think suicide as taking it on the cheek," I said more bitterly than I intended.

"Doll," Matthew hummed a warning under his breath.

"Oh, Nina..." Jane murmured, shaking her head.

But Eric wasn't angry. Instead, he just looked up in surprise. "Nina, do you think that Grandmother was responsible for Penny's death?"

I blinked. "Of course it wasn't her *fault*. She wasn't holding the *knife* or whatever the poor girl used, but—"

"It wasn't her fault at all," Eric cut in. "And Penny didn't kill herself. Jude Letour murdered her. He was sent by John Carson, a nasty fucking power play when I was first initiated into the Janus society. He confessed it this spring." His voice was short and curt. He obviously didn't like talking about any of this.

As the truth washed over me, I felt just as quickly like I was drowning in it. "But she—I thought—didn't they—"

Slowly, I melted, head into my hands, like a candle whose core was sinking in on itself. All my misconceptions revisited at once. Terror at being alone and pregnant and nineteen. Walking down the aisle with Calvin, seeing potential murder in my grandmother's eyes rather than the disappointed truth. Peppe, dead in Florence, and all the fear I had carried with me since.

"Oh, God," I whispered into my hands. "What...did...I...do?"

"Did you—is that why you married Calvin?" Jane asked in a kind, quiet voice. "Because you were afraid of what might happen if Celeste found out that you were pregnant?"

I looked up. "You knew?"

Jane shrugged. "I wondered. I can do math. Olivia was pretty early, and Calvin has never said a thing that indicates he has ever spent an hour in Italy, much less the month or two you claim he did." She turned to Eric. "Last week I asked him if Marcus's Negronis measured up to the ones he had in Florence. He said he didn't drink Greek beverages there."

Eric snorted. My mouth felt dry. Matthew had stilled completely, his only movement the meditative swirl of his brandy snifter as he watched the revelations unfold.

"So, Grandmother didn't...the family didn't...they weren't responsible for Penny's death?" I finally managed.

Eric swallowed, then scooted forward in his seat. "Look. I'm not going to pretend our family is full of saints, because it's not. Our grandmother in particular was a conniving, power-hungry, narcissistic old bat. But she wasn't a murderer. And in her fucked-up way, I think she tried to make amends for her disapproval of Penny by bringing Jane and me back together."

I frowned. "Eric, she blackmailed you into getting married. You and the rest of the family would have been disinherited otherwise, isn't that right?"

But Eric, to my surprise, just laughed. "Nina, I had already disinherited myself. Do you really think I gave a good goddamn about the family fortune? I had my own business. I was doing fine. And I never once believed she would have followed through on the other half of that threat."

"Then—well, then why?"

"The truth is, I would never have said yes if it wasn't going to get me what I really wanted in the first place. She knew she was going to die, and in the end, Jane and I think she just wanted to see the family together and me happy." He reached behind him for his wife's hand and squeezed it, then ran his knuckle up the inside of her arm. "As much as I hate to admit it, I think she pressured me to get married because she knew *exactly* who I'd choose."

He gave Jane a look that squeezed my own heart in response, then raised her hand to his mouth and kissed her knuckles.

I ruminated on these revelations in silence for several minutes. Perhaps he was right. Grandmother had been the definition of manipulative when it came to doing what she thought was right for her family. She had also made no secret that while Eric thought he was a "free man" here in Boston, she had been keeping track of his whereabouts the entire time. Eric and Jane had met in law school and burned out there too. Undoubtedly, she was aware. Perhaps he was right, that at the end of her life, her ambitions for him were more altruistic than she let on. Perhaps her dying wish, then, was only to bring Eric back into the family and help him find happiness at last.

But then another question remained.

Celeste de Vries had two grandchildren. So why hadn't she done the same for me?

"The best thing I ever did was leave, though." Eric broke through my thoughts. "It showed me I could be my own man."

"It's good you were able to do that." I couldn't quite keep the resentment from my voice. It was difficult, when I considered how much I had needed him myself.

"But, Nina?"

I looked up and was surprised for once to find myself a target of Eric's penetrating gaze. This kind openness was something I had caught directed at his wife several times, but never anyone else in the family. And that included me.

"I'm sorry," he said quietly. "Not for leaving. I can't—I can't be sorry for that, considering everything it's given me." He squeezed Jane's hand, and it was clear what he meant. "But I'm sorry I left you behind. We were close once. I hope we can be again, you know."

I remained quiet for a long time, trying and failing to process everything he had said. I didn't know what to make of any of this. Not Eric's apology. Not his revelations before that.

"Thank you," I said numbly, keeping my eyes trained on the fire as my mind swam with confusion.

"It's not too late for you, coz. Not if you really want."

The conversation died, and for a moment, I could feel the other three pairs of eyes fixed on me—all of whom, it was clear, were eager to help me however they could.

Would they still feel that way, I wondered, if they knew all I had done to help Calvin?

It must have been clear I wasn't going to say anything, because after a moment, Jane turned to Eric and whispered something in his ear. My cousin's expression, which was generally unreadable, assumed a peculiar heat that I also wasn't used to seeing in my family, but which I knew somehow, his wife managed to produce regularly. It might have made me uncomfortable if I wasn't so happy for him.

And so very riddled with envy.

"If you'll excuse us," Eric said as he stood up to follow Jane. "We're, ah, tired. I need to put Jane to bed."

And without waiting for any response, they left Matthew and me to watch the final flickers of the dying fire. And each other.

CHAPTER THIRTY-ONE

"What are you thinking?" Matthew asked after Jane and Eric escaped to the house.

I was hypnotized by the embers left from the once-crackling fire. I wanted to watch the flames grow high again. Maybe throw myself into them.

But the embers just glowered with a soft, slow burn.

"What am I thinking?" I repeated as if in a trance.

The tips of Matthew's black sneakers shone on the other side of the fire, and like a magnet, my vision was drawn up his long legs, past the belt around his taut waist, past the chest just bared through a few undone buttons, and to his face, with those sooty eyes always cast with desire. The kind that echoed so deep in my bones, I could hardly breathe for want.

And then my reality came roaring back.

It wasn't Celeste's fault that Penny died.

Eric's voice was another echo, but instead of fading away, it only grew louder and louder. Along with another thought in the back of my mind.

If she didn't kill Penny...maybe she didn't kill Peppe either.

Suddenly, it wasn't just a thought, but a full-blown certainty. And the force of it broke me.

"What am I thinking?" I said again, now unable to keep the shaking from my voice. "I'm thinking…you really don't want to know what I'm thinking, Matthew."

"Yes, I do." His voice was strangely calm, almost choked. "Don't hide from me, doll. I want to know it all."

"Why?" I swallowed, feeling like a massive lump was stuck in my throat. Everything felt wrong. My skin was starting to crawl.

She didn't kill them. Oh, *God*. Was it really true?

"Because," Matthew said. "You need to spit it out, baby. I'm here. I'll listen."

"I'm thinking I've been the greatest, biggest fool on the planet." I choked, the words like fire in my mouth. "I'm thinking that all the reasons I gave up my entire *life* for ten whole years didn't exist."

"You mean what Eric said about Penny?"

I nodded miserably. "I thought…God, I can't believe I ever thought this. But I swear, Matthew, when I came home from Florence, pregnant with Olivia, I truly believed there was a chance that my grandmother would do something terrible to me. And then, a year later, when I was just thinking of leaving Calvin and going back to Italy…he was dead."

"Who?" Matthew leaned forward, tense with interest. "Who was dead, Nina?"

I hiccupped back a dry sob. "P-Peppe. Giuseppe. My—Olivia's father."

"You thought she killed him?"

"I don't know what I thought anymore."

I rubbed my face hard. Everything seemed to be stuck. I felt like I had been living inside of a house of mirrors that had just been smashed, but I was still buried under the shards.

"She didn't do it," I whimpered into my hands. "Oh God, she didn't do it. None of it was ever necessary. Not my marriage. Not any of it!"

"It's still not," Matthew said gently. "Or it won't be. Hopefully soon."

"As if that matters now," I said bitterly. "Look at me. I'm so lucky to be here. On this beautiful property. With these lovely people who also so clearly love each other. And I'm here with the man I want, the man I l-love more than anything too…"

My voice cracked over the words as several large tears spilled down my cheeks into my palms.

Suddenly, through the lingering ashes and charcoal, filtered the scent of light fresh cologne, paper, and man. I looked up to find Matthew crouched beside my chair, waiting patiently for me to breathe again. Funny. In my anguish, I hadn't even heard his footsteps on the gravel. He was a cat, slipping through my life and my heart with such feline grace.

In this state, I was more like a bull in a china shop.

"I'm thinking about how cruel fate is," I whispered. These emotions, they were all too much. Regret, remorse, anger, desire. "Because I'll never love anyone like I love you, but I c-can't have you. Not now. Not…not ever. And it's all my own *fucking* fault."

If my sudden profanity shocked him, he didn't show it. Instead, Matthew slipped a hand around my shoulder and threaded his fingers into the hair at my nape, massaging lightly. Comforting.

The effect was immediate. I sagged toward him, seeking more.

"It's not your fault," he said quietly, his deep green eyes demanding mine in return.

"Of course it is. It's completely my fault. It's my ignorance that's to blame, and no one else's."

Matthew leaned in and pressed his forehead to mine. "Nina. You didn't know. It's. Not. Your. Fault."

I didn't respond. I felt as if all the life I'd ever had, what little of it was left in me, had been sucked out by Eric's revelations. Matthew had no idea what I had given up to keep the peace. To keep my daughter safe. To keep my family happy.

And it was all for nothing. *Nothing.*

"Tell me one thing," he said, eyes closed, as if he were almost scared to see the response in mine. "Is it—would it—" He took a deep breath. "If you had to make a choice, which would it be? Your husband behind bars? Or me?"

I blinked through a lace of tears. "You, of course. But to be honest,

Matthew, I—I don't want anyone to get hurt. I'm so, so tired of all this pain. For everyone."

I found that it was true. Matthew, however, didn't seem to agree. In an instant, he went through a transformation similar to the one in Newton. His tenderness vanished, replaced by a steely edge I had only seen directed at me a few times before.

"Is it because you actually do care about him?" he asked. "That you love him?"

My lower lip trembled. "What? How can you ask me that?"

"You've been with him for a decade. It's not out of the realm of possibility. You might feel loyal after everything he's done."

"Loyal?" The word felt foreign on my tongue. "To Calvin?"

Matthew sighed, then stood up and returned to his chair. Picked up a stick, tapped it viciously on the ground a few times before hurling it into the woods. Then he glared at me.

"Do you still fuck him, Nina?"

I gaped. Where had this conversation gone? What was happening? "I'm sorry, *what?*"

Matthew's eyes glinted like a knife's edge, all sparkle of kindness gone. "I have to know. You fuck me. You fuck me every chance you get—"

"I'm sorry, but I do not *fuck* you every chance I—"

"But I never asked, did I?" he rattled on. "I didn't think I had the right."

"You still don't," I seethed, despite the fact that I would have been equally upset—and had been—about his sexual partners.

"I don't care. I want to know. Do you fuck that simpering, lazy, no good son of a bitch?"

"He's my *husband*," I said, though the word made me ill. "What do you think we do?"

"I don't know!" Matthew shouted, causing me to jump in my seat. "You live with him. You do whatever he asks. You don't argue, you play the good little wife, even check on his pro—"

He cut himself off suddenly and rubbed his face hard, like he was trying to rub out a stain on a piece of tarnished silver.

"I don't know," he said again, this time more quietly, but no less dangerously. "That's why I'm asking. I don't know."

We glared at each other across the fire. The light was so dark here at the edge of the orchard, Matthew looked more like some shadowy devil than the polished attorney. But, strangely, no less himself.

As angry and confused as I was, I had never wanted him more.

"We are married," I said, inwardly begging my jaw not to quiver.

Just tell him, an inner voice said.

Tell him what? I asked it right back. Tell him that at first I fought it, but after years, he wore me down to the point where it seemed easier to let him have his way than to risk cracking my ribs again? Tell him that since January, I hadn't been able to numb my body that way anymore? That once again, I allowed my husband to hit me and shove me and kick me like I was no better than a stray dog because I would rather he did that than cross that final line with my body, which now, after Matthew's touch, somehow felt sacred again?

I closed my eyes as memories came back unbidden.

A hand between my legs.

Hair torn from my scalp.

Body slammed into a mirror.

Do not fight me on this, princess.

You'll lose, princess.

You frigid bitch.

When I opened them again, I was swimming in shame. Years ago, I had made myself a promise, and then broke it so many times. Turned myself into a ghost of a person until I was revived by the man in front of me.

How do you tell a man who brought you back from the dead that the price of your love was also your life? How do you face the possibility that he might hate you for it?

"Nina." Matthew's gaze felt like fire. "I said don't hide from me."

"Then stop looking at me like that," I said. "Stop it."

But he did not. That blackish-green gaze. That face like a pirate's. That soul of an artist.

God, I loved him and hated him so, *so* much. For everything we were. For everything we couldn't be.

"I could never stop looking at you," he said. "Not in a hundred years. Not in a thousand."

That was when I knew I believed everything Matthew had ever said.

And I knew he loved me.

Because I knew that if he ever discovered the true nature of this marriage, its mercurial faces behind closed doors, its real costs...he would crash through every barrier stopping him from protecting me. He'd throw away his job, his career, everything he had ever worked for if he thought he could save me from pain.

And it would ruin everything for him.

The only problem was...I loved him too.

Just as fiercely. Just as much.

So I did as I'd always done.

I told the truth I could. And kept the rest to myself.

"No," I said quietly. "No, I do not...sleep...with my husband. Not —not since I met you."

Matthew sucked in a tortured breath, almost like he was afraid that my response wasn't actually real.

I stared at my hand, suddenly shaking.

"Nina," he called quietly from the other side of the fire, which had died now into a soft orange glow.

"Yes?"

"Baby. Will you please just look at me?"

"I can't," I whispered.

"Why not?"

"Because," I replied. "Every time I have to stop, it hurts that much more."

Lord, even just to say it was a knife through my heart.

"Nina."

His voice was a siren's call, male or not.

"Nina, don't hide from me," he said again. Softer this time. A request, not a demand. "Please."

The simple, kind, frank courtesy undid me completely. I looked up, and found that guileless love back on his face. And I knew I couldn't fight this anymore.

Like a woman in a trance, I rose from my seat. Matthew's gaze didn't break as I walked around the fire toward him. I felt like a fish being reeled on an invisible line. Called by a song I couldn't hear to push him back into his chair, carefully sitting astride him until my skirt was bunched around my hips. I placed my hands on his shoulders, so I could be closer, as close as I could get, to this man who owned my heart.

"So it's like this, is it?" he asked quietly, almost sadly, as I settled in his lap. His warm hands slipped over my bare thighs as the skirt bunched up, the broad span of his palms fitting naturally atop my skin.

"Yes," I said. "It is."

It was truly as if we had no choice but to touch. Like magnets, we were drawn to each other no matter how much time apart, no matter what obstacles were in our way.

We'd be separated again. Tomorrow, probably. And every day after. But perhaps that only emphasized the need to take advantage of the rare moments like this.

Written in the stars, he had said. Perhaps this, right now, was what he meant.

"Are we—are we truly protected here?" I asked, looking up at the sky. Just beyond the heavy canopy of the trees, a few stars blinked above us from the night sky. Stars we could never see in Manhattan, suffocated as they were by the city.

"As protected as we'll ever be."

I looked back down, overcome with clarity. Then, without saying anything else, I pushed his tie over his shoulder and began the process of unbuttoning his shirt. The crisp white parted to reveal his skin, a deep, glowing bronze, like a Roman hero come to life. I stripped off my own shirt and bra until we sat face to face, skin to skin under the night sky. Despite the lingering heat of summer, only *his* warmth could thaw my wintry chill.

"I love you," I told him, for once unafraid of the words.

"I know." Matthew's gaze didn't waver, as solid and unmoving as the statue he resembled. But so much warmer. So wide and open.

His eyes drew a long, slow blaze up my torso, tarrying a moment on my breasts and nipples, perked in the night, then continuing up my neck and face, to find my eyes once more. One of his hands slipped around my back while the other cupped my jaw to pull me close. My nipples grazed his chest, just enough that I sucked in a breath.

"For what it's worth," he said, the warmth of his breath sweet on my face, "I love you too. I have a feeling I'll never stop."

This time, there was no hurry. There had been so many goodbye kisses with this man that they were starting to blur together. Even so, this one felt different. There was no hurry to get through it, no frenzy to remove the rest of our clothes or devour each other whole. Instead, our mouths moved in achingly slow concert while the wind swished through the trees around us. Our tongues danced, slipping in and around, tasting, feeding, savoring each deep lick, each tangle and twist.

Matthew's hands ran up and down my back, tracing the grooves of my spine and ribs, then slipped between us to cup my breasts. He kneaded them while he sucked on my lower lip, then worried my nipples between his thumbs and forefingers until I was humming against his lips like a kitten.

When he broke away, I gasped at the sudden flush of air between us, but Matthew wasn't in a hurry to return. Instead, he settled his hands back on my hips and looked at me.

"What?" I asked breathlessly. "What is it?"

"I'm thinking..." He closed his eyes for a moment, then opened them, looking pained with desire. "I'm thinking you're the most beautiful woman I've ever seen, Nina. I'm thinking that you always will be."

I drew my hands up to cup my breasts the same way he had, then took my nipples and continued the long, luxurious tugs he had engaged in just seconds before.

"Anything—" I pulled again, enjoying the concurrent shudder that ran through his shoulders as he watched. "Anything else you're thinking?"

His eyes dragged up to meet mine. "Honestly?"

I bit my lip. "Please."

"I'm thinking I really don't want to be here right now."

That was *not* what I was expecting. Before he could say anything more, I stopped what I was doing and folded my arms quickly over my chest. "Oh." I looked down, trying to ignore the bite of rejection.

He knew. He had changed his mind because he knew.

But before I could get up, I felt his warmth against my back as his hands closed over my arms and slid down them, then around to pull me tight against him.

"Because," he continued, "I need more than just another quick fuck in the woods, Nina. I need four walls. I need a bed. I need a place where I can take my fucking time with you again."

I stilled. "Well, then. Why don't you take it?" I did, after all, have an entire cottage at my disposal.

"Just tonight," he said solemnly. "But tomorrow? Cards on the table, Nina."

I bit my lip, unsure of what he meant. Perhaps he could see through my half-truths. Matthew was better at reading me than anyone else. I was too scared tonight, but at some point, I'd have to tell him everything.

"Agreed," I said. "Tomorrow, we'll talk."

He kissed me again, and then I felt my shirt drawn back up over my shoulders.

"Put your shirt back on, doll," Matthew murmured against my lips. "It's the last time you'll wear it until morning."

CHAPTER THIRTY-TWO

W e ran through trees and meadows of the spacious property like children in the night, toppling into the guesthouse with something akin to glee but which extended to someplace deeper. Someplace darker.

Matthew knew this house, of course. Had even stayed in it a few times over the years. For some reason, knowing that this too was a place he came to for its warmth and security, a place where he felt at home, only made me want him that much more. It wasn't either of our homes, but it was better than a hotel room, or Central Park, or a public beach. It was a space that offered privacy and security, a place where both of us could trust that for the night, at least, we were safe.

As soon as the door shut behind us, Matthew kissed me once more, then resolutely set me apart from him.

"Strip," he ordered, even as he began loosening his tie.

I licked my bottom lip, unable to respond from want.

"I'm not fucking around tonight, Nina," he proclaimed as he yanked it off. "Do you understand?"

I honestly wasn't sure I did, but I was too transfixed by the sudden expanse of brick-like muscle that appeared when he removed his shirt completely.

"Nina."

I looked up. "What?"

Matthew yanked me to him and delivered another kiss that made my head spin. I barely noticed as he wrenched my blouse off my body and my skirt fell away like a shed chrysalis. All I knew was his mouth devouring mine. And the warmth of his skin under my hands as they slid over his shoulders and into his hair to pull him that much closer.

And then, just as quickly, he stopped again.

"Matthew!" I sputtered. "P-please!"

He wrenched his belt from his pants and the leather hit the wall with a loud thwack. Two seconds later, the rest of his clothes were on the floor, I was swooped off the ground, and Matthew was carrying me eagerly into the bedroom at the other side of the cottage.

"I'm so fucking tired of this," he muttered as he let my feet drop back to the ground.

"Tired of what?"

"Needing you like this." His kisses were so much more urgent now, desperate attempts to quench something burning within us both. "It never stops, Nina. It never. Fucking. *Stops*."

"I know." I took my share as well, grabbing his handsome face and yanking him back to me again and again. "I know, my love, I know."

He buried his face in my neck, teeth drawing roughly over the delicate skin until he came to the base and sucked, hard. He trapped both of my wrists to the bed as he worked, pinning me against the soft, cool linens. I couldn't have been more content.

And then, suddenly, he stopped.

"What?" I breathed, back arched, nipples inches from his mouth.

The hands around my wrists squeezed tighter.

"Fuck," he muttered. "*Fuck*. I can't fucking focus."

"What?" I asked. "Why—why not?"

I was slightly hurt. I had practically tumbled down the rabbit hole just from his kisses alone, but he was losing interest?

He turned and felt around on the floor for something, then popped up holding his tie.

"Put your arms above your head," he commanded.

Taken aback, I did as he asked. He pulled the fabric taut between his hands and grinned like the rake he so resembled at times. The rake he *thought* he was, though I knew better.

"Stay still," he said as he began wrapping the scarlet silk around my wrists, binding them first together and then to the slatted wood headboard behind me.

"How can I give you what you want if I can't touch you?" I wondered.

"This is what I want, doll." He continued with his task, brow adorably furrowed, until my hands were securely bound. "There. Now you can't go anywhere. Not until I say."

"You were worried?"

"I'm always afraid of that," he said quietly. "Because it always happens in the end, doesn't it? One of us always leaves."

I didn't have an answer for that. Because, of course, he was right.

"Not tonight, though." He pressed his face between my breasts, inhaling deeply as though his life depended on it. "Now you can't leave until I say."

"Why do you always want to see me in red?" I asked when the red of the tie caught my eye above us.

Matthew's hands slipped up my arms to my bound wrists, then back down again.

"Because you're so pale," he said as he drew kisses down one arm, then the other. "It's beautiful. This scarlet splash against your purity." His smile curved wickedly inside my elbow. "And I *really* like knowing I'm the one who corrupts you."

"But I'm not pure," I said. "I have my sins, Matthew. Just like everyone else, I bleed when I'm cut."

He paused over the bruise just above my breast, the one I never allowed to heal. Not completely. He licked it, lightly at first, then again with one long, languorous swipe of his tongue.

I shuddered as he moved between my breasts, tongue tickling the sensitive skin between them.

"I like it when you sin, Nina." His voice rumbled against my skin, causing goose bumps to rise in its path. "I like to see you get a little dirty. With me."

His mouth closed over one nipple, and he sucked, hard.

"Ah!" I cried. "You'll—you'll have to be careful. Someone is going to hear us."

"Who?" he asked as he moved to the other side. "We aren't sharing any walls here, Nina. It's just us and the damn trees. So go ahead, baby. Make that sound for me again."

I did, and then I watched, transfixed, as he drew a trail of kisses down my belly, pausing just below my navel to press a particularly tender one to the sensitive skin there.

"Baby," he murmured, then continued further.

"Oh!" My heels dug into the mattress, hips arching upward as his mouth found my clit.

Hands wrapped around my ankles this time, securing me to the mattress on both ends.

"Take it, Nina. I want your pleasure. I want to feel you fuckin' writhe, baby."

And writhe I did, as his tongue twisted and lips sucked, as he savored every buck of my hips like I was a horse he was trying to tame. Every so often he would hum, and the delicious rumble against that most sensitive part of me made me jerk, not in an attempt to escape. I wanted to get closer.

My fingers flexed, aching to sink into his silken hair. His tongue dipped into me.

And suddenly, I flew.

"Matthew!" I shouted, loud enough that I was sure anyone within a five-miles radius must be able to hear me.

He released my feet in order to grab my thighs, hold me down while I shook and shivered and thrashed until I couldn't anymore. At last, his iron grip softened. He placed his chin on my hip and smiled sweetly while he waited for me to recover.

"You okay?"

"Please," I gasped. "Please. I want you."

"Not yet." He pressed one more kiss to my leg before sitting up on his heels, looking for a moment like a king surveying his kingdom.

"Why?" I whined shamelessly. "Matthew, please."

"First I want to see those beautiful eyes while I slide into your mouth."

I licked my lips eagerly, utterly shameless for the way his words drove my desire. He crawled up the length of my body, drew his impossibly hard arousal over my stomach, between my breasts, as if he wanted to feel every modest curve I had touch *his* most sensitive part as well. Then carefully, he straddled my shoulders and held his erection to the seam of my lips, a deliciously greedy gleam shining in his dark eyes.

Obediently, I opened.

How is it possible? I wondered as he slid inside, inch by inch. Despite the fact that I was literally bound and tied while this man unabashedly took his pleasure from my body, I had never felt more free.

Perhaps because I knew that however he judged himself, Matthew never judged me for embracing my animal nature.

"Fuuuuuuck," he groaned as I sucked hard, relishing the taste of him. "Goddammit, Nina. It's too much."

But before I could do it again, he pulled out of my swollen mouth, then bent to retrieve a condom from his pants. When he returned, he covered me completely, his long, graceful body a secure cage against the bed.

I couldn't have been happier to be trapped.

"Are you ready for me?" he murmured against my lips just before he stole a few more kisses. When he slipped against my slick entrance, he shuddered. "God, *please* tell me you're ready, baby."

Dying to pull him to me, I instead arched my hips upward in invitation. "Please."

He fit himself to me, then grabbed my chin with one hand, holding me perfectly still as his lips closed over mine and he began the delicious, excruciatingly slow process of sliding inside me.

"Mmmmfftttt?"

I moaned lightly at the way he teased, then reluctantly, broke the kiss. "What did you say?"

His lips curved into that deliciously wicked smile against my mouth. "I said, 'Is this all right?'"

"Oh—ah!" I tensed again as he pressed forward perhaps an inch more, then stopped. "Why do you always ask me that?"

"You know why." He slipped in a little more, taking his time, giving me a few moments to adjust at each stage. Another tender kiss. Another inch forward. "I don't want to hurt you."

I lifted my head, capturing his lower lip between my teeth, biting lightly. "You won't. Just do it." I bit again. "Matthew, I need you."

He hissed his accord and then captured my mouth with his all over again as suddenly, he rammed the rest of the way inside.

The sudden force knocked my head against the wood slats, but I didn't notice. Suddenly, he was moving, steady and deep, and I could not think of anything else but the fact that I was here. He was in me, filling my deepest, secret spaces.

"Squeeze me," Matthew ordered in a ragged voice as his hands found my thighs and urged them around his trim waist. "Tight, Nina. Put all that Pilates to good use."

Without thinking twice, I hooked my heels together and squeezed as hard as I could, pulling him inside completely. He needn't have waited. I was slick with need, had been ready for him for hours.

"*Fuck!*" he croaked as he surged into me again and again.

"I want to touch you," I moaned with every deep thrust. His body was slippery against mine, the friction of our meeting driving me closer and closer.

But I didn't want to do it alone. Something was wrong. I didn't want to be trapped anymore. When I toppled over that nameless edge, I wanted to bring him with me. In my arms, not just carried in his.

"Then free yourself," he said, breath warm, voice low against my ear. "You want your freedom, my gorgeous girl? You gotta fuckin' earn it."

I shook my head from side to side, unable to take much more. "Please, Matthew. Just let me go. I want to come *with* you."

But instead of doing what I asked, he just kept going, merciless in his rhythm. "You didn't even fight, duchess. Why don't you find out what happens when you do?"

His eyes gleamed as he pushed himself to his knees, still keeping my legs around him as he moved, a bit slower now.

He was the carrot, I realized. All I had to do was grab.

And so, tentatively at first, then a bit more insistently, I started trying to work my wrists out of the tight binding that trapped them. I wriggled and moved, and to my surprise, the silk began to loosen.

"It's coming free!" I grinned as with each movement, the tie around my arms loosened until it had unraveled completely. At last I was free, and the energy from that feeling caused me to fly up and into his arms, forcing him to topple onto his seat as he caught me. We were still joined, but now I was the one on top, the one who drove the pace.

I ground down, taking him even deeper, and his mouth found my breast once more, sucking deeply, echoing the rhythm of our bodies.

"Oh, God," I cried as my head tipped back. His strong arms kept me upright, along with my fierce grip on his thick hair. "Please, Matthew. Oh *God*, I'm so close!"

Matthew's hand slipped between our bodies, but I didn't need it as I flew again and, this time, took him with me. This man in my arms, and me in his.

It was and would always be enough.

CHAPTER THIRTY-THREE

The moon had risen high above the trees by the time we stopped to catch our breath again. Matthew and I lay together in the big, rumpled bed watching the shadows from the moonlight slowly cross our bodies while casting us both in its cool blue glow. For the first time in days, I was able to enjoy the plush, yet comfortable surroundings of the guesthouse, decorated as it was with oversized pillows, bright white and gray paints, and farmhouse furniture with just the right amount of weathering.

"This is what I used to want my home to be like," I said, waving a hand around the cabin.

"This small?" Matthew joked. "I can't really see you making do with a thousand-square-foot cabin, doll."

I shook my head. "Well, no, not that part. Although in New York, there are plenty who do."

He grunted in response, clearly feeling that should have been self-explanatory.

"I meant the feel of it," I elaborated. "The decor. Comfortable, yet chic. Luxurious, yet lived in. Bright whites, farmhouse furnishings."

"What's your apartment like, then?" Matthew wondered as he

drew his knuckle down one of my arms. "Is it much like Eric and Jane's place?"

I considered my cousin's large townhouse on the Upper West Side, with its loft-like space and colorful, modern furnishings. "No. Jane has much more eclectic taste than I do. I forget that you've never actually been in my home." I smiled to myself. "It belonged to some distant cousin who died a few years before I was married and then was gifted to me. I never changed any of the interior, so it looks very dated. And very formal."

Matthew lay on his side, watching me carefully. "You never wanted to change it?"

I shrugged. "It was never my home."

He remained quiet, watching our fingers toy with each other against the soft white sheets.

"It's a wreck now," I said sometime later, "but the house you saw—the one in Newton—that was my dream home. When I bought it, anyway. I imagined Olivia there. The backyard was this lovely meadow. You couldn't see it through all the overgrown grass, but there's actually a creek running through the far corner, with a willow tree and a thicket of raspberries alongside it." I closed my eyes. "I used to imagine sitting in the back, living this idyllic—not quite rural, but something calmer—life. I even had a place secured for Coral, my horse, at a farm in Concord."

"It sounds like it would have been nice."

"It would have been safe." And then, because for some reason, I hadn't been able to stop thinking about it: "How long did Skylar nurse Jenny? Do you know?"

Matthew screwed up his brows. "Ah..."

I giggled. "I'm guessing you didn't keep track?"

He snorted. "No, I don't really 'keep track' of what Skylar does with her tits, doll. And if I did, I'm pretty sure Brandon would kick my ass." He lay back in the bed, looking up at the shadows from the ceiling fan that striped the plaster. "It's hard to say. I'd guess around the same amount of time Lea does, which is about a year and a half, maybe longer. I remember her leaving the room to do it when Jenny was about to walk. That was around fall, when I visited for Thanksgiving."

"They made me stop," I said.

His whole body stilled. "What do you mean, they made you stop? Who's 'they'?"

"My husband. My grandmother. I don't know. People."

He sat up, causing the sheets to fall down his broad chest, like Dionysus rising from his slumber. "How does someone make you stop feeding your kid?"

I shrugged. "It's hard to explain. You didn't know my grandmother, but—"

"I've heard enough stories and met your family. I have a pretty good idea."

I swallowed. "I was really young, remember. I had a hard time speaking up for myself."

"You don't seem to have a hard time doing it around me."

I smiled. "I—you seem to bring that out in me. I'm not sure what I think about it."

"It's good. Very good."

"You like that I'm difficult?"

Another kiss. "I like that you're *you*."

The kiss deepened. And maybe I would have let it sink into something much more, but my mind was still lingering on the topic at hand. Matthew seemed to sense it, and eventually, he released my chin and settled us both back onto the blanket while he pulled me close.

After a few minutes, I finally spoke again.

"She was almost six months old. The doctor said she could eat. I fought it until then. My grandmother never nursed either of her children—a lot of women didn't back then, and she said it would ruin my figure. And my hus—Calvin, he...well, he just didn't like it. Maybe it meant I would not be available to him for even longer. I honestly don't know."

Matthew didn't say anything for a long time, just kept his dark eyes trained on me in the dim light. I didn't look away.

Then, he reached out and drew the sheets down to my waist, baring my breasts again in the moonlight. He took a long time to examine them, cupping each small, pale globe in his hands, brushing his thumbs lightly over the coral pink topography of areola and nipple. Then he leaned down and pulled one of the tightened buds between his lips. His mouth worked in long, slow sucks, once, twice, three times on one side, then repeated the motion on the other. With each tender pull, something inside me opened up. More keys turned in the secret locks that had been closed my entire life. This wasn't about sex; it was about truth. Compassion. Love.

A tear trickled down my cheek, followed by another. Then another.

"Baby," Matthew whispered as he gathered me close again. "Why are you crying?"

"It's silly," I said, wiping the tears from my eyes. "I haven't thought of it in years. But at the time, I was so crushed. I—I wanted so badly to give her s-*something*, you know? And I couldn't. I couldn't..."

"You gave her a lot, Nina. You gave her all the opportunity in the world. You kept her safe."

"I tried," I said sadly. "But I never gave her what I wanted. Never a home. And how could I? I never had one myself."

"You could have done it. You still can." He brushed the hair out of my eyes and continued to stroke my cheek, wiping away a few more errant tears.

"I went from my mother's to my grandmother's and back, these great, formal houses full of priceless antiques and immaculate surfaces. They groomed me and dressed me like I was just another fixture. I think that was why they made me stop feeding her, you know. Too messy." I sighed. "But I also think that was when I really wanted out. Not just of my marriage, but of all of it. So I decided to go back to school, bought the house, had the papers drawn up."

"So, what happened?"

I swallowed. "Well, you know what happened. Giuseppe died, Matthew. I had no reason to go back to Italy then."

"But the rest? The house? School? You let it all go. For what?" His tone sharpened slightly—out of anger on my behalf, I thought.

I shrugged. "I was scared."

"Because you thought they killed him."

I closed my eyes, and for a moment, I was taken back to that terrible day in Calvin's office. "Because I didn't know what else they might do."

Matthew remained quiet for a long time, holding me gently, brushing back my hair until both of us gradually dozed off in our lovers embrace. A temporary shelter for the rest of the night, but the best one I'd ever had.

When I awoke again, it was still dark outside. But Matthew wasn't beside me any longer, instead he was sitting on the edge of the bed, broad back facing me, elbows perched on his knees, clearly in deep thought.

"Matthew?" I asked. "Are you—is everything okay?"

He turned around but remained where he was. His eyes looked hollow and worried. "This can't wait until morning. I thought it could...but it can't. Nina, I need to ask you something. And I need you to tell me the truth."

I sat up too, clutching the sheets to my chest. "Okay..."

"Is the name Katarina Csaszar familiar to you?"

I frowned. "I already answered that question last week, Matthew. Why, who is she?"

Matthew's eyes narrowed. "You're sure? Never a Kate or a Katie? Nothing similar?"

I tipped my head as something occurred to me. "Well, the woman who answered the door mentioned a Kate, like I told you. Was she talking about this Katarina?"

Again, he didn't answer. Just pressed on. "How about Károly Kertész?"

I couldn't have said why, but something about the name sent a shiver running through me, like someone had run a wet finger down my back in the middle of a snowstorm.

I gripped the sheets harder. "Matthew, what is going on? Who are these people?"

Again, he didn't answer my question. Instead, he just shook his head back and forth and rubbed his face hard.

"It doesn't make any fucking sense," he muttered as he got up to get some water, but not before he grabbed his phone off the nightstand and took it with him.

"Matthew," I called after him. "What's wrong? Who is Károly Ker-Kertész?" I stumbled over the unfamiliar pronunciation.

My answer was the door shutting behind him. But instead of following, I remained in bed, content to ruminate. The names sounded vaguely Eastern European. Did they have anything to do with the people in my house?

My phone buzzed on the bedside table. The small clock next to it read sometime past one in the morning.

"What in the world…" I murmured.

Caitlyn: Drinks this week? I miss you.

I frowned at the text. I wasn't sure why she had been so friendly lately, and now that I was away from New York, I wasn't sure I cared enough to rehabilitate this relationship. Certainly not at one a.m. I thirsted for friendships, for a life that was real. It hadn't happened yet, but strangely enough, here I felt support for those dreams from people who barely knew me, far more than those I had been around most of my life.

Nina: Sorry, classes start next week. I'm trying to sort out a place to live before then.

Caitlyn: You are awake! I thought you were coming back soon. Silly me!

She thought I was coming back? Why? I set my phone on the nightstand and pulled the blankets back over me, waiting for Matthew to return.

A few minutes later, my phone buzzed again. I scowled at it. It wasn't like Caitlyn not to take a hint.

But it wasn't Caitlyn. It was my husband.

Calvin: What in the hell were you doing in Newton today?

Immediately, I froze. How did he know about that? Calvin knew I was planning to go back to school, but I hadn't said a word about moving back into the house I'd purchased years ago. There was no way he would have known I was there.

Unless...the man at the door had told him. Or he was having me followed.

And if the latter was true, he may have also known that Matthew was with me too.

But my heart iced over completely as something else occurred to me.

The foreign accents. The sleeping bags on the floor.

Calvin had lied all those years ago, and now he was using my sweet, small house as a stopover for smuggling people into the country illegally. The stacks of documents and passports I'd seen in his office that day reappeared in my mind's eye. He had continued that business. He had built his own meager fortune on these illegalities. And what's more, he was still doing it, attached to my name, despite everything he had promised.

At that moment, Matthew walked back into the room with three frown lines that looked permanently etched over his brow.

"All right," he said. "If you tell me you don't know anything more about these people or that house...I believe you."

He was shaking his head with the look of a man still figuring things out. But then, all of a sudden, his expression cleared.

"I believe you," he said again. "And I love you. Enough that you and I are more important than this case. Nina, I think it's time I stepped back and—"

"I do know who they are," I cut in before he could finish.

He blinked, stunned, then sat heavily on the bed again to face me. "You do?"

"I—" I shrugged. "I have an idea."

He frowned. "Wait. You do know who Károly Kertész is or you don't? Katarina Csaszar?"

"I'm guessing they're illegal immigrants," I said. "Smuggled in by my husband through one of those houses in Brooklyn. Or any number of properties he has around the tristate area that are likely owned by that company, Pantheon."

Matthew's jaw dropped.

"I have to tell you something else," I said softly.

And then I proceeded to tell him everything I knew. I told him about the money I'd given Calvin out of my trust when I was young. The additional cash he'd requested, again and again, from my grandmother's accounts. I told him about finding the cache of dirty documents and how many of them had my forged signature, along with the deeds and other property-based paperwork.

I didn't mention the beating. I didn't mention the fear. After all, he knew how terrified I'd been of my own family over the past ten years. I hoped that would be enough for him now to understand my motives.

He was quiet for a long time after I finished. I hugged my arms around my chest, waiting to hear him tell me it was over. That I wasn't the woman he thought I was. That I deserved to be locked up with my husband and every other criminal in New York.

After all, he would have been right.

Instead, his response was the last one I expected.

"That's it?"

I looked up in shock. "What do you mean, 'that's it'? I just told you I'm complicit in an illegal immigration scheme Calvin has been running for years. That's very, very bad, Matthew."

"It's bad," he agreed slowly. "But...Nina, you gave him some money and kept his secrets because he trapped you into this. And I don't for a fucking minute believe it was just to keep your daughter's home life intact. Not when you send her away for months at a time."

"Andover is a very good—"

"You love Olivia," Matthew interrupted me. "If I hadn't known it before, I definitely do now, after seeing you with her. You had a broken heart when you got back into the car this morning. I knew then that you would never send her away if you didn't believe she was safer somewhere else. Somewhere without you. I..." He squinted, like he was trying to see something clearly a long way away. "Look, I've already decided to recuse myself from your case no matter what."

"What?" I reared. "I thought you were the only one who—"

"Derek and I have been making some contacts with the Newark PD and in Connecticut. Even here in Massachusetts. There are a few other white hats out there." He shook his head, thinking. "I think it's fair to say that *if* you did decide to turn yourself in, the DA is likely to grant you a pretty small plea deal. You'll be forgiven pretty quickly, especially if you offer evidence against your husband."

"Can I do that?" I asked. "I thought you said he would claim spousal privilege anyway about anything I said."

"All bets are off if you're an accessory or co-conspirator," Matthew said. "But I still think you'll be forgiven quickly. You might even be able to negotiate immunity, given everything you know."

"And you?" I was almost afraid to ask. He was still so far away, on the opposite side of the bed from me. "Would you forgive me?"

He was quiet for a good while, making no move to reconnect. Every second that passed felt like a dagger to my heart.

"You promise that's it?" he said finally. "That's *everything* you know?"

I nodded, suddenly desperate for his touch. "Yes. Matthew, yes, I promise."

"Nina," he said. "If you tell me the truth, I'd forgive every mortal sin in the book." Slowly, he reached out and took my hand, then placed a reverent kiss over my knuckles.

I melted, then pulled on his hand, urging him close again. Light shined within us both. This would be a hard road ahead for both of us. But if Matthew was there to support me, even if it was just with a small kiss like this, I knew I could do it.

"Come back to bed," I said, tugging on his arm. "Please. I need you."

He leaned in to kiss me again. But just as it was deepening into something much more, it was his phone that buzzed this time on the floor, still in his pants pocket.

Matthew swore. "I'd better get that. If someone's messaging this late, it's important."

But, apparently, it wasn't. Matthew stood up and shoved his legs into his pants as he read the text on his phone. Immediately, he swiped through and brought the phone to his ear.

"Derek, it's almost two in the—" he started to snap, but then stopped, eyes popped open. He then turned to me as he covered the mouthpiece. "I'll be right back, okay? And then...we'll come up with a plan, baby. I promise."

I lay back down in the bed, wondering just why everyone we knew wanted to contact us in the wee hours of the morning. Eventually, though, my mind wandered. Back to the house in Newton, or maybe a red brick house in the middle of Brooklyn. To Olivia swinging by Matthew's arms in a green backyard or nearby park. And maybe another dark-eyed baby nestled to my breast, cooing while we watched his beautiful father laughing in the sun.

I closed my eyes, and for the first time in many years, really let myself dream.

But dreams, as they say, aren't real. And mine died almost as quickly as they were born.

The bedroom door banged open, and I turned to find Matthew striding in with a face full of fire.

"What's wrong?" I asked, sitting up once more. "Is everything all right? Is Derek okay?"

Matthew snatched his shirt off the ground and began violently shoving his arms into it. "You. Fucking. Liar."

I recoiled, almost as if I'd been struck. "What? Matthew, w-what are you talking about?"

He snatched his tie off the ground, scowled at it, then shoved it into his pocket. "I'm talking about the fact that your shitty house in Newton wasn't the only place you visited on Sunday, was it? Derek just finished going through a ridiculous number of files sent over from the Hartford PD. Surprise, sweetheart. You're on camera."

He held out his phone, and I watched a video that looked eerily familiar. There was my Volvo, pulling up in front of a different New England house. And there, of course, was me, walking up the drive, knocking on the door, and delivering one of the envelopes Calvin had sent with me as a clear price of my limited freedom.

"Hartford," Matthew said. "About two hours from here. One of your 'errands,' I see."

"Matthew," I said. "Please listen. Calvin sent me to give the tenants a notice to vacate. He's planning to liquidate everything before the trial. He wanted to get rid of all the evidence, and—"

"Then how do you explain this one?"

He flipped to another video, this time of a different, rickety town-house, the black Escalade I knew and loathed pulling up to the curb instead. But again, a tall blonde woman exited the car dressed in off-white clothes, carrying a familiar Celine handbag, and wearing my favorite waterfall-colored pumps. She was...me.

I stared, dumbfounded, as I strode up the path and knocked on the door, which was quickly answered by the same man I had met yesterday at the Newton house, stepping out onto the front porch of a different New England address. We embraced briefly and chatted for several moments like old friends before I left. But I had no recollection of this event. I had never been to that house or met that man before yesterday.

And yet...that was me...wasn't it?

"That's not—that's not my car," I stumbled as I watched the Escalade drive away.

"It's not? Because the plates match, Nina."

"I've been driving a Volvo here!" I protested. "You know this!"

"I don't think that matters, considering this was from three weeks ago," Matthew snapped. "Jesus Christ, how stupid do you think I am?"

I watched miserably as a few minutes later, the door opened again, and the man emerged, followed by several skinny pale girls with mousy-brown hair and haunted faces. Not the same ones I had spied in my house in Newton, but similar. Too similar.

"Who—who are they?" I asked, unable to look away.

Matthew laughed dryly. "It was my mistake, holding you back today. I should have let you knock on the door, if only to be an eye witness to the little charade you and your friend Benjamin put on together."

"Who *are* they?" I demanded, hysteria rising quickly. "Who are you talking about?!"

"Please. Like you don't know. Tell me, how long have you been recruiting girls for Ben Vamos, Nina? Or any of the other *four* separate prostitution rings run specifically for Ivy League shits that John Carson and Jude Letour have been running for decades? Have you been working for the Janus society all this time, or just since you got married?"

I slid back in the bed, a cold, icy finger of fear sliding down my back. "I don't—Matthew, I swear to God, I don't know what you're talking about."

"How about this?" he said as he held his phone out again.

It bore a different picture, this one taken somewhere in New York, from the look of the brownstones. Another safe house, I gathered. Another site for Calvin's crooked dealings.

"Here's one of the ones in Brooklyn. Look familiar? See anyone you know?"

He flipped through the pictures, and I watched aghast as another stream of girls poured out from a basement-level entrance.

"In 1989, a Hungarian kid named Károly Kertész moved into a house rented by Ben Vamos in Paterson, New Jersey," Matthew narrated as he paged through the stills. "He lived there with a woman named Sara Berto and her daughter from her first husband, Katarina Csaszar. Two years later, Sara went back to Hungary and took her daughter with her. Kertész stayed and went into business with Vamos. They provided fake papers to girls in the Eastern Bloc, brought them to the States, and then quickly forced them into prostitution, funneling them across the Northeast. They started working out of one property here and there, but quickly realized that trafficking girls wasn't the best income without real money to back the enterprise. So first, to access the big names needed for a job like that, our friend needed a new identity. He changed his name. I think you'll recognize it."

He flipped to the next picture, in which a familiar man was exiting the house in the previous photo.

"Meet Károly Kertész, Nina," Matthew said. "Otherwise known as Calvin fucking Gardner. Your husband."

"Oh, God." My voice was cold and wooden, just like the rest of my body as I pulled the blanket tightly around my shoulders. "I had no idea. I swear it, Matthew. I had *no idea*."

"You had no idea? The houses. The fake passports. The fucking girls? Jesus Christ, Nina, some of them aren't that much older than Olivia! By our estimate, there have been hundreds of children and young women funneled through these properties over the last decade. Your family is up to their necks in this secret society shit, and you had *no* fucking clue?"

"They were just supposed to be for the immigration papers," I whispered. "That's all he said they were for."

"You can't have *really* thought that. Even you aren't that naive."

Matthew looked thoroughly disgusted. It was something I knew well. That contempt. That derision. Like I was nothing more than something on the bottom of his shoe.

I just never thought I would see that expression from him.

Tears started welling before I could stop them. "I swear it," I whispered. "Oh, *God*, Matthew, I swear it. That's all he bought them for."

"You swear it, when you signed the papers for every single one of these deeds?" he asked. "Christ, Nina, you just fucking admitted it! All fifty-three of them are under Pantheon, LLC."

I swallowed. Another house of mirrors. Another pile of shards. "What?"

"Come off it, Nina. Stop with the big-eyed Pollyanna act."

Hastily, I swiped at the tears that threatened to fall. "No, really. What are you talking about? I'll own up to having my name on that LLC, but *fifty-three* properties? My trust provided a down payment for two properties in Brooklyn outside of the house I bought in Boston with my own savings. And there were perhaps ten deeds in that office that day. That's all."

"Just because we fucked a few times, sweetheart, doesn't make me an idiot. I'm not falling for those big gray eyes again."

My jaw dropped. "Matthew! I swear it, I don't know *what* you are talking about."

"Then how the fuck do you explain all of these?"

He exited out of the pictures and began scrolling through the other evidence he had been sent.

"Derek has weeks of this shit," he said. "Video after video of you visiting every one of Pantheon's properties. Giving instructions. Sometimes you actually walk the girls to their car. Sometimes you even bring some of them in."

Again and again, I watched the woman in the waterfall-colored pumps exit the black Escalade.

She had my hair.

My shoes.

My dress.

She was…me.

"I—what—how—" I stumbled over every word.

Beside me, Matthew shook his head. "Do you have any idea how many of these Derek has? Most of the time, you never get out of your car. But on Sunday, you did."

My jaw quivered. "I—I don't know what to say. Matthew, these aren't real."

"That's your car, isn't it?"

I stared. "I—yes, but, I never—"

"And those are your clothes, aren't they?" Matthew shook his head. "You were wearing those shoes the night we met. And I'd know those legs anywhere, Nina." He sounded disgusted with himself.

"Matthew," I said slowly, feeling my heart drop—first from relief, then from sadness. "This isn't me. It can't be. I *never went to these houses*. The one in Connecticut, yes, but that's all!"

"It *is* you, Nina. In every single one!" Then he turned, and with a roar, hurled his phone against the wall, where it splintered immediately into the plaster. "Don't *fuck* me, Mrs. Gardner!"

Tears flooded down my cheeks. I didn't know who that girl was. I didn't know why we looked so alike or what she was doing in Calvin's business. But as my heart pounded so hard it shook my entire body, all I could wonder was why Matthew didn't believe me. How, after all this time, could he think that was me unless he *wanted* it to be?

The thought ruined me all over again.

"That isn't me," I said again and again. "I swear, it isn't me."

But Matthew just stared at his broken phone. Then, in a mad dash grabbed his shoes and socks off the floor and made for the bedroom door.

"I trusted you," he said in a creaky voice. "They said I shouldn't. They even sent me here to find out what you were hiding."

I shrank even farther into the covers, my nakedness somehow so much more than skin deep. "They? Who's…they?"

But he only sniffed loudly, and it wasn't until he opened the door to the bedroom that the light from the hallway showed the streaks of tears running down his face.

"I trusted you, Nina," he said again. "But this…goddammit. You just broke my fucking heart."

"Matthew!" I cried, suddenly finding my voice. "Matthew, please! Stay. Let's talk about this. I don't know what's going on, but I *know* we can figure it out together!"

But he just shook his head viciously, then stood up straight. His features hardened into a stony expression, a fierceness somehow only enhanced by the last tear streak sliding down his left cheek. He took one final look at me, and I could have sworn in that moment, I was turned to stone.

"You better use that dirty money of yours to get a damn good lawyer, Mrs. Gardner," he said. "Because after tonight, you're going to need a fuckin' army to escape a life in prison."

Before I could respond, he slammed the door of the bedroom and did the same as he sprinted out of the cabin, clearly trying to put as much distance between us as possible. The second bang rocketed me into action. I sprang up from the bed, grabbing the first thing from the armoire I could find—a plush terry bathrobe put here for guests. I shoved it on, then ran out of the cottage in my bare feet, prepared to chase Matthew down until he would come back and talk some sense again.

But as soon as I reached the other side of the orchard, I came to a stop behind a big oak.

The front porch light of the big house had turned on. Skylar appeared, tiny and disheveled in a black nightgown, followed by Jane, wearing only Eric's shirt.

"Matthew," Skylar said, again and again, though the rest of their conversation, I couldn't decipher beyond a few words.

"Stay."

"Wait."

"Listen."

"Time."

But Matthew was a force as he rocketed into the house, then back out again, carrying his bags and briefcase. He looked so far from the smart, stylish man I knew and loved. Only half his shirt was buttoned, and his hair was standing up in the back, like someone's hands had been running through it all night. *My hands.*

I hiccupped back a sob, but remained behind the tree.

The sound of tires on gravel drowned out their conversation before a taxi appeared. I watched as Matthew dropped reluctant kisses on both his friends' cheeks, then ducked into the cab and left.

Skylar and Jane turned toward the cabin. I shied farther behind my tree. Jane shook her head, then slipped an arm around Skylar's shoulder and guided her back to the house, where they both disappeared.

And then I returned to my bed, to lie there alone. Listening for the return of a car, but only hearing silence for hours until morning striped the walls with color and light. That was when my phone rang.

I answered, too weary not to. "Hello, Calvin."

"Where have you been?" Calvin demanded.

"Sleeping. It's quite early still."

"The property manager called me. Said there were some vagrants in the Newton house, fucking freeloaders. Are you all right?"

I frowned. I could count the number of times my husband had inquired about my well-being on one hand. And all of them were related to when he wanted something.

"I'm fine," I said.

"So, listen. The DA has been really quiet, so I've convinced the lawyers to get a speedy trial back on track," Calvin said. "Maybe get it scheduled by the end of the year or early spring."

"That's good," I replied numbly as I touched the indent on the pillow where Matthew's head had been. "Get it over with."

"I'm going to need you to do something," Calvin said.

"What's that?" I mumbled. At this point, I wasn't sure I cared.

"I'm going to need you to offer an alibi for a few separate dates. Under oath."

At that, I sat up. "You want me to be deposed?"

"I want them to put you on the stand, yeah," Calvin said. "If it comes to that."

"I-I don't understand," I replied. "I thought—I thought spousal privilege was supposed to keep me out of this trial."

"Only if I assert it," Calvin sneered. "Lawyers think I should, but they don't know jack shit. As of last night, my privilege was waived. I told them you're Nina de Vries. There's no better alibi in New York, and you're going to give it to me."

Privilege. Waived.

Just like that, I saw the imaginary shackles around my wrists unlock. Perhaps I'd be trading them for newer ones. But it would be an imprisonment I determined. Not him.

"Of course," I found myself saying, but then realized it would be suspicious if I acquiesced without any kind of fight. "Wait, Calvin. What do you mean, exactly, as an alibi?"

"You're going to tell them what I do, just like you've always known. That we flip properties. That we buy and sell real estate at a profit. And there will be a few dates where, I don't know, you can talk about some dinner we had at home."

I swallowed. "What about the papers? The passports." *The girls, you lying piece of garbage.*

There was a long pause. Then: "It's not a problem. The statute of limitations expired a long time ago. Besides, you have no evidence that I ever did that sort of thing. And they obviously don't either."

I hummed in acknowledgement. My entire body still felt numb, but something deep inside me was ticking again.

"I was also thinking about that vow renewal. I want to make it happen in the next week, two at the latest. I've already called a planner, and she's getting us into St. John's on a cancellation. You can wear your old wedding gown or get a new one. You just need to look the fucking part. Do you understand?"

I hummed again in accord, though I had absolutely no intention of walking down any sort of aisle with this man ever again. I would have rather died.

"And, Nina?"

I swallowed. "Yes?"

"If you don't? Everything will come out in the open. Is that clear?"

I understood so much more than he thought.

And so, I found myself nodding.

"Yes," I said softly.

"That's right, princess." Calvin's voice struck a strangely hypnotic note. "Now do as you're told and get back to New York. We have some work to do before your deposition."

The line went dead as he hung up. I sat on the edge of my bed for several minutes, hand pressed to my heart as I tried to calm it down to a normal rate.

Not because I was afraid anymore.

Because I was full of knowledge.

There was only one path forward for me now. For the first time in my life, I knew exactly what I needed to do. And I finally had the courage to do it.

POSTLUDE
DECEMBER 2018

Matthew

I approached the corner office at the end of my hall with lead in my feet and my stomach.

"Hey, Shirley," I said to the assistant manning the desk outside.

The small, gray-haired lady I'd seen most days for the past seven years smiled at me. "Hi, honey."

"He in?"

She clicked a few screens on her computer. "Yes, he has a minute or two." She pressed a button on the intercom. "Matthew Zola out here."

"It'll just be a minute," I told her, though I wasn't sure why. I needed to tell someone, I guessed. Someone had to know what I was about to do.

Shirley just gave me a sympathetic smile, but didn't look surprised. "Go on in, hon."

I walked into the office of Greg Cardozo, executive assistant district attorney and head of the Bureau of Organized Crime and Racketeering. My boss for the last three years, and before that, the guy who trained me when I was as green as the trees waving in the park a few blocks away. Rumor had it he was up for promotion, and he hadn't made much of a secret that he was grooming me for his job.

"Greg," I said.

Cardozo looked up. "Zola, hey. What's going on?" He frowned, suspicious. Yeah, I wasn't ever one for hand-holding, or to be loitering around anyone's office.

My throat felt thick. Like it had been coated in paste.

"I—" I cleared my throat. Better get it the fuck over with. "Here."

I slid the paper I'd typed up and signed just before walking down the hall onto his desk. It was still warm from the printer.

Cardozo frowned at it, then looked back at me. "What's this?"

"It's my letter of resignation." I had to look out the window and immediately hated myself for it. A real man looks another man in the eye when he's full of shame. Even if he does have his tail between his legs. But here I was, staring at everything but my boss like one of the perps we interrogated regularly.

"For what?" Cardozo asked.

I sighed. "You're not going to like this."

Cardozo sat back in his chair and folded his hands. "Try me."

So I sank down into the chair opposite him and proceeded to tell him the whole story. Well, most of it. Greg was a good boss. Partly because he knew how to listen. He sat back in his chair while I told him the story of me and the de Vries family, starting with that night, nearly a year ago now, when I'd gotten the call from Jane about her father. I skimped the details, of course, but recounted how and when I had first met Nina. And then described when I'd met her again, only to learn exactly who she was.

"I'm not proud of it," I said glumly. "I knew she was married. But that was *all* I knew at that point, I swear."

Greg only nodded and gestured for me to continue.

So I told him the rest. About how we had finally planned to be together. About how the night of John Carson's death, things were about to turn around. Until I learned about her husband's part in all of it, and how that had led to months of trying and failing to keep our relationship separate from the case. For her sake. For mine.

I had failed on both counts.

"So," I said at the end. "There it is." I pushed the paper toward him again. "Please accept my letter of resignation," I requested formally.

I had never wanted anything less.

Greg scowled at the paper, rubbed his knuckles into one palm, then switched and did the other, like a boxer getting ready to train.

"No," he said at last.

I balked. "No?"

His mouth spread down and out, a silent expressive rebuttal. "Nah, no. I don't think so."

I frowned. "Greg, did you hear everything I just said? I was involved with the *defendant's wife.*"

"So recuse yourself from the case," he argued back. "Don't cost me one of the best prosecutors I have. You have more convictions than anyone else on my team, Zola. Two more years, you could end up department chief."

"Convictions aren't everything," I replied. "Some might say that just makes me a dirty cop."

"Yeah, well, yours are also fairer than everyone else's," he said grimly. "You and Derek make a good team. You always have."

I sighed. "Greg, I don't think you're hearing what I'm saying. I was in love with her. And because she royally fucked me over, I think it's pretty clear I can't do this with a clear head. If I ever could. My judgment is compromised, probably always was. We're going to lose on that alone."

Again, the nonchalant shrug that was starting to become really fuckin' infuriating. "Again, so you recuse yourself. This case hasn't gone to trial, Zola. Did you lie about how any of your evidence was obtained?"

I swallowed and shook my head. "No, but—"

"Did you depose her? Were you planning to call her to the stand during the trial?"

"Well, no, because we assumed they would claim spousal privilege, so—"

"And was your pursuit of justice in any way corrupted, for better or for worse, because of her relationship with Calvin Gardner?"

At that, I remained silent. I wanted to say no. I wanted to say that my dogged pursuit of Calvin Gardner over the past several months had been purely because he was a rotten fuckin' guy who deserved to have the book thrown at him for the things he had done.

But that would have been a lie.

Greg tapped his fingers on the desk like he was tapping out numbers. "Look. It's not good, I'll grant you that. But, Zola, you didn't break any laws here. Sure, you crossed some ethical boundaries, but from what you said, it doesn't sound like Nina Gardner was manipulating you in any way to benefit her husband, considering she probably hates the motherfucker more than anyone. Extortion. Kidnapping. Fuck, his behavior at the beginning of their relationship sounds a lot like grooming to me."

I ground my teeth at the word "grooming," then willed myself with everything I had not to run out of the room and chase Calvin Gardner with a baseball bat.

I blinked. No, sympathy for her was *not* what was needed now. "She's still implicated in the crimes."

"Do you know that for sure?"

My hands gripped the edges of the chair. "She all but said it. We have the video confirmation. But I can't prosecute this anymore. I probably never should have."

"So, you won't." He wrote something down on a legal pad. "I'm taking it on personally, given the sensitivity of the case. I'll need all the files immediately, and meanwhile, someone from IT will erase the remainders from your hard drive. But we'll get that conviction, Zola. And we'll help the Newark ADA get hers too."

I wanted to bury my head in my hands. "Anyone who takes it should probably call me to the stand too."

Greg shrugged, unconvinced. "I think you're being a little hard on yourself. You didn't actually witness anything, so technically, your statements would all be hearsay. Do I think you should have kept your pecker to yourself? Yeah. Do I think you should have given this to me the second you realized who she was? Definitely. But given the circumstances around the Carson case, I also understand why you didn't. Hell, Ramirez was pretty clear with you about it, wasn't he?"

Grimly, I nodded. "Yeah, he wanted it done under the table when it was focused on Carson. We couldn't risk the Manhattan DA or the Feds who were bought off by John Carson stepping in. So I was fully responsible for that one. We had nowhere else to turn."

"Well, there you go."

Cardozo grabbed my resignation letter off his desk and dropped it into the shredder by his feet. We both watched as the machine sliced my guilt to ribbons.

"Last thing," Greg said. "I don't want to lose you, but this wasn't good, Zola. I'm probably going to have to put you on unpaid administrative leave until things die down. I'll let you know. Can you handle that?"

I swallowed. It wasn't great. I'd probably have to pick up some shifts at Jamie's just to make my mortgage. Christ. I never thought I'd go back to waiting tables and bartending to get by after I finished law school, but here we were. Still, it was better than what I imagined when I first walked in here.

"Yeah," I said. "Yeah, it'll be fine."

"All right," said Cardoza. "Get your things together. Figure out how to divvy up your caseload. And then we'll see you in a few months, good as new."

———

"Banks, how's everything looking in there?"

"Looking good, Cap. A little quiet, though."

I frowned at Percy, my second, who stood next to me with the same quizzical look on his face.

"Quiet?" he echoed. "Quiet in Fallujah?"

It was supposed to be a raid. They were supposed to go in and come right back out.

"All clear up here, Cap—oh, fuck!"

BOOM. The upper quadrant of the already-crumbling apartment building exploded.

"Fuck!" I shouted, jumping out of the shadows where I had been sitting with the only three members of the platoon I'd held back with me. "Goddammit." I yanked my radio from my shoulder and called for backup.

The reply was immediate. "Roger, stand by."

I scowled at the phone. "Fuck this."

"Cap, what are you doing?" Perkins shouted as he watched me strip off the radio and toss it to him.

"There are three other Marines in there, Perkins, and I'm not leaving them to a slaughter when I'm the one who sent them!" I shouted. "Stay on the line and wait for orders. I'm coming out with my men or I'm not coming out at all!"

Without waiting for a response, I hurtled into the building, ignoring the rubble raining down above me and the rattle of gunfire that was suddenly everywhere.

I found two of them.

"Snacks! Bancroft! Grab my hands; let's get you guys out of here."

With more strength than I knew I possessed, I pulled the two men up from the stairs, thankful that they were both at least able to walk, even if their faces were badly burned.

"Cap," Bancroft muttered. "It's Napoleon, he was upstairs when it went off. We got most of them, but he's still up there."

I helped them out of the building where two of the men who were waiting outside ran across the street to help their platoonmates to safety.

"Cap!" shouted Perkins. "Artillery is here in six minutes!"

"I gotta find Napoleon!" I shouted over my shoulder even as I headed back into the building, gun drawn.

There was smoke everywhere—the fire that the bomb started had quickly caught on the cheap wood furniture and dry surroundings.

"Napoleon! Yo, Pletford, where are you?" I called through the smoke, stepping over civilian bodies and trying not to think too hard about whether they were dead or alive. I was halfway up the crumbling stairs when I saw the Marine's legs limp at the top.

"Plet!" I yelled as I sprinted up toward him, praying I wasn't responsible for a third dead Marine today. "Fuck, Plet, come on. Let's get you out of here."

I rounded the corner and dove for my compatriot, not even bothering to check for vital signs. I just needed to get him out.

"Come on," I grunted as I threw one of his arms around my shoulder and tried to maneuver his dead weight over my back.

A loud moan emitted from Pletford's body. His head lolled back, and his helmet fell off, revealing a long mane of golden hair dangling over my shoulder.

"What the..."

I pushed Pletford's body against the wall so I could look into his face.

But it wasn't Pletford.

A pair of pained, silver eyes gazed back at me atop a straight, elegant nose and a pair of lips that were red again, but for all the wrong reasons.

"Matthew," Nina whispered as blood stained her mouth. She coughed, and more came out.

"Oh, fuck," I cried. "Oh, fuck, no, no, no, baby, no..."

Nina lunged forward, her body sinking into the too-large uniform of the Marine I'd somehow lost to the fire.

"Matthew," she said as she wasted away. "I'm so sorry."

And then her eyes sank back as her body dropped limp in my arms. I shook her, trying to revive her there in the hall as another round of bombs sounded in the square outside.

"Nina!" I shouted. "No, no, no, we've got to get you out of here! Nina, goddammit, stay with me! NINA!"

"MATTIE! *MATTIE!*"

"Huh? What?"

I shook awake with the rush of a dog shaking water off his coat and almost twice as wet, given the sheen of sweat that covered my body.

Frankie stood next to the bed clutching the edges of her bathrobe, tired eyes wide with concern.

"What is it?" I asked. "Is everything all right? Where's Sofia?"

"Mattie, everything's fine. Sofia's sleeping. You were shouting in your sleep," she said. "I didn't know you were having nightmares again."

I didn't respond. The fact that I was having nightmares again was news to me too, but it wasn't something I was ever going to complain about. Most of the guys I knew who came back from Iraq suffered a lot worse than a bad dream every now and then.

I blinked, trying to get the image of Nina, bruised and battered, out of my head.

Put it away. You're done with her now.

Maybe if I said it to myself enough times, I'd actually start to believe it.

"Anyway," Frankie said. "I actually woke up because your phone was ringing."

"Oh," I said, still bleary from sleep. "Okay, um, sorry. I'll silence the ringer."

When she didn't leave right away, I frowned. "Something else, Frankie?"

She just watched me for a moment. "Must have been quite a dream for you to sleep right through your ringer."

Again, I took a deep breath. "I'm fine, Frankie. Go back to sleep."

She gave me another long look, then trudged out of the room to her own across the hall.

I flopped back onto the bed. Five missed calls. Jesus, no wonder it woke her up. *Five* missed calls. All of them from Derek.

When I called him back, he picked up immediately. "Jesus, where have you been?"

I frowned. "Do you have a death wish? Can you ever call me at a normal fuckin' time, man?"

There was a long sigh. "You're going to want to come down here."

I rubbed a heavy palm over my face, ignoring the scratch of three days' worth of stubble there. "Derek, come on. Whoever you got, it can wait until—"

"Zola," he interrupted curtly. "It's Nina Gardner."

At the sound of the name, I sat straight up in bed. It echoed around my head—no, my *soul*—like a church bell, heavy and resonant.

"What?" I said, convinced I'd misheard him. "Did you just say you have Nina…"

"Gardner, yeah. She's turned herself in."

Holy shit.

I could imagine her clearly in the middle of the local precinct, sitting primly in the mint-colored interrogation room, hands folded on her lap over her designer dress. Wedding ring gleaming, hair glossy. Acting like the queen of her new, gritty domain.

"And, Zola, there's more," Derek said. "She asked to look at the videos you showed her. The ones of her running the properties with Vamos. I let her. I wanted to see what she'd do. She says she's not actually in them."

"I'm sure she did," I said crabbily.

"But she says it's someone she knows," he continued. "Someone named Caitlyn Calvert."

———

To be continued…in *The Honest Affair*

Coming Fall 2020

Thank you so much for reading *The Perfect Woman*. Nina and Matthew's story concludes in the upcoming novel, *The Honest Affair*. You can preorder here: www. nicolefrenchromance.com/thehonestaffair

ACKNOWLEDGMENTS

Ho-ly crap. This book is done. I don't think I'm alone in saying this year has presented some of the most massive challenges to writing I have ever faced, so many of which have to do with the extraordinary times we are living in. As a result, I was forced to delay the book's publication not once, but twice in order to offer my readers the best I possibly could. So, first and foremost, **my thanks must go to them**. Thank you for your patience and for sticking by this story while it came to be. You are beloved and cherished.

I also must thank a few other critical people without whose help this book would not exist:

My alpha readers, Danielle and Patricia, who were appropriately demanding, yet endlessly patient, especially considering how many times I made them re-read whenever I changed the chapter order AGAIN. My beta readers, Dawn and Erika, whose gloriously detailed reading truly helped this story become the best it could. And my ARC team, whose constant excitement for Nina and Matthew's story drove this forward, inch by inch, until it was done.

My nebulous but ever-growing group of authors peers. If I've sent you a random message over the past few months and you answered, thank you. What would I do without those contacts in a world that is becoming increasingly contact-free? Even if we haven't explicitly talked about the books, your energy buoys me. In particular, Jane, Laura, Kim, Crystal, Claudia, Parker, and Harloe—I appreciate you more than you know.

The team of incredible women whose professional help keeps me on track and focused: my publicist, Dani, and the entire team at Wildfire; my editor, Emily Hainsworth, who juggles my multiple drafts with the ease of a circus performer; my proofreaders, Shauna Stevenson and Judy Zweifel. What would I do without you all? Probably nothing at all.

Lastly, my husband and step kids, who so helpfully juggled the constraints of homeschooling and childcare for a six-year-old in the Time of Corona to help me finish this book. I realize I haven't exactly been a joy to be around the past few months, and your bottomless patience and love is astounding. I hit the jackpot with you.

To anyone else I may have forgotten while writing this, please forgive me. You matter so much more than I could possibly say. Thank you for your support and for reading in any way.

Made in the USA
Monee, IL
26 October 2020